ROUGH DRAFT

"A thoroughly satisfying thriller . . . Strong and engaging characters."
—*The Washington Post Book World*

"Good, old-fashioned, hideously violent fun. . . . remarkably original . . . The creepy hit man Hal is one of Hall's best psychos."
—*Miami Herald*

BODY LANGUAGE

"*Body Language* seduces you, then it grabs you, and it never lets you go. This is a first-rate thriller by a masterful writer."
—James Patterson

"Alexandra Rafferty is a fabulous addition to the ranks of law enforcement. She is smart, competent, the consummate professional, and her job as a Miami P.D. photographic specialist places her at the heart of the crime scene, with a cold eye for detail and a passionate commitment to justice."
—Sue Grafton

"*Body Language* is a sizzling tale of sex, blood, and obsession."
—Stephen Coonts

"Hall fans will be more than reimbursed by his poetic imagery in the landscapes and love scenes. Alex is a heroine with enough endearing attributes to sustain yet another long-running character series."
—*Publishers Weekly* (starred review)

"Suspense and forensic detail with a near-flawless grasp of character."
—*Booklist*

ALSO BY JAMES W. HALL

ACCLAIM FOR JAMES W. HALL
AND HIS NOVELS

"James Hall's writing is astringent, penetrating, and unfailingly gripping long after you read the last page. Explodes with the brilliance of chain lightning." —Dean Koontz

"The king of the Florida-gothic noir." —Dennis Lehane

"No writer working today . . . more clearly evokes the shadows and loss that hide within the human heart." —Robert Crais

"James W. Hall's lyrical passion for the Florida Keys, his spare language, and unusual images haunt us long after the story has faded." —Sara Paretsky

"A master of suspense . . . James Hall's prose runs as clean and fast as Gulf Stream waters."

—*The New York Times Book Review*

"James Hall is a writer I have learned from over the years. His people and places have more brush strokes than a van Gogh. He delivers taut and muscular stories about a place where evil always lurks beneath the surface." —Michael Connelly

MAGIC CITY

"A gripping tale of dirty politics, love gone wrong, murder for hire, and international intrigue that is impossible to put down. Highly recommended." —*Library Journal*
(starred review)

"The quintessential South Florida novel."

—*Fort Lauderdale Sun-Sentinel*

MORE . . .

"Further solidifies Hall's mastery of an element that eludes many other contemporary mystery writers."   —*The Miami Herald*

"Fast, entertaining . . . Hall offers lively characters, livelier dialogue, and an excellent depiction of contemporary south Florida."
     —*Publishers Weekly*

"Another outstanding chapter in one of the genre's most consistently first-rate series."   —*Booklist* (starred review)

"Hall's action scenes are starkly poetic."   —*Baltimore Sun*

"From an opening scene that charges out of the box like a greyhound on amphetamines, to the climactic denouement that will leave the reader as limp as two-month-old kale, the pace . . . never slows."   —*The New York Sun*

FORESTS OF THE NIGHT

"Complex . . . chilling . . . [Hall's] prose style becomes almost cinematic . . . don't put this one aside as a beach read. A long winter's night is a better bet."   —*New York Daily News*

"A successful departure from [Hall's] usual style . . . [Hall] leaves the reader wanting more."   —*Cleveland Plain Dealer*

"The sort of first-rate thriller we have come to expect from Hall . . . in *Forests of the Night*, Hall again exhibits mastery of the craft. He knows, perhaps better than anyone in the genre, how to tap into the fundamental passions that drive us: ancient, dark, mythic passions, like those spoken around a fire at the dawn of storytelling . . . Hall has given us a thriller of the first magnitude."   —*Miami Herald*

"[Hall is] a writer who carefully measures out the answers in clean yet elegant prose. Hall used to be a poet. In all the important ways, he still is."   —*Denver Post*

"A multilayered, richly characterized, and compulsively readable story . . . Is it too early to pick a best book of the year?"
—*Rocky Mountain News*

"A suspenseful, sharply detailed blend of history, family drama, and thriller, *Forests of the Night* cuts a wide literary swath, and does it with élan and passion." —Russell Banks

"*Forests of the Night* moves like an arrow—lean and swift—toward its amazing target. James W. Hall is at the top of his form; he's a wonder to watch." —Reynolds Price

"Compelling . . . with action scenes that bristle with visceral intensity . . . nearly everyone has real depth, and the author's appreciation for history and its reverberations adds further complexity."
—*Publishers Weekly*

OFF THE CHART

"In the crowded and talented pool of South Florida suspense writers, James Hall pretty much has the deep end to himself. Out of reach for most, it's a place of nameless primal fears and murky evil, from which Hall shapes compelling characters in riveting stories. You get caught up in the light and color, the movement of the unfailingly taut action, but you are always aware of something very old and dark beneath it all. His latest novel is wonderfully disturbing in just this way . . . all of which make the carefully crafted, darkly resonant *Off the Chart* stay with you."
—*Miami Herald*

"After years of tussling with metaphorical pirates of every stripe, fly-tying South Florida swashbuckler Thorn finally gets to go up against the real thing . . . the combination of world-class villainy, exotic locations, quick-march pacing, and studly heroism also suggests Thorn's channeling James Bond."
—*Kirkus Reviews*

BONES OF CORAL

"Hall takes this high adventure a step beyond the limits of the traditional action novel . . . a thoughtful, multifaceted novel that should not be missed."
—*Library Journal*

"Brilliantly suspenseful . . . Hall raises mystery writing to its rightful place of honor alongside the best of American fiction."
—*San Francisco Chronicle*

BLACKWATER SOUND

"Nautical action sequences [are written] with cinematic vigor."
—*The New York Times*

"Compelling . . . A well-crafted thriller." —*Miami Herald*

"From dramatic beginning to chilling ending, Hall's never been better . . . the result is suspense, entertainment, and high-quality literature." —*Publishers Weekly* (starred review)

"Terrific." —Scott Turow

"I believe no one has written more lyrically of the Gulf Stream since Ernest Hemingway . . . a wonderful reading experience."
—James Lee Burke, author of *Bitterroot* and *Purple Cane Road*

"Sleek and relentlessly propulsive." —Dennis Lehane

"With beautiful prose and a heavily muscled story, it moves with the grandeur and unpredictability of a hooked marlin. Make that a killer marlin." —Michael Connelly

MAGIC CITY

JAMES W. HALL

St. Martin's Paperbacks

This is a work of fiction. All of the characters, organizations, and events portrayed in this novel are either products of the author's imagination or are used fictitiously.

MAGIC CITY

Library of Congress Catalog Card Number: 2006050913

ISBN: 0-312-94747-X
EAN: 978-0-312-94747-7

Printed in the United States of America

St. Martin's Press hardcover edition / March 2007
St. Martin's Paperbacks edition / February 2008

St. Martin's Paperbacks are published by St. Martin's Press, 175 Fifth Avenue, New York, NY 10010.

10 9 8 7 6 5 4 3 2 1

For Les, brother in arms

ACKNOWLEDGMENTS

Michael Carlebach's wonderful photographs of South Florida were my original inspiration for this story, and they continue to inspire to this day. A special debt of gratitude goes to Geoff Colmes, the best damn fishing guide in the Keys and boon companion. Thanks to Charlie MacNeil for his assistance in all things medical and to Richard Schaffer for his excellent lessons on search-and-rescue dogs. And to the citizens of South Florida, wherever they may currently reside. Never has there been such a stimulating, spicy, and marvelously weird collection of folks. And to Evelyn, a true Miami original.

On the flat coastal swamps of South Florida . . . there has evolved . . . a settlement of considerable interest, not exactly an American city as American cities have until recently been understood but a tropical capital: long on rumor, short on memory, overbuilt on the chimera of runaway money and referring not to New York or Boston or Los Angeles or Atlanta but to Caracas and Mexico, to Havana and to Bogotá and to Paris and Madrid.

—JOAN DIDION, *Miami*

MIAMI 1964

Outside Snake's window a slice of Miami moon hung like the blade of a freshly sharpened scythe. It was February 25, 1964, the night a dozen armed men in stocking masks came for the Morales family.

Snake was twelve. Christened Manuel Ricardo Morales, early on he was tagged Culebra, or Snake, for his long, sinewy body. A lean kid with a quirky brain. At a clinic on Calle Ocho a Cuban *médico* put a name to his condition. The boy recorded everything he heard or read or saw and could recite it back flawlessly. Its scientific label: eidetic memory.

"A gift from God," the medic said.

His cross to bear, Snake would come to believe.

Snake's joys: the everlasting Miami heat, lush ocean winds. Exploring the city streets on his Schwinn Sting-Ray, circling out from his Little Havana neighborhood mile by mile. But more than anything: the golden hours he spent in the company of his sister, Carmen. A girl devoted to Christ and the purity of her soul. She and she alone could ease Snake's lonesome heart.

After midnight on that airless February night, Snake lay awake. Beside him in the dark, the radio buzzed with Cassius Clay's triumph. The brash Clay had humiliated Liston, exposed him as a clumsy oaf and quitter.

Clay was Snake's idol, had been for the past few months while he trained on Miami Beach and showed up daily on the sports pages of *The Miami Herald*. A tall young man, handsome to the point of prettiness, a loudmouth, unafraid of any man. Everything Snake was not.

As the announcers babbled about the new champ, Snake reran the six rounds, every punch and duck, Clay taunting, backpedaling, side-wheeling, jabbing, jabbing, staying just out of range. Two cuts opening around Liston's eyes in the second round. Slinging blood, he struck wildly. Clay danced and punched, jab, jab, hook, right cross, straight right hand, smearing the bloody face, his own eyes wide. Liston striking air and air again. Jab, jab.

Next round, cuts repaired, Sonny came out brawling. Clay ducked and dodged. Punch after furious punch grazed Cassius but did no damage. Falling back, falling back, Cassius let Liston tire himself out.

Les Keiter's radio voice called every feint and bob, every thudding strike.

Between rounds four and five Cassius rubbed furiously at his eyes, complained he was blinded by something evil on Liston's gloves. The goop used to seal Liston's cut, the wintergreen liniment on his shoulder, or something more devious.

Eyes on fire, Clay wanted to quit, but Dundee dragged the stool away, shoved him into the ring, Dundee screaming this was his chance, his one and only. Blind or not, he had to fight.

Clay stumbled out and Liston attacked with chopping lefts and rights, trying to finish it. Cassius wiped at his stinging eyes, backpedaling, stiff-arming, but getting hit again and again. Biggest, baddest heavyweight of all time throwing bombs at a sightless man. Liston stalked and Keiter cranked his voice higher, Sonny was close to a knockout, body blows, fists slammed chin and nose.

But Cassius survived. Somehow he held on, survived.

In the sixth his eyes were clear and it was his turn. Snapping left after left, jab and hook and straight right hand, smacking Liston. While the champ, flat-footed, gasping, could only paw at Clay. An empty shell. Done.

When the bell rang to start the seventh, Liston stayed on his stool.

"Wait a minute, wait a minute," Howard Cosell yelled. "Sonny is not coming out, he's not coming out. Clay's the first one to see it. It's Cassius Clay, Cassius is the winner and new heavyweight champion of the world."

And Clay roared, "I am the king. I upset the world. Give me justice."

Snake pumped a fist, joining with Cassius in celebration for all newcomers, all outcasts, all those who were gravely underestimated.

Later during the postfight chatter Snake heard noises outside, and rose to see. Two cars rumbled into the driveway and doors flew open and men poured out. Glint of metal in their hands. They swarmed the house.

He woke his brother, Carlos.

"It's happening," Snake said. "Get up, it's happening."

Over and again his father warned that Fidel's reach was long. Snake's dad was from Varadero, Cuba, an exile strangling on hate, enraged at the injustice, the terrible disaster at the Bay of Pigs. Forever ranting. Happy for Kennedy's assassination. That traitor, he said. That coward.

Snake's dad was no dad. His mom, no mom. No baseball in the backyard, no Saturday trips to the beach. Not a kiss good night or questions about his day. A father who spent every free hour organizing a militia. Dozens of exiles rode with him into the Everglades each weekend in boots and camouflage to target practice, rehearse assault plans.

Back in Cuba, Jorge Morales was a *machetero*. A simple cane-cutter who swung his long blade twelve hours a day down the endless rows. Now earning his wage as a barber on Flagler Street, but his real work was commanding his two dozen men, each on fire with the same fury. Crush the tyrant this time. Liberate their homeland. Do it without the gutless Americans. Snake's mother went along, cooked for the troops and smiled, fighting for a place in Jorge's heart. Nothing left over for her children.

"There's another woman," Carmen told Snake. "I hear them through the walls, fighting about her."

"Another woman?" Snake was bewildered.

Carmen shook her head. Snake too innocent to hear more.

If it weren't for Carmen, Snake would not have known love's name. She was two years older, fourteen. Asleep down the hall. Long raven hair, brown eyes glistening with confidence, a faithful glowing smile, a body swelling toward womanhood. Carmen recited her prayers and saved her pennies for Sunday candles at St. Michael the Archangel. She had surrendered her heart to God. In the Morales house, that residence of rage, guns, and camouflage, Carmen was the soft, true core. The shine, the goodness. Snake's soul.

So certain was Snake's father that Fidel would one day try to crush him, he rented a room in their cramped house to two brothers in arms. Always a sentry awake by the front window, gun in hand, waiting for just such a night.

But on that evening his father's bodyguards had gathered by the radio, listening to young Clay dethrone the brute Liston. Hours later all of them were still lounging in the Florida room at the back of the house. Drinking rum, puffing cigars, paying no attention to the dangerous night.

As Snake brought his brother awake, the intruders broke inside. Blasts in the living room. Screams and howls and answering gunfire. A crater exploded in the boys' wall and a chip of plaster carved a bloody groove across his brother's forehead. Before Carlos could wail, Snake clamped the boy's mouth and stood listening to the thunder of handguns.

Beneath his feet the terrazzo trembled. Snake hissed Carlos quiet, then went to the window, pushed out the screen.

One man stood guard, stocking over his head. Snake ducked.

"Under the bed," he said. "Get under the damn bed. I'll get Carmen."

"I'll kill them." Face bloody, Carlos drew from beneath his bed a long machete. It was their father's, still holding a gleaming edge. Weeks before, Carlos had smuggled it out of the cluttered garage and hid it below his mattress so he could toy with it in the moonlight each night before sleep.

"Give me that," Snake said, and pried the heavy blade from Carlos's hand. "I'm going for Carmen. You stay here."

Snake shoved Carlos into the dusty hideaway below the box spring.

At the door, Snake peeked out to see men in the living room. Stocking masks and dark clothes. Their backs to him as they fired at the last resisters in the Florida room. Snake pressed against the wall and inched toward Carmen's room, carrying the machete's dreadful weight.

One of the invaders turned his way. Snake flattened into the shadows. When the man swung back to fire at the hold-outs, Snake threw himself forward, made it to Carmen's open door, and lunged inside.

A man was there. Blocky head, thick shoulders. His hair cut in a burr.

The man was sitting on the side of her bed, his right hand moving under Carmen's sheets. In her white nightgown his sister was suffering the assault in silence. Her eyes found Snake's as he entered the room.

Snake raised the cane-cutter and stole forward until he was just behind the man.

Her eyes on Snake, Carmen said, "Hail Mary, full of grace."

The machete was cocked high when the blocky man swiveled, his face hidden in shadows. Snake faltered for a heartbeat, then emptied his lungs of a scream, and brought the blade down, striking the man's outstretched hand. Metal clashed bone, and the machete spun from his grip.

The man made no sound, just stared at his mutilated hand, the first two fingers hanging by threads of gristle. Blood washing down his sleeve. On the man's pinkie finger, a large diamond ring sparkled. A fat, ugly diamond.

When the man dropped to his knees, Carmen tore out of bed.

"Come on, Snake. Come on."

She scrambled out the window and dropped into the long spring grass. A second later, machete in hand, Snake landed beside her, and from the adjacent window Carlos jumped onto the lawn and rolled to his feet.

The sentry spotted them as they neared the street. Sprinting through the warm night air, Snake heard gunfire, three blasts, four. Snake slowed when he heard the shots, falling back a step behind Carmen, and out of the darkness his sister slung her arms around him, tackling, dragging him to the lawn. They fell side by side, and her face came to rest inches away, blood pouring from her temple. Her eyes lingered on his for a second, then rolled upward to make the acquaintance of her God.

Snake drew a breath, the black night spinning. Then he grabbed the machete and found his feet.

The attacker was stalking toward them, head craned forward, peering through the silk stocking. A shiny pistol wavered before him.

Carlos fled across the street. By then neighbors were spilling from their houses, calling out to one another through the darkness.

Snake charged the man.

A slug whisked by his ear; another plowed into the soil at his feet. Snake flew across the yard and gored the man's belly, drove him backward. The two fell, and Snake rolled away and drew the blade free and hacked at the man, chopped and chopped until the killer no longer moved.

When Snake looked up, the invaders were fleeing the house. One of them saw their fallen comrade and started toward him, but a woman called out, "Leave him, let's go."

A woman.

They ran to the cars, slammed doors, roared away. Beside him a neighbor squatted over the body of Snake's victim and rolled back the stocking that covered the dead man's face. He was a short, narrow man with a thin mustache. Snake stared into his empty eyes but did not know him.

Then sirens.

While a medic treated Carlos's gash, detectives questioned Snake. Had he seen any of the bad men? Could he identify them? Snake said nothing.

It didn't matter. Nothing mattered. Old Snake was dead. New Snake was emerging from sloughed-off skin.

"You boys have relatives in Miami? Aunts, uncles?"

Snake shook his head. There was no one. The police officer eyed him strangely, this child, this killer.

A sharply handsome man with a birthmark on his cheek leaned close to the policeman and whispered and the officer nodded, then said to Snake:

"This good citizen has offered to look after you boys until the state of Florida in its infinite wisdom decides what the hell to do with you."

Snake voiced no protest. Going home with the man was what came next. Resisting was useless. The world's machinery operated according to laws absolute and unstoppable.

The man drove them away in his black Cadillac. His large house faced the dark shimmer of Biscayne Bay. Silk sheets on the beds, plush pillows. Carlos fell instantly asleep, but Snake stared into the darkness and thought.

For days the massacre filled the news. Before the killers left, they'd painted slogans on the walls of the Moraleses' house. *Viva la Revolución. Viva Fidel.* Death to all traitors. This was clearly Castro's work, the TV people proclaimed. His spies were everywhere. The bloodbath was meant to stifle dissent and put fear into the dozens of other exile groups in Miami that were organizing small armies to stage attacks on Cuba.

The man Snake hacked to death was named Humberto Berasategui. Though he worked as a Miami plumber, it was clear that Berasategui was a communist sympathizer, an agent in league with the dictator.

Local Cubans called for U.S. retaliation. Full-scale invasion. Hundreds rallied in the street and marched with placards, chants of hate and war. Eight people, including Snake's parents and Carmen, had been butchered by the pack of devils.

Snake saw himself on television, led away by the man with the birthmark. The mayor of Miami, Stanton King, had charitably opened his Coconut Grove home to the two orphaned boys.

"We'll find the boys a good family," the mayor said to the camera. "No matter how long it takes."

"Be good, Snake," Carlos whispered. "I like it here."

The day following the murders, FBI agents interviewed the boys while King chatted nearby with police. The same questions as the night before. What had Snake seen? A big man with a square head. That's all? He no longer has two fingers on his right hand, Snake said. The men looked away as if chilled.

Later he heard Gladys, the housekeeper, gossiping with the yardman.

"Those FBI boys'll catch the killers," she said. "You mark my word, G-men are as smart as they come, they'll get to the bottom of it."

"No, ma'am. Not with them Cubans mixed up in it," the gardener said. "Them people got so many secrets, so much bad blood going back to that damn island, back to the dawn of time, you watch, there ain't going to be no bottom to it."

That evening King didn't speak to the boys, just sat in his study and drank can after can of Country Club malt liquor.

At dawn the next morning another group of federal men arrived. Secret Service, the housekeeper whispered. Dark suits, rigid haircuts. They scoured the mansion, poked through closets, inspected the hot, dry attic.

Late that night three black limousines rolled up. A tall man with a belly climbed out of the largest car, surrounded by agents. Stanton King met him in the drive, shook his hand.

"Look there, boys. The president of these entire United States. Mr. LBJ himself. Most powerful man in the world." Gladys stood beside them at the front window as the two men mounted the steps.

"Big deal," Carlos said.

"You gonna remember this all the rest of your life. Isn't many people get to see the president up close in their own house. That's how important Mr. King is. They saying he run for governor next. That's why LBJ came over after his Democrat get-together. Pay his respects to Mr. King. Talk business."

The group came inside and went into the study and shut the door. Lyndon Baines Johnson. February 27, 1964. Two days after Cassius. Two days after Carmen died, trusting in the grace of a merciful God. Snake prayed she found him.

Snake lay down on his bed and switched on his radio. Through the wall he could hear Carlos's television set blaring Napoleon Solo's voice in *The Man from U.N.C.L.E.* On his own radio was one of Carmen's favorite Beatles song, "I Saw Her Standing There."

With the radio playing softly, Snake was staring into the dark when a Secret Service man appeared in his doorway and summoned him downstairs. Snake wore new Superman pajamas, blue and red with elastic cuffs at the ankles and wrists. Gladys stood on the landing, watching Snake descend the stairs, her face slack with astonishment.

In the study, the president came to his feet and walked over. A large man with a congenial smile, iron gray eyes. He bent forward and held out his paw, and Snake raised his hand to shake. The man's flesh was cool and dry. He seemed both radiant and weary, as if his great storehouse of vitality was under heavy strain, drawn down by responsibilities too enormous to imagine.

"I'm awful sorry to learn of your loss, son. Awful sorry."

When an interval passed, Snake withdrew his hand from the president's grip and stepped back. Barefoot, in his cartoon pajamas, feeling foolish. The three Secret Service men were looking away from the scene. Stanton King stared at the rug, as if the president and the boy gave off a painful glare.

"Nobody can replace a boy's father and mother, but I'm certain Mr. King will do his damnedest. You'll be well taken care of, son. Count on it."

"My sister, Carmen," Snake said. "No one can replace her." LBJ nodded solemnly.

"You're right, son. Your sister, too. A terrible loss." LBJ looked around at the other men, then turned back to Snake. "You're a brave boy. It took courage to fight back like you did. You're a hero, a credit to your nation."

Snake had nothing to say. He'd killed one man, maimed another, but it had not been enough to save Carmen. All he felt was the black chokehold of guilt.

When Mayor King told Snake he could go, the boy turned from Lyndon Johnson and went back to his room, shut the door, and lay down, inhaling the heavy scent of night-blooming jasmine that clogged the air beyond his window.

He devoted that sleepless night and many nights to come replaying what happened. Searching for a clue he had missed, anything that might give his life direction. But the yardman was right. There was no bottom to it. Like a cavern branching down endlessly into the limitless black heart of the world.

In the hours of that everlasting night Snake made a vow—his own mission. Inch by inch he would wriggle to the bottom of that bottomless cave, and one day shine his light in the face of the monster who resided there. Find out what happened and why. Then take his vengeance.

Whatever it took. However long. Until then, he'd be Cassius. Wait for his eyes to clear, backpedal, stay out of range. Survive, survive.

CHAPTER ONE

"You hate Miami."

"It's not my favorite dot on the map," Thorn said. "But I don't hate it."

They stood on the pine dock that rimmed the boat basin.

Sugarman set his new laptop on the seat of a canvas deck chair. He'd been showing off the computer, and Thorn had been trying hard to feign interest as Sugar flashed through dozens of digital photos of his twin daughters, zoomed in and out on their beautiful smiles, showing Thorn how to filter away messy backgrounds, crop off the edges.

Now Sugar took a swallow of his Bud and watched Thorn tug his red-and-white bobber toward the center of the basin. It was a muggy April afternoon, closing in on suppertime with the sun drifting behind the sabal palms on the western edge of Thorn's property. A gust off the Atlantic riffled the lagoon, and for a moment the water went opaque, then a moment later the breeze died and the rocky bottom came back into focus fifteen feet below.

"You ever spent seven consecutive days in Miami?"

"Not that I recall."

"You'll freak, Thorn, you'll break out in boils."

"Oh, I'll survive."

"So what's the deal? Alexandra's quitting her job? Going to do search and rescue full-time?"

"She and Buck have to pass final certification. But yeah, Miami PD is setting up a team. She's first in line."

"Lost children, old people wandering off? Cadavers?"

"That's the idea."

"That's why she hasn't been down lately? This extra work?"

"Part of the reason, yeah, but I've been going up there. All of us slogging around the Everglades. I mind Lawton while she and Buck search for scented dummies."

"First I heard of that."

Thorn gave another light tug on the line.

"It's interesting work. Puzzle solving, following clues."

"Not just the dog sticking its nose up in the air, then taking off?"

"A little more complicated than that."

"Well, that mutt's smarter than I thought he was," Sugarman said.

"He's a Lab. Even the dumb ones are smart."

Thorn watched his bobber drifting with the incoming tide.

"Twenty years snapping photos of corpses, working around hard-ass homicide cops, I see how she'd find search dogs more stimulating."

Thorn was silent, focused on the bobber.

Sugar said, "Why doesn't Lawton come down here, spend seven nights at scenic, relaxing Club Thorn?"

He gestured at the house behind them, the one-story Cape Cod where Thorn had grown up. Tucked in an insolated cove, it faced into the steady Atlantic winds.

Fifteen years ago when Kate Truman, his adoptive mother, died, Thorn shuttered the place and settled into a stilt house a few miles south on the opposite side of the island. Then last year a fire turned his stilt house to cinders, and all these months later, he still hadn't found the heart to clean up the debris, much less rebuild. So he'd returned to the white wooden house where he'd spent his youth, opened it up, aired it out, and for the past few weeks he'd been adjusting to the ghostly echoes. Scenes from his youth replaying at odd moments, a whiff of a baseball glove, a moldering fishing rod, would set off long rambles through his teenage years.

"While she's in Tampa taking her tests, she gave me a list of projects she needs done, a roof leak, that kind of thing. So I putter around while Lawton's at day care, take charge of him in the evening. Seven nights, how bad is that?"

"Alex never really liked the Keys, did she?"

"She likes it fine, but all the driving back and forth gets old, an hour each way, traffic getting worse all the time. Her life is up there."

"In Miami."

"Yeah, Miami. The streets, the hum."

"And your life is here, the water, the hush."

"You trying to say something?"

Sugarman tightened his lips.

"All right. You want the barefaced truth?" He drew a wary breath. "Ever since Alex stopped coming down here, you've been seriously gloomy."

"Oh, come on."

"I'm serious. Bleak. Moodier than usual."

"Funny, I thought I was feeling pretty bubbly."

"You? Bubbly?"

"Relatively speaking, I mean. Relatively bubbly."

"Okay, so when's the last time you tied a bonefish fly?"

Thorn tugged his line, scanned the basin.

"A month ago? Two months?"

"Two's about right."

"So what've you been doing for income?"

"I'm getting by."

"You're surviving on chunky peanut butter and beer. Raiding the penny jar. Can't even afford Red Stripe, drinking Budweiser, for godsakes."

"You volunteering to be my financial planner?"

"Tell you what I will do," he said. "I'll go up there myself, babysit the old man. Lawton and I get along fine. You stay here, get to work."

"Nice try," Thorn said. "But I need to do this."

"What you need is to get back to what makes you sane."

"So now I'm insane?"

"You're mopey, Thorn. And you been hitting the long-necks hard. Starting early, a six-pack before the sun goes down. You need to get your groove back, my man."

"My groove?"

"Oh, jeez, now I get it." Sugar shook his head. Something so obvious taking so long to dawn. "You're thinking about moving up there, aren't you? That's what this is about. Desert the Keys, move in with Alexandra. Jesus, Thorn. That's it, isn't it? Live in freaking Miami."

"Here it comes." Thorn nodded to his left. "Ten o'clock, five yards."

He angled to his right along the dock and tugged the bobber so it was floating a few feet ahead of the big snook's path.

"And, hey, what's with the bobber?" Sugar said. "Where's your fly rod?"

"I want to catch this fish, not play with it."

Sugarman leaned out and watched the snook swim past the finger mullet that dangled below the bobber.

He and Sugar went back to grade school. Though it felt like they went back further than that. Brother yin and brother yang. Sugar was the only guy on earth who could give Thorn the level of shit he did. Tell that kind of truth.

He'd been a Monroe County sheriff's deputy, now a security consultant, a term he liked better than private eye. Half Jamaican, half Norwegian. Pale blond mother, Rasta father. A lucky blend. Inherited the laid-back genes of the ganja man and the chiseled cheekbones and long limbs and elegant moves of his lovely mom. Her cold focus. After those two abandoned him when he was still a toddler, his scruples were shaped by a foster mom who raised him in the tropical poverty of Hibiscus Park, Key Largo's ghetto. Crack houses and heroin dens, rusty cars up on blocks; the only lawful neighborhood business was a hubcap stand along the overseas highway. After a childhood like that, Sugarman had developed an indestructible gristle at his core. He grew up quiet and clear-minded, a man so strictly principled, so secure in his humane convictions, that on countless occasions he'd served as Thorn's true north, hauling him back onto the proper path just as Thorn was about to lurch over some fatal precipice.

Sugar peered into the lagoon.

"Damn, that's no snook. It's Orca, the killer whale."

Thorn watched the snook glide across the basin to the mangrove roots that curved into the basin like the bars of an underwater cage.

"It's checking an escape route. It'll try to cut me off on those roots."

Sugar said, "Did I see that right? All those leaders streaming off her mouth? There must be a dozen hooks in her lip."

"At least."

"What do you figure? Fish that size, it's got to be ten, twelve years old?"

"Closer to twenty-one," said Thorn.

"Twenty-one? And how'd you arrive at that?"

"One of those leaders is mine."

"Same snook? Oh, give me a break."

"I was standing right here when she broke it off. Kate and I were fishing together. That fly was one of my first attempts at a ghost streamer."

"So that's what this is about, fixing some youthful error?"

"I saw it a couple of weeks ago, all those leaders dangling. I figured I should clean her up. Been out here every night since. Sort of a project."

"Well, that's a first. Thorn getting emotional about a fish."

"A creature like that, it's entitled to a decent old age without dragging around a nest of monofilament."

"Maybe those are her medals. An old warrior, she might be proud of them. Shows 'em off to her snook friends."

The snook curved away from the mangroves and made another pass at the finger mullet, checking it over, then once again coasting off.

"You might be about to add one more hook to the collection."

"I'm a better fisherman than I was twenty years ago."

"She could be a better fish."

Thorn stepped out on the dock and towed the bobber closer to a rotting piling. Trying to reassure the fish, make it feel secure with structure nearby.

A second later the snook reappeared and in a flicker it crashed the bait, then ran so fast that it almost snatched the rod from Thorn's grip.

Instead of charging to the mangrove roots like she should've done, the fish headed for the mouth of the basin and the flats beyond. But hauling all that heavy line wore her down fast. The drag was set light, reel shrieking as the big fish tore toward open water.

"Not a smart move," Sugarman said. "For an old warhorse like her."

"Gotten lazy. Cutting corners. She didn't do that twenty years ago."

Thorn tightened the drag, then pumped the rod, reeling on the down stroke. As the hook dug in, the fish broke from the water, jumped high into the rosy evening air, twisting and trying to buck loose. She flopped hard on her side and startled a school of baitfish into a flurry of pirouettes.

That one jump was all she had.

As the snook reached the entrance of the basin, Thorn leaned back on the rod and turned her around. The snook made a couple of halfhearted zigzag runs, but as Thorn worked her back toward the dock, it was clear the old girl's iron will had melted. As he cranked her the last few feet, she was docile.

"Getting old is hell."

"Tell me about it," Sugar said.

Thorn hauled the fish to the dock and handed the rod to Sugarman. He knelt and found a safe grip on her lower jaw, then heaved her up onto a wet towel he'd laid out and began to work with his pliers, clipping, prying, snapping the barbed ends off the hooks, curling them free.

Half a minute later when he was done and the snook's lip was clear, he lowered the fish back into the water and stroked it back and forth until it recovered and glided for-

ward and was on its way without a backward glance or nod
of gratitude. Left behind in the water was a faint cloud of
blood.

"Sometimes you have to hurt them to fix them."

"Words to live by," Sugar said.

"She'll be fine in a day or two."

"Your good deed for the year." Sugarman knelt to the
basin and washed the slime off his hands. "You're hereby
absolved, my son, and are now free to return to your dis-
solute ways."

Thorn watched the satin gloss of the sunset water, gold
and pink ripples spreading out in perfect V's behind the departing snook.

"You're right about Miami."

"Which part?"

"That I'm considering a move."

Sugarman was silent, staring at the darkening horizon.

"I'm trying it out, is all. An audition. Driving up tonight;
Alexandra leaves first thing tomorrow. I'll give it a week, see
how it feels, if I can cope. Maybe stay a little longer after
she gets back. But even if it works, Sugar, I'll always have
one foot here. I'll never leave the Keys, not really."

"This her idea or yours?"

"Mine. Alex wouldn't ask me to do it."

"She means that much to you."

"She does. Yeah."

"We're talking marriage here? Picket fence, weekend
barbecues?"

"I'm talking about seven days in Miami. See how it
feels."

Sugarman nodded and looked up at the dying blush in
the sky.

"Well, promise me one thing."

"Name it."

"It's a big bad city, and you're an island boy, Thorn, spent
your entire life on this damn rock, which makes you just one
notch above a country bumpkin. Promise me you'll keep
your head down, okay? Stay cool."

Thorn smiled. He'd been dreading this conversation, the effect it would have on Sugar—and on him, too—speaking the words out loud.

"I'll be good," Thorn said. "Flowers in my hair, peace and love."

Sugarman lifted an eyebrow and gave him a dubious smile.

"Weird shit goes on up there, Thorn. And I do mean weird."

Sunday afternoon on South Beach. Across Ocean Drive the art deco hotels stood like a row of sno-cones drizzled with tropical syrups and speckled with peppermint.

She was there to shoot a man.

Her only requirements: He had to be Hispanic, tall and slinky. The slinkier, the better. Tall and slinky. Like him.

Cloudless sky, surf splashing, ocean spangled with white diamonds. Nearby a radio thumped with rap music, loud enough to cover the percussion of her Walther Red Hawk.

Men strutted the strand, where sheets of surf unfurled before them. Gusts scented with sea foam and baking sand, coconut oil. The riotous screech of gulls.

An electric buzz inside her head. A buzz. A buzz.

She had no schedule. Only came to shoot when the dark column of static rose up her spinal cord and the drone began around her head, the hateful buzz.

She sat in her aluminum beach chair. A floppy straw hat shading her face, hair tucked under. Hiding behind sunglasses with white square frames. A brown towel lay across her lap, concealing the sleek black pistol with its smooth molded edges, lustrous black frame, eight-shot rotary magazine.

Loaded with pellets. Lead lumps with cinched waists and pointy tips. Shaped like minarets. Twice the weight of BBs. Sent flying by spurts of pressurized gas.

Lethal, oh yes, if the muzzle was snug against an ear, fired into the soft interior channels, one after the other, or into an eyeball. That could bring death or leave them pleading for it.

From the distance she was shooting, no, not fatal. Oh, but at five hundred feet per second, what a beautiful, vicious sting.

Her days of killing were finished. All done. No more guns and blasts of gore. This was more fitting. Sting, not kill. More fitting for a woman her age, her station. Her twisted history.

So many targets on parade today. So many men in their cocky Speedos, the bulge of crotch. The flaunting display. They swaggered by. A mouth like his. Like his.

An unbroken pageant of nearly naked men. So many, many Hispanics. The dark hair, insolent smiles, long lashes. Sensual macho lips.

She saw one coming. Red clingy suit. Head high, dark wraparounds.

Tightened her finger. Tensing to a pound of pressure, two, then backing off. Letting this Speedo pass. This bulge of prideful meat. She wasn't ready yet. Too quick. Too early. No reason to rush.

Drew her hand from beneath the towel, wiped her palm dry. Slid it back inside, fitted her fingers to the molded stock. The molded stock.

She waited, watched them pass. Looked down the beach. The crowd around her drowsing, talking, reading paperback novels and magazines. She was simply one of them, a lady in late middle age, basking in the sun. No one knew. No one ever knew.

Five minutes passed before she spotted an even better one. Forty yards off, ambling the hard-packed sand, with gold around his neck; long, loose limbs; a gaudy lump in his black thong. Watching him approach, that smug stride. Deciding, yes, this was the target for today. To hush the drone, the nagging hum inside her skull, the buzz buzz buzz.

Curling the finger.

Fifty feet, forty, coming into range. She aimed for the crotch, the tender thighs. Navel to knees, that was her zone.

He slowed, then halted, stooped for something in the retreating surf. A white chip of shell. He stood, holding it. Examining. A sensitive fellow. A willing target.

She squeezed and squeezed again, then once more. Three quiet plonks lost amid the noise around her.

He dropped his shell, slapped a hand to his thigh, looked down to see the blood drooling from a tiny hole. He crumpled to his knees, a husky roar.

"I'm shot! Someone shot me!"

At the brim of his thong, a second puncture in the flesh. Then she saw the ragged slash in the nylon crotch.

Three for three, a notable day. Sting, sting, sting.

As once she was stung.

Shrieking women ripped up their towels and blankets, fled.

A panicked exodus, which she joined. Simply another woman padding up the hill of sand toward Ocean Drive. A Jeep roared up. Beach patrol. It had been happening for years. Blamed on gangs, soulless teens. A dangerous prank. Police were on alert but always came too late.

She mounted the dune. The buzz had toggled off. Sweet silence swimming up her spine. Brain quiet. Buzz gone. Just the ocean, the restless sea.

While on his knees on the hard-packed sand, the man, the random man, screamed and screamed and screamed.

CHAPTER TWO

Eight o'clock on Sunday evening, Stanton King trailed his lovely wife, Lola, through the snooty throng at Merrick Gallery. As usual when Lola passed by, men nodded in approval and spoke her name, women smiled with icy politeness and edged closer to their partners. It was the same performance Stanton had witnessed for the entire span of their marriage, and he took more than a little pleasure in watching it unfold.

After all these years, Lola King had lost none of her power to excite. As they made their way across the gallery, male libidos drummed in counterpoint to the hiss of female envy. At times such as these, in crowded rooms, Stanton took an honored place beside his wife, matched her step for step, received her cool hand on his offered arm, feeling more intimate with her in such public gatherings than he ever did when they were shut together in private.

Nearly once a week they were similarly engaged. Gallery openings like tonight's, or dedications of halfway houses, fund-raisers for homeless shelters and historical-preservation-league functions, environmental campaigns, thousand-dollar-a-plate dinners for one or another of Lola's charitable causes.

It delighted Stanton that even in her sixties Lola was the object of such palpable lust and that he as a result could bask in covetous esteem. Sadly, the display was all pretense, for

Lola had not shared her bed or body with Stanton in decades and they rarely engaged in conversation on topics more intimate than the grocery list, but still, the wave of arousal that rippled through the gallery cheered him. It was the reason he accompanied her to these stuffy events, simply to live out the public version of what he no longer enjoyed in private.

Tonight Stanton's white frizzled hair was unruly as always, an electrified mass that bore a resemblance to Einstein's. He wore a blue aloha shirt decorated with white oversize hibiscus blooms. White slacks and white shoes. A costume that in Miami was considered formal wear.

Lola was tricked out in a pastel pink sheath dress with a scooped neckline that displayed the ample cleavage she'd possessed since her twenties. Her waist was slim and the swell of her hips still well within ideal proportions. For tonight's occasion she'd swirled her red hair into a dramatic display, and her complexion, an unblemished creamy white, was undusted by powder.

Within her blue eyes, a dark light fluttered like a volatile magnetic field. It was Lola's custom to fix her gaze on whoever was closest at hand. She was not one of those annoying women always scanning for a better circumstance. It was part of her charm, part of her wondrous attraction, that she could bring the full force of her allure to bear on a single individual.

After greeting several acquaintances, Stanton and Lola joined the line that moved in a slow clockwise amble around the perimeter of the gallery to view the artwork. Behind him Lola settled into quiet pleasantries with Miguel Marquez Estefano, a squat, silver-maned Cuban gentleman who operated the largest Toyota dealership in the city. Lola and Estefano occupied seats on several boards together, and after a brief acknowledgment of Stanton, Estefano held Lola's attention as the conga line progressed past the black-and-white photographs that were the cause of the evening's celebration.

In the far corner of the room Stanton noted Mr. Alan Bingham, the photographer whose work they were honoring tonight. Stanton identified him from the snapshot on the printed program, a gaunt man in his fifties, surrounded by well-wishers and friends. He seemed a quiet sort. Wispy and unassuming. The type of individual who could slip here and there and snap his photos without stirring the air around him.

His exhibit displayed the seamy edges of Miami with a wry, good-hearted slant. Strippers and drunks, obese tourists frolicking inelegantly, forlorn immigrants trapped behind razor-wire fences, all of them staring frankly into the lens and revealing some angle of themselves that was cocky or profoundly desperate or just plain goofy. As the line moved forward, Stanton entertained himself by looking past the obvious subjects of the photos and trying to place the locations where each was shot. Krome Detention Center, Miami Beach, Opa-locka, a strip club on Biscayne Boulevard. All of them rendered in the unsparing black-and-white manner of Diane Arbus but tinged with a hearty humor Arbus never managed.

Midway through his journey around the large hall, with Lola and Estefano trailing behind, Stanton confronted a shot of Cassius Clay and Sonny Liston poised mid-ring on that night in 1964. He halted briefly and craned forward for a sharper view, his heart rising quickly to a hammering percussion. A wave of chilly sweat broke out across his back.

Beyond the fighters, in the third row of the Miami Beach Convention Hall, sat a group of fans who were watching the proceedings in various degrees of attention. Framed perfectly by the rope rings, these fight fans were most certainly the focus of the photograph. Five of them sitting side by side.

It was, Stanton saw with horror, a collection of notorious people who might easily be recognized by any of a dozen patrons in the gallery tonight if they bothered to stop and take a longer look and burrow back into their memories for faces and events from forty years ago.

Stanton slid forward, his breath tight, and behind him Lola and Estefano passed by the boxing photograph, unaware of its import. But as they were edging forward to the next selection, Lola halted and reversed course. For several seconds she absorbed the image before her.

When she turned to Stanton, the faint smile that had been fixed on her lips all evening had vanished. Her eyes were blurred and her features tensed into a grim, rubbery mask. Her lips drew open as if she meant to scream.

"It's nothing, darling, I'll take care of it," he assured her. "Would you excuse me for a moment?"

Stanton broke from the line and headed for a rear exit. The moment he was in the alley, he drew his cell phone from his trousers and made the call.

In his panic he misdialed and got an angry man who clicked off as Stanton was apologizing for the wrong number. He looked up and down the dark alley, drew a long breath. He counted to ten, then to twenty.

He focused on the keypad and punched the numbers, and after a single ring the familiar voice answered.

"I have a job for you," Stanton said. "It's of the utmost importance."

Stanton stepped farther from the rear exit.

"It will involve illegal acts. It must be done tonight. Are you willing?"

One in the morning, in the alley behind Merrick Gallery, Carlos Morales splashed kerosene on the heap of framed black-and-white photographs. Snake stood watching. When he'd emptied his can, Carlos scratched a match with his thumbnail, flicked it into the pile, and they watched as the flames meandered through the photos.

"Now for the good part," Carlos said. "Mr. Photographer."

As he was turning to leave, Snake glimpsed an image he hadn't noticed before. The photo lay on top of the pile, flames moving around it. He went back, leaned over the fire. A shot of a boxing ring, two black men at arm's length, behind them the crowd. Cassius and Sonny. February 1964.

"What the hell're you doing?"

Without thought, Snake thrust his hand into the flames. Gripped the frame, but the heat crippled his fingers and the photograph slid away, wedging deeper into the bonfire.

As it was consumed, he studied the image, watched it darken and crinkle, turn to red and yellow ribbons of fire twisting into the night. Cassius up on his toes, Liston heavy and slow. Behind the boxers, rows of men in suits and white shirts and narrow ties, some with kerchiefs in their breast pockets.

Then he saw the two men sitting side by side, and his heart roared.

Three rows from the ring was a man with a birthmark on his cheek, Mayor Stanton King. Next to him a stocky man thrust a cheering fist toward the boxers. A diamond flashed on his pinkie finger. Exactly like the ring on the man Snake had confronted in his sister's room forty years before.

By the time Snake noticed the stocky man and his diamond, the flames had eaten away his face, and seconds later the fire consumed the rest of him.

CHAPTER THREE

"Your hand, man, doesn't that hurt?"

"Don't worry about my hand."

On a middle-class street, South Miami, with stucco houses on small lots, Snake parked his Friendly Service yellow cab and they walked along the sidewalk toward the man's home. Tile roof, big oak out front.

Snake was trying to reconstruct the photo, bring it up from the hazy developing pan of memory. The way his brain worked, he absorbed every image passing before him, stored it away. Things he didn't register at the time, he could go back and pick out, see as fresh as the original moment. But not this time.

The stocky man's face wouldn't coalesce. It remained a shadowy smudge. Stanton's features, yes, those were sharp and clear. A frown of tension. A troubled look Snake had rarely seen him wear, this congenial man who'd raised him, fed, clothed, housed him and Carlos for the past four decades.

One house away, Snake halted and whispered to Carlos, "Look for that boxing photo, I want it."

"The old man said burn everything."

"Our mission has changed."

"It has?"

"This is no longer about what Stanton wants. It's about what I want."

Carlos said, sure, that was cool, whatever.

"I need to study the image," Snake said. "Grasp its meaning."

"Yeah? Why's that?"

"It's the answer. Why Carmen died and our parents were killed."

"Oh, shit, Snake. That's so over. Fucking ancient history, man."

"It's not over, Carlos. Not by a long way."

It was nearly one in the morning. Nobody around. Even the dogs asleep. Snake rang the man's bell. He rang it again, then again.

Finally there was a voice behind the door asking what in the world they wanted. A mild-mannered guy.

Snake kept his face close to the peephole.

"It's a neighbor," Snake said. "There's a fire. I'm warning everybody."

"A fire!"

"A fire," Snake said. "It's moving this way. Fast."

The man inside the house weighed it for a few seconds, then unbolted his front door, and that's when Carlos kicked it into his face and the two of them went inside.

Once they trussed up the man with plastic ties, they took their time.

One by one Carlos smashed all the man's cameras and pulled out the film, then they opened each drawer and checked for photographs, and when Snake made sure the boxing photo wasn't among them, Carlos piled them up and set them ablaze in the man's fireplace.

They had the man tied up in his darkroom, center of the house. Heavy curtains, thick stucco walls. Better than a dungeon, scream all he wanted.

Snake's brother was a thick-chested man of medium height with a head one size too large for his body, a square face and dense black hair that he kept shaved in a bristly skullcap. He had the bloodshot eyes and puffy cheeks of a pro wrestler gone to seed. His eyes juked constantly, and every minute or two he waved a hand in front of his face like he was swiping at a cloud of mosquitoes. Except there were no mosquitoes there. None at all.

After the night their family was slaughtered, the Morales boys were ruined in different ways. Carlos lived on constant high alert, forever vigilant of things whisking at his face, seeing danger where there was none, his hand lashing out to squash imagined creatures, taking offense when none was meant.

Snake's memory was his curse. At least once a day, a stray moment from those long-ago hours flared to life. The same ancient images recycling. A bullet blasting through the bedroom wall. Snow of plaster in his hair. Carlos sobbing. Carmen lying dead in the long spring grass. Cassius and Liston, LBJ unfolding from his limo, his cool dry hand enclosing Snake's.

"What is this about?" the man said. "What do you want?"

"Your photos," Carlos told him. "We already did the museum, all those are taken care of. Now we're doing these."

"You went to Merrick Gallery?"

"Just came from there," Carlos said. "Nice place, all that marble. Not much of an alarm system, but they'll probably upgrade after tonight."

"And you stole my photographs from the show?"

Carlos waved an imaginary gnat from his face.

"Piled 'em in an alley and torched them. Sorry. That's just how it is. Nothing personal, just doing a job."

"I don't understand."

"So this is all your photos?" Carlos said. "What we're seeing here? You don't have an office, a warehouse, there might be more stashed in boxes?"

"I work at home."

"Hey, don't be getting jiggy with us."

Carlos got his face up close to the man's, gave him a stare, then swung around, and with a wave he cleared a path through the cloud of bugs and marched into the house to resume his search.

The man's name was Alan Bingham. He was in his late fifties. Tall and lean like a distance runner, still with a good head of silvering hair. Wearing faded jeans and a white T-shirt.

"Look, Alan," Snake said. "Don't make this difficult."

Carlos was in the living room, rummaging.

"You break in, tie me up, destroy my cameras. I'm supposed to cooperate like none of that happened?"

"Yeah, I know. It's disgraceful, smashing your fine equipment. My partner gets carried away. You've seen him. He's rash and volatile."

"Every single photograph? Is that what you're saying? You want to know where every single one of them is?"

Snake could hear Carlos wrecking the furniture in another room.

"Okay." Snake took his voice lower. "Here's the truth. We don't care about *all* your photos. What we care about is one particular shot, okay? One that was in your show at Merrick Gallery."

"Which one?"

Bingham was peering into Snake's eyes like he was trying to bond. Or maybe searching for some fiber of humanity. Good luck with either.

"Cassius Clay and Sonny Liston."

"You want that photograph? Why, for God's sake?"

"What were you, about twelve when you took that?"

"Fifteen," he said. "My first real photo."

"I listened on the radio," Snake said. "Nineteen sixty-four Miami Beach Convention Hall. Louisville Lip versus the Big Ugly Bear. Seven-to-one odds against Clay. Liston had an eighty-four-inch reach. Bone breaker for the mob, in and out of jail, everyone thought he'd kill Clay. Howard Cosell doing the color commentary. Les Keiter on the play-by-play. Ref was Barney Felix."

"You're a boxing fan."

"No. I just remember things. Useless trivia. When I was a kid, I saw Clay a few times. I watched him work out at the Fifth Street Gym, saw him on the streets in Overtown, strutting around. Later on after he won the title, driving that tomato red Cadillac convertible."

"He was a beautiful young man," Bingham said.

"But in the photo you weren't interested in him. It's more about the crowd. I just got a peek. Couldn't make out all the faces, but a couple of guys in one row looked bored. How the hell could they be bored at that fight? A night like that. History in the making."

Bingham nodded.

"But then, you never know it's history in the making till it's over, do you? Living your life, you got no perspective. That's what you were after, I bet. Being part of something big, but not knowing it at the time."

Bingham shook his head, not believing this.

"What was it about the boxing shot made you put it in the show?"

"Just what you said. The looks on the people's faces."

"That's it? Nothing more than that?"

"That's a lot. All those different points of view."

Snake gave Alan a reassuring pat on the shoulder.

"I made a pledge to myself," Snake said. "On that very night, the Cassius-Liston fight. I made a pledge, but then I kind of let it drift away."

"A pledge?"

"A promise to myself, a life mission. But after all these years, I lost hold of it. It's hard to hang on to one idea that long. Keep your focus."

Alan was peering uncertainly at Snake.

"But you did it, didn't you, Alan? You held on to your pledge. You were taking photographs at fifteen, here you are, all these years later, you're still doing it. You stayed devoted to your quest."

Alan Bingham's face softened, his eyes drifting toward the wall.

"There's always ups and downs," he said. "Passion is hard to sustain."

Snake nodded. His own fervor had melted away, nearly vanished, but just tonight, it was back.

"I want that boxing photo," Snake said.

"Jesus Christ. You could've just come in and asked for it.

You didn't need to get rough." He shook his head, squirmed against the restraints.

"I've been patient with you, Alan. This doesn't have to get messy."

"All right, damn it. In the oak cabinet. The studio, two doors down. There's negatives of everything." Alan's eyes were muddy, body limp.

Snake was turning to the door when Carlos rolled into the room, sweating—his green polo shirt with a dark butterfly of sweat on the front.

"Your freaking air-conditioning broke?" he said. "Or you just cheap?"

"I don't have air-conditioning," Bingham said.

"What're you, crazy?"

"Alan's old-school," Snake said. "Living close to nature like the pioneers. Isn't that right, Alan?"

"Fuck nature," Carlos said. "And the camel it rode in on."

Alan Bingham said nothing, looking off toward the far wall.

"I think I got 'em all," Carlos said.

"And the one I want?"

Carlos shook his head.

"Well, there's negatives," said Snake. "Oak cabinet, two rooms down."

"I burned 'em already. They're history."

"You didn't check them first?"

"Check them?"

Snake cursed and pushed past him and found the oak cabinet. Drawers empty. He hustled to the fireplace, but it was too late. Just ash and rubble.

He walked back to the darkroom. Carlos swished a hand through the air.

"Okay, man, it's go time."

"I need that photograph," Snake told him.

"Aw, shit. The old man says burn 'em all, we burned 'em all. This is getting to be a major buzz kill. Let's just go."

Snake turned to Alan.

"Tell me, Alan. Where can I find a copy?"

Alan shook his head, mouth clamped.

Snake said, "Show him the pistol, Carlos."

Carlos dug the .22 from his waistband, pressed it to Alan's temple.

"Where, Alan?"

Bingham swallowed again.

"All right, all right. There's one I can think of. But it's not here."

"Where?"

"If I tell you, you have to promise you won't hurt the man."

"Have we hurt you, Alan?" Snake said.

"We're cool with that," Carlos said. "We look like stone-cold killers? Hey, we're pulling a job for a guy. Torching some snapshots. He gave us work, we're doing it. That's all. A little harmless destruction of property."

"Who would hire you to do such a thing? Why?"

"I said his name, you'd know it."

"Zip it," Snake said. "Alan doesn't need to know our business."

Carlos turned a make-believe key in front of his lips.

Almost fifty, Carlos had never matured past adolescence, as though some crucial hormone had failed to kick in. A dash of gray sprinkled his hair, wrinkles setting in around his eyes, but otherwise, he was still a junior-high punk.

"So who has this copy?" Snake repeated. "Tell us that, we cut you loose, we're gone like a bad dream."

Carlos lowered the pistol to his side and patted Alan on the shoulder.

Alan thought about it. Looking at Carlos, then shifting back to Snake, still trying to read him but getting nowhere. Finally he sighed.

"He lives across the street. He's an old gentleman losing his memory."

"How fortunate for him," Snake said.

"You've got to promise me you won't hurt him."

"It's all good," Carlos said. "We're straight up with that."

"His name, Alan," said Snake.

"He's a frail old guy. Look, I'll go over there myself and get it back."

"No," Snake said. "We wouldn't want to put you to the trouble."

"Just ask him for the photo, he'll give it to you. No rough stuff."

"Alan, his name."

"Lawton Collins. He's a sweet old man."

"Directly across the street? White house, tin roof?"

Alan nodded.

"He admired the boxing shot, so I gave him a copy. I'm longtime friends with him and his daughter. Nice neighbors."

"That's good, Alan. That's very good."

"Now you've got them all. A lifetime of work. Gone. Irreplaceable."

"There's nothing can't be replaced," Carlos said, shifting the pistol to Bingham's chest. "Not even you, dawg."

"No, Carlos, there's no need for that."

Snake lay a restraining hand on his brother's arm, but it didn't stop him.

The tiny pistol wasn't loud, which was a virtue, but the downside, a caliber that small, it took three shots to quiet Alan's gurgling.

CHAPTER FOUR

Lying beside Alexandra all night, Thorn dreamed of naked flesh, sleek torsos, fingers tracing across his skin, several persons attending to him, an orgy held in his honor, a dream that seemed to last for hours with bodies coiling like oily snakes around his own, his erection holding firm so long it began to ache. Such a vivid dream, it might have lasted only seconds but seemed to stretch back into the long hours of the night.

He was still lost in the erotic swoon when he felt Alexandra's long limbs raking across him, her arms and legs, thin yet strong from years of karate training and wind sprints across the soft dunes of Key Biscayne. Gymnast's calves and the long, smooth arm muscles of a distance swimmer.

Groggy, submerged in the ocean depths of slumber, Thorn registered her climbing atop, settling skin to skin, pressing flush against his contours. He opened his eyes, saw her smiling down. Then came a faint shifting and re-aligning until he was fully within her. Alexandra's glossy black hair fell forward and curtained his face. There was a wry twist in her smile, as if she'd seen into his dreaming mind and was pushing aside the others and claiming what was rightfully hers.

An April dawn in Alexandra's bedroom with gray light swimming beyond her lace curtains. Outside the open window a gardenia hedge flowered, its perfume thickening the air.

No kissing. Speechless. As though this were an encounter

between unknowns. A woman and a man in an anonymous bed. Some wordless song passing back and forth between their lips. The rasp of her skin against his. Her face nuzzled against his neck, the smell of her sweat, acrid and citrus. With his fingertips he sketched the knobs of her spine. Inside her, heated but not moving. Holding it there, that fit, that merge of tissue and moistness.

On the bureau across the room, an oscillating fan hummed and sent its periodic breeze. Her breath stirred the hair on his neck.

Her right hand cupped his neck from behind. He turned his face and touched the tip of his tongue to her wrist, licked at the dark wisps of hair. Tasted more of her salt. But some message her loins transmitted kept him contained, not even permitting a mild thrust. The two of them holding that tight grip. Their hips immobilized by some signal rising from their core.

She worked her other hand into the small of his back, touching a knob in his lumbar region. Just there. Pressing it with her fingertips. Top of spine, base of spine, making some electrical connection. Alexandra, the conduit.

And Thorn had a male vision. A dead bolt gliding into its slot. Swiss precision. Twin pieces coming together in finely engineered connection. A fit so flawlessly calibrated, no oil was required for its slide. An effortless mesh. A lock with two halves joined. Him and her, with a rising pressure now in her hands, one on the base of his neck, the other just above his rump, gripping, cradling, the heels of her hands digging in. He could feel her nipples prod his own. The smallest writhing worked through their hips. His or hers. He was lost now. Not there. Fused. Loins dissolved.

Then after an interminable moment, she flinched. Her haunches quivered; a rumble rose between them. Some forewarning below the crust of the earth. An ancient growl of awakening geologic plates.

And a final surprise: with no warning, there was a mutual gasp. A massive letting go of air and fluids, spasms of sphincters, gripping so hard that there surely would be blue and yellow finger bruises later, and then constriction. Painful, burning. And with a groan, Alex heaved herself up and rolled away onto the white sheets.

Breathless and panting, both of them. Something like laughter rolling up, a cough of breath, an astonished cheer.

The cardinal that had nested in a poinciana tree just beyond the gardenia bush sang for them. Riddling the silence, overfilling it with a lush melody, its one simple song. A bird in the delicate light, a stirring breeze. His heart was slowing, gravity returning to reclaim him.

When words were possible, Thorn said, "What the hell was that?"

She took several seconds before answering.

"I don't know."

"Where'd you learn it?"

"Here," she said. "We learned it together, in case you didn't notice."

"Something Oriental? Chakras, all that?"

"Is a name required?"

Thorn's right hand was resting on her thigh. Damp flesh still warm, still beating with blood.

"All right," he said. "Nameless it shall remain."

Alex rolled onto her side, resting her head in the shallow of his shoulder.

"Will it hold you for the week I'm gone?"

"A week? Hell, I may never need sex again."

"Oh, God, it wasn't that good."

"Close," he said. "Damn close."

"The female gender would be losing an important natural resource."

"I'm not interested in the female gender. I only have eyes for you."

"Yeah, right."

"It's true."

"For the moment maybe. Don't fool yourself, Thorn. Lifetime habits don't go away so easily."

Thorn was trying to recall a line of poetry he'd known once, something from John Donne about romantic constancy. But it wouldn't come up from the foggy back roads of memory.

"I hear Dad. We should get up."

"Your hearing's better than mine."

"He's in the kitchen, pouring milk into his cereal, talking to Buck."

She untangled from his arms and sat up.

"I'm glad you're doing this search-and-rescue stuff," he said. "This'll be good. A new direction. More upbeat. Not the same old thing year after year."

"It's fun, yeah, but there's stuff I'll miss."

"Crime scenes?"

"Believe it or not. The homicide guys, the other techs. Change isn't easy. You know how that is. You're pretty fond of your routines."

"Lately I've been feeling open to new possibilities. As a matter of fact, I've been feeling very open."

"Meaning what?"

"Oh, I don't know. Something more than a night now and then. You and me and a gardenia bush outside."

"Don't be stupid, Thorn. That's the sex talking. Your brain is addled. You couldn't give up the Keys. You've spent too many years up in that tree house, staring at sunsets, to ever walk away."

"I didn't say 'walk away.' But some arrangement we can be together more. I've been thinking about it. It could work, if we want it to."

They were quiet for a while, the cardinal asserting its territorial claim. On the window screen a lizard climbed halfway up and puffed out the red disk in its throat and did five or six jerky push-ups as if stimulated by the erotic afterglow radiating from the room.

"You don't have to go through with this, you know. Dad can sleep over at Harbor House. He's done it before."

"You're dodging the issue."

"Yeah, I am," she said. "But in a couple of hours I'm hopping on a plane and leaving for a week. A subject like this, we need time to discuss, don't you think?"

Thorn shrugged a yes.

"So, I'm serious. Dad can sleep over at Harbor House. You don't really need to do this."

"You want to back out. You don't trust me."

"I didn't say that."

"Okay, okay," he said. "My track record has been spotty. But any scrapes your dad and I got into, we lived to tell the tale."

"Barely." She snuggled deeper against him.

The aura of their sexual moment was dissolving, but still Thorn sensed that the charged particles that passed between them had changed the nature of their bond. He wasn't exactly sure how. For the better, he believed. But then again, every new high-water mark was a challenge to the future. The glow of the past always a rival to what followed.

He pushed away the misgiving and listened to a mockingbird who'd replaced the cardinal just beyond the window. Usurping its branch and its song—a cheaper version, repeating its melody four times, pausing, then going on from cardinal to blue jay to catbird, unspooling its repertoire, feeble simulations of the originals.

"Something's not right across the street. Alan should be in class by now. But his car is still parked where it was last night."

In blue-and-white-striped pajamas, Lawton Collins was leaning forward across the breakfast table, peering out the side window and over a pink hibiscus hedge toward the green house across the street. Buck's tail thumped at their appearance. The dog took a quick look at Alex, and when she gave no command, Buck resumed his watch with Lawton out the window.

A year ago when the yellow Lab first wandered out of the woods near Thorn's house, Lawton claimed naming rights. For the first few months, the dog was called Lawton. But Alexandra finally talked her father out of the name. Too much confusion with two Lawtons around the house. After a week of protest, Lawton relented and decided the dog would now be known as Buck. It was the name of Lawton's partner for twenty years on the Miami Police Department, Buck Gomez, recently deceased. A tribute to the man who'd covered Lawton's back for two decades. So Buck it was.

Alexandra sliced up a cantaloupe and handed Thorn a plate with five slivers, a soy sausage patty from the toaster, and a piece of whole wheat toast.

"Finish your breakfast, Dad. We're on a tight schedule this morning."

"Nobody listens to me," Lawton said. "I'm just some old fool. A moldy boot in the back of the closet. A wad of greasy hair clogging the drain."

Thorn and Alexandra exchanged a look. More and more lately her father had been breaking into these bleak rhapsodies. Haiku of woe.

"You're not a fool," Alex said.

"Some bad shit is going down at Alan's house."

"No, it's not, Dad. Everything's fine."

"I'm imagining things, that's what you're saying."

"I think there might be a little imagination involved, yes."

"Buck woke me up last night," he said. "He heard it and alerted me."

"Heard what?"

"Ask Buck. I'm halfway to deaf myself."

Buck turned away from the window and went over to his green mat and curled up, keeping an eye on Alexandra. Since he'd first appeared a year ago, the dog had made remarkable progress. Going from a starving, feral creature to a supersensitive member of Alexandra's household. An avid student, so thirsty for knowledge it was scary.

Sit, stay, come here, shake hands. That was Thorn's meager list of dog commands. Buck had graduated far beyond his abilities. For the past several months Alex had pushed him to new levels. These days Buck responded to dozens of one- and two-word commands, as well as hand signals. He could run the agility course head-to-head with the smaller, nimbler breeds, track a scent in the air or on the ground through woods or suburban environments, and locate well-hidden targets.

"That guy," Lawton said, "Alan Bingham, he could've been my son-in-law, but no, you get all swoony over this loser." He jerked his chin at Thorn.

"Dad," Alex said. "You love Thorn."

"This bum? Are you kidding? He doesn't even have a job. Unless you call tying fishing lures work. What do you make, kid, a buck-fifty apiece for those things? How you gonna get ahead, support my daughter in the style she's accustomed? A buck-fifty, Christ, you can't buy a gallon of piss for a buck-fifty. How you going to pay the mortgage, now tell me that?"

"Good question." Thorn was trying to smile his way past the moment, but Lawton was rolling full speed.

"Now, you take Alan. There's a guy with unlimited possibilities. University prof, big-time photographer, about to take his art show to New York, D.C., going on tour all around. My daughter's a photographer, too, in case you didn't know, for the Miami police. Full benefits, a retirement plan, the works. You got anything like that, kid? You got any benefits?"

"Not a one. But I have a few drawbacks."

"Now the guy's smart-assing me. In my own home."

"This is my home, Dad." Alex used her quiet but don't-push-it tone. "Now, stop this."

"Alan and Alexandra, that had a nice ring, but, no, my knucklehead daughter goes gaga over some derelict from the Keys, when right across the street she's got Prince Charming."

"Ignore him, Thorn."

"I'm trying."

She got up and took her plate to the sink.

"Alan and Alex were picking a date, writing their vows, all of a sudden this poltroon comes along. Thorn. What the hell kind of name is that, anyway? Your parents never bother to give you a whole name? What's the deal?"

"My parents died before they got around to it."

It was true enough, but it sounded needlessly harsh at that

moment. Alex gave him a questioning look, and Thorn raised an open hand in apology.

"Okay, Dad. The Harbor House van is coming in fifteen minutes. Have you shaved yet? Are you planning on wearing your pajamas today?"

"What's the difference? All those feebleminded buffalo parked in their wheelchairs, slumped over, drooling. I can run around that place naked, nobody notices."

Thorn listened to the hum of traffic. Seven-thirty in the morning and already the noise was wafting in from Red Road and surrounding highways. Overnight the buzz of the city seemed to have taken root in his bones, creating a grating resonance. The sirens, car alarms, barking dogs, motorcycles roaring on nearby streets, the screech of brakes. A ceaseless turbulence on the airwaves, the ragged hustling pulse of Miami.

From decades of living along the coastline of the Florida Keys, with the heave and swell of ocean breezes flushing away every unnatural noise and buffered by thick stands of mahogany, gumbo limbo, and Florida holly, Thorn had developed the hypersensitive antennae of the recluse. Touchy, thin-skinned. On perpetual alert for that off-key crunch of gravel or growl of motor that warned of approaching human contact.

Miami and the Keys were only fifty miles apart, but they occupied opposite ends of the galaxy. City of clamor and an island as still as the moon.

"So what did Buck hear last night?" Thorn had a last sip of coffee.

"Thorn. Don't encourage him."

Lawton shook his head and turned from the window, looking at his daughter, then at Thorn.

"Gunfire," Lawton said. "I was asleep, but that's how he was acting. Like he heard a gun going off. Pawed the hell out of my arm."

"I didn't hear any gunshots, Dad." Alex finished rinsing the dishes. "Did you hear anything like that, Thorn?"

Thorn shook his head.

"Of course you wouldn't hear anything. Going at it like a couple of overheated goats. All you could hear was the thumpedy-thump of your damn headboard pounding the wall."

Alex worked her jaw. When Lawton was in one of his moods, there was little to be done beyond summoning patience. The irritability and antagonism would pass, and in the next instant he could be sunny, even comical.

"Bingham's a photographer, you know, like my daughter. Only Alex takes photos of corpses, but Alan, his subjects are still alive. Not that one's better than the other. But I think it's a good match. You got two photographers, between them they cover the whole gamut, alive to dead. Match made in heaven, you ask me."

Thorn finished the last of his melon, gave Alex an innocent look.

"Picking a date, huh?"

"We went out a few times," she said. "The rest is Dad's invention."

"Went out a few times, yeah, and they stayed inside a few times, too," Lawton said. "If you catch my drift."

Alex shook her head helplessly.

"Alex and Alan," Lawton said. "A perfect fit, but does she listen to her own father? Oh, no, I'm just toe jam around here. Roach droppings."

Lawton rose from the table, then stood still with his head cocked to the side, staring at the wall as if it were a bank of fog he was trying to penetrate.

For the past few years he'd been fading in and out of lucidity on some timetable that was impossible to anticipate. One minute his memory was laser-sharp, the next he was whimpering in frustration, confounded by knotting his tennis shoes. After two MRIs and an array of other tests, the doctors wouldn't give a firm diagnosis. Only way to be sure, one doctor said, was an autopsy.

But it was clear to Thorn that Lawton was fast becoming a new concoction. One jigger of the tough, street-smart homicide cop he'd once been and one shot of some obstinate, bewildered gentleman oblivious to good manners and mortal danger and the simplest forms of logic. Dump that in the blender and liquefy.

"So, Thorn," Alex said, "what's on your agenda today?"

She had her back to him, loading the dishwasher with the breakfast plates.

"I'm going to start with a little flashing."

"You're not in Key Largo anymore; up here they arrest people for that."

She half turned, smiling at him over her shoulder.

"So keep it in your shorts, mister."

"Flashing is that stuff around the edge of the roofline. In case you haven't noticed, we roofers have a different vocabulary."

She went over and gave Thorn a kiss, a taste of melon on her lips.

"I have to fluff myself up. Then I've got to run." She settled a serious look on him. "You're sure about this, Thorn? You can handle things?"

"She means me," Lawton said. "Mr. Toe Jam."

"Trust me," Thorn said. "Lawton and I are buddies."

Lawton muttered something and marched away toward his bedroom, and Alex lay a hand on Thorn's shoulder.

"I think he's getting worse," she said. "He's cycling through the ups and downs faster than he used to."

"He doesn't seem too bad to me."

"I'm going to cancel the trip. I can't leave him like this."

"Oh, come on," Thorn said. "You can't let Buck down. Or yourself."

At the sound of his name, the Lab thumped his tail against the floor. Alex looked out the window for a moment, then sighed and turned back to him.

"You're sure?"

"I can handle this, Alex. It's only seven days. We'll be fine."

Her hand slid up the side of Thorn's neck and she cupped his face. She bent and gave him a fuller kiss. This one was good-bye for a week.

Then she turned and walked down the hallway to her

bedroom. She must have known he was watching because she put a little extra sauce in her hips, though Alexandra Collins required nothing extra to hold his attention.

Thorn finished his breakfast while Lawton and his lovely daughter readied themselves. He took a look out the window at the house across the street but saw nothing over there the least bit suspicious.

CHAPTER FIVE

In the foyer a few minutes later, with the suitcase at her feet and Buck standing nearby, they shared another kiss—one so warm and eager, it might have been the prelude to another hour of love if the taxi driver hadn't honked.

Alex pulled free, opened the door, and waved that she was coming. She had on gray linen slacks and a pink sweater set. Somehow managing to look both feminine and tough.

"Oh, I almost forgot." She gave him a wary smile, snagged her purse from the front table, dug through it, and produced a silver cell phone, flipped it open, and showed it to Thorn. "You ever use one of these?"

"I'm more of a pay-phone kind of guy."

She smiled and shook her head.

"You're such a Luddite, Thorn. Come on, join the new century."

"I was just warming up to the last one."

She demonstrated how to turn the cell phone on, use the speed dial to reach her own cell, then showed him the charging cord and where to plug it in.

"Why do I need this?"

"Do me a favor, okay? One week, it won't corrupt you. Leave it on in case I want to check in, hear your voice, see how Dad is doing. Just in case."

The cabbie honked again, and they embraced once more.

Buck stood close by and pressed his head against the side of Thorn's knee.

Thorn carried her bag while Alex followed with Buck on the lead. The cabbie got out and popped the trunk. He was a young black man in a green guayabera. As Buck approached, he backed away, and though his English was spotty, he let it be known he didn't want a dog in his cab.

"It's a police canine," Alexandra said, flipping open her department shield and showing it to the guy. "I'd be willing to bet this dog's cleaner than most passengers you carry. Not to mention smarter."

The man seemed confused, so Thorn gave him a short-hand version in basic Creole. "Police work. You have to do it."

The man scowled at both of them and got back into the driver's seat.

"Creole?"

"Years of fishing in the islands," Thorn said.

"Man of many talents."

They kissed again and Alex drew away and got in the back with Buck.

"Leave the phone on, okay? Humor me."

"The things I do for love."

"When I get back I'll find a way to reward you."

"Kick ass on the test. You, too, Buck. Sniff out the sneaky bastards."

The Lab wagged his tail and curled up beside Alex, resting his head in her lap.

After Thorn rinsed his dishes, he carried the extension ladder outside, clattered it out to its full length, and propped it against the roof edge. He set up his supplies, a roll of black felt paper, a box of roofing nails, and various tools. Toting the cordless drill and thermos, he climbed onto the roof to make his initial inspection.

The pitch of the roof was slight enough that he could work without handholds or ropes. For a while he prowled the aluminum surface, checking for any obvious faults, but found nothing in the panels themselves.

The water stains had recently appeared on the ceiling outside Lawton's bathroom, but as with any roof leak, the problem could have been weeks or months in the making and originate nearly anywhere. Water was devious. It could penetrate the house thirty feet away and follow some gravity-assisted path that was impossible to predict. Given enough time, a steady trickle could rot away the roof timbers or march down the joists like a trail of ravenous termites, softening crucial beams along the way before it ever showed up as a dark patch of crumbling plaster inside the house. Like senility. Like a lot of things.

So Thorn started with the obvious. One by one he pried off the rusty strips of flashing around the three vent pipes. But he discovered no sign of rot. While they clearly needed replacing, the problem just as clearly lay elsewhere.

After half an hour of work, shirtless, wearing only khaki shorts and boat shoes, Thorn paused for a moment to enjoy a rare breeze that tossed the fronds of a nearby royal palm and sent small licks of shade teasing across the roof.

His hair was clumped with sweat and he raked it out of his eyes. From countless hours on the water, fishing the creeks and flats of Florida Bay, Thorn had scorched his hair to the shade and texture of summer straw. At six feet tall, he was still as wiry as he'd been in his teens and as darkly tanned. Although lately he'd been feeling some middle-age creaks, a little swelling in the finger joints, he was still agile enough to spider-walk the roof without strain. And that bedroom incident this morning, something entirely rich and strange, it gave him a jolt of confidence about the aging thing. Undiscovered territory lay ahead. Whole continents yet to be explored.

For the dozenth time since mounting the roof, he touched the alien lump in his pocket. It was silly for the device to make him anxious. But he couldn't dispel the feeling that he was hauling around some living creature that might at any second squawk and demand attention. More than once in the past few minutes, he thought the cell phone had squirmed against his thigh and he'd fought the urge to snatch it out and heave it as far as it would fly.

For the next half hour he replaced the flashing around the three vents. When he was done he climbed to the peak to catch his breath and slug down some water from the thermos he'd hooked to the ridge seam.

With every degree the sun rose, the white aluminum glared more harshly. Sweat dribbled from his flesh and hit the roof and vaporized. He squinted into the brightness for a while, gathering himself for the next phase.

As he gazed out at Alexandra's neighborhood from that height, seeing each house planted neatly in the center of its fifty-by-hundred-foot plot, and the streets running in a grid exactly north and south or due east and west, he felt a twinge of claustrophobia. A milder version of what that doomed man in the Poe story must have felt when he awoke and became slowly aware that he was locked inside a coffin.

He forced aside the pang and reclaimed some of the buoyancy he'd felt earlier. By God, he was determined to make this work. Resolved to beat back the qualms and give the city a fair shot. There was no other option if he and Alex had a chance. A woman every bit his equal in toughness and independence, and one who awakened in him a mix of tenderness and sensuality he hadn't known he was capable of. He felt fresher around her, more confident than he had in years.

So this was his week to adjust, make last-second tweaks to his tranquilized Keys psyche before she returned. Find his place in this seething stew of humanity.

While he rested, a yellow cab drew over to the curb two houses away, parking in the shade of an oak. For an idle moment Thorn watched the taxi and listened to the snarl of several nearby motors. In the past hour three different gardening crews had descended on the neighborhood and were roaring up and down separate lawns like synchronized drill teams with their weed whackers and leaf blowers.

Thorn had another sip of the icy water, splashed some

over his hair, and got back to work. He used Alexandra's
Makita drill to back out the screws. A fine tool that fit solidly
in his hand and made a throaty purr that blocked out the leaf
blowers and the rumble of traffic from a thoroughfare a few
blocks to the west. One motor canceling out a dozen others.
Maybe that was a way to cope. Get one of those exotic machines that produced the rumble of artificial surf and keep it
running in the background.

He worked his way down the first panel, pocketing the
stainless-steel screws while his rubber soles squeaked against
the hot aluminum.

He slid the first panel aside and spotted the telltale rip in
the roofing paper. As he was congratulating himself on his
good fortune, a man's voice called out a hello from the
front yard.

Thorn rose and leaned forward, peering over the edge.

Standing on the lawn beside the front walkway was a
lanky man in a baseball cap and mirrored glasses. He had on
tight black jeans and a light blue button-down shirt with the
tail hanging out. Coils of smoky gray hair showed at the
edges of the hat. His flesh was a chalky brown, the shade of
cinnamon latte with a splash of extra cream. He was in his
late forties, maybe older.

"Can I help you?" Thorn said.

"I'm trying to locate a Mr. Lawton Collins."

"Lawton's not here."

"Might you know where I could find him?"

Thorn had been steeling himself for a heavy dose of the
brusque manner he'd come to know from the Miami hordes
who invaded the Keys each weekend, bringing with them the
buzz and tension of the city. It seemed that this town was
brimming with impatient, overbearing folks who were used
to brushing past the likes of Thorn.

So he was thrown off by the man standing in the yard below. His down-home drawl and the languor of his movements had echoes of the Deep South, as though he might be
a throwback, one of those mannerly crackers who long ago
populated the region, hacked away the dense native tangle

and made South Florida habitable for the lesser mortals who would soon swarm its landscape.

"What do you want him for?"

The man gave the question thorough consideration, all the while looking up at Thorn with an impassive smile.

"And who would I be speaking with?"

"Friend of the family," Thorn said. "And who are you?"

Thorn heard another man's voice come from below. He didn't catch the words, but the tone was abrasive—more like the city voice he'd been bracing for. Apparently the second man was pressed against the front of the house.

Acknowledging his partner's words with a slight nod, the man in the mirrored glasses kept his face tilted up toward Thorn.

"This gentleman, Lawton Collins, he is in possession of an item belonging to me. I've come to have it back."

"As I said, he's not here right now. Won't be home all day."

The second man's coarse voice sounded again, but this time the curly-haired man ignored his comrade, staring up at Thorn with a steady concentration as if Thorn had finally merited his full attention.

While the man himself was not openly threatening, the situation tripped a switch. The hidden partner, the studiously indifferent manner. Thorn felt the last vapors of his early-morning mellowness dwindle, his mood hardening into annoyance. He had promised Sugarman and Alex he would behave, and he'd prepped himself with calming thoughts, but all that flew away as the man in the yard and his hidden pal worked their game.

The bony man removed his sunglasses and looked down as he cleaned the lenses with his shirttail.

With no conscious thought, Thorn's finger crushed the Makita's trigger and the screw bit whirred. If the man in the yard heard, he showed no sign, just continued to clean his shades.

A few seconds later he tipped his head up in slow stages and finally allowed Thorn a clear look at his eyes—doing it with such dramatic emphasis, it seemed likely he'd used this tactic before to unnerve an adversary. His eyes were an unnatural blue with the silvery glint of one of those expensive martinis made with a dash of Curaçao.

As the man replaced the mirrored glasses, Thorn caught the second man's shadow moving toward the front porch.

Thorn took a step to his right, coming a foot closer to the ladder. It was a twenty-foot leap to the ground. Good chance he'd sprain an ankle or blow out a knee if he tried it. No tree limbs near the house, and no Tarzan vines to swing down on. If he was going to get back to earth without risking serious damage, the ladder was the only way.

"Tell your friend to step out where I can see him."

The man produced his smile again, showing teeth but no amusement.

"Up there on the roof, you're not exactly in a position to give orders."

Hearing the cold authority in the man's voice decided it for Thorn. To hell with good-conduct medals. He skipped sideways to the ladder, got a hand on it, and was turning backward to start down when the man muscled it from Thorn's grip. The ladder tipped to the right and fell, clanging onto the cement walkway.

"Now take a deep breath, count to ten," the man said. "We'll be finished shortly and scoot along. This is no affair of yours."

Thorn backed away from the edge of the roof.

Across the street at Bingham's house an old Buick had pulled into the driveway and a dark-skinned woman in jeans and T-shirt got out. She opened the trunk and pulled out a sponge mop and a bucket full of cleaning supplies. She glanced at Bingham's car, then went to the front door and flipped up the lid of the mailbox and felt around inside.

But she found nothing, so she rang the bell, then used the clapper. After waiting a few seconds more, she marched back to her car, stowed her gear, and drove away.

The smoky-haired man missed the action across the way because he was focused on the front porch, where his accomplice's shadow was emerging.

"Got it," the invisible man said.

Thorn waited till the top of the man's head appeared, waited a moment more until he came down off the porch and stepped onto the lush lawn, then dropped feet first onto the shorter man's back.

CHAPTER SIX

Thorn and the man collapsed in a grunting tangle.

His split-second plan was to club the man with the drill, but in the jumble of thrashing arms and legs and the scramble to their feet, a photograph fluttered from the stocky man's grasp and he clawed a small revolver from his waistband and was tipping it toward Thorn's stomach.

Thorn, on his feet, shot out his hand reflexively, rammed the screw bit into the man's upper arm, and mashed the trigger.

The man howled and buckled to his knees, and the pistol fell from his grip. Scooping it up, Thorn stepped back and directed it at the taller man.

"Raise your shirt," Thorn said. "Turn around slow."

"I'm unarmed," the man said.

"I'm not saying it again. Raise your goddamn shirt."

The man complied and made a slow rotation. Flat, hairless stomach. No sign of a weapon.

He knew he might regret it, but he'd had more than his share of misfortune with loaded guns, so he broke open the revolver, spilled the rounds into the grass, and sailed the pistol across Alex's hedge into a neighbor's yard.

He turned back to the tall man.

Blue Eyes hadn't budged. He simply stared at Thorn with his eyebrows raised a notch as if he were pondering some lofty issue that had nothing to do with the events unfolding before him.

Whimpering, the other one struggled to his feet, his left hand clasping the bloody wound.

When he caught sight of Thorn, his lips drew back in a snarl and he staggered in Thorn's direction.

Thorn lifted the drill and gunned the screw bit at his face.

"Want the next one in your forehead?"

"You bastard, you're going to regret the shit out of this. When I'm done with your ass, you'll wish you never laid eyes on me."

"I'm already there," Thorn said. "Now get out of here. Both of you."

The chunky man glanced at the black-and-white photo lying faceup in the grass, then looked at his partner.

"You're standing there not doing nothing. You're supposed to be my ace boon coon. Have my back."

Keeping a watch on the two, Thorn walked over to the photo and snatched it up.

"I'm going into the house now and I'm dialing the local constable. Maybe you'd like to stick around and explain this little episode to him."

"Some tough nut you are, whining to the po-po." The dark-haired man glared. "Why don't you stay out here, dawg? I'm about to open up a super-size can of whoop-ass."

Thorn squeezed the trigger again, and the dark-haired guy drew back. His hand came away from his wound and swept in front of his face as though dragging aside a cobweb. There was some gray in the guy's hair. He was maybe three or four years younger than Blue Eyes. Though his speech and manner were more suited to a delinquent in his teens.

The tall one squinted at Thorn through the brilliance. Despite the circumstances, he gave off an air of stillness and resolve that struck Thorn as more menacing than his cretinous partner.

"Having that photo is a matter of great personal importance to me."

"Yeah? Well, that doesn't cut a lot of slack with me."

On the man's lips a wistful smile appeared.

"I can see we've employed the wrong approach. You're an

honorable man. Sneaking inside your home was an affront to your civility."

He spoke the words with a rational disinterest, as though he were reminding himself of the strange moral codes followed by others.

"Why do you want that photograph?"

"I seriously doubt you'd understand."

"Try me."

"I'm dying here, Snake," the other man said. "I need a fucking doctor."

"It's a family matter, none of your concern."

The small man doubled over and retched into the grass.

"Snake?" Thorn said.

Snake spoke to the other man in a tone one might use with a slow child, while his eyes never unlocked from Thorn's.

"Go get in the car, Carlos. We're finished here."

Carlos wiped the spittle from his lips and marched across the lawn, then down the sidewalk toward the cab.

In Thorn's pocket the phone buzzed.

"Last chance to give me the photograph," Snake said.

Thorn stared at the man but said nothing.

"All right. Then we'll have to complete this transaction later."

Thorn waited till he'd covered twenty yards before digging out the phone. He flipped it open and found the ON button.

"Thorn?" Alexandra said.

With a leisurely stride, Snake crossed the lawn.

"I'm here."

She hesitated a moment, as if registering his tone.

"What's wrong? You okay? What's happened?"

"I'm fine," he said. "Everything's cool. Nice town you got here."

"Talk to me, Thorn. I'm on the plane; they're about to shut the doors."

Thorn watched Snake catch up to Carlos and fall in step beside him, heading back to the cab. Snake and Carlos, the names echoed somewhere in the dusty warehouse of Thorn's memory.

"Thorn?"

"It's okay," he said. "I slipped off the roof. But I'm fine. Not even bruised."

"Fell off the roof?"

"Listen, it's okay. I landed on my butt. Nothing's hurt."

"You're lying to me, Thorn. Don't do that, don't lie. I can tell."

The cab U-turned and rolled slowly past, neither man looking his way.

"Everything's cool. It's this damn phone. It makes me sound weird."

"The phone?" she said. "It sounds like more than the phone."

She was silent for several seconds, and Thorn could hear the murmur of passengers around her. He hadn't lied to her before, not about anything major. And he was trying to stay faithful to that history. Nothing but the truth, just slightly less than the whole of it.

Maybe he hadn't handled the two guys with the most dexterity. He'd have to sort that out later, critique his effort. But at the moment he wanted to keep Alexandra on her way to Tampa with a minimum of anxiety. Tell her as much truth as possible without alarming her.

"I'm gone for an hour and you fall off the roof."

"The good news is, I found your leak. First panel I removed, there it was, rotted roofing paper."

He raised the photograph and gave it a look.

"I don't believe this," she said. "You could've broken your neck."

"Hey, while I got you, let me ask you something. That photograph in the house, I was looking at it earlier. The black-and-white glossy of a boxing match, looks like Cassius Clay and Liston. Where'd that come from?"

"Photograph?"

"Yeah, Cassius Clay, before he became Ali."

"It's Dad's," she said. "Alan Bingham gave it to him, the guy across the street. A gift. Why?"

"Oh, nothing. It's a nice shot. I was looking to see if I'm in it."

"What're you talking about?"

"February 1964. I was in the crowd that night. Dr. Bill was a big fight fan. He took me and Kate along. I think we were on the other side of the auditorium from this shot. We stayed that whole week in Miami. Very exciting time. Very memorable."

"I'm getting off the plane," she said. "You don't sound right."

"I'm fine, I'm good," he said. "Call me when you land in Tampa. I'll be wrapping up the roof about then."

She weighed it for a few seconds. Thorn could hear an announcement over the plane's intercom. Seat backs and tray tables upright.

Alex sighed.

"Promise me you're not going to slip off any more roofs."

"You have my word," Thorn said. "I've had enough thrills for one day."

"Okay," she said. "Be careful, damn it. I love you."

"Love you, too."

Thorn shut the phone and slipped it in his pocket.

He plowed through the hedge and into the neighbor's yard and found the pistol. A .22 revolver. He sniffed the barrel. He was no expert, but it did have a smoky tang as though it might've been fired recently.

He went inside, set the pistol on a kitchen counter, then poked through the house until he was satisfied nothing had been disturbed. He paused at the refrigerator door where the Harbor House monthly schedule was fixed with colorful magnets. Printed in bold letters across the top of the schedule was the facility's address.

Snake and Carlos wanted the fight photo for a reason powerful enough to draw a gun. They'd known Lawton's name, but even though they seemed to have no special interest in him, just the same, it wouldn't hurt to drop in on the old guy. Maybe spring him for the day. Thorn would carry along the photo, see what Lawton had to say about it. It was, after all, his primary assignment this week, to look after the old man, make sure he was safe.

In the bedroom Thorn dug a denim shirt from his duffel and found Alexandra's car keys and went outside. He surveyed the street. All quiet, the taxicab gone, the lawns mown and blown.

He started down the walkway, then halted and went back to the house. He found the right key and locked the front door. For a moment he'd forgotten he was in the big bad city, land of locked doors and security alarms.

According to the address on the schedule, Harbor House was south on Old Cutler Road, almost to Black Point Marina. From his vague recollection, he made that roughly a twenty-minute drive.

The flight attendant blocked the aisle and raised her hands to halt Alex.

"Ma'am, we're about to shut the door and push back from the gate. We'll have to ask you to take your seat."

A man in an aisle seat reached out and petted Buck behind the ears.

"I'm getting off the plane," Alexandra said.

One of the male flight attendants was locking down the door.

"No one gets off once the door's shut."

For the second time that morning, Alex dug into her purse and brought out her Miami PD identification. She opened it for the flight attendant to see.

"I'm getting off the plane," she said. "Now step aside, please."

The woman frowned and took a step backward.

"The door's closed," the flight attendant said. "Now take your seat, or I'll have to call the captain."

The queen had roused herself from winter hibernation.
Paper wasp. Order Hymenoptera, *family* vespidae, *genus,*

polistes. *Slender, narrow-waisted, with long legs, reddish-orange body banded with yellow. A stinging wasp. Capable of multiple venomous strikes. Flex her abdomen, arch her back, drive the stinger into flesh, then pump toxic antigens from the venom sac. Dissolve red blood cells.*

Withdraw, then thrust and thrust again.

It had been her father's obsession and became hers. Hymenoptera, *wasps, ants, sawflies, hornets, yellow jackets.* Nesting insects that lived in regimented colonies. Queen, worker, drone. Her father admired their industry, their mindless dedication to social order. No frivolous individualism. Their hives, their tidy world. Their happy obedience.

Her father wished the human race could be so ordered and industrious. Wished his daughter was so dutiful.

Now on this warm spring afternoon, she was in the attic, the dry tight space above the air-conditioned house, sitting in her rocker in the shadows, observing the newly awakened queen as she scraped grooves in the soft rafters, then chewed the wood pulp, mixed it with her spit to build her papery nest, cell by cell. Comb of hexagonal compartments, a frail gray flower blooming, attached by a single filament to an old pine beam.

The queen would attack if her nest was disturbed. To defend her hive, the female wasp stings and stings and stings.

At other times her pointed spike doubles as ovipositor, used for laying eggs. Same tube for birth and death, eggs and venom. Only the female of the species holds the power to replicate or kill.

With the loaded pellet gun lying in her lap, she rocked her wooden chair and observed the queen, the diligent queen scraping furrows of wood from the rafters and chewing it to sticky mush, then sculpting the insubstantial nest, cell by cell. The soft buzz vexing the quiet, dusty light.

Her daddy taught her all she knew of wasps and other things.

Sting, sting, sting.

Her daddy taught her more than any girl should know.

CHAPTER SEVEN

"The deltoid muscle is torn, and there's penetration of the humeral circumflex artery with significant pulsatile bleeding when the drill bit exited."

Dr. Javier Lopez-Lima dabbed at Carlos's wound with a gauze pad, then drew his hand aside so Carlos could take a look. Which he didn't.

Lopez-Lima was in his late sixties. The cigars stuffing his shirt pocket bulged through his lab coat. Half a century ago the guy had worked in Havana, before Fidel gave him the heave. A man whose surgical skills were honed by tweezering bullet fragments from the hides of American mobsters. A guy who'd seen his share of payments peeled off rolls of hundreds. That's where he learned his English, too, back in Cuba, from Trafficante and his boys.

"Luckily, the humeral circumflex artery is not large enough to allow total exsanguination. It appears the muscle itself has compressed the puncture and provided counterpressure to the arterial flow."

"So you're not going to bleed to death," Snake told Carlos.

"But I'm about to blow chunks again," Carlos said.

The nurse who'd been standing at Snake's elbow extended the stainless-steel pan, and Carlos emptied what was left in his stomach.

While he retched, Snake gazed at the anatomical poster on the far wall. A man stripped of skin, his bright pink muscles exposed and all their Latin names noted. This was the clinic where Snake's mother had brought him, the clinic where his eidetic memory was diagnosed, and for that reason it was the only clinic Snake ever used.

Lopez-Lima turned back to Carlos.

"You finished whining?"

"My goddamn arm hurts."

"The pain will go," he said. "You'll be able to lift your arm in a day or two. Just be glad he didn't hit you in the armpit. You would've bled out by now. We'd be disposing of a corpse."

"You believe this fucking Cubano?" Carlos grimaced at Snake.

Snake and Carlos were a hundred percent Cuban themselves, but over the decades they'd become more Anglo than Hispanic. Because of how they were raised. Lost their Spanish. Got a long, slow transfusion of cool, standoffish American blood. As much as Snake resisted, even some of Stanton King's southern gentleman bullshit rubbed off.

Snake walked over to a metal folding chair and sat. He watched Lopez-Lima bandage Carlos's arm while the nurse stood guard. His burned right hand was salved and wrapped in gauze. Snake looked around at the sterile room, the white walls, inhaled the tangy medicinal smell.

That harsh aroma whisked him back to the spring of 1963.

It is two years after the Morales family first arrived in Miami. He is in the examining room and the doctor has just diagnosed his condition.

"Remembering is good," the doctor says. "It is a blessing you have received from our almighty God. You should be grateful, my boy."

Nineteen sixty-three. He remembers every second. Every day. Snake is eleven years old, and wave after wave of his countrymen are washing ashore. Changing Miami overnight from what it was—a quiet town, no traffic, an easy tropical pace. Jewish grandmas and pale-faced Yankees milling around on the beaches and piers in summer clothes and silly smiles. Pinching themselves at their good fortune for landing in paradise.

But all that is changing.

Snake is pedaling his bike. It's nighttime. He's cruising down Biscayne Boulevard, whooshing fast, his legs pumping, he's full of spunk, down and down Biscayne to Pier 5, "World's Finest Fishing Fleet," with the neon sailfish over the entrance. Smelling the salt water, and the tang of fresh-caught grouper and sharks and giant marlin hanging up.

Then he goes a few blocks west through the city center, dead at that hour of the evening. He heads into the black ghetto of Overtown, wanting to catch a glimpse of his amazing hero, Cassius Marcellus Clay, who lives in there while he trains at the Fifth Street Gym, a second-story sweatbox out on the beach. Living next to the Famous Chef restaurant, Clay thrives on the rowdy nightlife. Snake has seen him twice, bopping the streets, Pied Piper, doing magic tricks for trailing kids, while through the open front doors of the nightclubs boom the honeyed voices of Ella Fitzgerald, Count Basie, B. B. King, Nat King Cole. Nineteen sixty-three Overtown is Harlem with palm trees.

Cassius is smack in the middle, reveling in the hot nights, the hot jazz. Sleek, handsome teenage kid who'd won Olympic gold, while to most local whites he's just another no-account nigger. Gaseous Cassius, the Louisville Lip. In 1963, Miami might as well be Mississippi, or anywhere in Old Dixie.

The crackers had hated niggers forever. Now they expand their hatred to include Cubans. Cubans like Snake. Anglos drive by with bumper stickers, WILL THE LAST AMERICAN LEAVING MIAMI BRING THE FLAG? Over time, most of those idiots leave, move north to some white-bread town where everyone agrees on everything. Good riddance, as far as Snake is concerned.

Snake pedals for a while and he thinks he sees Cassius in the distance, but the slender man in white pants and loose shirt ducks into the Harlem Square nightclub, a place Snake cannot go. Snake pumps to where he disappeared and, yes, a sizzle still hangs in the air like free-floating electricity. Music is shaking the ground. People are whooping. Cassius was there, all right.

Snake stays a moment, hair on his arms standing up, then he turns back and pedals from Overtown toward his home in Little Havana, just off Flagler. Heading west, the sky is a plush blue suede. Snake tastes the cinnamon air. Like inhaling spun candy.

Then he's home. His father and two of his men are in the Florida room in the chairs surrounding the Magnavox TV. They're smoking Chesterfield Kings, longer length, milder taste. He's holding forth on communists. In particular a Russian poet, Evgeny Evtushenko. Jorge Morales fancies himself a literary man. It is part of his romantic costume.

Jorge is explaining to his men that Nikita Khrushchev has permitted a few chosen writers to travel abroad, hoping to curry approval from the world's cultural elite. But Evtushenko takes advantage of this permissiveness and writes poems that harshly criticize the heirs of Stalin. Even better, while traveling through Europe, he wallows in Western decadence, attending parties on the arms of movie stars. Jorge Morales admires him for mocking Soviet repression. As Snake watches from the doorway, his father recites lines of the Russian poet: "I stride on, straightforward, irreconcilable, and that means—I am young." He can quote "Baba Yar," "There are no memorials at Baba Yar—the steep slope is the only gravestone. I am afraid." His father knows every word. The air is thick with cigarette smoke, and Jorge Morales intones the words with deep-voiced bravado.

When he is finished the militiamen mumble in feigned respect. One of them claps feebly. It is clear to Snake they do not comprehend Jorge's enthusiasm. May even find it effeminate.

Behind Snake, Carmen has been watching the spectacle, and when he turns, he finds her there. Her mood is somber.

At her whispered request, he follows her to her room and she shuts the door behind them. She stands before him for a moment and Snake is afraid that she will do something sexual. He does not know how he might respond.

"What's wrong, Carmen? What's happened?"

"Will you promise me something, Snake?"

"Anything."

"You need to make peace with the Lord."

Snake says nothing.

"I won't always be here to guide you. You need to know Jesus Christ."

"What do you mean you won't always be here?"

"When I'm gone," she says.

"When you're gone?"

She looks away. Surely she must've been referring to the convent and had no premonition of what horror was coming only a few months away.

"Promise me, Snake. I can't bear to think of you living in sin."

"I promise. Yes, of course."

It is 1963. Carmen is overflowing with the Holy Spirit. Jorge is ablaze with political passion. Snake feels his own world teetering on some momentous brink. All around him the city he now calls his hometown is transforming. It is departing America, joining the larger world. The moment is thrilling and scary, and Snake feels voltage in the air. It is Magic City, where overnight the poor can become rich, weak become strong, where refugees produce white doves and wildly colored scarves from their meager hats.

Miami is up for grabs, and Snake is sitting front row.

Nineteen sixty-three. Richard Burton and Elizabeth Taylor are Antony and Cleopatra. Their romance is heroic, more grand than anything a movie screen can contain. Everything that year is bigger, louder, faster. Chrome behemoths with giant fins and supercharged engines cruise the highways. The Beatles and Cassius, Elvis, Reverend King and Malcolm X and the Kennedys crowd the stage. Men in space suits lift off from Canaveral and soar into the heavens. The mushroom cloud blooms darkly on the horizon. An era when everything is immense, passionate, more cataclysmic than ever before, and Jorge Morales and his daughter, Carmen, in their own ways are competing with those heroic proportions. Miami is their stage. Revolution, danger, excitement, the amazing power of Christ, all of it pulses in the walls of the house near Flagler Street. It is 1963. Before the fall. The tropical air is sugary with innocence and hope. Anything can happen. It is Magic City.

"Hey, Snake. You still with us?"

It takes a moment for that time to vanish. Like Snake is rising up through deep waters, seeing sunlight in the distance. Some shreds of memory linger. The jazz beat, the female voices filtering into the balmy night, the rumble of horsepower.

Carlos held out the cell phone. The doctor and nurse were gone.

"It's him," Carlos said. "Wants to talk to you."

Snake took the phone, closed his eyes.

Stanton King's voice was tense.

"What happened, Snake? Don't leave anything out."

Snake drew a breath. Calmed himself. He needed time to sort this out before he confronted Stanton King with what he suspected. That only a few hours before Snake's father and mother and sister were slaughtered, Mayor Stanton King had been sitting thigh to thigh with one of the killers.

Snake was, above all else, methodical. A man whose passions were subordinate to rational consideration. He would find the photo, decipher its meaning, then do what was necessary, accomplishing each step with dispassionate focus. As Cassius had fought. Aloof, above the fray, deliberate, calculated, and merciless.

Snake kept the rage from his voice as he described the previous night's events.

Merrick Gallery, the fire in the alley, breaking into Bingham's house, destroying the photos, the cameras, shooting Bingham. Snake told him how he and Carlos waited till sunrise, watching from down the street. How they watched the old man leave in a nursing-home van, and later a young woman, probably his daughter, left as well. Then while Snake kept the roof guy occupied, Carlos snuck inside and found the photo. Then the roofer turned heroic, jumped on Carlos's back, disarmed him.

Carlos still sat on the stainless-steel table. He waved away a bug or two and gritted his teeth against the pain.

"And you left the photo behind?"

"The man was a badass. He assaulted Carlos with an electric drill."

"An electric drill?"

"The Liston-Clay match. That's what a man got murdered for?"

King was quiet for a moment. Snake tamping down his fury.

"Destroying all the other photos, that was just a smoke screen, wasn't it? All you cared about was that one. Am I right?"

"It was not my intention that anyone should die," King said softly.

Snake looked over at the muscle chart. A man completely skinned, his organs exposed to sun and air. How Snake felt at that moment.

King said, "You're smart, Snake. But you left that photo in the hands of a man who can identify both you and Carlos. That's not what an intelligent man would do. You also managed to make that picture even more important than it was before. Now it's evidence in a homicide investigation. The police will want to examine it. It will be scrutinized."

"Carlos needed medical attention."

The line was silent for several moments.

Then King said, "Well, thanks for your help, Snake. You two can resume whatever was occupying your attention. I'll take it from here."

Snake hung up and Carlos said, "So?"

Snake unwrapped the gauze from his hand and dropped it on the floor.

"We will find the man who attacked you," Snake said. "And do whatever is necessary to take possession of the photograph."

Carlos grinned through his pain.

"That fucker," he said. "I'm gonna put the smackdown on that butt face, for real."

CHAPTER EIGHT

Pauline Caufield's cover was as extravagant as the Agency got. Her current front was TransAmerica Construction, an American-based corporation that ostensibly provided engineering assistance to Latin American businesses. In her role as CEO of TransAmerica, Pauline traveled for weeks at a time throughout Central and South America. A wonderful perk.

As an NOC, her diplomatic status was defined as nonofficial cover in the directorate of operations. Which meant, when she was traveling, she had no immunity to protect her if she was exposed. At her age, she should have been frightened. In the more dangerous countries of the Southern Hemisphere where drug trafficking and political corruption drove the economies, what rule of law existed was maintained with a capricious combination of bribery and brute force. Yet over the decades of her service as a covert operative, the thrill of roving through such places had never diminished.

Her stateside duties were less adventurous but vital. When she returned to TransAmerica headquarters, it was only natural she should host dignitaries and industrial bosses from a wide array of tropical nations. Though in truth, the parade of men and women were usually in her office to swap information for cash or favors, or else to apply for an increase in their Agency remuneration.

It was a multimillion-dollar cover, an investment Pauline had richly repaid with a reliable stream of information and years of successful operations.

Foremost among her missions was the decades-old effort to undermine the stability of communist Cuba. On that front one of her recent triumphs was Machado Precision Tool, a manufacturing enterprise in Venezuela that was a wholly owned subsidiary of the CIA, and Pauline's own creation. Late last year Machado Tool had filled an order from Cuba's Ministry of Basic Industries for half a dozen steam turbines that were to be used to power the three-phase generator at the Antonio Guiteras electrical power plant. One of seven plants that supplied electricity to the island's 11 million citizens, Antonio Guiteras contributed only 11 percent of the total 3,200 megawatts used on the island. However, it was a crucial 11 percent.

A month after delivery, when half the steam turbines Machado Tool delivered seized up right on schedule, the Guiteras plant had to be taken off-line. It stayed out of action for a total of eight months. Blackouts began to roll throughout the island. Without the Guiteras plant, the Ministry of Basic Industries could produce electrical power at only 50 percent capacity when 65 percent was needed to meet the nation's demand. Machado Precision Tool closed up shop shortly after the problems were discovered, and as far as Pauline knew, the Cubans never discovered the CIA's involvement.

While sabotage against Cuba was not official U.S. policy and might not have played well in middle America, it served a crucial purpose in sustaining the support, financial and otherwise, of the fervently anticommunist Cuban-American community. A central feature of Pauline's job was to keep the exile population under the impression that their concerns were being honored. Miami was the only American city with an official foreign policy—to make Castro's life as miserable as possible. The pressure to fulfill this mandate had grown steadily over the years as Miami's Latinos gained increasing muscle.

TransAmerica Construction's corporate headquarters occupied the upper two floors of the south tower a few blocks from downtown Miami. Pauline's own suite consumed a third of the top floor. Leather furniture in muted grays, swanky architecture—several generations more refined than the *Miami Vice* style that still plagued the city skyline. Those outlandish buildings with their gaudy primary colors and chest-thumping innovations—like the cut-out sections mid-building, as though an errant missile had opened up a wound that never healed. That was all so passé.

Claughton Towers consisted of four smooth barrels of smoked glass and gunmetal steel, staggered in height like the pipes of a church organ sprouting along Biscayne Boulevard. Pauline had been told by the architect that her floor-to-ceiling view commanded exactly three hundred degrees. To the south were the downtown spires of banks and legal offices and insurance firms, and to the east across the glimmer of the Intracoastal Waterway she could keep abreast of the daily count of new high-rises soaring along Miami Beach. Northward there were the posh man-made islands, the sprawl of North Miami and the blue haze of the Atlantic.

Though she mostly ignored the wraparound view through the long hours of her busy days, Pauline was not indifferent to its symbolism. In her business, such a sweeping vista was as close to an acknowledgment of status as she would ever have. Anyone stepping into her office for the first time quickly realized that Caufield had clout unequaled by anyone in the Agency outside of Langley.

It was ten-thirty on Monday morning, a new work week well under way, and Pauline was finishing her fourth café con leche and had toiled halfway through the latest stack of intercepts that had come in overnight from Ecuador. American oil executives were growing anxious at the gathering crowds in the streets. The throngs of demonstrators had been moving inexorably from peaceful displays to window breaking and rock-and-bottle attacks on the national militia. From the intercepted cell phone calls and e-mails, it was not completely clear what stage the citizen outrage had reached. Was a coup attempt imminent, or were they simply looking at more marches?

The two agents working out of the Quito station were in prickly disagreement about the level of opposition to President Manuel Cevayano, the general whose government had been cooperating so smoothly with Gulf + Western for these past three years. So far the current U.S. administration had put its chips squarely on Cevayano, but Pauline was tasked with moving those chips the instant the situation tilted the other way. One of her tasks. One of hundreds.

When her console buzzed she was just dashing off an e-mail to Silma Herrera, the Quito station chief, requesting that she shake the banana trees a little harder. Surely they had more penetration into the leadership of the opposition. If they didn't have a source inside, why not?

"Can't talk right now," Pauline said. "Take a message."

"It's himself, Ms. Caufield, the Big Cheese."

Pauline's hand drew back from the console.

Big Cheese was the handle they'd given Hadley S. Waters. A Wisconsin native, and die-hard Packers fan. More important, Waters was a forty-year vet of the intelligence service, now occupying the top spot at Langley. In this tricky election cycle, Waters had emerged as a top contender for the Republican presidential nomination. Although still two years out, the campaign was already under way, broadsides being fired, and Hadley Waters had grown touchier every week. Finding fault with veteran agents, even terminating a couple of highly placed clandestine ops working out of the Beijing station for a trifling slipup. Though Pauline and Waters went back four decades, they hadn't spoken in years. A call from him during his period of intense public scrutiny didn't bode well.

Pauline reached out and clicked open the secure line.

"Director Waters. What a pleasant surprise."

That's when she first learned of the photograph. Cassius Clay–Sonny Liston, 1964, Miami Beach.

And the floor beneath her chair began to sway.

CHAPTER NINE

On his way to Harbor House to pick up Lawton, Thorn got lost. Double, triple lost.

Turned north when he should've gone south, east instead of west. Crossed highways he'd never seen, headed toward landmarks he thought he remembered but didn't recognize once he got close. He drove into suburban neighborhoods, mazes with one cul-de-sac after another, the sidewalks deserted. No one to ask.

Twice he stopped for directions at gas stations, and both times got directions in machine-gun Spanish, but must've confused a *direcho* for a *direcha,* got even more lost, and found himself stuck on a freeway, heading in the wrong direction, traffic inching ahead for ten minutes till he reached the cause of the bottleneck.

Some guy standing beside the highway holding up a sign:
GOD IS PISSED

Thorn thinking, Yeah, if he's paying attention.

An hour after Thorn left Alexandra's house he located Old Cutler Road, a shady, winding historic lane that connected Coconut Grove with points south and snaked along the coast through lush neighborhoods. Ten minutes later he was pulling into the parking lot of Harbor House.

He found a space, switched off the engine, and sat for a moment to gather himself. From the east a breeze carried the sweet, rank scent of brine and seaweed and exposed tidal flats. Years earlier Thorn had spent an entire summer exploring the fishing grounds out there on Biscayne Bay, an hour's boat ride from his home in Key Largo. A summer of poling his skiff around the mangroves of Elliott Key, within sight of the gleaming towers of downtown Miami. That weird clash of wilderness and urban flamboyance.

There were bonefish in the skinny waters of the bay, good fishing. That summer he spent every daylight hour peering across the dazzling sheen until he spotted the telltale shadows of schools of bones muddling across the flats, the riffle of their wake. Then he poled to intersect, get within casting distance.

For a hundred consecutive days, Thorn fished those shoals, always the long, slow hours of hair-trigger vigilance, drinking in the quiet and the endless underwater theater. A hundred days, with no two identical: the tenor of the light, the flood of scents carried on the breeze, the riffles, the tricky geometry of that landscape was always fresh, always rearranging.

It had been a while since Thorn indulged in such daydreams. He'd been holding fast to discipline—fixed on his goal. Making a new life in the city, one that embraced Alexandra, one that came to terms with asphalt and traffic and density. As focused as he could manage, maintaining a strict partition between his old ways and the world he was entering. He could have both. This wasn't either-or. That's what he'd told Sugar and what he continued to remind himself, his fortifying mantra. But his resolve was starting to fray.

Maybe Sugar was right. He should pick up Lawton, haul him down to Key Largo, entertain him for the week, delay major decisions.

If it hadn't been for the screeching tires, he might have done just that.

Two lanes over, a yellow cab fishtailed across the parking lot, heading for Old Cutler. Same kind of taxi the two tough guys used. Thorn slammed the Toyota in reverse, peeled out of the space, and caught up to the taxi a second after it found a gap in the traffic and swerved north onto the two-lane road. Thorn made out two heads in the car, both in the front seat. Maybe a third slumped down in the back, but he wasn't certain.

At the nearby corner, the traffic light had turned red and the cars formed an impenetrable wall, blocking Thorn's exit, nobody even looking over to acknowledge his honking.

At the last instant, as the taxi fled, Thorn got the number off the side of the Friendly Service yellow cab: 4497. But the car was probably stolen, and with such a head start, there was no way he was going to catch them.

Of course, he wasn't sure these were the two shitbrains from earlier, or whether they'd abducted Lawton. Could be just a stray paranoid synapse firing.

Cranking the wheel, he cut back into the lot, reclaimed his space, and trotted to the entrance of the two-story pink building.

"Lawton Collins!" he bellowed at the lady behind the front desk. She looked up, startled.

He was huffing from his sprint, and when the woman didn't immediately respond, he jogged down the main corridor, into the heart of the building.

A glassed-in aviary filled one corner of the reception area, parakeets and songbirds thrown into a wild fluttering from limb to limb at Thorn's sudden approach. An ancient woman in a wheelchair was parked before the glass cage, watching the action. Around the corner, lunch was being served in a cafeteria with two televisions blaring the noon news.

Thorn scanned the dozen tables—lots of silvery hair, pale faces, people slowly munching, but no sign of Lawton.

As he reached out to tap the shoulder of a woman in an official-looking smock, two arms grabbed him from behind and squeezed Thorn into a breathless bear hug. The voice at his ear had the jingly lilt of Nassau.

"We backing up now, mon, you with me? Backing up, getting you around this corner, where you don't distress the folks eating their Happy Meals. Okay, we together on this, are we? Say yes, why don't you?"

Thorn planted his feet and tested the man's strength with a hard wriggle, but the guy tensed his meaty arms and Thorn's rib cage crackled.

"Okay, okay," he grunted as the guy dragged him out of view of the lunch crowd.

For half a minute he was in the solid embrace of the orderly. In that time he got down a single swallow of air and was starting to feel woozy when finally the lady in charge came marching around the corner.

She was taller than Thorn, with broad shoulders and a clipboard gripped tight against her bulky chest. She wore a black pantsuit and had the scowl of someone whose greatest joy was handing out demerits.

"Let him go, Marvin."

The man released him, and Thorn stepped away and looked at his captor. Marvin gave Thorn a gold-toothed grin and crossed his arms over his chest.

"Welcome to Harbor House," the woman said. "I'm Marion Davies, the director of the facility. Is there a reason for this disturbance?"

Thorn managed to drag down a full breath.

"I'm looking for Lawton Collins."

"Popular guy," Marvin said.

"And what business do you have with Mr. Collins?"

"I'm his guardian for the week," Thorn said. "Is he here?"

A small gathering of noontime diners had assembled in the hallway nearby. A couple had carried their plates and were still spooning their food while they spied on the ruckus.

"Look, I appreciate your caution. I don't have any ID. But my name is Thorn. Alexandra Collins and I are friends. I'm up from Key Largo, staying at her house in South Miami for the week while she's in Tampa doing some police work. I just need to know Lawton's here and okay."

"What makes you think he's not?" Ms. Davies said.

"Were there two men here looking for him?"

For a moment the woman's gaze roamed his face as if searching for some fault line in his innocent expression.

Then without a word, she headed down the hallway beside the aviary.

Thorn followed and Marvin stayed close behind.

"Those two guys," Thorn said. "They were here, weren't they?"

Marvin's smile fluttered on and off like a loose connection.

"A couple of bad mamma jammas," he said. "Tried to bullshit their way in but, no, sir, not with Marvin on duty."

Lawton was perched on a high stool at a round desk. The room was sunny and spacious and had a high ceiling. Lawton was using pinking shears to snip the tips off flower stalks before handing them one by one to the ladies assembled around the worktable.

In front of each woman sat a vase with a bouquet that more or less resembled the one displayed on a podium in the center of the table.

As Thorn and his custodians approached, a wave of cooing and rustling erupted. Crookedly applied smiles turned his way and widened, while here and there a hand reached up to touch a white coiffure.

Ms. Davies walked over to Lawton's side.

"Mr. Collins, do you recognize this gentleman?"

Lawton shot Thorn a look and shook his head more in disgust than denial, then snipped the tip off a daffodil and handed it to the white-haired lady beside him.

"Looks like common street scum to me," Lawton said.

"He says his name is Thorn and he's your guardian."

"My guardian?" Lawton looked around at the assembled ladies. "Hell, this nitwit couldn't guard a dead possum at the side of the highway."

A couple of his elderly fans tittered.

Davies tapped Thorn on the shoulder and steered him a few feet away.

"He's playing games," Thorn said.

"Yes," she said. "Lawton's famous for his humor."

"In half an hour or so Alexandra will be landing in Tampa. You can call her, double-check."

"That won't be necessary. She left your name, description.

Even said you wouldn't be able to produce any ID, which I still find exceedingly strange."

Thorn offered no explanation. Like a lot of Keys citizens, he'd never bothered to register his presence on earth with the federal government or the state of Florida. With his property taxes paid by a trust Kate Truman set up before her death, Thorn didn't even require a bank account. No doubt he had a birth certificate filed somewhere, a high school transcript, but as far as he could figure, that's the only trace he'd made. No other bureaucratic fingerprints. Thorn was ghosting through, without a nine-digit number dragging behind. Living happily an inch below the sweep of radar.

For him, keeping a low profile was no paranoid fetish. He wasn't running from anyone or trying to hide. He wasn't some secret agent changing his name every day. Thorn was only living as simply as possible, maintaining a pleasant isolation, staying clear of the sticky web of officialdom for which he had no patience. Why should he carry around half a dozen plastic cards to prove who he was when everyone he truly cared about or who cared about him knew exactly where to find him?

"I'm taking Lawton out of here till we find out what this is about. That okay with you?"

Inside Marion Davies's jacket a cell phone played the opening notes of Beethoven's Ninth. She flipped it open, spoke her name and listened, then shut it without a word and slid it back inside her coat.

"Marvin, would you please escort Lawton out to Mr. Thorn's car?"

And she was gone without a fare-thee-well, which suited Thorn just fine.

A minute later, waiting for a break in traffic at the edge of Old Cutler, Thorn said, "Flower arranging?"

"It's where the babes are. Ones that still remember their name. You got a problem with that?"

"Kind of surprising for a hardened old homicide guy like you."

"A man makes do the best he can."

Thorn saw an opening and peeled into the heavy flow heading north.

"Why isn't my daughter picking me up? What'd you do with her?"

"She's in Tampa, Lawton. She flew up this morning."

"Yeah? And what's your game? Do I know you?"

"I'm Thorn," he said. "You and me, we're old buddies."

"You look like a certain peckerwood I arrested back in the eighties. Bad checks, breaking and entering. Possession of a controlled substance."

Thorn slowed for a car turning left. He glanced over at Lawton, who was massaging his forehead as if trying to ward off a headache.

"Okay, now listen, here's the plan, Lawton. We're driving over to your house, pick up some clothes, then head down to Key Largo. Stay there a few days, go fishing. You like fishing, right? Snook, grouper."

"Don't go switching subjects on me. I know that game. Used to run it myself, getting the lowlifes to talk. It won't work, peckerhead."

Lawton's detour into hostility seemed to tire him out. His head slumped against the headrest, a look of melancholy weighting his features. Alex had coached Thorn on these sudden mood swings, telling him to stay on course no matter which direction Lawton veered. Be consistent, don't respond to the outrageous accusations. Be a beacon of normalcy so Lawton could use Thorn to chart his way back to safer waters.

"Me, a beacon of normalcy?" Thorn said. "You're kidding, right?"

"Yeah," she said. "But try to fake it, okay?"

At the next red light Thorn reached into the backseat and got the black-and-white photo and laid it on Lawton's lap.

Lawton picked it up, gave it a long look, then in a singsong voice said, "If you want to lose your money, bet on Sonny. I'm the champ, you the chump. Round eight to prove I'm great. If you wanna see heaven, you'll go down in seven."

Thorn stopped for a light under the shade of a giant banyan.

"This is yours, right? This photo."

Lawton grumbled and his eyes lost focus, as if he'd been ambushed by a sorrowful memory.

"What is it, Lawton?"

"I worked that fight. Three-fifty an hour."

"You did?"

"You wouldn't know about overtime, guy like you never drew a paycheck in his life. But I had a daughter and a wife. Back then I worked lots of nights. Rock concerts, football games. I never liked Clay much—all that smart-mouthing. But I came around. Hell, everybody did eventually."

"Lawton, listen. This morning two guys came by the house. One snuck inside while I was on the roof and he tried to steal this photo. You have any idea why?"

"What the hell were you doing on the roof?"

"Repairing it," he said. "You have any idea why somebody'd try to steal this?"

"Now I remember," he said. "Reason why Alan didn't go to class today, why his car's still there." Lawton set the photo on his lap and stared out the windshield. "He's got a show at Merrick Gallery in the Gables. That's where he went. He canceled his class so he could be at the opening. He gave me an engraved invitation. I got it at home in my sock drawer."

"But, Lawton, listen, do you have any idea why anyone would try to steal this from you? Is it valuable in some way? Did Alan say anything about it?"

Lawton gave the photo a look and pointed at another man.

"This one I know," he said. "Fifth row, skinny guy chewing on his fingernail right there. Guy ran a sports bet out of his Miami Beach condo. Billy Freestone, that's his name. Cheap hood, probably dead by now, got whacked by somebody. That's the kind of guys came to boxing matches. Gangsters, hoods, underworld types. Here's another one. This guy here."

Lawton tapped a fingernail against the photo.

"This fellow, now this is some top banana. Forget his name, but he was a big-deal potentate of one kind or another.

Probably dead, too. Not a profession you live a long time, gambling, loan sharking, dealing drugs."

Thorn looked at the man Lawton was pointing at. Little guy with dark wavy hair and a squirrelly face. He wore a gray sports coat over a gray polo shirt. He was watching the action in the ring but didn't seem impressed.

"Before we go down to Largo, maybe we should have a word with Bingham. Find out what this is about. Why a couple of punks would want this thing enough to break in the house, draw a gun on me, come looking for you."

Lawton said, "Alan was going to be my son-in-law till what's-his-name, that Keys weasel, came slithering along, stole my little girl's heart."

Thorn stayed on Old Cutler, driving past the slapped-up housing projects with phony wilderness names: Hawk's Nest, Heron Harbor, Manatee Cove. Here and there he caught a glimpse of the scrubby palmettos and pinelands that once covered the southern peninsula, bulldozers parked nearby. The road became shady, houses growing formidable, disappearing behind hedges, coral rock walls, down curving drives.

At the next light he asked if Lawton knew the way to Merrick Gallery.

"Hell, boy. I've lived in this town seventy years. I know nooks and crannies the cockroaches haven't found."

"Well, lead on, my friend."

CHAPTER TEN

The photograph had slipped through Snake's fingers three times already. At Merrick Gallery it burned up before his eyes, at Bingham's house Carlos had stupidly destroyed the negatives, and during the bungled encounter with the roofer Snake lost it yet again. Further humiliation came at the old-age home, where he and Carlos had been thrown out by a single black security guard.

It was clear to Snake that he needed to step back, regroup, and plot his next step more carefully.

The Church of the Little Flower in Coral Gables had served as Snake's sanctuary for decades, and it was there he went to soothe his turbulent mind.

He planted Carlos in a rear pew and walked straight to the confessional, shut the door and knelt, and waited for Father Meacham to greet him.

Roughly Snake's age, the priest had been hearing Snake's confessions for over twenty years. It had been a trial for Meacham, listening to Snake recite the same admission several times each week. It was not for the machete killing of Humberto Berasategui for which he asked absolution, nor the maiming of the man who'd worn the big diamond ring. He felt no guilt for those acts and considered them no sins at all. But guilt still gripped him.

On the night when the killers came and the three children

were sprinting across the lawn, if Snake had only run a step faster, only a single step, it would have been him that was shot, not Carmen. If it had been Snake who died, Carmen would have dealt with his death better than he had dealt with hers. She would have given the weight of her suffering to her God, and even if that had not relieved her of all her pain, it would have relieved her of most of it.

A hundred times every day he blamed himself for falling back half a step in fear when the bullets began to fly. Wishing over and over that he had gone down that night. His last sensations could have been the smell of the grass and Carmen's cries as she ran unhurt into the safety of the darkness.

No penance Father Meacham ever prescribed relieved Snake's burden. Yet he returned and returned again, carrying inside a Ziploc bag Carmen's small weathered Bible. Aside from a single photograph of her, the Bible was the only possession of hers that survived.

He had tried his best to honor his vow to Carmen, but Snake had long ago lost faith in God and any hope for atonement. Still, over the long years, the unvarying tranquillity within the high-domed chapel and the ritual of Father Meacham's blessings had provided Snake a modest relief from the turmoil of his shame and heartache.

The priest and Snake had come to a silent understanding. Snake would not be saved, would never enter the kingdom of heaven, and Father Meacham was under no further pressure to bring about his religious awakening. It was a mutually agreed-upon stalemate.

Meacham turned his head and looked through the tiny window at Snake.

"Yes, my son?"

"I have a question of some urgency, Father."

"What is it, Snake?"

"Is there any prohibition from seeking the truth?"

"Of course not. None whatsoever. You are encouraged to do so."

"The truth will set me free, isn't that the holy word?"

"John 8:32, yes. 'And ye shall know the truth, and the truth shall make you free.' God will move heaven and earth to help you see his face."

"And I am permitted to move heaven and earth myself?"

"Whatever it takes, my son, to know your Lord and master."

Snake opened Carmen's small Bible and located the passage.

"I found this in Numbers, Father, 35:17. 'And if he smite him with throwing a stone, wherewith he may die, he is a murderer: the murderer shall surely be put to death. Or if he smite him with a hand weapon of wood, and he die, he is a murderer: the murderer shall surely be put to death.' "

"Yes," Father Meacham said. "This, too, is God's word."

"Then the next verse," Snake said. " 'The revenger of blood himself shall slay the murderer when he meeteth him, he shall slay him.' "

Father Meacham was quiet for a moment with his head bowed, eyes closed. When he opened them, he turned and looked directly at Snake.

"What exactly are you asking me, Snake?"

"The Bible doesn't have a problem with revenge. That's how I read it."

"It's more complex than that."

"But those are the words. Those are the Bible's words: 'The revenger of blood himself shall slay the murderer when he meeteth him.' That sounds very simple to me, Father. Very simple. Very clear."

Before Father Meacham could further contradict him, Snake rose and left the confessional. Carlos was waiting in the back pew near the door, paging through one of the girlie magazines he took with him everywhere. Snake slipped into a seat beside him.

At the rail across the aisle, Sister Madeleine was lost in prayer. A nun whose lustrous black hair sometimes showed at the edges of her hood. Hair as black and radiant as Carmen's. A nun who meditated for hours in the Church of the

Little Flower. As devout, beautiful, and pure of heart as Snake's lost sister.

Incense floated through blades of sunlight beaming through the high window slits. The chapel had a hollow resonance that absorbed the sharp edges of sound. It was a timeless space where Snake felt the weight of his earthly cares lighten. The church had existed before he was born and would outlast his petty trials, his guilt, his anger and frustration. A place of suspended animation where the ancient rituals were unchanging, where the raging voices beyond those walls were muted to inconsequence.

Though he knew that when he walked out into the hard sunlight, all his sorrow and fury would begin to roll and crash again through his bloodstream, for those serene minutes in the sanctuary, he could sense Carmen's spirit wafting through the high warm air.

Years earlier he tried repeatedly to pray to God, to share in that holy union Carmen had discovered. But only dead silence answered Snake's deepest pleadings. Then one day, in a fevered state, he made the slightest shift in his prayers, directing them no longer to an indifferent divinity but directly to his lost sister. It felt like sacrilege, but in an instant he was rewarded with a swelling in his heart and a breathtaking rush of sweet air into his lungs. It was miraculous. By simply addressing his prayer to her, Snake had reestablished a fragile communion with Carmen.

Since that first instance, his sister had answered him only sporadically, as if she were measuring out her aid in tiny increments so as not to overwhelm him. What he got was a hallowed whisper that floated down from the vaulted ceiling, not words, not specific counsel, but the delicate murmurs of an all-knowing adult reassuring a child.

At first Snake worried he might be going insane and this voice he heard was nothing more than self-induced hallucination—produced by a longing so deep and abiding, it had begun to mimic real sound.

Though finally Snake settled on the belief that whether it

was Carmen speaking within his head or Carmen out there in the sacred vapors, it was clearly her, and she was surely trying to console him. Just as certainly it was this soundless voice of his lost sister that was the single force that restrained Snake from buying a handgun and directing its blast into his vacant heart.

"So what's the play, big man?" Carlos said.

Snake pulled his eyes away from Sister Madeleine. So quiet, so at peace.

"We're going back to the house where the roofer was."

"And do what?"

"We'll wait," Snake said. "See who shows up. Get it right this time."

Alex paced for ten minutes at the curbside before a cab picked her up. On the airport loop road, they got stuck in an unmoving line of cars. She kept trying Thorn's cell, but apparently he'd switched it off.

The five-mile drive to her home in South Miami that should have taken fifteen minutes took forty-five. She paid the cabbie and he hauled the bag out of the trunk and without a word roared away.

Her Camry was gone. Thorn's rusty, spavined VW Beetle hunched at the curb. A ladder lay across her front walkway, roofing equipment scattered around the lawn. At least Thorn had the sense to lock the door before he left.

She unlocked the door, stepped into the foyer. She tried his phone again, got no answer. She stepped into the kitchen. All cleaned up from breakfast. The Makita drill sat on the kitchen table, dark tar on the drill bit.

Buck tugged on his lead, ready to be free. Not understanding why they'd made the journey to the airport, worked through the long obstacle course to the gate, boarded the plane, taken up a position in the rear emergency row, the only place where service dogs were allowed. Five minutes later they got up, made a sudden exit, riding home in another cab only a couple hours after they'd left.

"Okay, okay, easy does it, boy. We're home."

Alex squatted down and unsnapped his leash. He shook himself hard and cantered away to the rear of the house in search of Lawton and Thorn.

Alex called out Thorn's name even though the car was gone and she knew he wasn't there.

Something was off-key. His voice on the phone, the disarray in the front yard, Thorn abandoning his work in the middle of the day, and some other edginess in the air she couldn't identify.

She dialed Harbor House and got Lilly the receptionist. Before she could get the question out, Lilly said, "There was a young man here, handsome fella. He took Lawton off with him."

"Thorn?"

"Blondish hair, dark tan, boat shoes and shorts. Rangy guy."

"Why did he take Dad?"

"I think it had to do with the other two fellas that were here before him. Real sleazy types. They were asking for Lawton, but Marvin ran them off."

"What's this about, Lilly?"

"That's all I know. Two seedy guys, then this rugged guy in boat shoes. Is that your boyfriend? Nothing personal, but I was wondering if he's taken."

"Is Marion Davies there?"

"At a luncheon with the board of directors."

Alexandra thanked her and hung up.

She left her bag in the foyer, walked down the hallway, and was punching in Thorn's cell number again when she heard Buck snarl, then a commotion in one of the back bedrooms, a man grunting, furniture overturned.

The dog yelped, then made a helpless squeal that ceased abruptly.

She didn't keep a handgun in the house, so she swung around, dropped the phone on the counter, threw open a drawer, snatched a carving knife, and crept down the hallway.

She halted outside the door of Lawton's bedroom, stilled

her breath, listened. Heard nothing. She was lifting her leg to give the door a side kick when a man's arm locked around her throat and dragged her into Lawton's room. He whacked the knife from her grasp.

For the past two years she'd been neglecting her karate training, so was slow in her reaction, but the instincts were still there. She seized the man's thumb and cranked it backward against the joint.

He cursed and his grip loosened a notch. Then there was another man standing in front of her. Tall and thin with a bony face and silver-blue eyes. Behind him she glimpsed Buck lying on the Oriental rug. Tongue out, panting, a gash near his ear.

"Are you going to be nice? Cooperate with us?"

"Put the smackdown on her, dawg. Bitch is breaking my thumb."

Alex gave the joint a sharp tug, and the man's grip gave way. She ducked free and pivoted to put all her weight behind a backward elbow into the guy's solar plexus. A stocky man. Sheathed in muscle, but the point of her elbow found the tender zone below his sternum. Blew the air from his lungs, sent him staggering.

She was swiveling back to block whatever the tall man was throwing her way when the butt of a pistol flashed at her skull. She shot up a hand to deflect but was late. It struck her square in the temple, and the jolt sagged her knees and locked the air inside her lungs. The sunlight danced.

She had enough wattage for a front kick to the guy's groin, but it was too slow, too late, too feeble. He slid to the left and drew back the pistol and hammered the butt against the same patch of skull as before, and Alex felt her muscles soften and heard a whistling shriek like a teapot at full boil, then the floor came flying up.

Carlos drew his shoe back to kick the woman, but Snake halted him.

"My thumb, man, she almost tore it loose."

"Leave her alone," Snake said.

"Nice-looking broad," Carlos said. "She's out cold, we could do whatever we want."

"Forget it, Carlos. None of that."

Snake stood over her body. He was weak in the legs. Striking the woman had sent tremors down his arms, echoes of the clash of the machete blade against flesh and bone.

"Don't be getting spooky on me, Snake. What the hell're we supposed to do with this woman?"

"What we're going to do, Carlos, is trade her for what we want."

CHAPTER ELEVEN

"We're here to speak to Alan Bingham," Thorn said.

"Well, he's not here."

The willowy man who opened the front door of Merrick Gallery was about to shut it again in their faces when Lawton shouldered ahead of Thorn and plucked his wallet from the back pocket of his plaid Bermuda shorts and flashed an ID at the man.

"Homicide," Lawton said in his old cop voice.

"I just put the phone down thirty seconds ago and you're here already?"

Lawton didn't skip a beat.

"Famous for our response time. What's the problem?"

"We were robbed. Or, I don't know, plundered, ransacked."

The man half opened the door but didn't move, still deciding what to make of Lawton and Thorn. Two guys in short pants. He was not more than thirty but already bald except for a fringe of blond hair. He wore a dapper yellow silk shirt embossed with bamboo stalks. His mannered tilt of head and sulky tone suggested the irritation of someone whose station in the world was less than he believed he deserved. Another unappreciated genius.

"I called Coral Gables police, but your ID says Metro."

Thorn had wanted to speak to Alan Bingham briefly, get his story on the photo, and head off to Key Largo, but now he was becoming intrigued.

"Thing like this," Thorn said, "we send our best."

"And who are you, sir?"

Lawton said, "This guy, he's one of our street punks working undercover. He's *supposed* to look like a dirtbag."

"You want our assistance or not?" Thorn said.

The man heaved a world-weary sigh and swung open the door.

"My name is Marcus," the man said. "Marcus Carbonnel."

"So give us the tour, Marcus," Thorn said.

"I unlocked the place five minutes ago. And this is what I found."

Marcus strolled into a cool, shadowy room with high ceilings. He flicked on the overhead halogens and the room filled with a stark, flawless light. Except for the neatly spaced picture hangers, the white walls were bare.

"It's all out in the alley. Someone tore them down and made a bonfire."

"Alan's photos?" Lawton said. "Somebody destroyed them? Why?"

"I believe it's your job to answer that, isn't it?"

So far, Lawton was holding himself together, but Thorn saw the old man's eyes begin to mist—the first signs of a meltdown. A crying jag or some rambling discourse on the degenerates he used to toss in the slammer.

Thorn stepped around Lawton and took over.

"Mr. Bingham have any enemies you know of?"

Marcus drew back and stared at Thorn as if he'd uttered a heresy.

"Everyone adores Alan. He's a sweet, dear man. I mean, yes, his work has a slight political edge, a kind of liberal sympathy for the downtrodden, but he's certainly not someone who would inspire this kind of . . ." Marcus gazed around at the empty walls and drew a fortifying breath.

"Violence?" Thorn offered.

"I suppose that's the word, yes," Marcus said. "Of course, in this town sooner or later everyone in the arts is a target. You know how it is, anything that might be construed as the least bit pro-Castro, we can expect pickets and boycotts, political pressure. The Merrick has had its share of bomb threats, and the board of directors were bullied once into taking down an entire show. But, as I say, nothing in Alan's work arouses that kind of hatefulness."

Carbonnel touched a hand to his white throat and kept it there as if taking his own overstimulated pulse. He looked over at Lawton, who was wandering the gallery, staring at the walls. The old man paused and hooked his finger over a hanger and tugged to test its worthiness.

"Just last night," Carbonnel said, "we had a VIP reception, a private viewing with members of virtually every segment of Miami society, and I heard nothing but positive remarks all evening."

"You hear that, Thorn?" Lawton called. "That's who Alan is. That man can draw the black-tie limo crowd. And what about you? You think any VIPs would show up for something you did? I sure as hell don't think so."

Thorn figured they might have a minute or two more before the real cops arrived. It'd be tricky trying to explain why he and Lawton were impersonating police officers.

"Hey, Marcus," Lawton called again. "You trying to pass this stuff off as art? All these blank walls. This some kind of joke?"

Thorn smiled.

"Don't mind Detective Collins, he's a joker."

Marcus gave Thorn a sour look and seemed on the verge of trotting away to his office to make another phone call to the Gables cops.

"Did I see your badge?" Marcus said. "I don't believe I did."

Thorn raised the boxing photograph.

"Was this part of the exhibit?"

Marcus examined the photo, then looked at Thorn.

"Where'd you get that?"

Thorn repeated his question, and with a huffy frown Marcus nodded.

"Look, Mr. Carbonnel, is there anything unique about

this photo, something that sets it apart from the rest of the show?"

"You're not policemen, are you?"

Thorn held his gaze until Marcus couldn't bear it anymore, and with a grimace, he cut his eyes away. Not used to losing stare-downs.

"Here's the deal, Marcus. Detective Collins and I may already have a lead on the two guys who did this."

"You do?"

"But we need your help. So stay with me, okay?"

Thorn glanced over at Lawton. The old man was almost finished circling the gallery. He'd tugged on every hanger and was shaking his head at the blank walls.

"The photo," Thorn said, bringing it into Marcus's line of sight. "Is it distinctive in any way? Different than the others in the show?"

"Alan should be here by now," said Marcus. "I phoned his home but got no answer, so I suspect he'll show up any second. You can ask him these questions."

"I'm asking you," Thorn said.

"Oh, I don't know. I mean, yes, I suppose it's unique. Uniquely inferior. Don't repeat this to Alan, of course, but that boxing shot is quite immature, technically sloppy compared with where he is now. More of a snapshot than an artistic effort. To be honest, I'm not sure why he decided to include it. The lighting, composition, even focus. It's amateurish. Has none of the elegant structure, the aesthetic tension he evolved over the years."

"What about the people in the audience? Anything jump out at you?"

Marcus squinted for a moment, then shook his head.

"Fight fans, typical dress of the time. Somewhat quaint."

"Why quaint?"

"Except for that one woman, it's all white middle-aged men. Everyone wearing suits and ties like they were dressed for church. That's not what you get in a boxing audience today."

"Besides that?"

Carbonnel shrugged and looked over at Lawton, who seemed to be studying a particularly blank part of the wall.

Thorn caught a glimpse out the front window of a patrol car pulling up.

"Detective Collins," he called out to Lawton. "We should wrap it up."

"What?" Marcus said. "A couple of questions? Not going to dust for fingerprints? You don't want to see the bonfire in the alley, take a look at the security video?"

"There's a video?"

"Of course," Marcus said. "Before you arrived I took a peek. Two men. Hispanic, I think. One was tall and thin, the other short and husky. I just looked at a few seconds, then you showed up."

"Those are our guys."

"You're sure?"

"Is there a back door to the alley?"

"Through there." Marcus motioned with his chin to a narrow corridor.

"Listen," Thorn said. "That VIP thing last night. Was that the first time these photos went public? They weren't on display before?"

"Oh, no. Alan's work has been shown a great deal. This show was a retrospective covering four decades of his career, more complete than anything he's done before. That's what made it so special. The breadth and scope of his presentation of Miami life, history, culture, crime. Everything."

"This one, too, the boxing shot? It's been exhibited before?"

A uniformed cop was rapping on the front door, shielding his eyes from the sun as he peered into the tiny window.

Marcus made a move that way, but Thorn took a grip on his arm and held him fast.

"That's Mulroney, don't worry about him. He'll wait."

"But . . ."

"What about it?" Thorn said. "Has it been shown before?"

"Not that I'm aware of. Alan must've pulled that out of a drawer in a moment of sentimental weakness."

Thorn patted Marcus on the shoulder.

"What about a guest list from last night, this VIP thing?"

"Do you have a warrant?"

"Do I need one?"

Marcus glanced over at the patrolman at the door.

"It's in the office."

"I'll wait."

Marcus returned a moment later with a sheet of names. Thorn took it, folded it into quarters, and slid it into the back pocket of his khaki shorts.

"I really should let him in," Marcus said.

Thorn gripped the young man's shoulder and steered him toward the rear of the museum.

"First the bonfire," Thorn said. "The patrolman can wait."

CHAPTER TWELVE

"Meyer Lansky," Lawton said when they were back in the car, heading south through a shady neighborhood.

"What?"

"This guy." Lawton tapped the little man in the gray sports coat and polo shirt, dark wavy hair, sitting three rows back from the ring. "It's Lansky, all right. And that guy next to him whispering in his ear, hell, anybody with a diamond on their pinkie, they got to be a gangster."

They were working their way south through the Gables, driving beneath a canopy of oaks and ficus, passing tile-roofed mansions that backed up to a golf course. Hovering in the west was the glittering spire of the Biltmore Hotel. Part palace, part fortress, the hotel dominated the Mediterranean fantasyland surrounding it.

"My memory," Lawton said. "It's spotty, I'll grant you that, but faces, no sir, I see a face once, zap, it sticks forever, like fuzz on Velcro. Names and faces. Faces and names. My specialty."

Thorn kicked it around for a few blocks. Then, when they were stopped for a light at Bird Road and Granada, he said, "We're dropping this, Lawton. It's none of our damn business. We'll go to your house, pack some clothes, drive down to Key Largo. I'll call Alex later, tell her what happened. She can pass it to her cop friends at work, have them sniff around."

"I *am* a cop."

"You *were* a cop, Lawton. You're retired now."

"Hell with that. A guy like me can't retire. Can you picture me, Jesus, sitting around all day in some retirement home? Hell, they'd have me doing flower arranging with a bunch of biddies before you know it. 'Cause that's what happens. Minute you quit the force, they ship you off to flower arranging."

"I've heard that, yeah."

"Lansky wasn't a killer per se," Lawton said. "He was the financial guy. He set up the front businesses. Down in Havana, that was his big deal. He squeezed out Bugsy Siegel, made a bargain with Batista, the dictator before Castro. They were going to build fifty hotels together, a Riviera of sin, gambling, prostitution, drugs. Then the communists came along and tossed him out, and old Meyer wound up back in Miami Beach. Not even his CIA buddies could help him. He was pissed. But what could he do? I saw him once before he died of cancer. Out walking down Collins Avenue with his blind shih tzu. Shriveled-up little guy. Didn't matter he was worth four hundred million. He died like the rest of us."

"When was that? When did he die?"

"Had to be, I don't know, twenty years ago. In the eighties sometime."

"So why the hell would two punks care about a picture of him at a boxing match?"

"Punks," Lawton said. "Who knows how their minds work? I got close to forty years working with slimeballs, I still got no idea what makes them tick. Anybody says he does is full of shit. Way I see it, slimeballs come flying in from the far end of the universe. Some perverted planet produces them and launches them one after the other. *Whoosh, whoosh.* Dead of night, they zoom down out of the sky, crash-land in the desert, the Mojave, Death Valley, Sahara, they're closed up inside those pods, you know. A few hours later, up they pop. Ready-made slimeballs. They're raining down every night, hundreds of them, thousands maybe. Who knows? Deserts all around the globe."

Thorn felt a wave of ripples pass across the flesh of his shoulders.

Snake. The name had been itching in his head since he'd heard it earlier that morning. And now like some faint echo that finally comes rolling back across the canyon, the name clarified, attached itself to a place and time. There had been only one Snake in Thorn's life. Only one.

When the light changed, Thorn wheeled left onto Bird, then left again, heading back the way they'd come.

In that week following the Clay and Liston fight, he and Kate and Dr. Bill had stayed in a Miami motel to take in the sights. During those seven memorable days, two boys' names were on the news again and again. Two orphaned kids. They were the sole survivors of a mass murder, which was graphically recounted in the press. It was to be Thorn's first clear memory of the horrors men could wreak upon one another. And since Thorn himself was an orphan, losing his natural parents in a violent car crash when he was an infant, those two kids, Snake and his younger brother, made an indelible mark.

Thorn weaved north, picking his way toward Coral Gables Library, listening to Lawton work out his intergalactic theory of evil.

Maybe Thorn was starting the slide toward senility himself, because by the time he drew into the library parking lot, Lawton's outer-space invasion idea was starting to sound as plausible as any explanation of evil Thorn had ever heard.

Millicent Wharton, the reference librarian for Coral Gables Library, was in her late sixties and must have threaded the microfiche machine for idiots like Thorn ten thousand times before. But she did it with a happy smile nonetheless, chatting all the time about the year he'd selected, 1964. A wonderfully innocent period, according to her. Miami was such a lazy, happy town. So polite and full of promise.

"You couldn't have been more than five years old," Thorn said.

The white-haired woman gave him a pretty smile and hooked the spool of film onto the sprockets and ran it forward. The pages flashed by on the screen like a herky-jerky newsreel.

Millicent's unstated implication was one Thorn had heard hundreds of times before. Think of what a paradise Miami would be today if Castro had never come to power and Miami was still an English-speaking southern city instead of the unofficial capital of Latin America. The attitude was a sly mingling of nostalgia and racism. Most in South Florida had long ago come to some sort of détente with the Latin takeover. Many, like Thorn, even embraced it, found its food and scents and cacophony of languages a stimulating alternative to the bland middle-American sensibility that once ruled the region. But Millicent's delicately stated bias was common. It sneaked into the conversations like a wisp of toxic gas. It was offered as an invitation for a full mean-spirited conversation about the Hispanic invasion and all its irritating consequences.

But Thorn let the invitation pass.

At a reading table nearby, Lawton was hunched over. He'd fallen into a dark sulk and was staring at the empty mat before him.

When Millicent had the machine primed and ready, Thorn slid the boxing photo onto the desk in front of her.

"Cassius Clay?" she said.

"You're good."

"He was the champ. Who could forget?"

"What about the audience? Anyone you recognize?"

Millicent studied the image for a while, then turned to Thorn with a look of mild surprise.

"The mayor. Stanton King. All of twenty-seven years old."

She tapped the man sitting two down from Meyer Lansky. His left cheek stained with a red birthmark.

"Well, now," Thorn said. "Isn't that interesting?"

"Oh, back then Stanton King was a boy wonder. Everybody loved that man. Such a charmer. Until he got married, then he just sort of disappeared."

"Marriage can do that, I hear."

"Especially if it's to someone like the woman he fell for."

"Oh, yeah?"

"Oh, listen to me. Gossiping about one of the pillars of our city."

"Who'd he marry?"

"Well, her name is Lola."

Millicent made a face. The slightest roll of eyes, her lips flattening in mock horror. The look a respectable woman might give a tramp who'd just sashayed into the drawing room with her garters exposed.

"Would you like me to help your father find something to read?"

"That'd be nice," Thorn said. "But he's a little cantankerous."

"Wouldn't be my first." The librarian smiled and drifted away to take charge of Lawton.

Thorn cranked the machine through the early days of '64, speeding past photos and headlines and page after page of classified ads. After a while it felt a little like pawing through a tomb. The transitory goodies of an era so far removed that probably little if anything advertised on those pages still survived.

He homed in on the last week of February, scanning the items quickly.

The sports pages were full of prefight articles and photos. Cassius with his mouth and eyes wide-open, jawing at the press, at whoever would listen. Cassius with the Beatles, clowning around inside the ring of his training camp, throwing a fake punch at Ringo. And several shots of Sonny Liston glowering into the lens in a hateful, wordless gloom. Edwin Pope was the writer of most of those sports stories. A man who still covered that beat for the *Herald,* still clipped his sentences short and brutally precise. Thorn loved his stuff and he'd forgotten that it was Pope's coverage of Cassius that he'd read at the breakfast table each morning when he was just a kid.

Then he rolled the machine forward to the Morales murders. The shocking events shared the front page with Clay's victory. And just as Thorn's flickering memory had whispered, the two surviving sons of Jorge and María Morales were named Carlos and Snake.

He rolled the loop of microfilm forward to the days following the bloodshed and found pictures of the boys settled into Mayor Stanton King's Coconut Groves estate, a fine old Mediterranean villa where the photographer had posed the newly orphaned kids in front of a vast swimming pool and the spread of Biscayne Bay. The tall, wiry Snake, and the thick-necked younger brother, Carlos. There was no mistaking it. The two boys in the newspaper photos had become the two men at Alexandra's house earlier that morning.

Even in the fuzzy black-and-white newspaper photos, it was clear the two of them had experienced their loss in starkly different ways. In every shot young Carlos was smiling broadly, while Snake was slumped and heavy and refused to look into the camera lens. A few days after their entire family was murdered, the younger kid was celebrating his good fortune while Snake seemed to be tormented by the unspeakable demons of grief.

Off to his right Thorn heard Lawton's grumpy voice coming from the far corner of the back shelves. Library patrons were glancing that way as Lawton came stalking across the big quiet room with Millicent's hand fixed firmly to his upper arm.

"He was trying to tear out a page," she said as she sat Lawton down at the microfiche machine next to Thorn.

She was holding a coffee-table book of photographs. *The Life of Muhammad Ali*.

"Page seventy-five," said Lawton. "Look at it, Thorn."

Millicent settled the heavy book on the desk and flopped it open. Thorn leafed through the glossy pages: Cassius growing up in Louisville, Cassius at the Olympics in 1960, Cassius training in Miami Beach for his showdown with Liston. And then a single shot of the fight itself.

"Upper right corner," Lawton said. "I told you I was there."

Thorn peered at the photo of the crowd. A different view

of the big auditorium from the one with Meyer Lansky and Stanton King.

"I don't see you," Thorn said.

"Right there." Lawton leaned over and tapped a finger against a pair of legs standing in the aisle. "Those are my shoes. See how polished they were? That's me. Spit-shined. Nobody ever got their shoes as glossy."

Millicent looked at Thorn and smiled.

"They *are* shiny," she said.

"Yes," said Thorn. "Shinier than anybody else's."

"And you thought I was lying," Lawton said. "But look. I was there. I watched the whole damn fight. 'If you want to go to heaven, you'll drop in seven.' I was there, damn it."

"Yes, you were," Thorn said.

When Lawton had quieted down, Thorn asked Millicent how to make Xerox copies of some of the newspaper pages. He might want to read them through more carefully later on. Millicent led him through the process, feeding several dollar bills into the machine. Together they printed out a couple of dozen pages. Millicent Wharton found a manila envelope and slipped the copies inside, along with the Clay-Liston photograph.

"Good luck on your research," she said at the door.

Thorn thanked her for her help and stepped outside.

A shower had passed while they were in the library. The sidewalk was steaming and water pattered from the branches overhead. The light filtering through heavy clouds turned a misty yellow as they walked back to the car. Summer was coming. Its seven months of relentless heat, the airless breezes, the merciless clouds of mosquitoes.

Usually Thorn was cheered by that first taste of humid air. He thrived in the summer heat. But today the thickening breeze seemed oppressive and full of menace. His lungs were unaccountably laboring.

He'd staggered into somebody else's nightmare. A mayor and a mobster sitting at a boxing match forty years earlier. The boys whose parents had been murdered that same night were grown men now, and apparently the two of them had ransacked an art gallery, destroyed a photo exhibit, then come gunning for Lawton to steal his copy of that image of their adoptive father and the Mafia boss.

Maybe it was Thorn's vivid memories of that week in Miami after the Clay fight. The newspapers full of the murders. The TV and radio prattling on about nothing else. As Thorn and Kate and Dr. Bill had driven around the city, soaking up the sights, half a dozen times they'd been halted by blockades. They sat in the car and watched as hundreds of Cubans marched down main thoroughfares, carrying posters and chanting for an American attack against the communist devils who'd committed this atrocity.

Or maybe what was pushing Thorn's buttons was the orphan angle. The explosion of brutality those two kids had suffered had fused with his own experience of a similar grief and isolation. He identified with those two boys, knew the weight and texture of their hurt, the devastating sense of injustice and desertion of losing both parents in a single bewildering catastrophe.

Whatever it was, the significance of the photograph and the passions it had aroused were absolutely none of Thorn's goddamn business. Yet it was all starting to feel very personal.

CHAPTER THIRTEEN

"Here you go, Mr. King. Whole wheat bagel, cream cheese, café con leche."

Sammi set his food before him, and Stanton King rewarded her with a smile. For the past two months she'd been his waitress. College girl, nineteen, with wide hips and an unflagging resolve to flash her bejeweled belly button. As was her habit, Sammi stole a glance at the port-wine stain that marked Stanton's right cheek, then blinked and looked away.

Vascular lesion. *Nevus flammeus.* The vessels and capillaries were enlarged and dilated. As the decades rolled by, the color had deepened, and nodular and papular hemangiomas developed, causing increased disfigurement and irregularity of the skin texture. Classic case.

To make matters worse, that patch of skin seemed directly wired to his emotional switching station. When he was calm, the stain merely tingled, but in times of stress it became a scalding sore, pulsing brightly as if to broadcast his agitated inner state.

Once a South Florida power broker, Stanton King was now reduced to a mere Coconut Grove eccentric who each day at this late-morning hour pedaled his bike from his estate on St. Gaudens Road up the bumpy bike path, along Main Highway, past Ransom Everglades School, into the shade of towering banyans that had been giants even when Stanton was a boy. To onlookers he no doubt seemed to be yet another ancient hippie cruising the streets in search of his stoned youth. Few locals knew his name, or the role he'd played in shaping the city's destiny, not to mention the influence he once wielded in matters more far-reaching.

His grandfather was a two-term governor of Florida and his father a congressman and golfing buddy of a Democratic president. Even as a child, Stanton had been groomed for higher office. Though certainly the position his ancestors had in mind was loftier than the only one he'd attained. Mayor Stanton King. One brief stint in the limelight of city politics. A boy wonder whose meteoric career fizzled just as suddenly from a single disastrous misjudgment.

Now his only striving was to disappear into the sameness of each day. At exactly eleven Stanton rode his Schwinn to Café Europa. Same tiny table, same teetering metal chair out on the sunny sidewalk. He had his café con leche, his bagel, his dollop of cream cheese, and watched the world pass. Each afternoon he whiled away the hours at the Japanese Gardens on MacArthur Causeway, an oasis of quiet.

As Sammi departed, Lola appeared and drew back a chair and planted herself across the table from him. Her jaw was locked as though she were clamping back a rush of hateful words.

Despite her fuming mood, and even in the harsh full sun, Lola was still beautiful. Finely boned with untamed hair, bright red that was lately streaked with lightning bolts of gray. She dressed with stylish casualness in the Hepburn manner. Tailored slacks and linen blouses in quiet tones. A Yankee princess whose dear departed father had been something of a religious fanatic. It was, in fact, his pious devotion and severity that sent Lola off into a lifetime of rebellion.

When Stanton first met her at a gala at the French consulate, she was only twenty-five but was already notorious in the Miami social scene. That first night she was making introductions between men in gold-trimmed robes to men in dark silk suits. Touching each with familiarity. Moving with the bright and fluent ease of a koi through those exotic waters. She had lovers. Lovers in the room that night, lovers in distant lands. Young lovers and old lovers, and Stanton had heard talk of princes and dictators.

That night he watched her from afar. She noticed him, made fleeting glances, even granted a private smile to the young mayor everyone was talking about. But she didn't cross the room to speak. Stanton took that as a demure invitation. At that moment he resolved to win the heart of this extraordinary woman at any cost. A price, it turned out, far exceeding anything he might have imagined.

Now decades removed from those heady days, late at night after a sip or two of sherry, if Stanton tried very hard, he could imagine he and he alone engaged Lola's heart. But the thrill of that fantasy never endured long. For the foul odor of his true circumstance always came sneaking back. Stanton might be the man Lola married, but he had certainly never been the man she loved.

"I thought you had a United Way luncheon."

"Are you going to tell me what's going on, or sit there like a damned fool?"

"You mean the photograph."

"Of course that's what I mean."

"I sent Snake and Carlos to destroy it and all the copies. I don't think it turned out so well."

"You sent our sons? You got them involved in this?"

"Yes. It was a stupid thing to do. An impulsive overreaction. It came at me so fast last night, it knocked me off balance. I wasn't thinking straight."

Sammi came over to ask if Lola was having coffee, but Lola was looking off at the treetops across the street and did not reply. Stanton shook his head at the girl, and she let them be.

"It's just a photograph, dear. Two hundred people got a look at it last night at the gallery, and apparently no one registered a thing."

"It's starting again," she said. "I always knew it would. Something like that won't stay buried. It scratches its way out of the ground and there it is, the monster is staring you in the face again."

"I called the Agency," Stanton said. "A couple of hours ago."

Lola brought her eyes back from the trees, but there was still a great distance in them, as if she were peering past the flimsy veneer of this moment.

"The Agency."

"Yes, Langley."

"Who did you speak with?"

"No one. I left a message for Pauline."

"Oh, God. Not Pauline."

"There's no one else to turn to, darling. If we're going to make this right, we have to involve Pauline."

"They wouldn't take your call at Langley?"

"No, but it was early. I'm sure the message will work its way up. They can't ignore this."

"What did you tell them?"

"Just the general outline. A photograph of Liston-Clay. The potential to implicate the Agency in matters it would rather not be made public."

With the table knife, Stanton glazed his bagel with cream cheese.

Lola stared at him in disbelief. Eating at a time like this.

He'd just begun to chew the first morsel when he noticed the large man crossing Main Highway without concern for the traffic.

The man's grim and familiar gaze was fixed on Stanton.

So it was happening already. Two hours. Far quicker than he'd imagined.

Though he had to be nearing seventy, Edward Runyon had aged damned well. Head shaved and well tanned, mustache neatly clipped. Muscles plumped and firm, head held high. No wattles, no shadowy circles beneath his eyes. Garbed in a bright green Hawaiian shirt, baggy tan slacks, and clunky sandals, as though Runyon had just been delivered to Miami by cruise line.

Stanton searched for the telltale bulge of a handgun, but the shirt was too loose-fitting to be sure. There might be others nearby as well, of course, Runyon's confederates. They frequently worked in pairs, sometimes in larger groups to swarm their target. Though Stanton doubted a man of his age and fragility warranted anything so extreme.

"In fact, I believe my message was delivered," Stanton said.

"What?"

"Must be off," Stanton said to Lola. "Ta-ta."

Ten yards away Runyon stepped onto the sidewalk.

Stanton palmed a piece of silverware, rose from his metal chair, dropped his napkin in his plate, and led the man away from his wife in what might very well have been a final act of chivalry.

She called out to him, but Stanton didn't reply. He kept an unhurried pace, drifting away from Main Highway, up Commodore Plaza toward Grand Avenue. At that weekday hour the sidewalks were nearly deserted.

Within half a block Runyon was beside him, step for step.

"Long time," Runyon said.

"Not long enough."

"You look like death, old man. Some reprobate on welfare."

"And you have the appearance of a condo commando. What is it, Boca Raton, land of self-righteous privilege?"

"Bingo," Runyon said. "Yanked from the sixth fairway to wipe the shit off your ass."

"Why you?"

"Why not me? I got a stake in this, right? And I'm local. Makes sense."

"Please tell me, old friend, this is not wet work?"

"Don't piss your shorts, King. If they wanted you dead, you'd already be on a slab."

"They can't remove me. There'll be consequences."

"Whatever you say, old man. Got a preference where we talk?"

"Suddenly I'm not in a garrulous mood," Stanton said. "Maybe later after I've gathered my wits."

Locking a grip onto the back of Stanton's neck, Runyon steered him into an alcove at the front of a kitchen shop. A CLOSED sign hung on the door. In the windows were shining copper pots and pans, the tools of a pampered chef.

Runyon shoved Stanton forward, crushing his face into the storefront.

"You called, we came," Runyon said. "What'd you expect?"

Stanton couldn't speak, his teeth sliced into the back of his lips, the glass was cold and unyielding. Tasting blood now. A clump of his frizzy hair was caught in Runyon's clasp, and Stanton's scalp burned as roots tore loose.

Runyon relaxed his grip enough for Stanton to turn his head and speak.

"I tried to handle it myself. But it didn't work out."

Runyon drew Stanton's face away from the glass and held him in place for a moment. His reflection came back to him as a ghostly echo. An ethereal Stanton King who stared at him with eyes so desolate, it was as if this other self were looking back from the land of the unliving.

Then Runyon slammed his face into the wall of glass. Across the black heavens of Stanton's mind, holiday sparklers spewed and flickered.

"That's for fucking up forty years ago," Runyon said. "Putting a giant turd in my file. That cost me, old man. You waltz away from the stunt without a bruise, I get docked five pay grades."

Stanton groaned but couldn't muster a coherent reply.

"And this is for fucking up today."

He drew Stanton's head back for another jolt against the glass.

Before he could administer that act, Stanton jammed his hand backward and the table knife he'd pilfered entered Runyon's belly just above the belt line, sliding into the big man's spare tire with only slight resistance. What a pleasant surprise to find Runyon more blubbery than he first appeared.

Though it was an awkward strike, backhanded and coming at an oblique angle, it accomplished its goal. Runyon dropped his hold on Stanton's neck and stumbled back. An inch or two of the knife handle gleamed through his shirt, not a fatal blow by any means, but blood was already staining the crotch of his tan slacks.

"You fuck," Runyon grunted. "You fucking fuck."

"Brilliant, Edward. Such eloquence."

Stanton reached out and tugged the knife from Runyon's love handle. The big man retched, staggered backward against the opposing window, and gripped his gut with both hands like a woman feeling the first jolt of labor.

Then Stanton eased forward into the brute's striking range and wiped the blade, one side, then the other, against the sleeve of Runyon's surfer shirt.

"Shall I finish you now? A swipe across the throat?"

Runyon growled, but the rage in his face had collapsed. He blinked erratically, as if only seconds from blacking out. Stanton fingered his nose. A stab of pain rang through his sinuses, but apparently the nose was not broken.

"I'll speak with Caufield," Stanton said. "And no one else."

With his back flat against the window, Runyon slid down until his butt thumped against the sidewalk.

"Pauline Caufield doesn't waste time with trash like you."

"It's either talk to me or the whole bunch of you are going down."

"Big talk."

"Oh, this threat is well grounded, my friend."

Runyon drew a precise breath.

"Listen to me, Edward. Listen well. Back in the old days when you and I were in our prime, I filed away certain paperwork that passed through my hands. That fiasco you mentioned. I still have every last document."

Runyon closed his eyes against the pain and growled, "You don't blackmail these people."

"Oh, it's not blackmail, Edward. It's life insurance. If I'm killed or disappear suspiciously, poof, our misspent youth is in the headlines. Splashed in bold print across the heavens. Names, dates, all of it. Just imagine the newspaper stories, the gleeful bloodletting. Oh my, think of the drama."

"You're lying. Shit like that never trickled down to riffraff like you."

"You forget, Runyon. Before my excommunication, I was

their fair-haired boy. The next big thing. For that brief time it all flowed through me."

Stanton King glanced back to see if his spectral other-half was still witnessing from the windowpane. But no, the phantom had vanished in the mid-morning glare. Retreated to his haven in the beyond.

"The files are put away in a safe location, Edward, so it will do no good for a pack of goons to tear apart my house. Pass that along, if you would."

Runyon's tan was turning milky. He swallowed and swallowed again.

"But rest assured, old friend, I'm fully prepared to take everyone down with me. So tell Pauline, won't you? I want a sit-down. Just the two of us. Like old times, a couple of spooks chewing the fat."

"You're fucked, Stanton. Royally fucked."

"Yes, yes. But then, who among us isn't?"

CHAPTER FOURTEEN

In Alexandra's front yard a flock of white ibis probed the lawn for cutworms and grasshoppers. Foraging well inland from the mucky tidal flats and moist prairies that were their usual hunting grounds. Hunched backs, red faces, long curved bills, stalky crimson legs. Five white ones grouped together, and standing several feet away was a slightly smaller ibis tinted a dark brown with a white belly and a white rump. An immature bird, as gawky and uncertain as an outcast teen. Tagging along but keeping his distance, as if mortified by his uncool parents.

It cheered Thorn that even with the sprawl and gridlock, bits of wilderness still leaked in. Weeks ago on a morning walk, he and Alex came across a pair of manatees wallowing upstream through the Coral Gables canals, and Alex assured him that snook and tarpon still cruised those same waterways past the seawalls of the multimillion-dollar villas. Lately he'd heard the cry of ospreys and seen great blue herons soaring on the parking lot thermals. Foxes roamed the dense foliage of Coconut Grove, and giant iguanas and parrots and pileated woodpeckers roosted in the underbrush in almost every Miami neighborhood, snakes and possums and raccoons prowled even through the snipped shrubs and hedges of the newly minted condos. The more fragile species had departed long ago, but the tough ones managed to dig in and adjust to that overpeopled terrain. Apparently it was possible.

Thorn was well acquainted with the doomsayers who made careers out of lamenting the lost Florida. There was a lot to lament, of course. But like it or not, Darwin had a point. The bitter truth was that every species either adapted or disappeared. Nothing complicated about it. For Thorn, the creatures worth celebrating were those still hanging on, the tough birds, the resourceful reptiles, the sluggish manatees dodging propellers. Bully for them. Finding their way through the maze, outliving their delicate cousins. Burrowing into a niche and making do. If this land he loved was to survive, it would be because the native creatures hung on, won their daily skirmishes with bulldozers, managed to cope and multiply. Thorn was rooting them on.

The ibis turned to watch Thorn and Lawton climb from Alexandra's Toyota, then fluttered a few yards away and resettled in the tall grass next door, not far from where Thorn had pitched the revolver.

Across the street Alan Bingham's car was still parked in the drive. The street was quiet. No mowers, no cars passing by, no one walking a dog. A working-class area with the ghostly feel of a neighborhood recently evacuated for some dreadful cause that Thorn and Lawton were oblivious to.

Lawton halted on the sidewalk and stared off toward a swath of cobalt blue beyond the rooftops.

"They wouldn't let Cassius try on a shirt."

"What?"

"A short-sleeve shirt lying on a sale table, two dollars, ninety-nine cents," Lawton said. "It was in the newspapers. Happened at Burdines, the downtown store, sales clerk refused to let Cassius try it on. Company policy. Negroes couldn't try on clothes 'cause it would contaminate them and no white person would ever buy anything there again. Cassius didn't make a stink out of it, just left the store. Here's this kid, he's got an Olympic gold medal hanging around his neck, and they wouldn't let him try on a frigging shirt."

"Things have changed in forty years," Thorn said.

"Oh yeah?" Lawton headed down the front walk. "What planet you been living on?"

Thorn unlocked the door, stood aside for Lawton, and when he stepped inside himself, he found the foyer blocked by Alexandra's roll-on bag.

"It's about damn time she got back," Lawton said. "Leaving her old man in the hands of an unreliable doofus, what kind of daughter would do that to her defenseless old dad?"

"Something's happened. She just left a few hours ago."

"My ass. It's been weeks. Don't try to play with my head, boy."

Thorn stepped past him, took a quick glance around the kitchen, and saw that the pistol was gone. He headed at a trot down the hall, calling out her name.

He pushed into her bedroom but found it empty. He called her name again, but all he heard was the raucous voice of the television that Lawton had switched on in the Florida room. Flicking through the channels in an endless search for some show he could never find.

Thorn walked across the hallway to Lawton's bedroom and opened the door, realizing as he did that he'd never seen it shut before.

When he stepped in, he was confronted by piles of Lawton's clothes scattered about the floor, drawers yanked out, contents tossed, the mattress flipped off the bed and gashed open in several places. Pillows disemboweled, paintings ripped from the walls, their backings torn off. The side table was on its face, chairs overturned, the tiny bathroom ransacked as well. Apparently by the time the looters reached the green-tiled lavatory, they'd lost patience and changed from searchers to destroyers. The mirror was shattered, toilet seat broken off, shower curtain dumped in the tub, tubes of toothpaste and shampoo and hemorrhoid cream had been squeezed flat, their contents smeared across the countertop and the windowpanes.

Thorn headed for the door and had one foot in the hallway when he caught movement to his right. He swung back and scanned the small room but saw nothing. He bent down, flipped aside the mattress, revealing only more of Lawton's garish collection of Bermuda shorts and peacock shirts.

He stood and listened. Then ticked his gaze from one side

of the room to the other until he thought he saw a small shrug of the white comforter that was humped by the over-turned dresser.

Next to the comforter a kitchen knife was stuck in the oak floor. It was cocked at a severe angle, its point buried half an inch into the wood.

Thorn grabbed the edge of the spread and yanked it aside, and Buck, the sweet, intelligent yellow Lab, wobbled to his feet and trudged toward Thorn. He made it about a yard before he groaned and settled back to the floor.

Thorn squatted beside him and explored his coat gingerly until he found the damp spot behind one ear. The dog yelped and drew back.

"What the hell're you doing!"

Lawton stepped into Thorn's field of vision. He was grip-ping an aluminum baseball bat in his right hand.

"Look at this place. You goddamn weasel. You attack my dog, you tear up my bedroom. That's the last straw. You're doing some hard time for this."

Lawton pointed the baseball bat at him, but his words had no muscle. Going through the motions. Exhausted from his grueling day.

The bat was a memento from his police softball league in the final years of work. He'd batted lefty, averaging .340 against much younger men. A few weeks back Alex had told Thorn about his athletic feats, her smile full of a daughter's pride.

"Listen to me, Lawton. Those same guys were here again looking for the photo, and they ran into Alex and Buck."

"Yeah? Who're you all of a sudden, Dick Tracy?"

Thorn squatted beside the dog and touched his ruff. The Lab looked up at Thorn, eyes still fogged. He fingered Buck's skull near the blood-matted patch and the dog winced and be-gan licking his lips.

"Got to get him to a vet," Lawton said.

"We will, but we need to find Alex first."

"Alexandra," Lawton said. "She went to Tampa. Her and Buck."

Thorn went room by room through the rest of the house. It took five minutes, every closet, under every bed, behind every door. Nothing out of the ordinary, except Lawton's ransacked room, Alexandra's luggage at the front door, that carving knife, the missing pistol.

The only scenario he could assemble was that she'd arrived, heard the two shitbirds tossing Lawton's room. Maybe Buck beat Alex back there and the two men snared the dog and clubbed him. Alex heard the fuss, grabbed the knife from the kitchen, and confronted them. After that, it could go anywhere. She could've chased them off, or captured them, hauled them away to jail.

But he knew those story lines weren't likely. She'd never leave Buck in such condition. The only other choices were ones he wouldn't let take shape in his imagination. Alex hurt, Alex kidnapped, and goddamn it, Alex dead.

Back in Lawton's bedroom Thorn found Lawton slumped on the edge of his box spring. Buck stood over a water bowl, lapping.

Lawton raised the bat and took a loose-gripped, easy swing.

Buck finished with his water and went over to the comforter and lay down, watching Thorn with a bleary look. Head up, chin tipped down, the dog's ears drew back in a cringe of guilt. He'd failed to protect his master.

"That dog's not right. He needs medical attention."

"He's tough, he'll be okay," Thorn said. "We need to get started. You up to this, Lawton? Or should I take you back to Harbor House?"

"Up to what?"

"We have to find Alex."

"Yeah, how you planning on doing that?"

"We've got an excellent search dog, and you're a first-class police detective," he said. "That should be enough."

Lawton found a lost smile, and his lips held it for several seconds.

"Ready, Buck?"

The dog lifted his head, thumped his tail. It was Alex's command, prepping the dog for work.

From the clothes hamper, Thorn retrieved the blouse Alexandra wore the day before, and in the foyer he squatted in front of Buck. He passed the material below the dog's nose and Buck stiffened to full alert. His eyes were sharp and questioning. Her? Not her?

Thorn got the dog's lead from the table by the front door and clipped it on, and the three of them walked outside into the grass where the flock of ibis had been dining on worms and beetles.

Lawton tagged along, running his palm up and down the smooth cylinder of his bat.

"Used to love them low and inside," he said. "Crank those suckers a hundred yards. Never played high school ball. No time for that fiddle-faddle, but I could've made the team if I'd tried. Coach was after me all the time to come out, and I wanted to, but times were rough and I had a bakery job. Sweating my ass off with all those ovens. Man, that was work. That was the real McCoy, that job, sweat and more sweat. But those smells, oh man, I loved those cinnamon buns."

Buck swung his nose back and forth a few inches above the ground and led Thorn to the end of Alexandra's sidewalk. Then turned left and followed the trail up the walkway toward the spot where Snake had parked earlier.

The dog kept tugging till he reached the shade of a gumbo limbo and pulled Thorn off the sidewalk, across the grassy swale to the curb.

Then halted. Trail's end.

Thorn looked up and down the empty street.

"They took her away in a car," he said.

Lawton cocked his bat over his shoulder, took aim at the trunk of the gumbo limbo, and did a slo-mo swing that ended in a tap against the tree. Then he looked off at the distant sky as if following the ball's trajectory.

"Going, going, gone. Downtown, baby, downtown."

Buck looked up at Thorn, awaiting further orders.

But Thorn had none. Standing on the curb, staring out at the deserted street, he was trying to remember what Alex said one afternoon about Buck's abilities in urban landscapes, all that asphalt and concrete where scent trails were continually contaminated by foot traffic and car tires, and even the very bacteria that scent was composed of was destroyed by so much carbon monoxide floating on the breeze. Alex had once mentioned cases of dogs tracking scent trails while hanging their heads from the windows of moving cars. Guiding their master through freeways and city streets. Improbable, perhaps, but at the moment it was all Thorn had.

"Let's get the car, Lawton, come on."

As he bent forward to turn the ignition key, the cell phone in his pocket dug into his waistband. Thorn eased back and pried the phone from his pocket.

He didn't remember when or where he'd done it, but somehow he'd managed to switch off the phone.

He punched the ON button, waited till the gizmo tinkled and came fully alive, then pressed the speed-dial number for Alexandra and listened to it ring.

After six buzzes he was about to punch off when there was pickup.

He pressed it hard against his ear.

"Alex? You there? Alexandra?"

For a moment he heard only silence.

Then Snake Morales spoke in the languid cadence he'd used earlier.

"Would this be Mr. Thorn I'm speaking with?"

"Snake?"

There was a pause, then Alexandra's voice came on, strained but unhurried.

"I'm okay, Thorn. Bring them the photograph. Just keep it simple. No one has to get hurt."

CHAPTER FIFTEEN

"The shitbirds kidnapped Alex?"

"That's right."

Thorn pressed the tiny cell phone to his ear while he drove north on I-95. Just one of the gang now. Every second driver blowing past him was doing the same thing, yakking away on his phone. Giant SUVs roaring up behind him, braking hard a few feet from his bumper, the driver one-handing the wheel at eighty-five, then cutting around him. Thorn, a newly converted city guy: When in Miami, do as the assholes do.

"Did you make a copy of the damn thing?"

"I don't give two shits about the photo, Sugar. They want it, I want Alex. It's a simple swap."

"Doesn't sound simple to me, man. Sounds like you need some serious backup. This is nuts, Thorn, you and Lawton and that banged-up dog. I wouldn't do it, man, way too risky."

"I can handle these two."

"I won't even try to convince you to call the police."

"Don't know what it is about me and the cops. Oil-and-water thing."

"You're up there, it's less than a day, and you're into this shit."

"I was minding my own business. This found me, Sugar."

"You're always minding your own business."

"You in your car yet?"

"I'm doing seventy-five on the Stretch, passing a Winnebago at mile marker one-eleven. I'll be there in forty-five minutes, tops. You can wait that long."

"Waste of your time, Sugar. Appreciate your concern, but I'm going ahead. I just thought you should have a heads-up in case we get a bad outcome. A place to start if I don't come back up for air."

"Aw, shit, Thorn. Pull over, man."

"I'm just jerking your chain, Sugar. This is a simple business deal. We each want what the other one has. Nothing complicated. Low-risk."

"These are bad guys. And it's two against one."

"They're a couple of sad cases."

"Hey, wake up, Thorn. They kidnapped Alex, they nearly killed Buck, they pointed a gun at you."

"But I had a super-healthy breakfast this morning. Big plate of fruit and soy sausage. They're the ones in trouble."

"Listen to me, you jerk, stop being cute. You go running in there half-cocked, you put Alex in danger, and Lawton, not to mention your own damn self."

A guy in a black-windowed Hummer cut in front of him, missed his bumper by a whisker, then swung into the next lane, flying.

"It was a very little pistol they had," Thorn said. "Bullets so tiny, they wouldn't scratch my leathery hide."

"Jesus Christ, Thorn."

"I'll be fine, Sugar. I'll handle it with my usual dexterity."

Sugarman was silent for a long moment.

Then he said, "The Liston-Clay fight? Back in 'sixty-three?"

"It was 1964. But yeah, Clay-Liston. The first one."

"And Meyer Lansky is in the shot?"

Thorn said yeah, him and the former mayor, Stanton King, back in the sixties.

"So this is a mob thing?"

"I don't know and I don't give a rat's ass. But these two guys that have Alex, they're the ex-mayor's adopted sons.

Forty years ago their parents were murdered by Cuban spies, same night as the boxing match. So I'm thinking more likely this is about some Cuban political bullshit. Not boxing or Lansky. It could be a coincidence the mayor and Lansky are in the same row."

"Did you talk to Alex? You sure they have her?"

"Yeah, they got her all right."

"That's all? Just 'meet us at the graveyard, swap the woman for the photo'?"

"Gave me a one-hour deadline. And, oh yeah. Don't bring the police."

"That's original."

Thorn looked in the rearview mirror. In the seat behind Lawton, Buck had his face out the window, ears flapping, sucking down seventy miles an hour of scent. Lawton was snoring. His cheek against the headrest, chin touching his shoulder. A sad, faraway look.

"Make a copy of that photo. Stop at a Kinko's, it'll take two seconds. Give the punks the original, get Alex back, we can figure it out later."

"I'm telling you, Sugar, I don't give a shit what it's about."

Thorn put on his blinker and moved into the far right lane. Since he'd been on 95 he hadn't seen anybody use his blinker. Cars darting and weaving so fast, there was no time to blink. Signaling intentions, another obsolete courtesy.

The blood was drumming in Thorn's throat. Jacked up over Alex, now the insane drive up I-95. He couldn't remember the last time his reflexes were firing at such a rate.

"Man, I need to go back to driving school. I'm a few steps behind the state of the art."

"You're acting like this is a joke, Thorn. That's a bad sign."

"It's how I cope, Sugar. You don't want to know how I really feel about putting Alex in the middle of this bullshit. Okay?"

Sugar was silent. Letting Thorn's outrage hang for a moment. When he came back, his voice was quieter than before.

"Give me the address again. West Dixie, I got that. The number."

"It's a cemetery. North Miami, couple of blocks west off Biscayne Boulevard, south of 163rd. Go straight into the graveyard, take the first right, and stop halfway down the row. Those are my instructions."

"I know that place," Sugar said. "Jamaican gangs machine-gunning Haitians for turf. Crack houses. It's a war zone, man."

"It just gets better and better," Thorn said.

"Look, man, don't go crazy on me. Pull over where you are, side of the road, wherever it is, and just wait for me. Do that for me, a favor for a friend. Pull the hell off and wait half an hour. It's nuts to go charging in there all wild-eyed."

"I'm calm," Thorn said. "I'm solid ice."

Another NASCAR hero slashed into Thorn's path from two lanes over and braked hard to make his exit. Thorn had to double-pump his brakes and his hand went on the horn, but he stopped himself.

"I'm relaxed," he said. "I'm the goddamn Buddha."

"Listen, I'm at the second passing lane. It's three-fifteen— this time of day, it'll be thirty, thirty-five minutes max, till I'm there. What's the difference, Thorn, thirty minutes?"

"I'm on the clock, Sugar. Like I said, they gave me an hour."

"A few minutes more or less, they're not going to do anything."

"Hey, I'll tell you what's truly dangerous, Sugar. Driving one-handed on this freeway with all these lunatics. Yammering away with a phone at my ear, now that's life-threatening. All these daredevils out here. Man, I'm going to have to hang up, Sugar, use both hands. I'm getting the willies."

"Thorn, goddamn it!"

Thorn clicked off. He exited I-95 at 135th Street and was heading east at a moderate clip when Lawton came awake, rubbed his eyes. Looking over at Thorn blankly.

"Where you taking me now, you weasel?"

"We're going to pick up Alex."

"You're the guy from Key Largo. That idiot lives in a tree house, ties fishing lures."

"Guilty as charged."

Fingering the butt of the aluminum bat, Lawton looked out at the neighborhood. Bars on the windows, lawns eaten away by exhaust fumes and cinch bugs, flaking paint on the houses. Even the trees were stunted by some essential lack of nutrients. There was too much sky showing, the land parched. Traffic and more traffic. Sidewalks swarmed with high school kids, black teenagers, the guys wearing baggy jeans, triple-extra-large T-shirts hanging down like skirts, scuffing along, crossing against the red lights, daring motorists to run them down.

A few blocks east, they passed the public school where the kids originated from. Graffiti covered the walls, Styrofoam cups tumbling down the middle of the street, a house here and there with a flower box out front and a green lawn, surrounded by tall, spiked wrought iron. Folks making their defiant stand.

The cell phone peeped and Thorn picked it up, checked the blue screen. Sugarman again. Thorn set it back on the console, let it ring.

"What's my daughter doing in a neighborhood like this?"

"Good question," Thorn said.

Lawton continued to babble, but Thorn focused on navigating the congestion. Kids cutting across the street, cars packed tight but clipping along.

Spotting the turn for West Dixie up ahead, Thorn swerved into the left lane and barely missed the front bumper of a red pickup truck. The guy honked and shot Thorn the finger. Ahead of him the light turned red, but Thorn bulled ahead, making the left onto Dixie against oncoming traffic, drawing a couple more honks. Fitting right in.

A block down Dixie, Buck lurched across the backseat and thrust his head out the window behind Thorn and let out a single woof.

"What is it, boy?"

The dog went quiet, nose tilted up. In the outside mirror

Thorn watched Buck swinging his head from side to side
through the half-open window. The cemetery was still ten or
fifteen blocks ahead, but Thorn guessed it was possible Buck
had already caught a trace of Alexandra. From what he'd
seen of Buck's search-and-rescue skills, nearly anything was
possible.

People shed dead skin cells every second of the day. Human bodies were like smokestacks pumping out particles
nonstop. Body heat sending everyone's personal soot up in
the air, each flake of skin carrying a microscopic trace of
bacteria—the body's aromatic signature. Sit in one place
long enough, the particles of smell pooled up around the
chair. Skin rafts, they were called. Every flake carrying a
grain of scent. And dogs swam endlessly through that torrent
of odor. A few parts per million was all they needed to catch
the trail. A few more parts to home in.

The way Alex explained it: a person walks into someone's house where a pot of stew is simmering, he can name
the scent, no problem. Beef stew.

Take a search-and-rescue dog into that same house, if the
dog could talk, he'd say, "Pinch of oregano, dab of thyme,
cup of onion"—every ingredient.

Thorn kept one eye on the road, one on Buck. The dog
was swinging his head from side to side. He had something.
A trace. A whiff of Alex.

The neighborhood turned grim and commercial. A few
two-story apartments with broken windows and missing
roof tiles, hard-luck pawnshops, an open-air Laundromat,
check-cashing shops, a boarded-up Taco Bell. An occasional
twenty-four-hour market or cut-rate gas station with cashiers
stationed behind bulletproof glass. A purple-and-green fu-
neral home. Strip malls with liquor stores, topless clubs, and
gun shops. All your basic needs.

Six, seven blocks in the distance Thorn could make out
the white-columned entrance to the cemetery. He was slowing for a red light when Buck freaked. The dog tried to pry
his head out the window opening, and when that failed, he
began digging his claws against the glass.

"Whoa, Buck. Hold on, boy, hold on."

Thorn skidded to a stop in the parking lot of a shabby concrete bunker called the Bamboo Lounge.

"You stay here, Lawton. Stay right where you are."

Lawton thumped the head of the bat against the floorboard at his feet.

"Yeah, right. Like I'm going to take orders from Mr. Weasel."

"I mean it. Lock the doors, keep the windows up. And don't get out of the car, no matter what. Goddamn it, do what I say for once, you old fool."

Lawton stared at Thorn for a moment, then his face caved in. Eyes brimming with hurt. In that instant Thorn saw Alexandra's features emerge from Lawton's bone structure, a ghostly appearance of the woman he loved. Her eyes were shadowed with unspeakable rebuke.

"Christ, I'm sorry, Lawton. But stay here, please. Stay here."

The old man shook his head with such finality, it was clear no simple apology was ever going to undo Thorn's words.

No time to make amends. Thorn threw open the back door, grabbed Buck's collar and hitched him to the lead, then let the dog jump out.

As Thorn shut the door, Buck yanked him sideways across the sidewalk and into the busy thoroughfare. Stumbling into the northbound lane, Thorn threw up an arm to halt the traffic. A motorcycle whisked by Buck's nose, but the dog advanced without a flinch.

Cars flashed around them, more horns and obscenities flung his way. Fixed on the scent trail, the dog hauled Thorn across four furious lanes of traffic and into the parking lot of a shopping plaza and heaved forward toward a windowless one-story building with flashing neon out front. As large and gloomy as a slaughterhouse, the structure was painted a washed-out red.

PINK GOLD—ADULT EMPORIUM. PEEP SHOWS, FULL LENGTH MOVIES, ADULT TOYS, LINGERIE, TRIPLE X. On the marquee above the door a lit sign advertised this week's double feature: *Ass Traffic* and *Nuns in Leather*.

Buck towed him to the front door. The wrought-iron security bars were latched open, the solid inner door shut.

Two black men stood a few feet away, smoking cigarettes and sharing a pint in a paper sack. Both of them desperately thin with the weathered hides of vagrants punished by endless hours of sun and fiercer weather from within.

"Yo, white boy, what's up with dat dog?"

The tall one pushed himself away from the wall and staggered toward Thorn. Buck shoved his nose against the doorjamb, then turned his head and fixed his eyes on Thorn's. It was called an alert. The dog displayed that signal only when he was closing in on a target.

"Take a fucking dog in there," the other man said, "perverts'll be humping that thing before you can spit."

Grinning at Thorn, the shorter man joined in.

"You can't be taking no animal in there. Ain't allowed."

"Watch me," Thorn said, and shoved the door open and stepped into the fluorescent interior.

CHAPTER SIXTEEN

Carlos Morales paced in front of the three grave markers, two large, one small. Next to those gravestones were two empty plots, a patch of grass waiting for the rest of the family.

One by one, Carlos mumbled the names and dates off the three headstones. Snake looked at the slabs, the date of birth and date of death with a short line between them.

Depressing thought. That was all it came down to. A slab of marble in a sunny field. A life summed up by a dash between the dates.

"Tell me something, bro," Carlos said. "They're off in heaven, got all the fucking time in the world, why the hell don't they send messages or something? Like clue us in how it is up there. How they're getting by."

"Maybe they do," Snake said. "But you just don't get that channel."

Snake stood in the shade of a small oak. He looked down Dixie, watching for the gray Camry he'd seen in front of the house in South Miami. The roofer was still within the hour deadline. Thorn was his name. A tight-lipped bastard. Hard guy.

Snake came up with the hour time limit so the guy wouldn't have the leisure to throw together something with the cops. Though Snake didn't make him for that kind. Struck him more as the freelance type. Swagger in his walk. The way he'd handled Carlos this morning, that probably jacked him up even more, gave him confidence he could handle this alone.

Snake and Carlos were on foot. Taxi parked a block away, the porn emporium eight blocks south. Five pedestrian exits out of the cemetery. If the cops did show, he and Carlos could wander off, one of them head east, the other west, disappear into the warehouse district or the scumbag neighborhoods. If they made it, fine; if they didn't, that was okay, too.

Worst case, the cops managed to surprise them, throw them on the ground. Two unarmed guys at a graveyard.

What the hell were they going to say when they found out the two guys they were manhandling were Stanton King's adopted sons, and Snake and Carlos Morales were simply paying a visit to the graves of their own long-departed parents and sister?

Yeah, he'd like to see that.

"What're you, crazy? Ain't no fucking animals allowed in here."

The woman behind the counter was closing in on seventy. Her hair was bleached platinum and hacked and gelled into a spiky mess with streaks of neon red and green. Piercings in her face and ears. Her black tank top showed off the tops of her deflated breasts and a tangle of green and blue tattoos crawled from her wrists to her shoulders. A biker granny.

"Turn around and get your punk ass out of here."

She drew a foot-long section of rebar from beneath the counter and tapped it against her open palm.

Buck pawed the linoleum, struggling for the back of the store.

"Don't worry," Thorn said. "He's housebroken."

"Take another step, shithead, I'll housebreak you."

Thorn relaxed his hold on the leash and let Buck steer him down the transvestite aisle past the gay paraphernalia, toward a door where a hand-lettered sign said EMPLOYEES ONLY AND THIS MEANS YOU JERKOFF.

As he was pushing through the door, he took a glance

over his shoulder, saw the biker granny on the phone. Calling in the troops.

Thorn hustled on. The lights in the big store seemed to be winking, or else Thorn's optical nerves were shorting out. Sharp pings chimed in his ear as if the submarine he was riding was free-falling into bottomless depths.

Maybe he'd been as full of rage once or twice before in his life, but he couldn't remember when.

Behind the EMPLOYEES ONLY door a narrow hallway stretched fifty feet and ended at a fire exit. Buck pulled him past the first few doors and came to a stop before the third on the left and prodded his nose against the metal knob, then pawed the slick concrete at its base. Buck looked back at Thorn with something like desperation in his brown eyes. What was the delay? Master in trouble. Master in trouble.

Thorn dragged open the door and stepped inside, and in that same moment Buck jerked free and loped away into the shadows.

It was a bigger room than he'd expected. He could hear the dog's nails on the concrete twenty, thirty feet away. Thorn turned and smoothed his hands across the wall until he found the switch. Flipped it and turned back.

A storeroom. Metal shelves stacked high with boxes of sexual equipment. Movies, dildos, inflatable dolls, cartons of magazines and DVDs.

Buck was at the far end of the room in an open space where a gray metal army surplus desk was shoved into the corner.

He saw Alexandra's legs stretched out across the floor. Lying on her back. Thorn felt the angle of the earth lurch forward, and he raced down the narrow aisle and dropped to his knees beside her.

Her eyes were shut. She was bound with the black nylon straps and the Velcro cuffs of a cut-rate bondage outfit. A red ball was wedged into her mouth and held in place with a web of black bands. On her forehead was a dark knot, and in the center of the bulge her flesh was puckered and split. Old blood smeared across her cheek.

Thorn spoke her name, and her eyelids cracked to slits.

He wrestled with the bands holding the rubber ball in place. It was just larger than a golf ball, smooth and hard, gouged with teeth marks. Thorn fumbled with the clips and metal rings, trying to figure it out, do it fast and light-fingered, to inflict as little damage as possible to Alexandra's already damaged mouth and cheeks.

He had to lift her head and cradle it with one hand while he unbuckled with the other, and finally he felt the device loosen. Buck stood watching nearby, his tongue out, his eyes hazy, head slumped with fatigue and pain.

The tangle of straps came free, and Thorn drew the hard rubber ball from her mouth. Her expression changed then, growing softer, as though she were about to take a deep breath and sink away into a swoon.

"Stay with me, Alex. We've got to get you out of here."

She groaned an attempt at language, but her jaw seemed to still hold the yawning shape of the rubber ball. She worked her mouth, then found the words.

"Where's Dad?" she said.

"He's outside in the car."

"Outside in the car, Thorn? You left him outside?"

"There weren't a lot of options."

"These guys want some photograph."

"I know."

"It's the one you asked me about on the phone, isn't it? The one Alan gave Dad."

"That's right."

"What the hell've you been doing, Thorn?"

"Nothing. It's just that one thing led to another."

"Jesus Christ, Thorn."

On hands and knees, Thorn set to work on the rest of the nylon straps. Velcro held some of them, and knots tied with haste and incompetence held the rest. He dug the knots open and stripped back the Velcro bindings and had her hands free and was working on her legs when he heard the voices.

Men running down the corridor.

"They're coming." He looked around at the narrow aisles,

the tall metal shelving stuffed with merchandise for unimaginable appetites. "I'll be over there. An ambush."

He nodded at an alcove sectioned off by fiberboard. A makeshift office consisting of a cluttered desk with an adding machine and a telephone.

"Close your eyes. Pretend." He pressed the ball back into her mouth and laid the straps across her face, close to their previous positions.

As the door blew open across the storage room, he herded Buck into the alcove and crouched down behind the desk.

Seconds later they were down the aisle. Snake and Carlos. Carlos held the pistol, and Snake was empty-handed.

They halted beside Alex, and Snake knelt down next to her.

"Where's your friend?" he said. "I know he's here."

Thorn rocked back to throw himself on Carlos, but Buck broke first, snarling and leaping at Snake's back.

Thorn was a step behind. He nailed Carlos with a forearm to the face and sent him sprawling into a shelf of dildos. The rack tipped and slammed into the one beside it, a row of clumsy dominoes cascading toward the far wall.

Lying on his back, Carlos brought the pistol up and fired. Buck squcalcd and fell away from Snake. Then the gun was aimed at Thorn.

"Bring it, pimp. Let's see you run into the machine-gun fire. Come on, where's your macho now, superdude? You make one move, you'll be tore up from the floor up."

Ten feet away, Carlos rose, keeping the pistol trained on Thorn.

"You okay, Snake?"

The tall man struggled to his feet.

Buck lay down beside Alexandra and shut his eyes. The bullet had grazed his right shoulder. Thorn could see the gouged flesh, the darkened fur.

"Where's the photograph, Thorn?"

"Let me pop him, Snake. Just one in the knee, show we're serious."

Snake glanced at Carlos and shook his head.

"Only if he tries anything."

"The photo's outside," Thorn said.

"Where outside?" said Snake.

"You'll get your damn photo. Right now the lady needs medical help."

"The photograph first." Snake stepped closer.

"Hey, pretty boy," Carlos said. "You're a tough hombre when you're flying off the goddamn roof, jumping on a guy's blind side. But not now, hey, roger dodger?"

"Shut up, Carlos."

"The dude messed with me, now the fucking tables are fucking turned."

"I said shut up."

"Yeah, shut up, Carlos," Thorn said. "Let Snake handle this."

"Let's keep this simple," Snake said. "Tell me where it is, Carlos will get it, bring it back, then your friend and you leave. Happily ever after."

Carlos was smiling at something over Thorn's shoulder.

"Well, looky here. Who we got now? Babe Ruth, Cal Ripkin?"

Lawton stalked down the center aisle. He had the photo in one hand, his aluminum bat in the other.

"Who buys this smut?" Lawton said. "That's what I want to know. What kind of pathetic loser needs to look at shit like this? Creepos and weirdos, that's who."

"Is he holding what I think he is?" Snake said.

"Stay right there, Lawton," said Thorn. "Right now. Stop."

Lawton halted a dozen feet away.

"Since when do I take orders from Mr. Weasel?"

"Please, Lawton. This man and I are having a conversation."

"Perverts," Lawton said. "That's who buys it. Guys with one hand in their shorts. Pond scum, that's who. Rapists, molesters. Stump dicks."

"Okay, Snake. There's your photo. Now I'm getting the woman on her feet and the three of us are walking out of here. All real civilized."

Alexandra called out, "Dad?"

She tried to sit up but groaned, then slumped back to the floor.

"Hey," Lawton said. "Is that my girl? Which of you punks did this?"

He focused on Carlos, took a couple of steps his way, let go of the photograph. It fluttered to the concrete floor.

"Put that cap gun down, boy. Do it right now." Lawton raised his bat and cocked it to his shoulder, coming forward. "I'm not playing games here."

"Dad, I'm okay. Stay right there, please."

But Lawton continued to advance on Carlos.

"Put the pistol down, hotshot. You heard me. I'm Detective Lawton Collins, Miami PD. You got till the count of three to drop that weapon."

"Snake?" Carlos cut his eyes between Thorn and Lawton, the pistol wavering. Snake ignored him and moved down the aisle toward the photo.

"And you too, skinny man," Lawton said. "Stay where you are." He tightened his grip on the bat. "Tell your little buddy to drop his weapon before someone gets hurt. I'm counting. One, two—"

"Lawton, hold on," Thorn said. "Hold on now, easy does it."

He thrust himself between Carlos and Lawton, blocking the angle of fire, but it wasn't enough.

Carlos ducked right and put two slugs in Lawton's chest.

The blasts halted the planet's orbit. A heavy finger pressed against the spinning phonograph record. Time decelerated, and the next few seconds became an interval of excruciating clarity.

When the two slugs tore into Lawton's shirt, he came to rigid attention, his bat clanged to the floor, and he gave Thorn a fleeting glance, a look of wry contrition as though in that instant he was taking back all his gruff attacks, his playful barbs. All in fun. Harmless tweaks.

Then he shifted his gaze to Alex, and there was a sea change in his face. His head lifted and he smiled with the vast pride of a father viewing his child. Radiating from him, a glow of satisfaction—his daughter all grown, doing good, a strong woman, smart, happy, her old dad taking a share of credit in that lingering moment of lucidity and peace. His eyes cleared, a fog lifting, a flicker of the man he must have been thirty years before. Tough, smart, devoted, the no-bullshit earnestness of a cop who risked himself every day, his blood and breath, on behalf of a set of ideals that men like him never owned up to.

Then with an awful lurch, the giant gears caught again, and the pace in that room quickened beyond a heart's rhythm or endurance. The planet resumed its relentless spin.

Carlos's jumpy aim swung toward Thorn and he fired once. But Thorn was already in flight, diving to his left, ramming into Alex, shoving her behind the jumble of fallen storage shelves.

With his arms around Alex, scooting her behind the heap of fallen boxes and metal cases, he heard the next the two blasts, and inside his embrace he heard Alexandra gasp and felt her body slacken. He drew back and saw the twin punctures in her blouse. Her eyes closed, mouth fallen open.

The room went white and began to whirl.

Thorn scooped up the bat, scrambled to his feet.

Carlos lifted the pistol and steadied it at Thorn. But Thorn was long past caring.

Much later, as he would replay the moment again and again to check his motives, he never pardoned his actions as any form of bravery. At best he was suicidal. Losing his own life would have been fair payment for the carnage he'd just caused. At other times Thorn would believe that it was animal fury pulling his strings. The ancient swipe of claw and mauling bite of some knuckle-dragging ancestor of Thorn, his brutish blood channeling down the ages and pooling inside his modern self to lie in wait for the proper catalyst.

Carlos had one shot left, and both of them knew it. Adjusting his aim, he hesitated a second too long. Thorn waded in and crashed the bat against his shoulder, lowered his aim and slammed the man's belly, then his knees, and finally rose up to pound his skull and level a blow across the face.

A bulge of blood erupted from Carlos's lips; teeth shattered and sprayed. The small man crumpled in a pile of softened bones and helpless flesh.

Thorn raised the bat to hack again but checked his swing. He'd gone too far already. He was not so crazed that he didn't grasp that. To push further was to step across a divide that even in that full flush of frenzy he knew meant losing connection with the world of man.

Thorn spun around and took aim at Snake's last position, swinging a wild roundhouse but hammering only the corner of a shelf.

Snake was halfway down the aisle. Deserting his kid brother. Thorn in pursuit. Carrying the bat of blood. Blood on his hands. Leaving slimy tracks on the floor. Snake at the door, running, sliding into the narrow hallway.

The biker granny at the other end stood in the entranceway to the store. Her tattoos wriggled as if alive; the hallway warped like fun-house magic.

Snake was fast, opening up distance between them.

Thorn halted, took aim. Two-handed, he raised the bat overhead, slung it like a long-handled ax, and end over end, it whirled down the hall and struck Snake in the spine and sent him sprawling headfirst, and the photo fell from his hand.

Snake struggled to his feet, took a glance back at the fallen photograph, saw Thorn sprinting toward him, then turned and slid and stumbled to the doorway, past the biker granny, across the store. Outside.

"Nine-one-one," Thorn shouted at the old woman. "Do it now!"

"Fuck you, dipswitch."

Thorn turned, seized the photo, stuffed it under his shirt, and ran back across the bloody trail.

Lawton lay on his back. His chest was still, eyes open, staring up at the fluorescent bulbs, beyond their light. Lips relaxed into a loose smile as though he were engaged in reuniting with the loving wife who'd been his partner for a faithful half century.

Alexandra had dragged herself across the room and

snugged against her father's body. Two ragged holes pocked her blouse. Left shoulder, left upper arm. Pale and shaky. Her eyes wet. A shiver in her jaw.

"Is he gone?" Thorn said.

She managed the barest nod.

"And you?"

"I'll live." Though her voice was frail, sleepy.

"God, Alex. I'm so sorry. Jesus, I'm sorry."

She tipped her head up slowly. Her lips were quivering, eyes hollowed.

There was the dry ache of helpless despair in her voice.

"What have you done, Thorn? What the hell have you done?"

"I tried to keep him safe. I did the best I could."

Her lips puckered and she blew out a puff of wind as though she were lifting an intolerable weight. As her arms tightened around her father, it seemed that against all natural laws, she was determined to keep his body warm.

The gray bleakness in her eyes was beyond measure. She held his gaze for several moments, then her head sagged and she looked down at the frail figure in her arms.

"A photograph, Thorn? Some goddamn meaningless photograph?"

She huddled her body around her father's, her long black hair falling across his face, hugging him tight against her.

Thorn dug out the cell phone, dialed 911, gave the address. He turned his eyes away from Alex and her fallen father. A sight he could no longer bear.

"Officer down," he said to the dispatcher. "Officer down."

CHAPTER SEVENTEEN

Pauline Caufield's secretary said five o'clock on the button, but it was five-thirty already and Pauline was nowhere to be seen. Measuring each breath, Stanton King sat quietly in the Zen garden and watched the Japanese caretaker pad serenely across the walkway till he was standing only a foot away.

"Mr. King, what happen to you?"

Yumi was holding the Zen rake. Just finished freshening the western corner, combing the sand back into perfect parallel lines.

"You mean my haircut?"

Yumi drew closer to Stanton King's bench. An hour earlier Stanton had visited a barber for the first time in years. He'd guided the hapless young lady through the process of buzzing away the unruly mass into a boxy military cut. The gray bristling look of an ex-Marine. Gearing up for what he suspected would be the final phase of his visit on earth.

"Haircut okay, but your face. Oh, sir, you have bad fall?"

"A fall from grace, I'm afraid," Stanton said.

His left eye was black and swollen from the morning's encounter with Edward Runyon and the windowpane. His forehead was a bruised lump.

Yumi of the flawless skin and unreadable features, bowed in acceptance of the mystery of Stanton King's transformation. He went back to his sand, resumed his task, raking with feathery precision, making subtle corrections in the furrows.

His perpetual duty and the ultimate test of his wisdom. Yumi kept the Japanese gardens in perfect harmonic accord with the natural scheme beyond the walls. A skill so rare that when Yumi passed on, no doubt the garden would, too. The modern world simply wasn't replacing men like Yumi.

Four decades earlier the dashing mayor of Miami, Stanton King, was instrumental in arranging the financial covenant between Mr. Shohei Ichimura, a wealthy businessman, and the city government. It was Ichimura's dream to bring to the city he had grown to love an art that expressed the essence of his native culture. The creation of the Japanese Gardens was indeed one of the few lasting contributions for which Stanton could take some credit.

Since he had dropped out of public life, nearly all of Stanton King's afternoons were spent in the Ichimura Miami-Japan Gardens. On a single acre snugged in beside the Parrot Jungle amusement park and bordered to the east by a finger of Biscayne Bay and to the north by MacArthur Causeway.

Just beyond that bustling freeway was Government Cut, the main channel out to the ocean, and sprawling on its shoreline was the port of Miami, with colossal cruise ships coming and going. Overhead a steady flow of single-engine planes towed advertising banners for Happy Hour Tequila parties and Coppertone lotion, on their way to parade up and down the coastline.

Yet somehow, even with the cars so close, the hurtling trucks, the motorcycles, boats in the bay, sky droning with planes, all that modern bustle dissolved to an exquisite silence within the high stone walls. Inside the garden a cone of peace prevailed. A pink orchid tree, coral walls, rock garden, pond, a three-hundred-year-old stone pagoda. His own refuge in the center of a city that had once been his domain. A place apart. A location as pure and empty as the heart of a guiltless man.

It was almost six o'clock, the late-afternoon sun dwindling into the distant Everglades, a rosy light saturating the sky, and still no Pauline.

Stanton had weighed the pros and cons of using the Japanese gardens as the rendezvous site. His major concern was karmic tainting. That Pauline Caufield with her manic vibrations, the stench of supremacy, would befoul Stanton's one pristine space. But he decided that the power of the garden to cleanse itself was greater than the contamination she could wreak. Above all else, if he had to die, this was exactly the place he would choose.

Before he heard her approach, she was beside him. Her faint perfume, something musky with a sunny tang of orange, filtered through the breeze.

"Is that who you're worshipping now, Stanton? The god of overindulgence?"

She took a seat on the bench.

"Hotei is the deity of contentment and happiness." Stanton did not look her way but kept his gaze fixed on the laughing Buddha. "That cloth bag he carries is filled with food and coins to feed the hungry and save the needy."

"A liberal," she said. "A fat, happy liberal."

"This garden," said Stanton. "Its original name was San-Ai-An. The abode of three loves. Love of country. Love of fellow man. Love of work. An ethic that you and I once shared, I believe."

"I didn't come for a lesson in Jap culture."

He turned then and looked at her. In the unsparing Miami sun, her skin had a faultless glow and she still possessed a boyishly trim body, no breasts or hips to speak of, but there was that same iron vigor in her posture, her brown eyes brimming with power and certainty. She wore her blond hair in a simple cut that teased her shoulders. Ragged bangs, and those same heavy masculine eyebrows and cheekbones that could slice a strand of barbed wire.

Stanton had gotten to know her in those weeks in '64 when events in Miami had her full attention. Even in her mid-twenties she had the air of command. Like Stanton, she was on the fast track to the highest rungs of her profession. Firm and precise, she could stare into the eyes of any man and back him down if it suited her. She answered to powers back in Washington, men whose names and rank gave Stanton chills. To the last man, the Joint Chiefs of Staff had signed off on their mission, and Pauline Caufield was made field commander.

Over the years he had looked her up in his Internet ramblings and tracked her movements in and out of a series of shadowy international corporations. She did business with a set of men and women who for decades circulated through different administrations and think tanks and political foundations. Power brokers who when they were not feeding at the public trough were sitting on the boards of the world's most prestigious corporations. Nuclear power, oil, aerospace, armaments.

It would have been easy to mistake Pauline Caufield for a second-tier functionary. An appendage to far more powerful and devious men. But Stanton would never make that error. He'd witnessed firsthand the extremes she was capable of. What risks she was willing to take with her own life and the lives of others in the interests of advancing her agenda and her career. She was not a woman to settle for anything less than full authority.

In the past few years during her latest tenure in Miami, their paths had crossed half a dozen times. He'd spotted her at social events and fund-raisers. And though they had only nodded at each other and moved on without a word, Stanton always felt a tremor in his blood when he caught sight of the woman.

She was staring at him now with that same unblinking gaze he remembered from long ago. He smiled, but she didn't return it. Try as he might, he couldn't sustain his own.

"Get to it, Stanton."

"You know, Caufield, you're disrupting the hell out of the feng shui."

"This photograph," she said. "Tell me about it."

"Always to the point."

"I'm not swimming in the rivers eternal," she said. "Like you, Stanton."

"Cassius Marcellus Clay versus Sonny Liston."

"I remember it well."

"And the rest of that night? Is it still fresh?"

She stretched her legs, heels digging into the pea rock. She set her leather purse on the bench between them, drew her skirt up a few inches as if to catch some of the fading Miami sun.

"We could sit out here all evening and do tit for tat, or you could simply tell me what the issue is."

"I have the complete file on Southwoods. I wasn't lying to Runyon. Names, dates, everything."

Her lips went flat and her cheeks hardened as if she were holding back the vilest threat she knew.

"I was young," he said. "Naive. I had absolute faith in my country. But even then I knew the risk I was taking. So I snagged those papers for leverage. Just in case."

"And this is the case."

"I sold my soul to you people. I risked everything."

"Speak, Stanton." She rose and her eyes flicked across the sculptures, the waterfall, the palms, the manicured sand, and he could see how shabby, how provincial, this holy place must seem to her. This woman who had visited the world's great shrines and taken their measure in the glow of kings and tyrants.

"It's a simple black-and-white snapshot," he said. "The photographer is well known locally, and his show was going on tour after a month here in Miami. Chicago, Atlanta, D.C., Manhattan. You and I sitting in the third row."

"That's all?"

"Someone would've noticed. Someone was bound to."

"I'm a boxing fan. No crime in that."

"Reporters looking for a story. Someone would've noticed, gotten out their magnifying glass, tugged on that thread till the unraveling started."

"Who else is in the photo, Stanton?"

"You were to my right, Meyer Lansky was two down on the left."

She looked at him. A flash in her eyes as she ran the possibilities.

"Miami was full of mobsters. Still is. Means nothing. Co-incidence."

"Between Lansky and me there was a square-jawed gentleman in a military haircut. Cheering, waving his hand. Big pinkie ring."

She held her tongue. Looking at him, waiting.

"While Runyon cheered, he was leaning over, whispering something in Lansky's ear, very chummy, just as the flash-bulb popped. And remember, Lansky wasn't just a run-of-the-mill mobster. He was, at that moment, one of the lords of the underworld. Murder Inc."

"And that's it?"

"Not quite," Stanton said. "There were others in our party that night. Don't you remember?"

Pauline Caufield stiffened, drew a breath. She looked out at Hotei, always laughing, always merry and bright. Belly full, arms uplifted.

"When Cassius was twelve," Stanton said, "a normal kid, no ambition to be a fighter, he left his sixty-dollar bike outside the Columbia Auditorium in Louisville to visit some bazaar. When he came out, his Schwinn was gone."

"What the hell are you talking about?"

"Clay was in a rage. He found a cop in the basement of a gym nearby and demanded this officer start a statewide search for his bike. He said he was going to beat the hell out of the thief when he found him. The cop, I forget his name, he asked Cassius if he even knew how to fight and Clay said no. That's how it started. Cop took him under his wing. Taught him some moves. Saw how quick he was, what a natural. All because his bike was stolen."

Caufield was eyeing him carefully now. In the presence of a madman.

"The moral," he said. "You never know what minor event will unleash the furies."

"Who else is in this photo, Stanton? Stop wasting my time."

"Do you recall a certain Cuban gentleman from Miami, a fellow with a pencil mustache? What *was* his name? I remember he was a plumber."

Caufield's lips parted with a soft snap.

"He was sitting beside you, Pauline, as though you were joined at the hip. His picture was in all the papers the next day. He made quite a stir."

"I forgot he was there," she said to herself. "The guy was a nobody."

Stanton looked back at Hotei.

"Perhaps he was a nobody when the picture was taken. But he was quite a celebrity twenty-four hours later."

"Jesus Christ."

"So you see. That's a stunning group. Lansky, you, me, Runyon, this other gentleman. Some sharp-eyed reporter digging around, who knows what else they'd find? Because don't forget we weren't the only ones in the third row that night. I'm sure you know who I'm talking about."

"All right. All right."

"I saw it hanging on the gallery wall and my heart flew out of my shirt."

"Where is this photo now?"

"Long story," Stanton said. "There's only one copy left, so far as I can gather. It's fallen into someone's hands. They don't know what they've got, I'm certain of that."

"Oh, this is beautiful."

"The sins of our fathers."

Hotei beamed. Stretching his arms up toward the Miami sky.

Pauline sat down again on the bench beside him. She was silent, eyes making calculations, a slow firming of her jaw. A woman hardened by trials and burdens he had no reckoning of. Not the Pauline he had once known.

"You and Runyon," she said. "You'll be the point men."

"Oh, come on."

"I'm serious. You and Runyon."

"With your resources, you'd rely on two old men?"

"Here's how it's going to work, Stanton. You know this town. You still have contacts. So I feel comfortable entrusting you with the role of facilitator. Runyon will handle the heavy lifting. You two find the photo, destroy it. I'll provide what cover I can. I have good relations with the FBI's Miami field office. They're not turf-conscious assholes looking for a fight. But any help I provide will still be limited. I'm sure you understand."

"Runyon and me. What can we do?"

"I have great confidence in you, Stanton. And Runyon may be long in the tooth, but even if I tried, I couldn't find anyone tougher."

Pauline resettled her purse on her lap and looked up at a fleet of white gulls navigating the invisible sea above.

"Forget it," Stanton said. "I won't do it."

Pauline swept a stray strand of blond hair off her cheek.

"Everyone has their secrets," she said. "But as I seem to recall, you and Lola have more than your share. Given Lola's high profile in the community, I'm sure public exposure of certain details of her past and your own would be the last thing either of you would want."

Stanton felt some part of his viscera shift downward.

"So it's blackmail. I do your bidding, or you out my wife."

"Characterize it as you will, Stanton. But Director Waters has charged me with making this situation go away quickly and completely. We'll provide backup assistance to the degree we can. Runyon knows the protocol. I'll give you both my private line, you can reach me in an instant."

"And you'll be staying well behind the lines."

"As you must realize, it's a delicate moment in the political cycle. If this photo were to fall into the wrong hands, careers would be finished. Think of this as your own personal second chance. An opportunity to clean up a disaster that all of us regret."

"Are you green-lighting me and Runyon to commit murder?"

She looked around at the Japanese gardens.

"This is critical, Stanton. The director has made it his highest priority. That image must be destroyed and the situation neutralized. So, yes, it's entirely possible you might be called on to perform some health-altering practices."

"Health-altering practices? That's what you call it now?"

She took a sip of the cooling air, held it, savoring it in her lungs for a long moment like a doper with his weed. When she blew it out, her eyes clicked to Stanton's and her lips tightened into something like a smile.

She unzipped her small leather purse and spread it open in her lap. The black glint of a molded pistol grip caught the dying light.

"Yes or no, Stanton? With us or against us? Speak now or forever hold your peace."

CHAPTER EIGHTEEN

Thorn waited in the porn-shop parking lot with a crowd of onlookers until Sugarman finally arrived. Sugar spoke to a couple of cops, getting the picture, then went over to Thorn with a dead look.

"I better get rolling," Thorn said.

"Cops might want to have a word with you."

"I'm not in the mood for cops."

"Where you going?"

"I don't know. I'll call your cell when I get settled."

"This isn't over for you, is it? You're just getting started."

Thorn watched the stretcher rolling out with the body covered by a sheet. Lawton's white tennis shoes specked with blood.

"I'll call you when I'm settled."

Thorn led Buck across the street and got into the gray Camry and headed off.

He drove back down I-95 into the Grove, and on south into Coral Gables. He found the motel where he and Kate and Dr. Bill had stayed that week in 1964. Riviera Motel. It was on the bank of a wide canal across from the University of Miami. It looked exactly as it had forty years before, though everything around it had changed.

He checked in to a room in the back, away from Dixie Highway, and managed to sneak Buck inside. He switched on the window air conditioner, turned the shower on as hot as it would go, stripped off his clothes, and got in and put his face into the scalding water. With the tiny bar of soap he washed his hair and scrubbed at his skin till it was raw. He dried off, put on the same pair of khaki shorts and denim shirt.

He found himself doing everything slowly. Rehearsing each step before he took it. As if he were drunk. Which he supposed he was. Cockeyed drunk. His head spinning, system working overtime to absorb the day's events. Lawton dead, Alex injured. He wasn't sure how bad.

And he'd been sent off alone, exiled from the kingdom he'd been trying to call home. Thorn went outside to the vending machines and bought a razor and blades and a cheap comb.

Back inside the room, he stared at the bathroom mirror. A wild man looked back at him. Red-eyed and confused and without direction. Thorn shaved. He broke half the teeth on the comb trying to part his hair.

Why shaving was so important he didn't know. Why it mattered so much to be showered and comb his hair. It was surely psychological. A need for order. A fresh start. Something basic and stupid like that.

He stood at the mirror and listened to the traffic. Buck was snoring on the bed. The dog was groggy, but he could walk steadily enough.

It was suppertime, rush hour, the workday done for most of the world.

Thorn picked one of the comb's teeth out of his hair and dropped it into the trash. He stared into the mirror and watched the darkness gathering about him, watched his image fade.

After a while he went to the desk beside the air conditioner, turned on a lamp, and sat down and spread out the contents of the envelope. The Xeroxes from *The Miami Herald,* February 1964. He drew out the photograph of the boxing match and set it to the side of the stack of Xeroxes.

Those five people in row three. Mayor Stanton King, Meyer Lansky, a thin blond woman, a chunky man with a diamond on his little finger, and a skinny Cuban man with a pencil mustache. Five people. Maybe they were together, maybe not. Maybe they had something to do with the Morales murders that took place a few hours later that same night, or maybe they didn't. Maybe the photograph was about something else entirely.

Thorn looked at the photograph and he looked at the pages of the old newspaper. He couldn't concentrate. He sat at the cheap wooden table and listened to the air conditioner and the rise and fall of traffic noise outside. Buck was snoring on the bed in the next room. The air smelled musty, as if ancient mildew had taken root out of sight somewhere.

Thorn couldn't remember which room he'd stayed in forty years ago. It might be the same one as he was in now. He'd had a room to himself that week, Dr. Bill and Kate staying next door. An independent kid. He couldn't remember what he'd done alone by himself in that room. So long ago.

At that same time Lawton was a young man. A cop. Picking up extra cash working security at the fight. Alexandra Collins was just a child.

Thorn stared at the photograph but saw nothing he hadn't seen before. Five people bracketed by the rope rings. Two he had names for. A gangster and a mayor. A man sitting between them with a blocky head and big diamond. A woman sitting beside the mayor, blond and young and intense. A small man next to the blond woman. Looking nervous and awkward, like he didn't belong.

Thorn stared at the pages from the newspaper. The old photographs, and the words some reporter had written, so full of the urgency and drama of the moment. Then the next day the reporter moved on to the next story and the one after that. Forty years of stories between that one and today.

Thorn couldn't concentrate. He wasn't sure he'd ever be able to concentrate again.

The eleven o'clock news was just beginning when Sugarman arrived. The Porn Shop Massacre was how they were tagging it. A big deal, even in that city of gaudy crimes. Fifteen minutes of coverage, going over and over the same sketchy details. A retired homicide detective shot dead, his daughter, a crime-scene technician with Miami PD seriously injured, and the adopted son of a former mayor of Miami brutally beaten to death in his own place of business.

The segment included a salacious camera pan across the porn magazines, a shot dreamed up by smirking juveniles in the newsroom. The shot replayed several times as the reporter spoke.

Sugar stood inside the door and watched in silence. They hadn't spoken a word yet. But Thorn could see from the rigid set of his jaw that Sugar's usual calm was under serious strain.

When the segment was over, Thorn switched off the set and drew out a chair at the desk and sat. Sugarman stayed put, his back against the door. Like he might be about to leave.

"She's at Baptist Hospital, in case you're interested."

"How is she?"

"Shoulder's busted up. They put metal pins in. Arm's in a cast, shoulder to elbow. Five months, six. She's going to be rehabbing awhile."

"Pain?"

"Doped up," Sugarman said. "Awake but groggy. Not feeling much."

"She recognize you? Say anything?"

"Said a couple of things, yeah."

"I suppose she mentioned a baseball bat?"

"She did, yes."

Sugar opened the miniature refrigerator, cracked ice from the tray and dropped two cubes into a glass, and filled it with water from the tap. At the Riviera Motel every room was an efficiency with a tiny kitchen tucked along a wall and separate bedroom.

Sugar drew out the other dinette chair, sat heavily, and stared into Thorn's eyes. Outside on Dixie Highway cars rumbled past.

"Goddamn it, I loved that old guy. Seeing him go down, I flipped out."

"You couldn't wait for me. You had to rush in there."

"Straight-Arrow Sugarman. Knows every word of the rule book by heart. Swears allegiance to all things honorable and good."

"That's not smart, Thorn, insulting the only friend you got."

"I'm going to see Alex," Thorn said. "I've got to talk to her."

"I don't know if that's a great idea."

"I'm going, Sugar."

"How in God's name did you get yourself into this shit-storm?"

"I jumped off the roof."

"What roof?"

"I jumped on Carlos Morales, the guy who shot Lawton."

"The one you killed?"

"Yeah, that one." Thorn slid the photo across the desk so Sugar could see it. "Carlos snuck inside Alex's house and stole this photo. He and his brother, Snake, were waltzing away, I jumped on the guy's back."

Sugarman tapped a finger on the tabletop. Looked toward the window. Keeping all judgment out of his face.

"Yeah, I know, Sugar. You don't have to say it. If I'd stayed put, let them walk away with the picture, none of this would've happened. They walk, I go about my business, Lawton is alive, Alex isn't facing months of pain, Buck is smelling the roses. All's right with the world. Any normal citizen would've waited till they left, climbed down, called the cops. But me, I fucking jump."

"You're Thorn."

"What's that mean?"

"Thorn jumps. We don't get to rewrite our genes. You're Thorn, you pull rusty hooks out of an old snook's lip. Risk killing some worn-out fish to spare it a little pain. And you're right. I climb down the ladder, call the cops."

"And everyone would still be alive."

"I don't know about that," Sugar said. "In my experience, jumping off the roof works about as often as following the rules. Neither has a particular advantage. And I don't think either one is morally superior."

"That's supposed to make me feel better?"

A siren passed by on Dixie Highway. Both of them looked at the window until it had passed. Not for them. Not this time. Not yet.

Lansky was only showing off by inviting them to the championship fight. His seats were three rows back, practically ringside. Such a smug man, making them all place bets, putting down as much cash as they could afford to wager. Saying the fight was rigged, a sure thing. Bragging.

She went along with the others. Something to do to pass the hours before the assault.

She sat and watched the two black men, the plodding one and the dancing one, the gorilla and the prince, watched them hit and sweat, plod and dance. Amazing. Around her all the men cheered as the fighters hammered each other. She was young and horny, and it was a carnal feast. While the men rooted, she imagined tugging the silk trunks down, pulling the jockstrap aside, exposing the prize. The prince and the gorilla. She pictured that while she watched them slam and dance and plod.

After the fight, passing a bottle in the tense car, a slug of bourbon each. They drove to the house, sat for a moment in the drive, readied their weapons. Got out.

The night was warm, the stars bright, a slice of moon. Up the concrete steps, halting at the door, looking into one another's eyes one last time. And she, the only woman, was first through. First through that door to the other side.

As she entered two men emerged from the sunporch. Cigars clamped in their mouths, looking at her, at the gun, then she fired and their round stomachs ripped open, eyes rolling back, a bark from each. Two fat men dying, then the others poured out with guns and she fired and fired but hit only two more. The husband, the wife. Meeting their eyes, killing them, the husband, then the wife. The dreadful wife.

She killed four that night. Lived with the memories for forty years. Over time it became just a high whine, a dentist drill buzzing far back inside her skull.

But now it was starting again. An intruder had poked the fragile nest. Threatening the colony. One by one the swarm gathered and the buzz grew. Ready to sting, to sting to protect the hive.

She loaded the eight-shot pellet gun and aimed it out of the slats of the attic vent, into the black heart of the night. She fired at nothing, fired at everything. Fired and fired, reloaded and fired some more.

CHAPTER NINETEEN

"That was Detective Mark Jacobs, Miami-Dade Homicide. He'll be here in five minutes." Stanton set the phone down and came around his desk.

"It's after midnight," Lola said. "It's too late for police grilling. Call him back; tell him we'll do it in the morning."

"I held him off all evening," Stanton said. "He's coming."

"I'm not talking to any cops." Snake rose and headed for the door.

Lola said, "No, stay. The three of us need to talk."

He minded his mother and went back to the love seat. He'd always minded her. Not that he feared or loved her. He obeyed out of instinct. Duty to the female race. Some vestige of his loyalty to Carmen.

They were in the study where LBJ had shaken Snake's hand. Two leather wingback chairs for Lola and Stanton, the white brocaded love seat for Snake.

Lola wore a simple navy dress. Her bright red hair was pinned up, a single coil broken loose and hanging down her right cheek like a strand of yarn. She'd been upstairs in her bedroom when the news came. Her adopted son dead, the victim of a savage beating.

Snake could see Lola's eyes were swimming. Her face hot and dizzy.

Through the evening helicopters hovered over the estate. News crews were camped at the front gates with satellite trucks and klieg lights, cameras trained on the front of the house, waiting for action.

Stanton made calls, managed to banish all but one of the choppers. A helicopter from the single local station where he had no pull was still hovering. Every minute or two its spotlight raked the grounds, and the beam passed across the velvet curtains and sent a slash of light into the study where they sat. Lit up the swirls of dust.

"That sweet boy," Lola said. "That innocent, damaged child. And look at you, Stanton, sitting there so detached, like it didn't happen. Like Carlos wasn't clubbed to death. Like it's all just some technical problem to be solved."

"He was an adult," Snake said. "Not a child."

Stanton sighed. He rose from his chair, went over to Lola, touched a hand to her shoulder, but she cringed, and Stanton removed his hand and returned to his chair and looked at Snake and shook his head.

Snake shifted his weight on the bench, and a quiet groan escaped him.

"Are you hurt?" Lola bent forward.

"The guy threw a bat at me. Same one he used on Carlos. It clipped me in the back. But I'm okay, I'm fine."

Lola closed her eyes and sank back into the chair, looking for a moment as if she were going to start weeping again. But she drew a fortifying breath and shook her head in a way that mingled sadness and disgust.

Stanton said, "Snake, this man. Describe him again. Anything you may have left out."

"His name is Thorn."

"First name or last?"

"He doesn't know," said Lola. "You've asked him that over and over like some stupid cop. Leave him alone."

"Guy looks like a boat bum," Snake said. "Dark tan. Works outside."

"About six feet tall?"

"That's right."

"One seventy-five, one-eighty?"

"Yeah, late forties, blondish hair. Some kind of blue-collar hero. A roofer maybe, but something tells me that's not his line of work. The boat shoes. I don't know, he just has the feel of a dock rat."

Stanton gave him a curious look, as if he'd detected the fury in Snake's voice. Snake was trying to hide it. Act the way he had for those long months after his family was slaughtered. Dead and cold and focused. He'd deal with Stanton King when all the pieces were in place. Hack off his head if he had to. But for now he was staying cool.

"Carlos had such potential," Lola said. "But he needed direction. He was lost. So lost." She shifted her eyes to the grand piano wedged into a corner of the room. An instrument that Snake had never seen opened.

"We did everything we could for both boys," Stanton said.

"Money," Lola said. "That's what you did. Your great solution to everything. Pour money on it."

True enough, by Snake's reckoning.

When he and Carlos each turned eighteen, Stanton presented them with a bank account, replenished it when it was empty. Using Stanton's political contacts and a chunk of cash, Snake had secured a taxi license and bought his own cab. A few years later Carlos acquired an interest in the porn business. Not the professions Stanton or Lola had in mind.

Snake had spent the decades roaming the city in his taxi just as he'd done as a boy on his Schwinn, mindless motion. Searching for something, he didn't know what. Some insight, some human revelation. In the meantime, distracting himself with empty movement, the clamor of the city. Surviving as Cassius did. Falling back, dancing, pushing the big ugly bear out of range.

In forty years he'd barely lived. He'd had only one lover. Back when Snake was twenty-five. The woman was ten years older, a dentist he'd picked up at the airport. Cindy Marcus. They struck up a conversation, and by the time they reached her South Beach condo, Cindy invited Snake inside. It lasted five years. Two nights a week. Snake in her bed, Snake taking her to dinner and clubs and the beach. Snake going through the motions. Cindy was short and blond and an atheist. Carmen's opposite. She said she loved him, and kept waiting for him to say the same. Five years. Snake couldn't bring the words to his lips. Couldn't lie. He drove his cab, picked up fares, went back to Stanton King's house each night. When she ended it, Cindy wept and beat her fists against his chest as if trying to bring his heart to life. It didn't work. Nothing worked.

Carlos indulged in flesh. Stuck in the soft mud of early adolescence. Fascinated by sex. Spending his nights with strippers and whores. Visiting swing clubs every chance he got, long nights of anonymous sex. Behind his locked bedroom door dirty movies played constantly, the fake grunts and moans of fake ecstasy. Nothing Lola or Stanton could do to pry him loose from his obsession. Carlos was Carlos. Bruised fruit. A boy whose bedroom wall had once exploded. Never the same.

Stanton tried money, Lola lavished them with affection. Coming into their life a few months after they were adopted by Stanton, she assumed a smothering familiarity with the boys. Tried to befriend them, coax their love. Carlos played along, milked what he could. Cash, toys, later a car, a speedboat, and clemency for his many transgressions. Snake gave Lola what politeness he could muster and was never openly hostile. But he could never answer her warmth with warmth of his own. That part of him was scooped out, buried in the casket with Carmen's body.

Lola's attempts at maternal passion struck Snake as desperate and foolish, as though she was driven by some emotion more complicated than motherly love. Nor had Snake ever grasped why a woman of such beauty and class would enter such a businesslike marriage with a man she showed no fondness for. What words she exchanged with Stanton were no more intimate than the chitchat of strangers on a bus. Once or twice he'd heard hints of her shady past. Lola the party girl. But he never saw a trace of that woman.

Across the room Stanton rose and poured himself an inch of scotch and leaned against the mahogany bar.

"Only got a few minutes, Snake. We need to get your story straight."

"I'm not wasting time with cops."

"Well, you might have to. If you do, then this Thorn fellow, leave him out. And no mention of the photo. We're going to call this a robbery attempt. I've spoken with the clerk at the store. She's cooperating."

Lola leaned forward to catch their words.

"The photograph?" Lola stood up. "Where is it? Who has it?"

"I'm working on that, darling. Be patient."

"You and I need to talk, Stanton. Alone."

"We will. I promise. But there are things I must handle now."

After a moment or two, Lola saw she would get nothing more from Stanton and sat back down with a helpless glower.

The spotlight blasted against the bayside window. It searched out the slit between the curtains, illuminated the frayed patches where the ancient fibers had worn to velvet cobweb. Then moved on.

A single lamp on a side table lit the high-ceilinged study. Snake glanced around at the furniture. Same pieces from the night with LBJ. Forty years and nothing had changed. Air the same, same dust circling in the slants of light. Aroma of leather and stale fabric and pipe smoke from Stanton King's father and grandfather. Same Oriental carpets, heavy mahogany furniture, pool table, deep-set casement windows. Stained glass, crystal chandeliers. Same port and brandy bottles positioned on the shelves of the study exactly as they always had been. Shadowy portraits of Kings going back five generations. The imperial style of a British outpost in the jungles of Malaysia.

Stanton finished his drink and set the glass aside as the single whoop of a siren sounded outside. Spinning blue lights brushing the heavy curtains.

"Before we let them in, I want a word with Snake. In private."

"Stanton, I have to know what you've done. What you intend to do."

"Of course. Soon, I promise, we'll have a long talk. Now please greet our guests and delay them a minute or two." His tone, coolly dismissive.

Lola lifted her gaze, staring into the shadows that hovered at the edge of the ceiling. Listening to the racing heartbeat of the chopper overhead.

She brought her eyes down from the gloom, showed them to the men. As bright and dangerous as shards of shattered glass.

She stared at Stanton with black hatred until he could weather it no more and turned away.

"Everything is going to be fine, Lola. Snake and I will put it right."

"You've never put anything right in your life, Stanton King. Everything you ever touched, you destroyed. Everything."

Stanton wouldn't look her way until she'd given up and marched from the room. With a shaking hand, he reached for the decanter, poured another glass, swigged it and refilled.

Snake waited for him to swallow the next slug, then said, "Who's the man with the diamond ring?"

"What?" Stanton bumped the glass and spilled liquor on his hand.

"The man sitting next to you at the fight. I recognized that ring, the clothes, the physique. It's the man whose fingers I chopped off. He was sitting beside you earlier that evening. What's his name?"

"You're insane, Snake. You've lost your mind."

"I always wondered if you were involved. Now I know you were. I just don't know how. Not yet."

"This conversation is finished. You've crossed the line."

"It had something to do with LBJ. The way you brought me in here that night and put me on display. You were trying to win the president's approval, weren't you? Because something went wrong. But LBJ didn't buy it. You fucked up, and that was the end of everything. No more politics. Career over."

In the hallway Snake heard the approach of subdued voices—men showing respect for Lola's loss.

But Snake wasn't running yet.

"You were planning to take it all to the grave, but this picture cropped up, brought it back."

"All this time, Snake, you lived under my roof, ate my food, wore the clothes I provided, and you harbored this hatred, these wild fantasies?"

"I don't hear you denying it."

"It's absurd. I won't even discuss such a thing with you."

"You saved me and Carlos, brought us into this house. I used to think it was just a political trick, taking in these two destitute boys, just a way to get reelected. But it was more than that, wasn't it? A lot more. You killed my parents and my sister, then you took me and Carlos in. Why? Was it just guilt? Your pitiful attempt at making amends?"

"You believed this, Snake, but did nothing, said nothing?"

"There was a woman that night at my house. I heard her voice. She was in charge. Running the show. That's her, isn't it? The one in the photograph. The blonde sitting next to you. What's her name?"

"Enough," Stanton said.

"Does Lola know what you did?"

Stanton bowed his head and refused to speak.

"I promised myself," Snake said, "that I would find out why Carmen died. And I'm going to do it. I'm finding out what this was about."

"Not that you deserve a response to these charges, but I had nothing to do with your sister's death. I had nothing to do with any of it."

"Who was the man with the diamond ring? Who was the blonde? Tell me or don't tell me, it doesn't matter. I'll find out, then I'll be back."

He heard the men speaking with Lola only a few feet from the door. Snake crossed the room, parted the heavy curtains, dragged open the window.

Outside, the helicopter's beam raked the grounds, probing the branches of the oak trees, lighting up the swimming pool and cabana.

The police were at the door, knocking softly.

"That lady cop that Carlos shot. She knows about the photograph. She's Thorn's lover. She's going to be a problem for you."

"Don't worry about the lady cop. She'll be dead within the hour."

CHAPTER TWENTY

Thorn ditched Alexandra's Toyota in a shopping center a mile from the Riviera Motel. The Toyota was the vehicle the cops would be searching for. Not Sugar's five-year-old white Taurus with a dent in the rear fender.

Sugarman drove; Thorn sat silent. Buck lay across the backseat.

"There's a twenty-four-hour animal hospital on Twenty-seventh Avenue, Knowles Clinic," Thorn said. "The dog first, then Alex."

He looked back at the Lab. The dog was panting. In the motel room before they left, Buck drank a full bowl of water. He wasn't bleeding anymore from his shoulder wound, but he'd lost the use of his front left leg. Gimping three-legged out the door to the car.

Thorn hoisted him into the back, and Buck groaned and stretched out.

"She's not going to talk to you, Thorn."

"Then I'll talk to her. And she can lie there and listen."

"There could be a cop waiting for you to show."

"So be it."

At Knowles Clinic they were buzzed in by a heavyset Cuban guy. Sugarman handled the paperwork, gave his credit card. Used Thorn's cell phone as their contact number.

Buck lay on the tile floor and watched them blankly.

Five minutes later they were in an examining room. A

slender woman came in, said a curt hello, then squatted down in front of Buck and inspected his shoulder. She shook her head and clicked her tongue three times.

"Gunshot? How'd it happen?"

"Don't know," Sugarman said. "We found him like this."

She looked up at Sugar, then at Thorn. She wasn't buying Sugar's story and wasn't much impressed with Thorn, either.

"His name is Buck," Thorn said. "You think he'll make it?"

"This wound is hours old," she said. "Lost a lot of blood. I don't know. If he survives the night, there's a chance."

"He's a good dog," Thorn said. "He's a damn good dog."

Buck looked up at Thorn and gave a single thump of his tail.

"They're all good," the vet said.

Sugarman drove south on Dixie to Kendall Drive and turned west. Twenty minutes. Finally a lull in traffic between one and five in the morning.

He found a space on the third tier of the parking garage.

"I'll be right here."

"Ten minutes," Thorn said.

Sugarman gave him the room number, directions.

"Tell her Buck's going to make it. Be sure to tell her that."

Thorn shut the door and fired a finger pistol through the windshield. Sugar didn't fire back.

They changed Alexandra's room. She didn't ask why. Couldn't if she wanted to. A disconnect between her brain and vocal cords. They moved her out of ICU into a double room with a hacking, wheezing woman, then an hour afterward moved her into a private one. Her medical plan kicking in.

Then she remembered her father. The memory bloomed like poisonous haze, choking off the air and light. She remembered him in her arms. His spirit departing. His body losing heft, a flutter in the air. It wasn't a dream or hallucination. A flicker of energy moving invisibly past her face.

In the murky light of her hospital room, gravity drew her deep into the mattress. Lungs laboring, heart trudging on. She felt again his body in her arms. The frail weight, his bones as delicate as the stems of wineglasses, an expression on his face, his last look into this world, first glimpse of the next. That second between. Stepping across. She'd seen that moment, the love leaving his face, the yearning and pain, and entering his eyes was a flush of boyish wonder. Something beyond this realm opening up. Leaving her behind. His face full of light, calm, and beauty.

Filtering in from the hallway was the noise of human traffic. Nurses speaking in normal tones as though the sick and dying, the injured and doped-up, would not mind, or could not object. Business as usual. Their days going on, their gossip, their light banter and laughter, the world Lawton had left behind. The world where his footprints were already disappearing. His scent dispersing so not even Buck could track him down.

Alexandra felt the drug, whatever it was. Felt the numb flesh enveloping her, lethargy, sadness clogging her veins. She listened to the voices, the electronic pings, the jangle and squeaks of passing carts and gurneys. The pad of shoes. A shadow, then another passing by. Her door was cracked open an inch. A narrow slit of light. Looking out from the dark room into that fluorescent world. The way her father must have done at the end.

Lawton Collins. A vital man. When she closed her eyes she saw him mowing the yard outside her childhood window. A vision of him pushing the lawn mower back and forth. The smell of fresh-cut grass thick in the air. He was sweating. His muscles showing, the mat of hair on his chest already going gray. Shirt off to the sunny summer day. She watched him, half naked, in his prime. Back and forth he marched in straight lines. Baggy gym shorts, laceless tennis shoes stained green by years of cutting that same grass.

He worked in choppy strokes around the legs of her swing set. Halting for a moment to wipe sweat from his eyes, propping a hand against the red metal bar of the swing set, taking a breather, then looking at the cylinder of metal beneath his hand, this apparatus he'd purchased for his only daughter, so she might rise into the sky, kick up her feet, come whooshing back, pushed higher and ever higher by his strong arms. Then her father, Lawton Collins, turned slightly and shifted his eyes to Alex as if he'd known she was watching at her window. He'd felt her gaze.

He stood there a moment in the sunshine of his manhood. Sweat glistening, resting a hand on the red swing set, the mower idling, air full of grass scent. That was all. A simple look passing between father and daughter on a summer afternoon. But it was everything. That flash across the humid air, that love in his eyes, that half smile of strength and certitude. It was everything he was. His essence. A man sweating in the summer sun, a weekend of chores. Keeping the grass trimmed, his family fed, his daughter reassured that she was safe and well loved, and that any dream she might have, any aspiration, that sweaty man in the yard would do all within his power to help her achieve.

Alexandra opened her eyes and her sweaty father was gone and the hospital reappeared. She gripped her right hand around the small oval of the cell phone. Before they started the IV, before she was wheeled into surgery, while she was still alert and could talk, could assert herself, "I'm keeping this," she told the surgeon. "Don't make me get physical with you."

Drawing a laugh from the female doctor.

So it was there in her hand. The battery running down. It might be dead by now. Under the dazzling lights of intensive care there'd been only two bars left on the battery signal. Probably dwindled away to nothing.

Not that it mattered. She couldn't see to dial, couldn't lift her hand, and if Thorn did think of calling, she couldn't answer. Couldn't speak, probably couldn't even punch the ON button. And the fact was, she didn't want to talk to him. Not now.

Light swung into the room. A nurse in her white uniform entered. Patty or Sarah. A name like that. Alex had been told but couldn't recall. A chunky middle-aged woman, a career nurse. Short curly hair, glasses. Going to check her chart, add a scribble, the late late shift. Efficient, a degree away from brusque. Seen it all, wiped up after. Whatever compassion brought her to this work had long ago burned off. Now she chattered, filled the room with white noise that Alexandra's brain was too slow to process. Caught a word, then another a moment later. Snatches. Something about the television. The news. Alex a big deal. Mayor King. A long time ago, but Patty remembered. Heard stories about the boys. A couple of losers.

Alex gave up trying to decipher it all. Closed her eyes, gave herself to the pillow, the drugs. Feeling the cold, empty presence of the phone in her hand.

Then a man in the doorway. His voice opened Alexandra's eyes.

He was older, a bushy mustache, bald head gleaming. White doctor's smock with a plastic ID clipped to the pocket. She'd seen him before. He was somebody. Somebody she knew but didn't know.

The doctor shut the door behind him.

The shadows deepened, the room lit by the glow of night-lights.

"How's our patient?" the doctor said to Patty. He had the exasperated tone of a man with better things to do.

The man was looking past the nurse at Alexandra.

Patty handed him the chart, and the doctor held it without looking at it.

The man smiled at Alex, something evil in it. Something inhuman. Then he turned the smile on Patty.

"Wait a minute," Patty said. "I know you. You're that guy."

"No, I'm not," he said. "I'm Ms. Collins's doctor."

"Well, you look exactly like that guy. That television guy, the politician."

"Oh, please, not a politician."

"Okay, yeah, not one of those. But government, FBI, something like that. On TV. Yeah, I know. You're the guy that stood up to Congress, didn't take any crap. That war down in Costa Rica or somewhere."

"You can go, Nurse. I'll take it from here."

"That *Hot Seat* show." She snapped her fingers. "*Runyon's Hot Seat.*"

"Oh, darn," the doctor said. "I wish you hadn't."

"You must get it all the time. You're a dead ringer."

Alexandra was staring at him, gripping the phone, trying to dig her thumb between the lid and body, open it.

"I loved that show," Patty said. "I guess they moved it to a different time slot. That, or switched networks."

"Canceled," the man said.

"My husband thought Runyon was a total nut job, but he watched anyway. He was into it, answering back, you know, arguing with the TV."

The man nodded.

And the smile came back. Malevolent. It was so clear to Alex. She wondered why Patty couldn't see it. Probably attention deficit disorder, her mind pinballing from one thing to the next. Amazing she was a nurse.

Beneath the white jacket the man wore a green Hawaiian shirt, khakis. His head shone in the light, bushy mustache. Wrong, very wrong.

Alex got the phone open. Used her thumb to feel for the speed-dial number. One for Thorn. A monumental effort that required her full concentration.

The man stepped close to Nurse Patty. She tightened up, tried to smile, squinting at his name badge.

"Dr. Blas? Reynaldo Blas? You're not him. I know Dr. Blas."

Something happened out of Alex's view, and Patty slumped into the man's arms.

Alex pressed the button. One for Thorn. Battery was probably dead. Or Thorn back home in Key Largo now. Hunkered down, disappearing into all that water and sky the way he always did. Becoming one with the blue.

Out in the hallway she heard a phone ring. Down toward the nurses' station. The identical ring tone she'd chosen for Thorn. First ten notes of "Yellow Submarine." Something goofy for the man she loved.

Down the hallway she heard those ten notes play again as the man, Runyon, stepped to the bed and lay a hand on Alexandra's throat. Testing to see if she would struggle. She wouldn't. She couldn't.

He wore surgical gloves. Dry and cool against her flesh. Unnatural. His right hand was malformed. There were hard stumps where the first two fingers should have been. A bony nub that prodded against her airway.

The man's shadow enveloped her. Alex smelled his breath. Green peppers, something meaty. Tacos, empanadas. He was going to strangle her one-handed. Didn't even require both to do the job.

Alexandra heard Thorn. His electronic voice in her hand.

"Alex? Alex? Hello? What room are you in? I can't find you. Alex?"

Thorn coming to save her. Delayed by her call. Delayed just long enough for Runyon to finish his work.

Runyon peeled back the sheet and pried the phone from her hand and clicked it shut. Then got back to work, his deformed hand pressing against her windpipe. Alexandra's hands fluttered beneath the sheets. She was a fighter, always had been. Scrapping for everything, having to try harder, being a female in that cynical man's world. Cops, cops, more cops. She held her own. More than her own. Traded jab for jab. She was tougher than most of the guys she worked with. The karate was one thing, but it was deeper down than martial arts. The spirit she'd inherited from Lawton, his gristle.

She pictured a move to knock Runyon's hand loose. She'd fire the heel of her right hand at his nose. Break it, send him reeling. She pictured it, what she'd do if she weren't drugged. But she could do nothing but wiggle her fingers feebly as if she were waving good-bye.

She kept her eyes on him, memorizing his face for later, for the lineup. Until after a few seconds, it began to come clear that there would be no lineup. No later. No more Thorn. No Buck, that smart dog, so eager to please. No more anything. And she shut her eyes because this man, this Runyon, was not what she wanted for the last thing she saw on this planet.

She closed her eyes and felt the pressure on her throat, felt her body shudder, but no pain, she was just fine down inside where it counted, still and quiet and accepting, then once again she saw Lawton Collins with his mower, marching back and forth in straight, even lines across the backyard. The air dense with sweet green cuttings. The sweat on his back sparkled and his muscles rolled. His mouth was shaped into a wide grin as he looked across the yard at her, an impossible distance between them, and he winked at her, father and daughter separated by such vastness, but in that second, no more than that, she snapped across those years, those empty miles, flying back to that hot summer yard into her father's strong arms. Her protector. Her shield.

And everything was fine again, exactly the way it had been on that Miami afternoon many years ago. Perfect. Just perfect.

Thorn saw the doctor bent over Alex. He went into the room. Stayed for a moment at a respectful distance. Didn't want to interrupt a procedure.

But something wasn't right. He saw Alex's foot wiggle hard beneath the sheets. Saw the man's thick neck straining.

"Hey," Thorn said. "Hey."

He went forward, saw the man's hands gripping her throat, then threw himself at the man and shouldered him aside.

The doctor who was no doctor swiveled into Thorn, throwing a looping right hand out of the shadows. Thorn took it on the cheekbone, his head snapping back, and he saw the spin and whirl of galaxies and felt the floor tilt beneath him.

Thorn grabbed the man's lab coat for balance, got his eyes to focus, and set his feet and slung the big man to the right against the bedside table. Just buying time till his vision cleared.

Glass shattered on the floor, and the man growled and came back at Thorn with another punch, this one to Thorn's gut. Hardened by long hours of poling his skiff across the flats, his stomach took the blow and took the next, and he was still standing. The light was coming back; the air had more oxygen.

Thorn crushed an overhand right into the man's jaw. Then hooked a left hard into his kidney, then another left to the same tender spot, and a right digging into the man's gut. The man belched up a string of spit.

As Thorn stepped in to deliver the knockout, the man snarled and drove his knee into Thorn's crotch. Thorn gasped and staggered backward, and the man pushed past him around the bed.

He was old and slow, but stronger than any man Thorn had ever fought. The man staggered out of the room, and made it to the hallway, turned left, and hustled away.

Breathing hard, Thorn went back to the bed, touched Alexandra's shoulder. Spoke her name but got no response. Her face was the wrong shade of white. She was cooler than she should have been, quieter.

He tilted her head back at the proper angle, bent over her, pinched her nose shut and pressed his lips to her lips and emptied his lungs.

Fighting off the dread, he found the rhythm and did it all again. And again. He pressed down on her chest, fit his lips to hers, and repeated and repeated again. A prayer he'd known as a child came into his head, and the words fell into the rhythm of his movements. Breathe, pump, breathe, pump. Hail Mary, full of grace.

CHAPTER TWENTY-ONE

Except for Carmen's gold crucifix hanging on the west wall, Snake's room was bare. Sheets on his bed, a single pillow, but otherwise a cell. The walls scrubbed clean, the floor dust-free, windows polished. Snake's daily ritual of exorcism, cleansing his cubicle of impurities. It was the room of a monk, a convict, a man deep in training. Snake thought of himself as some of each.

Two shirts in the closet, two pairs of jeans, running shoes. A wallet, key chain, and sunglasses. Traveling as weightlessly as a spirit, leaving no footprint, no evidence of his passage.

He needed a weapon fast and thought he knew where to find one.

It had been years since he had been in his brother's room. Carlos had kept the door shut, used multiple locks. Never admitted anyone, not Snake, not Lola, no girls, nobody. Part of his vast paranoia. Carlos's bedroom was thirty feet from Snake's. Neither had summoned sufficient motivation to move out, get his own place. Still boys, still orphaned kids. Suspended animation.

With another kick, Snake splintered the wood around one lock, and with two more jolts, another and another gave way, and with a final side kick the last two locks clattered to the floor inside the room. Snake leaned his weight against the wood and shouldered the broken door aside.

He stood in the entryway, absorbing the scene.

Carmen was everywhere. Carmen. Her long black hair, her brown eyes, her soft, rounded cheeks, those innocent lips. That look of happy resolve and joyous faith in God's generous, guiding spirit.

Carlos had reproduced the photo of Carmen from her thirteenth birthday. He had duplicated the image hundreds of times and blown it up or shrunk it, then grafted her smiling face to another and another and another cut-out photograph. Wallpapering his room with Carmen as a nun, Carmen with white angel wings, Carmen as a housewife minding three steaming pots on a stove, Carmen on a sailboat waving across the blue sparkle, Carmen driving a station wagon, piloting a fighter jet. There was Carmen's perfect smile sitting atop the bodies of Olympic gymnasts and movie actresses. An entire wall that set their sister's innocent face on the grotesquely inflated bodies of porn queens.

Snake stepped into the room and began to search. On a closet shelf he found a shoe box too heavy for shoes. He hauled it down and opened the lid. A .38 Colt with a four-inch barrel and a box of shells.

On his way to the door, Snake took a last look at the walls. Among all the photos, one caught his eye. Carmen wearing a red blouse and a white skirt. The same outfit she wore to her last Christmas Mass.

Christmas Eve 1963. Carmen is sitting next to Snake on a pew in the chapel of St. Michael the Archangel only a few blocks from the Morales home. In two months Jorge Morales will be murdered. So will his wife, María, and his daughter, Carmen. Five of his militiamen.

Snake sits in the aisle seat. Carmen is radiant in the red blouse and white skirt. Her bare arm brushes Snake's. He looks at her, but her rapt attention is fixed on the rituals of the Feast of the Nativity. "Glory to God in the highest: and on earth peace to men of goodwill."

Past Carmen's face Snake sees his father in a white shirt and dark tie. At this moment Jorge Morales turns his head and sneaks a look several rows behind them. Snake's mother notices and turns also, and her eyes settle on the object of her husband's attention. Carlos is babbling to himself and clicking together rubber soldiers in the battlefield of his lap.

In the middle of a prayer, María Morales comes to her feet. She snatches Carlos by the shirt and hauls him upright and motions for Snake to rise and lead the way out of the aisle. The rubber soldiers fall from Carlos's hands and he squirms to retrieve them. María Morales jerks him straight and herds her children toward the aisle.

They are causing a stir. People around them mumbling, others at the front of the church craning to see. Carmen is flushed with humiliation. Moving into the aisle, Snake snatches a look to see who is sitting behind them, the cause of this exodus, but it is all a blur, a clutter of faces, as he is jostled toward the exit.

Outside on the street, Carmen is aghast. Such a scene, such sacrilege.

María and Jorge Morales march ahead down the sidewalk. María speaks in harsh whispers near Jorge's ear. His face is forward. The children tag along. Carlos bawls about his abandoned soldiers. Snake turns to Carmen.

"Who was that?" he asks his sister.

"It was her."

"The other woman?" Snake says.

Carmen doesn't answer, but the affirmation is in her face.

Snake is two places at once. A child fumbling to understand, a man stretching back into the stillness of the past. Snake searches his mind for her face, this woman. This dark force haunting his family. He scans the rows of people sitting behind the Moraleses' pew, the faces caught in the flashbulb of memory. Going slowly, one by one down the benches. Row by row, holding them up to the harsh light of recollection, freezing them. Seeing the bald man in a tight suit, the pimpled teenage boy, the blond-haired baby in the arms of a young mother, then one woman sitting apart, a space on either side of her.

The revelation must have been coming for years, working upward like a wisp of superheated steam sifting through the hard strata of the past, finding fissures in the layers of rock, finally massing just below the surface, massing and massing until it was ready to erupt in a volcanic flash. On some unspoken, pent-up level, Snake must have always known who she was. The other woman. The woman whose face is hardening into focus.

Snake sees her exactly as she was that night at Christmas Mass, the third person from the aisle, two rows back. She wears a black hat cocked to the side and a burgundy dress. Her hair is a thick and lustrous red, falling over her shoulders, and eyes are dark blue and clear and have an eerie distance in them, as if she has stared too long at the horizon. A woman ablaze with desperate longing.

It is Lola.

Snake rocked back against the wall across from his brother's bedroom. He was breathing fast, the scent of church incense still lingering. The echoes of "Silent Night," the crèche, Baby Jesus in his crib.

Lola.

Outside on the lawn male voices approached, bickering and cursing. Cops coming to take his statement, trying to trick the truth from him.

Snake shoved away from the wall, scrambled down the stairs, cut through the garage, and exited out the door opening onto the bordering woods. He jogged along the property line to the neighbor's stone wall, mounted it, sprinted out their drive to the street, then stayed in the shadows to Main Highway, where he had left his taxi.

He was just unlocking the door, sweat trickling down his chest, when his cell phone jingled.

Snake dug it out, checked the caller ID: Friendly Service Yellow Cabs.

"You coming to work, or you quit?" Nelson Mendoza, the graveyard dispatcher, was as close to a boss as Snake had.

"I won't be there tonight. I'm into other things."

"Yeah, I heard about Carlos," Nelson said. "But people been calling for you. Thought you should know."

"What people?"

"Couple of reporters. Homicide cops. Some other asshole."

"What asshole?"

"Guy wanted you to pick him up. Very pushy."

"A regular?"

"No, some guy, *muy anglo*. He gives me your cab number, asks if you was the driver. 'Does Snake drive cab 4497?' That's what he says. 'Does Snake drive that cab?' 'Keep this to yourself,' he tells me, like you and him are long-lost buddies or some shit and he's going to surprise you."

"Didn't give his name?"

"No name, just the wiseass bullshit."

"Sounds like my buddy Thorn."

"Thorn?"

"He wanted me to pick him up?"

"That's what he said."

"He give an address?"

"Riviera Motel on Dixie, across from Suntan U. Room two-twelve."

"If this gentleman calls back," Snake said, "you didn't reach me."

"This about Carlos getting shot?"

"None of your damn business what it's about. Go back to sleep."

"Too bad about the kid. He was all right in a fucked-up kind of way."

Snake clicked off.

The Riviera Motel was about ten minutes away.

He got into the cab, dug out the .38, broke the cylinder open. He loaded it from the box of ammo, filled his pockets with the extras.

Snake started the engine, then sat for a minute, hands on the wheel.

A smart guy like Thorn had to know the dispatcher would check in with Snake, give him the address. Which meant it was a trap. On the other hand, Thorn would have to be an idiot not to know that dispatch would also tell Snake how he'd recited the cab number. Making the ambush obvious.

So either Thorn grossly underestimated Snake or the asshole was in such a hurry to do some head-butting that he didn't care. Then again, maybe there was some other angle Snake was missing.

He let the cab idle for another minute, rolling it around, then dug out his cell and called Nelson Mendoza back.

"Who's working tonight?"

Nelson gave him three names.

"Send Ignacio to the Riviera Motel," said Snake.

"Yeah? Why him?"

"Tell Ignacio his fare will be standing out in the parking lot. Honk if he doesn't see him. Keep honking till he shows his face."

"It's after midnight, man. That's the Gables, they throw people in jail for causing a disturbance."

"I know what time it is."

"What's this about, Snake?"

"Just do it, Nelson."

"I don't know about this. This doesn't feel right."

"Hey, Nelson, let me ask you something."

Nelson was silent.

"You ever meet my old man?"

"Your old man? You mean Mr. King?"

"The real one. Jorge Morales."

"What're you talking about?"

"I'm talking about my old man. You ever meet him, see his picture, read about him in the paper, see him on TV, anything?"

"Jesus, Snake. All of a sudden you want to start with the heart-to-heart?"

Snake gave him a few seconds of silence, then asked again: "You grew up in Miami, Nelson. I'm asking you if you happened to hear about my old man, read about him, anything like that. Form an impression of him? Jorge Morales."

Nelson sighed.

"An impression? I don't know. I was like fifteen. It was a big fucking deal in the newspapers and the radio, I remember that much, your sister and mother and old man getting whacked by Fidel."

"No impression?"

"Whatta you got in mind?"

"Like did he come across as a romantic hero? The kind of man who'd attract a certain sort of sappy woman?"

"Man, Snake, what've you been shooting up?"

"Call Ignacio," Snake said. "Give him the Riviera. Make it a rush job."

Pauline could've lived anywhere in town, trendy South Beach, the Gables, Grove, one of the towers on Bayshore, out on Key Biscayne, but she chose Belle Meade Island, off Biscayne at Seventy-sixth Street. A venerable fifties community, two-story Mediterranean homes. Staid, stuffy. She had a pool, a view of the bay. Five minutes from work. And what she liked best, her neighborhood rode the edge of Little Haiti. Which gave her a Third World buzz every day she drove to work through all that teeming hardship.

She was in her upstairs office, logged on to the Agency database, violating the hell out of Executive Order 12333, which expressly prohibited collecting intelligence information directed against U.S. citizens. Pauline was trying to pull up something on this Thorn character but was getting nowhere. A man with one name was proving to be impossible.

Scanning birth certificates, property ownership, brushes with law enforcement, credit rating, Social Security. Anyone with first or last or middle name of Thorn. Getting hits dozens of pages long, but having no way to narrow her search. Nothing to go on. Nothing to give her an idea how to approach this guy who was holding the photo for reasons known only to himself. What'd he want, for christsakes?

A Thorn in the lion's paw.

The lion being Hadley S. Waters. She'd gotten four phone calls from the Big Cheese following up his first one. Hadley was ready to call in a commando team, invoke national security, the Worldwide Attack Matrix, and start sterilizing the situation. He sounded serious. But she persuaded him to hold off, she was managing fine. Less troops, better control.

Then an hour later he's back on the phone and she had to convince him again.

Fact was, things didn't feel under control. The porn-shop fiasco. An ex-cop killed and his daughter, a crime-scene tech, shot up. Local Miami PD making a big deal. Turning their best homicide guys loose on it. The press was in full roar. Then just a while ago she learned of disaster number two at the hospital, Runyon bungling an attempt on the cop woman's life. She escapes, and runs off with this same Thorn character.

Pauline was trying to step back, stay calm. Just wait for Runyon to get it right. He'd once been the Agency's go-to man. Drop him anywhere in the world with just the name of his target and the job was as good as done. But this time she was starting to feel twitchy.

Looking out her window at the pool, the patio, the dark water beyond. Having another sip of the chardonnay that was warm now. Almost finished the bottle since supper. Not like her. Usually so cool. Covert operations on the verge of exposure, she'd seen it a hundred times. But this was something else. This was a goddamn tectonic plate buckling beneath her world.

She made a list, just a whim. Who she'd have to snuff to end this. Just to soothe her nerves. Names of the soon-to-be dead.

Stanton King, number one. He'd be easy, a man nobody would miss. His son Snake next. For sure, Lola. Unbalanced bitch. An entire family of loose cannons. Then there was Runyon. He'd have to go. This was too much inside information for even Runyon, a true-blue patriot. Too much gold for one person to have in his piggy bank. A year from now he could scoop it out, try to cash in. No, Runyon was on the list for sure. And she'd have to put Thorn's lights out. Pull the switch on the Collins woman, the injured cop. There was another guy in the mix, a black PI named Sugarman. He'd have to go. What was that? Seven in all.

Still one shy of the Morales murders. Take them off the table, one by one. She could do it. She still had the cojones. She could manage it in a day, two at most. Provided they didn't run, didn't hide. That would draw it out but wouldn't make it impossible.

Somebody might go squealing to the cops. Yeah, now that would be a complication. She had people inside Miami PD, people at Metro-Dade she trusted. She was working that angle already, putting word out in case the Collins woman checked in with her superiors at work. She even had a slime-ball she was tight with inside the local FBI field office if it got to that point.

Hadley Waters would okay anything she asked. He'd turn his eyes. Give support. That is, if she bothered to ask. But it would be far better to present it as a done deal. Keep Hadley's hands clean. Plausible deniability. He'd appreciate the hell out of that. It was leverage she could use later on. If he won the nomination, his seat at the CIA would be vacant. Who else could do that job as well as she could? First female director, that had a nice ring.

So that was it. Take all seven out, be done with it. Along the way the photo was bound to pop up. Burn that, get the Southwoods papers from King, burn those. If Stanton didn't hand them over, torture him, torture Lola in front of him. He'd cave.

Of course, she'd have to wait for Runyon or Stanton King to check in again to find out everyone's location. Play along with them a little longer. But once she knew where everyone was hiding out, she could start.

She looked at her list of names. It was just a game she was playing, mental chess.

She looked out the window at the pool, a blue shimmer in the darkness.

But the more she imagined it, the more she liked. Get involved, bull by the horns. It got her blood kicking. The way she used to feel every minute of every day, before she got old and started dialing back.

Yeah, why not? Seven scalps. Step way outside protocol. Out beyond the ozone. When the thing was done, Hadley would be forever grateful. Damn, the more she thought about it, the more her blood cooked.

CHAPTER TWENTY-TWO

Thorn was at the motel vending machine, feeding in quarters for granola bars and a single bag of pork rinds for Sugarman. Two cans of Coke. A freshly delivered *Miami Herald* from the bin.

While he stood with his food and newspaper, a current of air flooded the breezeway, carrying scents of hot pavement and chlorine from the motel pool and the aroma of warm doughnuts and coffee. It was still a couple of hours till sunrise, but Thorn could see the night clerk setting out a small breakfast in the lobby. He was tempted to go inside and help himself, but he expected his photograph might be on the TV by now, or somewhere in the morning paper, a suspect in the Porn Shop Massacre, or at least a drawing of his likeness, so for now the Coke and granola bars would have to do.

Back in the room Sugar was at the dinette table, studying the Xeroxed pages. He looked up when Thorn came in, and leaned back in the chair.

"Now we got three."

"Three?"

Thorn set the food on the table, popped open a Coke, and took a hit.

"You didn't look at these pages?"

"I scanned them," Thorn said. "Printed out everything around those dates. I haven't been over it in detail, no."

Sugar slid the boxing photo across the table and tapped

the slender man with the pencil mustache who sat beside the thin blond woman.

"So?"

He handed Thorn one of the Xeroxed newspaper pages.

The photograph had appeared on the second page of the lead article the morning after the massacre. The man Snake had hacked to death with his father's machete was named Humberto Berasategui. He ran his own plumbing firm in Miami. The grainy newspaper shot seemed to be a passport photo in which the man was wearing a dark suit and black tie. Same narrow mustache, same wavy black hair and skinny face.

"These people at the fight are the raiding party," Thorn said. "Having a relaxing evening's entertainment before they go murder eight people."

"Starting to look that way."

"No wonder Snake and Carlos want this thing. It's proof of who killed their parents."

"Don't know how much proof it is," Sugarman said. "Far as I can see, it's still just a photograph of a bunch of people. Mayor, mobster, plumber. There's nothing here that actually proves anything. Nothing says these people were in league, conspiring to do anything illegal. The plumber, yeah, it turns out he was one of the killers, but just because he's sitting next to these people, you know, it's not evidence of anything more than he was at the fight, sitting in the same row with some other people. Couldn't take it into court."

Thorn sat down and picked up the photo and tilted it toward the lamp.

"Maybe I'm playing tricks on myself."

"What?"

"The guy in Alexandra's hospital room, the one trying to strangle her."

Thorn pointed at the chunky man sitting between Stanton King and Meyer Lansky.

"You're shitting me."

"I didn't get a great look at the guy. It was dark, and our

scuffle was done in thirty seconds. He's forty years older. But it's the same build. Same blocky head. Meaty hands. I didn't see any diamond, but it could've been there. He had on latex gloves."

Thorn fingered the bruise on his cheekbone. Even his stomach muscles had begun to ache. The guy must be near seventy, but he had the punch of a heavyweight in his prime.

"Give Alex a look at the guy. See what she says."

Thorn leaned over to the venetian blinds and slid one slat up to see outside. He'd found a perfect angle to view the base of the stairway, the only way up to the second floor. If Snake got the message from his dispatcher and showed up, he'd have to pass that way going to room 212. It wasn't much of a ruse, but it would have to do.

"You watch for Snake, okay?"

"You think the guy's that stupid?"

"I think he wants this photo real bad. Stupid or not, he'll show."

Thorn picked up the photograph, walked to the bedroom door, opened it, and stuck his head inside. Alexandra's breathing was hoarse but regular. He stood for a moment in the doorway, then crossed the room and went to the edge of the bed and bent over and touched her lightly. Her forehead was damp and warm, and the scuffs on her neck were swollen and bruised. But she was alive. Very much alive.

He eased down onto the bed and took her free hand in his. It lay there for a moment, then came to life.

She blinked, took a few seconds to examine her surroundings. The cast on her left shoulder and upper arm seemed as heavy as a slab of concrete. She looked at him and withdrew her hand from his grip.

"Where am I?"

"A motel on Dixie Highway."

"Why?"

"Somebody tried to kill you. I got there in time, carried you out. You were pretty groggy, so I guess you don't remember."

"His name is Runyon," Alex said in a raspy voice. "I remember that."

"The man who attacked you? You know his name?"

"He murdered a nurse right in front of me."

"I saw her body," Thorn said. "Nothing I could do for her."

"That was Patty. She recognized the guy, called him Runyon. He used to have a TV show."

"Don't talk," Thorn said. "You're weak."

"He's one of the guys who took the fall for the illegal war in Central America," she said. "One of those fanatics."

"Okay." Thorn wasn't sure which illegal war she meant. "Where's Buck?"

"At an animal clinic. They're taking good care of him. He'll be fine."

Her eyes held his for a moment, then slid away.

"I need you to look at this."

He held out the photo and she turned her attention to it. With her good hand she rubbed the focus back into her eyes and took the photo from him.

"This is why Dad died?"

Thorn said nothing. She held it for a long while, shaking her head.

"Man with the diamond ring. Third row. Chunky. Recognize him?"

Alex handed the photo back.

"Runyon," she said. "Edward Runyon."

"That's what I thought, but I wasn't a hundred percent."

"What is this, Thorn? What the hell is this?"

"Has something to do with a mass murder that took place forty years ago in Miami. A Cuban family was killed: husband, wife, their fourteen-year-old daughter. Five other guys, too. Anti-Castro militia types."

"What does this have to do with us?"

"Lawton had this copy of the photo. The surviving sons of the murdered family came looking for it. More than that, I'd just be guessing."

"A goddamn photograph."

"I know, it doesn't make sense."

"Tell me something."

"Yeah?"

"After I left for Tampa, was there a point when you could have just handed over the photograph to these creeps and walked away?"

"Yes, there was."

"But you didn't."

"No, I didn't."

"That's what I thought."

"If I had it over . . ."

"Yeah, if we all had it over."

He stood up, watched her blink the mist from her eyes, then turned and went to the outer room and shut the door.

"She doing okay?"

"She'll make it."

Sugarman looked up.

"She's beating up on you pretty bad, huh?"

"Nothing I don't deserve."

At the hospital after five minutes of CPR, he'd brought her back. Maybe she'd been on the brink of death and his quick reaction saved her life. Maybe she was just unconscious and would have revived on her own. He wasn't in a credit-taking mood. He still felt a nasty clang in his hands from the aluminum baseball bat hammering Carlos Morales's skull. Probably be feeling that clang for a long time.

After he'd roused her from unconsciousness, Alex was too fragile to walk. Thorn phoned Sugar in the parking garage, filled him in, and Sugar came sprinting. Thorn helped her into her gray slacks and pink sweater, and with Sugarman running interference, the two of them smuggled her down an inner stairwell without a brush with security or staff.

"So we got names for four of the five?" Sugarman said.

"The man sitting next to Lansky is Edward Runyon. Some kind of soldier of fortune or something."

"Edward Runyon? You're kidding."

"Not a night for kidding."

"Christ, Edward Runyon is a world-class scumbag."

"I heard," Thorn said. "Some illegal war thing."

"Way more than that. Bay of Pigs, that arms-for-hostages thing, Watergate, you name it. All kinds of down-and-dirty bullshit our boys in Washington tried to pull off, Runyon's hovering around. One of those self-styled patriots, gun for hire, super-hawk. Few years back he had a dumb-ass TV show. Big talker. Bullying his guests. He's the guy who's missing his first two fingers. That's his trademark."

"What's that mean?"

"End of his show every night, he used to say the same thing. 'Don't forget, peace comes with a price tag, and that price isn't always pretty.' Then he'd flash the two stumps, and say, 'Peace.' Real sweetheart."

Thorn nodded, looking at the closed door of the bedroom.

"Guy's certifiable," Sugar said. "But there's people who worship him."

Thorn reached out, slid the Xeroxes over, and paged through them for a few minutes. He found the passage he recalled, reread it quickly.

"What if we can put Runyon at Morales's house?"

"How?"

"Snake whacked off two fingers of one of the attackers. Fingers were left behind on the floor in one of the kids' bedroom. Appeared to be first two digits of the right hand of a man who weighed somewhere around two hundred pounds."

"That's good. But it doesn't exactly nail it down."

"It does for me," Thorn said.

"Jesus, your boy Snake is a charmer. Hacks one guy to death, chops two fingers off some hulk."

"And he was only twelve years old at the time."

"This is the guy you're luring over to have a powwow with?"

"Snake and I have a strong common interest. I can give him four of the five people in this photograph. Two of the four were at his house that night. And he just might be able to give me an overview of what we got going on."

"You killed his brother, for christsakes. He's going to sit down with you and make nice?"

"I intend to give him that opportunity."

CHAPTER TWENTY-THREE

They sat for a while, Sugarman eating pork rinds, Thorn staring at the Clay-Liston photograph. Those five people sitting side by side. Four of whom they had names for. Only the blond woman was left.

Every few seconds while Sugar munched, he took a look out the blinds.

A minute or two later Thorn drew the cell phone from his pocket and dialed 911 for the second time in a few hours.

"Turning yourself in?" Sugar said.

Thorn said to the dispatcher, "I want to report a homicide."

Sugarman turned back to the venetian blinds.

"Name is Alan Bingham." Thorn gave her the street and approximate address. Then he hung up while she was asking him for more information.

"You're guessing these guys, Snake and Carlos, they killed Bingham?"

"They showed up at Alexandra's and knew Lawton had the Clay photo. Bingham gave it to Lawton as a gift. Who else would know that but Bingham? Lawton thought he heard gunfire at Bingham's last night, and I blew him off. Bingham didn't show up at his gallery this morning like he was supposed to, and didn't answer his phone when the gallery guy called. And when I was up on the roof I saw his cleaning lady arrive and the key wasn't in the mailbox like she was expecting. His car was there, but he didn't answer her knock. My bet is he's inside that house and he's dead."

"Aw, man," Sugarman said.

"Something else I want to know," Thorn said. "Why'd some seventy-year-old government goon show up in Alex's hospital room, trying to strangle her? I'm getting the feeling there's two different agendas working here."

"You're losing me."

Thorn stood up, dug the invitation list he'd gotten from Carbonnel out of his back pocket. Scanned it fast.

"Stanton King and wife Lola were at the gallery opening last night."

"You got a list? How'd you manage that?"

"Lawton and I dropped by there first thing this morning. I was just sniffing around at that point."

"You been a busy man."

"Okay, here's how it went," Thorn said. "Mayor goes to a gallery opening. He spots himself in a photo up on the wall. There he is, 1964, he's sitting two down from Lansky, cheek to jowl with these other people, two of whom, Humberto Berasategui and Runyon, were at the murder scene later on that night.

"The photo's hanging up on the wall for anybody to see. All it would take is one person standing there, noticing the young mayor or remembering one of these guys. Lansky was a public figure, so was the mayor, then eventually Runyon became one, too. A lot of people in this town might've even recognized Humberto Berasategui from the newspaper stories. If somebody identifies one of these people, starts asking questions, there's a reasonable chance it all gets exposed.

"So what does the mayor do? He freaks and sics his deranged sons on the thing. Snake and Carlos break into the gallery, destroy the photos, go to Bingham's house. Before they kill him, they squeeze Lawton's name out of him, somebody else who's holding a copy, bingo, we're off to the races."

Sugarman thought about it. He didn't say anything for a minute, looking down at his Coke can.

"That's means King has a different motive than Snake.

Snake wants to know who killed his family. He thinks the photo's going to show that."

"Yeah, I think that's it," Thorn said. "The two times I've been around him, he wanted to examine the photo, not destroy it. He and Carlos had it in their hands long enough, if they wanted, they could've just ripped it up right then."

"King and Edward Runyon coming from one direction, Snake coming from another. I don't like the sound of that."

"It's like Sophocles," Thorn said. "Oedipus."

"Oh, boy."

"A father tries to keep the truth from his son but accidentally winds up doing stuff that causes the son to discover the very thing the father's trying to hide. Cosmic irony."

"There's another way to read it."

"All right."

"There are no accidents."

"Stanton subconsciously wants to be exposed?"

"Maybe it's not something he can put words to."

"Well, if that's true, then I'd like to help him out."

Thorn stood up, carried the morning *Herald* over to a green chair near the tiny kitchen.

While Sugar kept an eye out the blinds, Thorn opened the paper and began to read the article on the Porn Shop Massacre. They'd printed an old police photo of Lawton and had run a fairly current shot of Alexandra posed against a white background like a school picture. She looked beautiful nonetheless. Black hair freshly brushed, a slight, knowing smile. Those dark eyes that Thorn found fascinating: probing one minute, alluring the next.

At the bottom of the front page the article mentioned a suspect wanted in the killings. A man of about six feet, medium build with dreadlocks.

Dreadlocks?

Thorn read the sentence again, then turned the page and there was the artist's rendering of the prime suspect in the porn-store murders.

It was a sketch of a black man, early twenties with a blocky face, a scar across his right cheek, and long Rasta dreads.

Thorn got up, carried the paper to the table, and lay it in front of Sugar.

"This is their person of interest for the porn-shop thing."

Sugarman looked at it for several seconds, then looked up at Thorn.

"They missed the twinkle in your eye."

"This isn't funny, Sugar."

Sugarman ate the last pork rind, had a sip of Coke, looked out the blinds, then turned back to the newspaper.

"Where'd they dig up this guy?"

"They invented him," said Thorn. "Article says two witnesses identified him as the killer of Carlos Morales and Lawton Collins. Old lady clerk at the porn shop and some customer. Their descriptions matched."

"Putting it on a brother, wouldn't you know?"

"Why doesn't this make me feel relieved?"

"What it means is, Snake or Runyon or somebody got to the clerk, gave her her marching orders. Send the cops wild-goose chasing in one direction, so Runyon or whoever is free to come after you. Neat trick."

"It's why they attacked Alex in the hospital. So she wouldn't contradict any of it. Last thing they want is for the cops to start digging around. Alex knows about the photo, she knows what really happened at the porn shop. She's a danger to them."

"So are you, Thorn."

Sugarman wiped his mouth on the back of his hand. Took a long drink of his Coke. Stifled a belch.

"Whole thing's getting complicated," Sugar said.

"We need the blonde," Thorn said.

"Maybe she's just a floozy, somebody's date."

"Doesn't look like a floozy to me. Looks like a tough broad."

"Forty years later, that isn't going to be easy, identifying some woman. A town like this, everybody coming and going. She'd be in her sixties by now. She could be a grandmother in Milwaukee. Waste a lot of time looking, and it might not explain anything."

"I know somebody I can ask. Guy with links to that time. Boxing, gambling, you name it, he was into it."

Thorn looked again at the sketch of the black man with dreadlocks. Then he folded up the paper and laid it on the floor by the chair.

"Who the hell do you know in Miami?"

"Remember Jimbo?"

"Jimbo? That old crook still alive?"

"I don't know," Thorn said. "But I know where to find him if he is."

"If it were me running the investigation," Sugar said, "I'd go confront the mayor. He's smack in the middle of this."

"I'll put him on the list."

"And this guy Shepherd Gundy."

"Gundy?"

"One of the investigators of the Morales murders."

"I must've missed that."

"It's in the pages you Xeroxed, a few days after the murders. Second Lieutenant Shepherd Gundy, military investigator based at Homestead Air Force Base."

"Military? Why was the military investigating this?"

"That's exactly the reason I'd want to talk to him."

Sugarman looked out the blinds again.

"Look, Sugar," Thorn said. "You and Alex need to get back down to Key Largo till this is over. Keep her out of harm's way. Take her to a doctor down there. She's going to need somebody to look at that arm."

"And leave you in the middle of this."

"It's my mess, Sugar. I need to clean it up myself."

"I'm okay with getting Alex somewhere safe. But leaving you on your own in Miami? I don't know, man. We've already seen how that turns out."

"You could keep on arguing. But you know it won't change my mind."

"Yeah, I know that. I surely do."

CHAPTER TWENTY-FOUR

"Your skills, Edward, they're in serious decline. You used to be such an efficient killer." Stanton took the last bite of his fish sandwich and pushed it aside.

"The guy ambushed me. I got the fuck out."

"Perhaps it's a precipitous drop in your testosterone level. I'd have it checked. You're going to lose your charter membership in Bullies of America."

"She was dead when I left."

"Well, she wasn't dead enough, Runyon. Her Prince Charming saved her and took her away."

Runyon's green aloha shirt was rumpled, but the burn in his eyes still simmered. An injured bull, more dangerous than a healthy one.

They were at an all-night Burger King, Dixie and Twenty-seventh, on the fringes of Coconut Grove. A booth in back. Except for the Asian kid mopping the floor, the place was empty. It was three in the morning. Runyon halfway through his second double cheeseburger and down to slurping the foam at the bottom of his chocolate shake.

"You've played one round of golf too many, Edward. Lost your edge."

Runyon drew a breath and said, "I know when I've killed someone."

"My source tells me otherwise. Security tapes show her

walking out with her arm over the shoulder of a tall sandy-headed fellow."

He folded three more fries into his mouth.

"You've got a spy at the hospital?"

"This is my hometown, Runyon. Sixty years, you make friends."

"The sandy-haired asshole is the one who ambushed me."

"His name is Thorn. I'm told he's the woman's boyfriend."

Runyon swallowed the last pinch of burger, wiped his lips on the paper napkin, missing a trickle of grease at the corner of his mouth.

"If she's still alive, then I'll just have to kill her again, and her boyfriend."

"How many would that make for you, Edward? Adding it up over the years. Do you keep count?"

"What do you care?"

"Just curious. It's a lot, isn't it? So many, you can't remember."

"I remember fine."

"Forty-odd years, a handful a year, that could be over a hundred."

Runyon pushed the food away and glanced at his reflection in the glass.

"You going to finish your fries?"

"I try to imagine how it is to be someone like you, Runyon. Blameless and self-certain. Triggerman for presidents."

"Prisses like you never get it."

"Oh, yes, I know all the clichés. You're on the frontline defense for democracy. Without you and your black-ops comrades, we wouldn't have burgers and fries. The only reason we enjoy the pampered life we do is because animals like you are prowling the perimeter."

Runyon picked at his mustache, eyeing King with a shadow of disdain.

"How many have I done?" Runyon said. "Face-to-face, it's not that many. Ten, fifteen. Other things I was involved in, bigger operations, that kicks the number up. But I don't keep track of those."

"You're amazing, Edward."

"Numbers don't mean shit. It's the fucking target that matters. Kill the right guy, you could be tipping the balance, save a million lives."

"Is that how they brainwash you? Get together on weekend retreats, sit around in a circle, and tell each other lies about how many lives you've saved?"

Runyon wet his finger and ran it around the inside of the empty box of fries. Getting his salt quotient.

"Here's what you really want to hear," Runyon said. "I get off on it. That creeps you out, doesn't it, old liberal pussy like you? All these years, taking someone down still gives me a hard-on."

Runyon grinned. He sucked his finger clean and dabbed it into the box for the last grains.

"I called Caufield earlier. Warned her we're in over our head."

Runyon met Stanton's eyes in the window.

"You stupid fuck. You don't play footsie with that woman. I met rattlesnakes I trusted more."

"She's giving us a bit more time to set things straight before she calls for reinforcements."

"Don't call her anymore. You want to talk to somebody, talk to me."

Edward turned the gaudy diamond on his finger. His eyes were as bitter and gray as thawing ice.

"You underestimate me, Runyon. I know you've been calling her, too. You want me to have no contact so you'll be in full control. Well, forget that. I have as much at stake in this as you. I'll consult with Pauline whenever I like."

Stanton King smiled. He couldn't help himself. All evening he'd been in a buoyant mood. An old weight finally lifting. He'd been thinking of Hotei, the happy Buddha, his arms thrown skyward in hilarious celebration. His large ungirdled belly jutting out. So absurd, all of it. Casting aside all his cares. What did any of it matter? The sins of Stanton's youth, the even more egregious sins of his nation's leaders, a poisonous boil that festered silently and out of sight for lo these many decades had been revealed by a random snapshot taken at a cosmically inappropriate split second. A wonderfully absurd coincidence.

A chance for Stanton to make amends in the twilight of his life for the one horrendous misstep he'd made forty years before. Let it all pour forth, let Humpty Dumpty come crashing.

"Tell me something, King. Nineteen sixty-four, that operation, I always thought it was suspicious, a guy like you, all-American Joe, apple cheeks, mixed up in that. Soon as you came into it, that operation started to stink."

Stanton's smile backed down.

He glanced over at the Asian kid tirelessly mopping the floor. The lad was going to run his own Burger King franchise one day. America was still grinding on, full of dreams and dreamers. Optimists, true believers.

"You're right about one thing, Edward. Murdering eight men, women, and children for a political pipe dream, yes, I'd say that smells. Even after all these years, it still reeks."

Runyon snapped the lid off his shake and tipped it up for a last swallow.

Digging the cell from his pocket, Stanton dialed Friendly Cab.

When the dispatcher answered, Stanton said, "Nelson, it's me again. You talk to him yet? Find out anything?"

"I was just dialing you," Nelson said.

"What do you have?"

"This is gonna cost you extra, Mr. King. Double what we said."

"Yes? And why's that?"

"I know where Snake is going to be in about five minutes. The exact address. And the other guy you mentioned, too."

"Thorn?"

"Same place," Nelson said. "What's it worth to you?"

Stanton shut the phone and looked at Runyon and smiled.

"You ready to ride?"

"You're not going to check in with your boss lady first?"

"Sure," he said. "Why not? I'll tell her where we're headed. Make her feel better."

"Don't do it, Stanton. The less she knows, the better."

Stanton smiled. He opened his phone and punched in Pauline's number. It rang twice and there she was. Stanton feeling a ripple of the old power. People like Caufield taking his calls again. Just like the old days.

Up in the dark attic. Aiming through the slats. The pool, the patio spread before her. A possum waddled from the woods. It snuck along the edge of the water, had a sip, waddled on.

From her sniper's lair, she'd brought down a handful of birds. Late one night she winged a rat and watched it crawl away to die. She'd nailed half a dozen cats, sent them yowling. Sharpening her aim. Sharpening.

She steadied on the gray possum, its hairy back.

Beside her the nest was quiet. The paper wasps were at rest.

Plonk, plonk, plonk. *Two out of three found flesh. The possum jerked. It skidded forward on the flagstone. Then pushed itself up on its tiny feet and toddled toward the safety of the woods.* Plonk *and again* plonk.

Its back legs failed, but it dragged itself on. Dragged itself on toward the dark woods.

She lowered the Walther Red Hawk, went back to her rocker. Sat.

Killing was no longer the point.

Stinging was.

Sting as she'd been stung.

The prick, the stab, the throb of pain. Sting, sting, as she was stung. There were worse fates than dying.

CHAPTER TWENTY-FIVE

The TV people had shut down for the night. Snake's street, St. Gaudens, was clear. He'd decided his taxi was too noticeable and wanted to switch cars. He dumped his cab in a neighbor's drive, stole back through the yards. Went inside the house, got Lola's keys from the desk in the foyer, then went out and eased her gray Audi down the drive.

He headed west on Poinciana, across Le Jeune into Coral Gables, and on to the Riviera Motel. Half a block away he killed the lights, eased down the street and into a church parking lot across from the motel. He surveyed the area and picked his spot.

Staying low, Snake slid through the shadows to a clump of bushes at the base of a tree. Foliage meant to shield the expensive homes from the distasteful sight of the motel and the busy highway. He had to shift around before he got the view he wanted. Lit up orange by the security lights, the parking lot stretched the entire back of the motel.

Two insomniacs were still up, lamps shining around the blinds, one room on the bottom floor, one on top. A dozen cars scattered about the lot.

He was settling into a squat, trying to pick out room 212, when a whippy stem sprang loose and flicked him in the eye.

Blinded, he rubbed his eye. Before him the parking lot, the motel, the cars became a blur, which sent him sailing back to Cassius again. Cassius and Liston. That night.

Snake is a kid, listening on the radio. He's a freshly minted American boy, rooting for his outrageous hero. But Cassius, noble Cassius, is blinded by something on Liston's glove. And he's lost hope, wants to quit. It is between rounds four and five. Cassius whines that he wants to cave in to the jeering fans, let Sonny Liston prevail.

Never mind the thousand grueling hours, jogging in street clothes and combat boots across Julia Tuttle Causeway, ten miles between his ghetto hotel and the Fifth Street Gym, running that ten miles in the morning, then again after a day of workouts and sparring and the heavy bag, jumping rope, ten more miles back home in heavy leather boots. Harassed by cops, stopped, questioned, searched, like a street thief running from a crime. Day after day he's done that, the punishing hours in the Miami sun, and now, with eyes stinging, he wants to quit. A little pain, and blurry vision.

Astonishing how a man with such deep-rooted passion can suddenly lose it. How fragile a strong man can be. One small splinter of doubt piercing deep into the tissues of confidence, whispering that you aren't going to succeed, that you'd better climb down from the ring while you still can, run for the exit. Start over in some other place, give up your dreams, abandon hope.

But his corner man, Dundee, won't let him quit. Blind or not, this is Clay's chance. It is fight or die. Endure the doubt, survive the blindness, and punch his way through. Dance and jab. A moment like this comes once.

As he settled back in his roost, a taxi pulled into the lot.

It idled for a few seconds, then honked twice.

Only a second or two passed before the driver honked again, then again. An hour before daylight, a stone's throw from five-million-dollar mansions, but Ignacio didn't give a shit. He honked once more, then held the horn down for a good thirty seconds.

"It's a trap, Thorn. Stay put."

"It's a trap I set. Snake's a little more creative than I thought."

The cab honked again and Thorn stepped back from the blinds.

"If I don't go out, this guy's going to draw a crowd, then we're screwed."

"You go out there, you don't have any idea what you're walking into."

"I want this over with."

"At least take my pistol, goddamn it." Sugarman drew his holster from the computer bag and extended the nine-millimeter to Thorn.

"You keep it. Protect Alex. I'll deal with our friend."

"Aw, come on, Thorn. Take it."

Thorn went over to the desk and picked up the photograph and went back to the door.

"This is all I need."

"Don't be crazy," Sugar said.

"If things go south," said Thorn, "get Alex out of here."

"Take the damn gun, Thorn. I'm not letting you out of here without it."

"Be careful, Sugar. Keep her safe."

And Thorn was out the door.

Alex heard the horn blaring.

The drugs had worn off and spikes of pain shuddered through her shoulder in sync with her pulse. Her throat ached, too, where Runyon had gripped her. Another kind of pain, every breath ripping at the wet tissues, a ragged, papery burn. She'd begun to taste blood in the back of her mouth.

She blew out a breath, pushed the sheets aside, slid her

legs over the edge of the bed, and rocked upright. A strobe light flared inside her skull and the room whitened and sent Alex's stomach rolling. Down her back she felt prickly trails of sweat like the march of insects. The flesh beneath the cast was already itching.

She held still until a wave of nausea passed and her vision cleared, then pushed herself to her feet and hobbled to the window and with a finger, opened a peephole in the aluminum blinds.

Thorn was walking across the parking lot toward a taxi. A swagger. Hot-dogging as she'd seen him do before when he was scared shitless.

He halted a few feet from the driver's window, bent forward, and spoke to the driver. Behind him, fifty feet or so, Alex thought she saw a shadow bob in the bushes. She craned forward and blinked but could make out nothing.

Alexandra returned to the bed and sat. She tested the flesh at her neck with a careful touch. There was a welt and some deep bruising, probably damage to her trachea. Her head wouldn't turn more than a few degrees left or right, as though a crick had taken root in the neck ligaments.

She eased the phone off the table and punched in Dan Romano's office number. Homicide detective, Miami PD, her cranky boss for the past decade. Officially retired but still pulling all-nighters three times a week, working some old cases he took personally. He claimed he wanted to tie up the last loose ends, leave a clean desk, but Alex knew Romano was having trouble letting go.

Four in the morning, Romano snapped up the phone on the first ring.

"Dan, it's Alex."

Dan was silent for a moment, then said, "I was getting worried."

Alexandra looked at the plastic card taped to the base of the phone.

"I'm at the Riviera Motel on Dixie. Across from UM."

"You in danger?"

"Not really."

"Why aren't you in the hospital?"

"Long story. I'll explain when I see you. I think Thorn's putting himself into some serious jeopardy, though. I need your help."

The line was silent for a moment.

"Hello?"

Romano said, "Honey, I'm sorry."

"Sorry?"

"I got orders about this."

"What orders?"

"If you should call in, there's a protocol in place."

"What? Who gave you orders?"

"Way it came to me, I'm supposed to pass on any info pertaining to your whereabouts. It's a national-security deal. I don't have a lot of latitude."

"Don't joke with me, Dan. National security, me?"

"Those were the words. All very hush-hush."

"What's going on? This is me, Alex."

"You ever hear the name Pauline Caufield?"

"No."

"Neither had I before today. Apparently she's got some serious weight with the feds. She's some major muckety-muck with one of the undercover agencies, NSA, Army Intelligence, FBI. They didn't say. But since she called earlier, the chief and his people are standing up a little straighter. Look like they're ready to salute."

"What're you saying, Dan? You're not making sense."

"Something you've done, Alex, you got the interest of some powerful folks. They didn't tell me all the details, but this is a big deal. They want you to come in and talk. I heard they're even going so far as to monitor calls around here. This call, for instance, I don't think my line's secure. So, you know, what you said earlier, your whereabouts, that might be compromised."

Alex slapped the phone down and stared at it as she backed away.

Sugarman was at her bedroom door.

"You okay, Alex? What's going on?"

"I called Dan. The feds are involved. They're after me for something."

"Local feds? You mean Frank Sheffield's people? FBI."

"No, this is somebody else. Pauline Caufield. You ever hear of her?"

Sugarman shook his head.

"They told Dan it was a national-security matter."

Sugarman scrubbed a hand back and forth across his hair.

"Before I knew they were listening in, I gave Dan our location. I think we should get out of here, Sugar."

"I'm getting that same feeling."

CHAPTER TWENTY-SIX

By the time he stopped a few feet from the cab's window and looked in at the driver, Thorn was feeling out-of-body. Like he'd already been shot dead, but his brain was lagging, neurons spinning out a little death dance as his body took a few seconds to go into total shutdown.

"You're not Snake," Thorn said to the Sumo at the wheel of the taxi. A man so big, he might need the jaws of life to get free at the end of his shift.

"No shit," the man said. "Where you want to go?"

"I want Snake, not you."

"Hey, man. You call the cab company, you get whoever comes. This ain't no fucking personalized limo service."

"Get out of here," Thorn said.

"Or you do what?"

The guy pushed his door open, but Thorn kicked it closed, then leaned his hip against it and brought his face down to eye level with the cabbie. He had the complexion of a rotten cantaloupe and around him there was the reek of whiskey that would've blown the sensors on a Breathalyzer.

"I'd say you got about ten seconds before the shoot-out starts. Stick around if you want, you'll make a nice target."

"What shoot-out?"

"The one your buddy Snake arranged."

The cabbie's testosterone wrestled with his common

sense for about five seconds, then he slammed the car in reverse and left a screaming track of rubber across the lot.

Thorn slipped the envelope with the Xeroxes and photograph under the front of his shirt and tucked it a few inches into the waistband of his shorts.

He turned around and appraised his exposure.

An open street on one side, a church in the distance. An adjacent parking lot. The only place a man could hide close by was in a clump of bushes on the south side of the property.

Thorn could try a sprint back to the motel room, but even if he made it, that would only draw fire toward Alex and Sugar.

As he headed back into the center of the parking lot, his head was still swimming, body braced for a dive to the pavement or the impact of a slug.

"That was cute, Snake, luring me outside with the taxi. Real clever."

Thorn took a sidelong glance toward the shrubs but saw no movement, no human shape. Wondering if maybe he had it wrong and this wasn't Snake's setup after all, that Thorn was out there alone in the dark talking to himself.

"I been studying the photo. Trying to figure out why it's so damn important. I identified four people already. Row three. Maybe you could give me a hand. The two of us together, we might solve this thing."

Thorn had been in the enemy's sights before. A familiar prickle crept across his flesh, a clench of sphincters. Like walking a narrow ledge with a mile-deep gorge on either side. Not the moment for any sort of wobble.

The door to their motel room opened and Sugarman stepped outside.

"We got to roll, buddy," he called. "We're lit up on the radar."

Thorn angled a few feet Sugar's way and got his voice down.

"You go. I'll be behind you in a few minutes."

"What're you going to do, hitchhike?"

"I'll go get Alex's car."

"Come with us, Thorn. This is turning ugly."

"Get the hell out of here. Go. Keep her safe."

"Then take my nine," Sugar said.

Thorn turned his back on the motel room and headed out into the lot. He stood in the center of the asphalt, staring into the dark perimeter, holding his position until he heard two car doors slam behind him, a motor revving and then Sugar's Taurus circling toward him.

The car pulled in front of him, two feet away, came to a stop and the back door swung open.

"Get in," Alex said.

Thorn went over and leaned his head down.

"I'll be fine," he said.

Sugar said, "The name Pauline Caufield mean anything to you?"

Thorn shook his head.

"She's some kind of super-fed. She's tracking us. She may be on her way here right now. Dan says it's a national-security issue."

"I got a few things on my plate already," Thorn said. "You drive safe."

He shut the door.

Sugar delayed a few seconds, but he knew all about Thorn's bullheadedness. Once he'd made up his mind, forget it.

When the car pulled away, Thorn began to move across the lot.

As bleak as his view of human nature was, mankind's penchant for depravity and malice, he also knew there was a sizable percentage of people with countervailing instincts, tendencies toward restraint. He'd heard that even soldiers on the front lines often misaimed on purpose, putting their own lives in danger rather than kill the enemy. A peaceful nature not even military drilling and foxhole pressures could corrupt. Whether it came from biology or culture, he didn't know. But what made his walk across that parking lot possible was some fraction of hope that Snake was one of those.

Or at least that he was a bad shot.

Thorn made an aimless meander of the lot, coming closer by small degrees to the bushes that were the only hiding place.

He raised the volume of his voice a click past conversational.

"A few hours ago when we first met, you said this photo was a matter of great personal importance to you. I believe those were your exact words. I believe you want to figure out who killed your parents and your sister, and why it happened.

"Well, that's fine, but the thing is, I got a personal stake, too. I need to know what this is about so I can take the necessary measures to walk away and be sure a year from now it's not going to pop up and whack my head off or endanger my friends. So what do you say? We make a truce, join forces. How's that sound?"

The voice came from farther out in the darkness than he'd been guessing. And it wasn't Snake. It was an older man, gruff voice, coarsened by age and strong drink: "Take out that fucking photo, lay it down on the asphalt, and step back. You got to the count of three."

Thorn halted and tried to track the direction of the voice.

"Is that you, Runyon?"

The voice was silent.

"How's that kidney feeling? A little sore, is it?"

Then another man spoke from the clump of shrubs a few feet away. Snake's syrupy drawl.

"If I were you, Thorn, I'd get flat on my belly quick as I could."

Thorn was lowering himself to his knees when the first shot whistled nearby and thunked into the fender of a parked car. Another followed it, and a third. A silenced pistol.

Thorn dove into the shrubs and tumbled into Snake's wiry body. Another slug tore a ragged groove in the tree a few feet overhead.

Snake held a pistol in his right hand, aimed into Thorn's gut.

"Who the hell is Runyon?"

Thorn disentangled himself and settled his rump onto a patch of sand.

"Maybe you should ask your dad that."

As Snake squinted in confusion, Thorn pitched forward and clipped a forearm to the side of his face. Snake fell back into the thick branches, and Thorn wrenched the pistol from his grip.

Another shot carved its initials in the bark overhead.

Thorn kept his head low and touched the barrel to Snake's rib cage.

"We both know what I'm capable of," Thorn said. "Now stay calm and don't fuck with me."

"I'm always calm." Snake's eyes seemed to absorb more than their share of the available light and store it in the silvery depths of his pupils.

"Where's your ride?"

"Across the street at the church. Gray Audi."

"This guy's not the best shot. We should be fine. Stay low and zigzag."

"I've seen the same movie," Snake said.

Thorn raised up and flattened himself against the trunk of the tree and let off two quick rounds. Snake was gone before the answering fire began.

The man could run, Thorn had to give him that.

"You know I'm going to kill you, first chance I get."

"Just drive, Snake. There'll be time to kill me later."

Thorn was in the passenger seat, the .38 held loosely in his lap. Snake at the wheel.

"My brother, Carlos, was helpless. You beat him to death."

"Make a U-turn by the Seaquarium, then it's your first right."

For the past hour Snake had been driving silently. Up Dixie Highway, then back south, Thorn looking out the rear window, trying to make sure they weren't being followed. If there was somebody back there, he was better than anyone who'd ever tailed Thorn before.

At dawn he directed Snake out to Key Biscayne, toward the only guy Thorn knew who might help.

"First right," Thorn said.

"The waste-treatment plant? What's there?"

Thorn stared ahead and didn't reply.

"You have no intention of showing me the photograph, do you?"

"Look, I'm taking you along because I want to hear what you got to say about the photo. Maybe clear up a few things, why people died because of it. I'll tell you what I know, and you tell me what you know. So yeah, you'll see it. When the time's right. Now put a cork in it."

Half a mile off the highway Thorn steered Snake into a gravel parking area. The breeze was out of the west, and the sulfurous reek of the sewage plant was flooding the eastern shore of Virginia Key. A hawk sailed overhead, on its way to the four-hundred-acre wildlife area. Virginia Key was a patchwork of good and bad ideas, tarnished legacies of the past and a living record of betrayed promises.

On the southernmost edge of the island near the causeway was a sandy strip that had once been Miami's segregated black beach. Sugarman had taken Thorn there back in the old days. A bathhouse and concession stand; Thorn, the only white kid for a mile around; the air ripe with barbecue and down-home recipes. Car radios playing boogie.

There was the high hump of a landfill a little north of that old beach. An unregulated dump that was now retired and overrun by vines and weeds concealing the toxic fuels and paints and solvents that generations of Miamians had unloaded there. All of it leeching through the limestone into the waters of Biscayne Bay. The western edge of the island, the side facing Rickenbacker Causeway, was dotted by marinas and restaurants with unhindered views across the water of the downtown skyline. The old Marine Stadium was there, too, on the bank of a horseshoe cove where rock concerts and boat races had once been staged. Raft up under the stars to hear the Rolling Stones boom across the water.

The stadium was closed now, and Thorn had read that it was the center of another tug-of-war between preservation-ists and developers. In that way and many others, Virginia Key was a mirror of Miami. Its best and worst impulses. An island surrounded by crystal blue, contaminated yet some-how managing to be the breeding ground for manatees and a shelter for rare hawks, eagles, and migrating birds.

Jimbo's Bar was a nice fit on that island of paradoxes. On the northeastern tip of Virginia Key, scattered about the hid-den lagoon where shrimp boats docked, was a collection of ramshackle bungalows. In the fifties the place had been slapped up as a set for some quickie sci-fi flick. Now it was a hangout for bikers and the BMW crowd, and a backdrop for TV and photo shoots. The ticky-tack bungalows painted gaudy Caribbean colors, with bocce ball courts and trash barrels full of iced-down beer, and the best smoked fish in South Florida. A movie set that had evolved into a funky bar.

The place was so convincing that every film crew that came to town believed it was a vestige of the genuine his-toric Miami. That was one of the city's special talents. With so many new arrivals pouring in every week, so many old-timers dying with their secrets, with the wrecking balls and bulldozers working constantly, Miami had no memory. So it was a paradise for frauds. An old movie set became a funky bar, which became a movie set again.

Snake wouldn't get out of the car.

"Show me the photo or shoot me, those are your choices."

Thorn reached across and snatched the keys from the ignition.

"Suit yourself. Stay here and miss the fun."

As Thorn crossed the gravel lot, Snake got out and tagged along. The sun was rising above the treetops and the sky was scuffed with frail clouds that streamed west on the shore breeze. The ocean was a stone's throw to the east, and its restless drone filtered through the Australian pines. Through a gap between the trees, Thorn saw a couple of fast boats slicing up the flat morning calm, their wakes peeling open the blue waters like beautiful flesh wounds.

He tucked the pistol in the pocket of his baggy shorts and waited for Snake to catch up. Cell phone in one side, .38 in the other. A fully converted Miami guy.

Thorn turned to watch Snake approach. There was a formal air in both his speech and manner, as if he were the product of religious discipline. His stillness seemed more deeply rooted than mere reticence. It didn't strike Thorn as caginess, either, but more like the icy vigilance of a shorebird who could wait for hours for his target to swim close by.

"Tell me something, Snake. Why didn't you shoot me when you had the chance?"

"Why did you stand out in the parking lot unprotected?"

"I didn't see another choice."

"Perhaps you're feeling suicidal after killing Carlos. Unless, of course, you bludgeon men to death every day."

"If I ever feel suicidal, I won't leave it for someone else to do."

Snake looked off toward the ripples of blue through the pines, his face slack with thought.

"I was standing out in the open. I had something you were willing to kill for. Why didn't you fire?"

"I didn't trust my aim," Snake said.

"What?"

"I saw you tuck the photo under your shirt. I don't want it damaged. Filled with bullet holes, it would be no use to me."

Thorn met Snake's silvery blue eyes. So much for the innate goodness of the human race.

Stanton King had already given Pauline a heads-up about the Riviera Motel by the time the Miami Police Department called her cell and relayed the same info. She made it crosstown in less than fifteen minutes and was just taking a position on a side street with a view of the motel when the action broke. A Taurus drove slowly out of the motel parking lot. Behind the wheel a black guy and in the passenger seat the lady cop. Then she saw muzzle flashes from silenced gunfire, and a few seconds later Snake Morales and the tall blond guy named Thorn came sprinting from the parking lot and crossed in front of her twenty feet away and jumped in a gray Audi and peeled out.

Over in the parking lot Runyon and Stanton King hustled out of some bushes. Runyon trotted to a white Cadillac, jimmied the door, had it running in ten seconds, and handed it off to Stanton King.

Runyon got in King's green Jaguar and headed north on Dixie, chasing after Thorn and Snake, while Stanton roared south to catch up to Sugarman and the lady cop. A path dividing in the woods.

Pauline had about two seconds to decide which fork to take.

She went with Stanton. He was first on her list, and he had the Southwoods file. She'd do the others after she finished with him. Made perfect sense.

Better not to overthink it. Better just to drive, tail her targets as she'd been trained. Several times today Hadley S. Waters, the Big Cheese, had tried to get her to open up about Southwoods. Angling for some kind of moral discussion. The ethics of the scheme, any pangs of guilt she might be feeling. But Pauline wasn't having any of that. Once you started weighing the moral fat grams of any given operation, you were fucked. You did what you had to do, then did the next thing on the list. Anything more than that, you might as well walk naked into quicksand.

The highways were thick with early-morning traffic, pickup trucks full of construction workers, and delivery vans, and schoolteachers heading to work in the dark, tourists in rentals trying to get ahead of the crush. Caufield stayed a safe five cars back of the white Cadillac. Even if she lost Stanton in all the congestion, she had his cell and could call and get his location if need be.

A few miles farther south she realized where their little convoy was headed. Sugarman leading Stanton, and Stanton leading Pauline, down the Florida Turnpike to Florida City, the turnpike narrowing to one lane, then becoming U.S. 1, the desolate highway that led into the Florida Keys. Not Pauline's favorite part of South Florida. Too much water, not enough land. Too many citizens who lacked the proper respect for legal authority.

CHAPTER TWENTY-SEVEN

In the morning gusts off the Atlantic, Snake's hair was a tangle of spirals and loops, stirring around like a nest of restless eels. Bony-faced and erect, he watched a couple of guys on Harleys rumble across the lot and park in the shade of the pines.

Thorn ordered him to walk a few steps ahead as they crossed the gravel to Jimbo's. The .38 was cold and heavy against his thigh. Riding the sea breeze were wisps of sewage mingled with the sweet stench rising off the shoreline, where seaweed and pinfish had been trapped ashore by the retreating tide and were already rotting in the sun.

From what Thorn recalled, the outdoor bar at Jimbo's never shut down. At dawn the all-nighters thinned out to make way for the breakfast beer crowd, one shift replacing another in an endless procession of drunks and merrymakers, the morose and the severely addled. The wooden stools and picnic benches were always warm; the cooking ovens where king mackerel and marlin marinated in heavy smoke were forever stoked.

They threaded through the bikers in jeans and leather vests and women with stringy hair and hazy eyes. A few dozen of them were scattered about the outdoor tables, chatting quietly and eyeing Thorn and Snake with bleary indifference.

He found Jimbo out on the docks, watching a shrimp boat easing up to its mooring. He was unstooped since the last

Thorn had seen him, ten, fifteen years back. A cigarette tucked in the corner of his mouth. He was barefoot and wore cutoff jeans that were one rip away from being rags. A white net shirt that showed his mat of gray chest hair.

His dome was bald, but his white ponytail hung to the middle of his back. Before he'd bought the fake bar and ridden it through the years into authenticity, he'd been a back-country guide in Islamorada. Not the best guide, not the worst. But a friend of Thorn's dad, and a local legend for his exorbitant feats of daring when it came to the poker table.

"Who's your friend, Thorn?"

Jimbo blew smoke into the breeze.

"Not a friend," said Thorn. "More like a prisoner of war."

"You're not here to start trouble, are you, boy?"

"If my buddy here minds himself, we'll all be fine."

Jimbo put out his hand and they shook. Snake got only a manly nod. Jimbo drew a deep drag on his cigarette and let it filter out with his words.

"Still tying flies?"

"When the spirit moves me."

"Always thought you had some kind of magic shit going on when it came to bonefish flies. Don't know what it is, but those goddamn fish just love what you do."

"You get out on the water much anymore?"

Jimbo squinted through the cigarette smoke.

"It's lost its appeal somewhat. The old bones are squeaking more than they used to."

They watched the shrimpers tie off their trawler, then amble over to the beer window. Snake stood quietly, looking out over the mouth of the boat basin toward open water.

"What brings you up to Miami?"

"You remember Liston versus Clay? Nineteen sixty-four?"

"The fight?"

"Yeah, the fight."

Jimbo said, "Do I remember it? Hellfire, I won more money on that boxing match than any bet in my life. Cassius made me a wealthy man. At least for a couple of weeks."

"I got a picture I'd like you to look at."

The old man flicked his butt into the lagoon and led them over to a picnic table apart from the others, parked beneath a coconut palm.

"My office." Jimbo sat on the bench, and Thorn dragged his shirttail up and drew out the envelope.

Snake was watching silently from two paces away.

"Now's the time, Snake. Take a gander."

Thorn drew out the photo and lay it before Jimbo and leaned in with a knee braced on the bench. Snake eased up to Jimbo's other shoulder. Thorn watched him bend forward and study the image, his mouth tensing, eyes tracking back and forth along the rows of fight fans. His first real look.

"I remember that week like it was yesterday. All the big names flocking into town. Christ, the Beatles were here, clowning around with Clay at the Fifth Street Gym. Joe Louis, Jack Dempsey, Godfrey, Gleason. Then you had all the politicians in the world coming down to hear Lyndon Johnson talk a couple of days later. Shit, Miami was the center of the universe that week."

"The photograph, Jimbo," Thorn said.

"So what am I looking for?" Jimbo straightened the photo against the rough wood planks of the table.

"Anybody you recognize."

"Sure. This guy, for instance."

He tapped the squirrelly faced man in gray.

"I got that one already," Thorn said. "Meyer Lansky."

"Oh, yeah. Lansky was a big-time badass. Not a killer himself, but he could give the nod. Still, all in all, compared to the trash we got now, old Meyer was a first-class gentleman. Played by the rules. Paid off when he lost."

"What about the blonde?"

Snake was standing erect again, eyes drifting away to the riffling water of the lagoon. He'd seen all he needed.

"What've you got, Snake?"

He opened his mouth, then closed it and looked at Thorn with something different in his eyes. The steeliness had softened into more malleable material.

"You were expecting a revelation and you didn't get it."

"Something like that," Snake said.

"This guy." Jimbo thumped a stubby finger against a man in a suit. His black hair was slicked back and his cheek was stained with a large red welt. "That's the goddamn mayor. What was his name?"

"Stanton King," Thorn said.

Snake looked at him.

"The man who raised me," Snake said.

Jimbo craned around for a longer appraisal of Snake.

"You're one of the mayor's boys, huh?"

"The only one left." Snake shifted his gaze to the sky above the rim of pines and was silent.

"Hell, I used to know your mom, Lola. Oh, now there's a classy lady. She could bring a room of men to their feet. Yes, she could. They still together, those two?"

"They are," Snake said. Then he turned to Thorn and said, "Why are you fucking with me, Thorn? If you know these people already, what do we need this old man for?"

"Easy, Snake."

Snake went around the table and faced them.

"The heavyset man with the diamond," Snake said. "Pumping his fist, whispering in Lansky's ear. "Who is he?"

"His name is Edward Runyon," Thorn said. "He's the guy who was shooting at us a little while ago."

"Shooting, as in guns?" Jimbo said.

Thorn nodded.

"I think the time has come for you to tell me what in fuck's name this is about, Thorn."

"Might be safer for all involved if I didn't do that."

"I don't much like those terms."

"Jimbo, I just need the blonde."

"Well, shit," Jimbo said. "I know the broad, I just can't pop her name."

"No hurry," Thorn said. "Take your time."

"I can tell you one thing. She's running this little extravaganza."

"How's that?"

"You don't see it? Sensitive guy like you. Look at her. Look at the other guys around her. I spent half my life staring at assholes across a poker table. You get so you can read their eyes, and I don't mean who's holding the high hand, either. You see little things happening in the group. One guy afraid of another guy, or some asshole so fixated on another asshole, he'll do anything to make sure the guy he hates loses. Things like that. That's what I'm looking at here. Group dynamics."

"I'm looking," Thorn said. "But all I'm seeing is a bunch of people watching a fight."

"Row three, these people are sitting together. Five of them, including the woman. They're a group. The mayor, Lansky, the woman, the pinkie-ring guy, and this little Cuban fellow on the end with the Clark Gable mustache. The blonde's holding four aces, and all these other guys know it. They're leaning her way like a bunch of daisies toward the sun."

"I don't know, Jimbo. I'm not seeing it."

"Look some more."

Maybe Thorn was kidding himself, but after a minute staring at the photo, examining their posture, the direction of their eyes, their expressions, Thorn detected the slightest of tilts in her direction. More than the attraction of a good-looking woman. In one way or another all of them were splitting their concentration between the action in the ring and the blonde sitting among them in the third row.

"So who is she?"

"Priscilla, Darlene. No, that's not it. Goddamn my fuzzy old brain."

"If I told you the name of the other guy, the one sitting next to her, would that help?"

Jimbo said he thought it wouldn't hurt.

"Humberto Berasategui," Snake said. "The small man on the end with the mustache. He owned a plumbing business in Hialeah. Berasategui came with the killers and stood sentry outside. A few hours after this picture was taken, I killed him. Out in my front yard, I hacked him to death with my father's machete."

Jimbo muttered something under his breath.

"What is it, Jimbo?"

"I think I'm starting to get the picture. What you boys are into."

He pushed back from the picnic table and climbed free. He looked around his property with an anxious frown as though expecting gunfire. But as far as Thorn could tell, there was only the usual assortment of harmless losers and drunks and a couple of firemen ending their shift.

"Her name's Pauline," Jimbo said. "I don't recall her last name. Don't know if I ever knew it. But that's definitely Pauline. I didn't run with that crowd. They stayed to themselves. But I knew 'em. Everybody knew 'em."

"Pauline," Thorn said. "You're sure?"

"Absolutely."

"Could it be Pauline Caufield?"

Jimbo blew a smoke ring down at the table and washed a hand through its remains.

"Sounds right. Pauline Caufield. Yeah, I think that's it."

"Who is Pauline Caufield?" Snake said.

Jimbo told them to wait just a minute. He headed over to the kitchen shack and went in the back.

"Who the fuck is Pauline Caufield?" Snake said.

"Easy, tiger. I'll give you what I got. Just relax a bit."

A minute later Jimbo came out of the shack with a scrap of paper in his hand. He went over and handed it to Thorn. A name and address scrawled there.

"Miguel Cielo?"

"I'm doing this only because I was close to your old man."

He dusted his palms against each other and stepped back.

"Who is he, Jimbo?"

"Maybe what I should do, I should put this in context for you, son. That time period. The year that picture was taken, back in the early sixties."

"Okay."

"For starters, you should know the CIA station in Miami was their largest outpost in the world, outside of their fucking headquarters in Langley. Nineteen sixties, those spooks ran three, four hundred front companies out of Miami. That's the kind of place this was. Next to tourism, CIA was the biggest game in town. More agents made their bones in Miami than anywhere else on the globe. Back then you pull out your pecker and take a piss, you'd wet some spook's leg."

"Pauline Caufield was CIA? That's what you're saying?"

"Well, now that's not the kind of thing you know for a fact," Jimbo said. "But it was pretty clear she wasn't in town to tan her butt on the beach. She ran with a crowd that was different than anybody else down here at the time. Short haircuts, military types, dead serious. And she was a hard-ass, and a woman of mystery. That's as close to knowing as you can come with their kind."

"What's the CIA have to do with this?" Snake said.

"How old were you the night it happened, boy? Ten, eleven?"

"I was twelve," Snake said.

"Well, they don't teach this in civics class, I guess. But as you might remember, back in 'sixty-four you had a few hundred thousand brand-spanking-new residents of our fair city. And guess what? Down to the last man and woman, every one of them damn Cubans voted.

"And guess what else? When it came to voting, they all voted exactly the same way. There was one thing and only one thing they cared about. You make them happy on that one thing, you get elected. I guarantee you, all those CIA folks, they were here trying like hell to make the Cubans happy. At least make them think the U.S. government was doing everything in its power to run the commies back into the Sierra Maestra where they came from, so all those refugees could go back to Havana. That's why the CIA was here then. That's why they're still here. Only now it's not just the vote. It's the money, too. A million, two million happy Cubans goes a long way toward deciding who sleeps in the White House."

Jimbo dug another cigarette from his pants pocket, lit it, and blew fretful smoke up toward the sky.

"And Miguel Cielo?"

"I don't want my name used," he said. "You didn't get this address from me, I never saw your ass today."

Jimbo's eyes cut away and strayed out to the lagoon.

"Who is he, Jimbo?"

"What he was called was El Padrino."

Thorn looked over at Snake.

Snake said, "Godfather."

"That's right," Jimbo said. "His outfit was known as La Corporación. The guy ran a *bolita* game, like the lottery. Made millions. Ran the show down here all through the sixties and seventies, split his time between Miami and New Jersey. If Lansky took a shit, before he squatted he cleared it with Cielo."

"How's he fit in?"

"Miami's like anywhere else," Jimbo said. "You want to get anything of significance done, you make deals with the devil. Cielo was one of the head devils. Cielo on the Cuban side, Lansky on the Anglo side. If the CIA was up to something, wanted their path cleared, Cielo would be out there chopping the underbrush. Lansky would be, too. The feds loved pitting one against the other. That's what our federal boys been doing ever since. Cielo and Lansky were up to their elbows in CIA shit. If anybody knows what this little gang of boxing fans were up to, it's Miguel Cielo."

"Cielo's still alive?"

"That's what I hear. Mean old son of a bitch still hanging on."

"He'll talk to us?"

"If he docsn't kill you first."

Thorn shook Jimbo's hand and thanked him for his time. He and Snake were halfway back to the parking lot when Jimbo called them to a halt.

They stood out in the sun and waited while he ambled over, puffing on a fresh cigarette.

"Just remembered one other item of interest."

Snake was massaging his right temple, as if a headache had taken root.

"Time that picture was taken, 1964, Lansky was quite the ladies' man."

"Yeah?"

"His main squeeze around then was a woman by the name of Lola Henderson."

Jimbo smiled at Snake with the quiet satisfaction of a man who's just fanned out a Royal Flush.

CHAPTER TWENTY-EIGHT

Snake sailed through Miami traffic as though he were telepathic, knowing where the openings would occur, which lanes were about to clog. Operating on his cabbie's instincts. They drove into Little Havana, then farther north, working their way around the sprawling Miami airport, then into the crush of Hialeah.

Snake was silent, but Thorn could see the grind of his jaw.

Thorn worked it around. What they knew, what was left to know.

At least two of the five people in the photo had been at the Morales house a few hours after the fight. Humberto Berasategui was in league with the big man, Runyon. More than likely everyone sitting between them was involved as well. With Pauline Caufield front and center, and the men tilting her way, it was tempting to believe she was calling the shots. That the Morales family died because of some operation the CIA was running. At the moment that's what the photo was saying.

But learning exactly what was driving each of those five people was what mattered now. And uncovering their motives was going to be a hell of a lot more challenging than simply learning their names. To untangle the web of forces that brought those five citizens together in that row and sent them forward into that black winter night on their mission of murder.

It was nine-thirty in the morning, the Miami sky was a bright, unbroken blue. Scents of broiling meat and harsh coffee filtered into the car. The farther north they traveled, the more congested the neighborhoods grew. Every store sign and billboard was in Spanish, tobacco shops and Latin supermarkets and cafeterias with serving windows that opened onto the sidewalks, drawing groups of leathery men in guayaberas with their paper cups of café cubano.

Thorn recalled that Hialeah was a Seminole phrase meaning "high prairie." Though as far as he could see, the only spaces that might qualify as prairies anymore were the vast asphalt parking lots.

"What's wrong?" he asked after Snake's third darting look in the mirror.

Snake shook his head.

"It's how I drive. Two eyes forward, one eye back."

Snake located the address Jimbo gave them and pulled into the dirt driveway of a tiny pink cement-block house. The windows were crisscrossed by security bars, and angry dogs prowled the backyard. All along the street old cars cluttered front yards. Green lawns and shade trees were in short supply.

"This can't be right," Snake said.

"Even godfathers fall on hard times."

A four-foot-tall Virgin Mary was planted next to the sidewalk and seemed to cast a disapproving glance Thorn's way.

"We need to talk," Snake said.

"About Lola and Lansky?"

"I don't give a shit about Lola and Lansky. So what if they were lovers? That has nothing to do with me or my dead sister."

"The mayor steals the mobster's girl. Sounds significant to me."

"Lola was a whore. She slept with my real father, too."

"Morales?"

"Yes, Jorge Morales," Snake said. "She was having an affair with him. I believe it ended at Christmas. My mother gave my father an ultimatum and he dumped Lola."

"Christmas 1963?"

"Yes, but it doesn't mean anything."

"Are you nuts? She's Lansky's girlfriend, she had an affair with your father, then a month later Morales is murdered and Lola winds up raising you and Carlos. Of course it means something."

"This is not about love affairs. It's about Cuba. And this woman Caufield. What else do you know about her that you haven't told me?"

Thorn was shaking his head. It was always about love. Always, always about love. Lost love, love denied, the obsessive hunger for love. Parental or romantic. Whether it was twisted or pure, fulfilled or unrequited, love was always at the source.

"Pauline Caufield, Thorn. What do you know?"

"I understand she's shown a strong interest in our recent comings and goings. That's all."

"Is that right? She's here in Miami?"

"I believe so, yes."

"How do we find her?"

"I don't think we can walk up to the CIA home office and ask for an appointment, if that's what you think."

"Don't mock me, Thorn."

"Look, I'm not hiding anything from you, Snake. It's all on the table. Do me the same."

Snake's gaze was fixed on the pink house before them. A young woman opened the front door and came out to stand in the sunlight. She was in her thirties, with hard cheekbones and dark eyes. She wore her black hair long and loose and had on tight jeans and a man's white business shirt with the tail out. In her right hand she held a small automatic. She raised the pistol. Not exactly aiming, but close.

"Who are you? What do you want?" she called.

Thorn got out the door and waited for Snake to join him.

"We're looking for Miguel Cielo."

She considered it a moment, chewing the edge of her lip.

"Just a couple of questions, that's all."

"About what?"

"A photograph."

"Who are you, what are you doing here?"

Before Thorn could answer, Snake stepped forward.

"My name is Morales," he said. "My father was Jorge, my mother María Gonzalez, and my sister was Carmen. In 1964 the three were slaughtered by men in stocking masks. My sister was fourteen years old. The assassins also murdered five of my father's militiamen. You may remember the event."

The woman lowered the gun.

"It occurred before I was born," she said. "But yes, I've heard of it."

Something happened to her body, a softening of her stance. She reset her feet, angling to the side and glancing backward through the screen door.

"Stay where you are. I'll pass on your request."

Eyeing them carefully, she gathered her hair one-handed, lifted it off her neck, then released it. She stepped inside the house, and Thorn could see her through the elaborate scroll-work of the security door as she spoke into a phone.

A moment later she came back out onto the porch.

"This is very unusual," she said. "He's willing to speak to you."

Thorn started forward, but the young woman raised her hand and halted him.

"He's not here. I'll take you to him."

"Who are you?" Thorn said.

"I'm Mariana Cielo, his granddaughter. I am the gate-keeper."

Snake touched Thorn's shoulder and bent to his ear.

"A green Jaguar sedan is parked a few houses to the south."

"What about it?"

"It's following us," Snake said. "It's my father's car."

Thorn caught glimpses of the green Jaguar in the traffic behind them as Mariana guided Snake south through the city.

It was a thirty-minute drive to Cielo's neighborhood, a wooded area rimming Biscayne Bay where the Grove and the Gables shared a border.

Thorn stopped at the entrance and Mariana drew a remote from her purse and rolled open the wrought-iron gate.

"This is more like it," Thorn said.

"More like it?" said Mariana.

"More befitting a man of your grandfather's stature."

The dwelling where Miguel Cielo lived was two stories with a red barrel-tile roof and a long brick drive lined with royal palms. The villa had spacious balconies, porticoes and slatted shutters, and the quiet, dignified feel of a Spanish convent. It was positioned in the middle of several acres of sprawling lawns and thick groves of bamboo and a pond where egrets and herons stood frozen in hunting poses.

Snake coasted up to the front door and they all got out.

Just inside the gleaming mahogany door two men met them, one with a shaved head, the other with wavy black tresses that brushed his bulky shoulders. Both had the stumpy look of shot-putters a decade past their prime. They wore jeans and body-hugging T-shirts, and each held a micro Uzi. Twenty rounds apiece, if Thorn's memory served.

Shaved Head said something in Spanish and Wavy Hair laughed.

The foyer they stepped into was larger than Thorn's old stilt house. Overhead an extravagant stained-glass window splashed rainbows across the terra-cotta tiles. The ceiling was planked with honey-colored oak, and the house wrapped around a central courtyard that filled the rooms with golden sunlight.

"Hands up, turn around, you first." Shaved Head was the leader. His sidekick stepped forward and Thorn did as he was told. No reason to get pissy with security. Especially with forty rounds between them and an IQ in the same range.

Wavy Hair frisked Thorn one-handed, holding the Uzi in his right. He extracted the .38 from one pocket, the cell phone from the other. Made another comment in Spanish, which drew a gruff laugh from his buddy. He lifted Thorn's shirt and found the envelope and drew it out. He looked inside and pulled out the photograph.

"What the fuck is this?"

"I'm hoping Señor Cielo can enlighten us about that."

Wavy Hair examined it for a moment, then showed it to his partner as if it might hold some hidden danger that escaped him.

"That Muhammad Ali?"

"He was Cassius Clay at the time," Thorn said.

"Never did like that draft-dodging asshole. He dead yet?"

"Give it back to him," Mariana said.

Wavy Hair looked at top dog for permission. The shaved one nodded.

Thorn took back the photo.

"Now you, skinny man, hands in the air."

Snake raised his arms and the shot-putter patted him down harder than he needed to.

"Stop showing off, Roberto." Mariana used the tone of a sister who long ago assumed maternal authority. "Abuelo wants to meet them."

Wavy Hair laid the pistol and the cell phone on a side table near the front door and trained the Uzi's sights on Thorn.

"These fine men are my brothers, Andrés and Robbie. Now my grandfather waits."

She led them through the door and down a hallway toward the sunny rear wing of the house. The tag team stayed close behind. Halfway down the hall, one of them goosed Thorn with the barrel of his Uzi.

The old man, Miguel Cielo, was dark-skinned and silver-haired and had the large, sensual features of one who has indulged deeply in the world's pleasures and now is paying the price. A wooden box of cigars lay on the table beside his chair. A large blue ashtray held half a dozen butts.

His chair faced a two-story-high glassed-in butterfly garden. The air inside the glass was alive with darting color, wisps of wing fumbling from blossom to bloom.

Mariana made the formal introductions and stepped back.

Cielo didn't bother with Thorn but studied Snake for several moments, grunted, and turned his eyes back to the trapped butterflies.

The brothers were watching Snake with interest, as if they were aware of his reputation, this childhood killer. A titleholder in their chosen profession.

Snake held the photo out to Cielo, and the old man looked at it for a while, then raised a stumpy finger and tapped the face of Meyer Lansky. He kept on tapping the glossy image, as if he meant to stab his finger through its surface.

Cielo's voice was soft and high-pitched, almost feminine.

"Lansky was a son of a bitch. An arrogant Jew."

Snake stood waiting with the photograph still held out before the old man, although Cielo seemed to have had his fill of it.

Cielo said, "There was an *oportunidad perfecto*. But it was wasted. Wasted on Jorge Morales. That *payaso*."

"My father, a clown?" Snake took the photo away.

Robbie heard Snake's aggravation and turned his weapon.

"I mean no disrespect. But the truth is, your father, Jorge Morales, was a ridiculous choice. He commanded no more than two dozen men in his militia. A gang of *obreros* playing soldier in the swamp."

Thorn glanced at Mariana, who stood near a window, looking at the butterflies dancing in the sunlight.

"Menial workers, dishwashers, carpenters," Cielo said. "There were other militia groups, well trained, from prominent families. Hundreds went into the street to protest the killing of this pitiful militia, but if I had been in charge, thousands would have been in the streets, a great tumult would have resounded through the entire nation. We would be back in Havana now."

"If you had been in charge?" Thorn said. "I understood you *were* in charge."

Cielo turned his head slowly and slid his gaze up and down Thorn's frame, as if sizing him for a coffin.

"Who are you?"

"I'm helping Snake find out who killed his parents."

"Why do you care?"

"I lost a friend yesterday," Thorn said. "He died because of something hidden in this photograph."

Cielo looked back at the butterflies. Solid purple, red and yellow, orange and black, iridescent green. Red admirals, swallowtails, monarchs, buckeyes, mourning cloaks, and others Thorn couldn't identify. They settled onto flowers that were not as bright or beautiful as they were, then twitched back into flight.

"I provided the CIA with advice, but the idiots ignored me and relied on Lansky to make the selection. They planned this *gran proyecto* and disregarded the people who knew the most. Lansky muscled me out of the plan. Told lies about my patriotism. He didn't care about the project. All he wanted was to take back his Havana casinos. He had no passion, no political understanding. He was a greedy man. He made a stupid mistake. Killing a nobody like Morales accomplished nothing."

"Was it Pauline Caufield who ran the operation?" Thorn said.

Cielo's lips twisted into a sour shape.

"That woman betrayed us. Her people have betrayed us over and over."

"Is it possible," Thorn said, "that Meyer Lansky put the hit on Morales out of jealousy? Removing a romantic rival?"

Cielo made a dismissive hiss.

"Meyer Lansky was motivated by one thing only," he said. "Not women, not politics. It was money and money alone he cared for."

Cielo looked at Thorn, then turned to Snake.

"Out of respect to your father and your mother and your sister, I have allowed you to come into my home. But I am an old man. I have little patience anymore for fools or foolishness."

"I understand, sir," Snake said. "One question more and we will go."

Cielo was silent, keeping a drowsy eye on his flock of beauties.

"If you could simply explain what it was the CIA was attempting to do."

"Those fools," he said. "They failed. They have always failed. They continue to fail."

"Stanton King," Snake said. "What role did he have in this?"

Miguel Cielo watched his butterflies dip and wallow. He watched them for nearly a minute before he spoke.

"Of all the traitors involved in this catastrophe, King was the worst."

"How so?" Snake said.

"He degraded himself, sacrificed his honor as well as the welfare of my countrymen. A transgression for which no payment would be sufficient. If he had not fallen so low in recent years, become so pathetic, I would have torn out his heart by now."

"How did he sacrifice his honor?" Thorn said.

"He sold us out for his own petty purposes."

"What exactly did he do?"

"That's a question for Lola, and for Stanton King. See if they have the courage to tell you."

And that was all El Padrino had to say.

On the way out, Snake arrived at the vestibule table a step ahead of Thorn and scooped up the .38. He turned and handed Thorn his cell phone.

"Power shift," Snake said. "You'll drive now."

Mariana led them to the drive, and Snake got in the passenger seat and waited.

Mariana put a hand on Thorn's arm.

"You must realize," she said, "my grandfather has only one cause. The desire to return to his homeland has burned in him for so long that I believe his vision of the truth has clouded in certain ways."

"So we can't trust what he said?" Thorn asked.

"I think there are others who might complete your knowledge."

"Like who?"

She pressed a slip of pink notepaper into his hand.

"What is this?"

"A house. Someone lives there who might be useful to you."

On the note she'd scribbled a street address.

"How do you know this place? What is it?"

"In this city my people have many memorials. Ordinary homes that have played a role in shaping Cuban history. We care deeply about our heritage. This address I give you is one of those. You would be wise to go there."

Snake rapped his knuckles against the windshield and motioned for Thorn to hurry up.

Thorn thanked Mariana and opened the car door, slid behind the wheel, and cranked it up.

CHAPTER TWENTY-NINE

In a rear bedroom at Thorn's Key Largo house, Alexandra used a pillow to muffle her sobs. Each time she thought the waves of grief had passed, another image came to mind: Lawton in the stern of the aluminum skiff, teaching her to cast plugs, or Lawton at the wheel of a Dodge Dart, driving her mother and her on a family vacation, singing that damn bottles of beer song.

She wept into the pillow while Sugarman went about the house, opening windows, airing the place out, puttering in the kitchen. And then another image of Lawton. His Sunday night ritual, shooing away her mother from the kitchen while he assumed cooking duties. Using the only recipe he ever mastered, Lawton melted a brick of Velveeta, mixed it with milk and liberal doses of paprika, and poured the pot of goop over crushed saltines. Welsh rabbit, he called it, and Alex loved it beyond any food she'd known.

She pulled the pillow away, struggling for breath, and stared up at the blurry ceiling, waiting for the next rumble to heave up from her bowels. But the flood of anguish seemed to have tapered off for now.

The truth was she'd been mourning her dad's loss for years, readying herself for this day. Though it was becoming clear that losing him in those torturous increments had not really prepared her for his final departure. Nothing could soften that.

She supposed there was some comfort in the way he'd died. He always claimed he wanted to go down swinging. Exactly as he lived, trying to bring order to an unruly world. Believing as he did that a man's honor was forever tested, his courage always under assault by those who would cheat and steal and betray the trust of others, and it was Lawton's sworn duty to represent the best that common man believed, to serve and protect his fellow man. A simple, sappy worldview. Welsh rabbit, crushed saltines, and cheese sauce.

Alex and Sugar were standing on the dock, watching mangrove snappers cruise the riprap wall. The four Advils she'd gulped were kicking in and the ache in her shoulder was down to a dull thump.

Sugarman brushed an insect off the front of his black polo shirt.

Even after the sleepless night, he was somehow unrumpled. Creases still holding in his tan slacks; even the shadow of beard on his smooth cheeks seemed tidy.

They stood for a while looking down at the snappers, then Alex said she had to return to Miami. This was all wrong, hiding out in the Keys.

Sugarman turned and studied her face for several moments, then said, "I'll whip up some eggs. We can sort it out over breakfast."

"No eggs, Sugar. I'm going back."

He nodded without enthusiasm. Sugarman's caution wasn't based on any degree of fear for his own well-being. He calculated risk and acted with measured responses that placed the safety of others far ahead of his own. On the other hand, he had a long-standing appreciation for impulsiveness and its occasional rewards. He was, after all, Thorn's closest friend.

"I'll get the keys," he said.

He'd been inside the house half a minute when a car rolled into the sandy drive.

"Sugar! We've got company!"

Alex heard the car door slam and a few seconds later the distinctive click of steel meshing with steel. She'd heard that same sound a thousand times at the pistol range—the magazine of a semiautomatic snapping into place.

Alex broke for the house. In the past twenty-four hours, two different men had tried to kill her. She wasn't about to let the third time be the charm.

As she entered the kitchen, she heard the intruder come through the front. She took the hallway that led to the north wing. It was a long corridor lit by transom windows and ran the entire length of the house. Thirty feet away down the hall, she heard Sugarman's piss ringing in a toilet bowl.

After entering the front door, there were two ways the trespasser could go. Straight ahead through the open living room and into the kitchen, perhaps drawn in that direction by the bank of windows, where he could peer out the back and check the grounds, or else he could take a hard left through a foyer, which meant at any second he'd appear at the other end of the corridor from where Alexandra stood.

She ducked into the first bedroom she came to. Thorn's boyhood room, little changed after thirty years, with bright posters on the walls, moose roaming across an Alaskan ice field, a hooked tarpon surging from the water. She scanned the room, saw nothing she could use, then drew open his closet door.

A flurry of gnats emerged from the shadows around his old clothes and shoes and fishing equipment. The leathery citrus scent of him was strong, radiating from the ancient boat shoes, the canvas gym bag, the collection of ancient poles and reels and tackle. She knelt down and pawed through the junk, looking for any kind of weapon. In the back corner, she uncovered a lead-filled wooden club. At the business end the wood was pitted and stained dark brown with fish blood. Not a handgun, but it would do.

She rose and fit the billy club to her hand, took a practice swipe at a slash of sunlight, then headed to the door.

As she cracked it open, the toilet flushed and she heard Sugarman washing his hands and whistling a low tune. Making enough noise to attract the intruder, and if the stranger had gone through the living room, as it now seemed, he would have to track past her door to locate the source of the noise.

With an eye at the crack, she waited. She heard the squeak of the faucet as Sugar shut off the water. Only seconds after that she felt the faint give of the floorboards beneath her feet and heard the slow creak of the man's approach. Sure of himself, he wasn't coming on tiptoes.

A breeze stirred through the room and shivered across the back of her neck. She stiffened and raised the club. With only one working hand, she'd have to toe open the door to get any kind of weight behind her swing. One shot was probably all she'd have. She blinked the film from her vision, imagined the blow of that heavy baton against the man's wrist or his skull or whatever crucial spot was most available. She'd have about half a second to decide.

At the other end of the hall, the bathroom door came open and then Sugarman's surprised grunt as he must have seen the man coming toward him. She angled her shoe into the opening of the door and tensed for the strike.

Rendered clumsy from the drugs and pain, Alex stubbed her foot against the door, took an extra beat to throw it open before she could lunge into the hallway with her good arm cocked.

By then the man had stepped back out of range and was aiming his .45 at the center of her chest.

"Can't we all just be friends?" he said.

He was about her height, in his early seventies with gray bristly hair. Wiry body packed tight inside black jeans and matching long-sleeve T-shirt. On his right cheek there was a bright red splash, as if he'd been slapped by a bloody hand.

"Relax, Mr. Mayor," Sugar called. "We mean you no harm. Isn't that right, Alex?"

Her hand wavered. She stood two steps from the man with the .45. He could nail her twice before she got within striking distance.

She turned and tossed the wooden club into Thorn's room.

"What're you doing here? What do you want?"

"I suppose it's too much to hope for, but do you happen to have the photograph? I think you know the one I mean."

Outside the Key Largo house Pauline Caufield knelt and watched. She had infiltrated to thirty yards. Isolated house, no neighbors anywhere she could see. She'd discovered an excellent vantage point, shielded by shrubs, the rear of the house spread before her—patio, lagoon, three sets of French doors that exposed the kitchen and dining area. Everything was well within range of the Glock 23.

She ran the Zeiss across the back of the house, thumbed the focus. It had 5×10 magnification, housed in a unit the size of a fountain pen.

Thirty feet to the center of the patio, forty to the interior of the kitchen. Shooting through glass would hurt her accuracy, but if anyone presented themselves, she was secure in taking the shot. On her last range test she'd consistently grouped them in three-to-four-inch clusters within the chest circle of the silhouette, and that was at fifty feet with the same Glock 23. A little wider spread at a hundred feet, but still within the target, and most were lethal hits. Not bad for an old broad.

Her only shooting problem: it sometimes took her one or two to warm up, get rid of the flinch. But with this vantage point working in her favor, she had the luxury of wasting a couple before she got the kill.

Doing it this way was making more and more sense. Simply go down the list, execute her plan, take whatever countermeasures were necessary, and be done with it. She'd been crazy to pass the assignment to Stanton and Runyon in the first place. That was sloppy, unprofessional, an easy way out.

Naturally she had some qualms about this approach, the repercussions it would have, the inevitable investigation, the press. Seven more deaths on top of all the rest. But she blocked that out. She'd been schooled in every aspect of crime-scene obliteration. She knew exactly what they looked for, knew exactly how to defeat them. And on this mission she had no doubt that Hadley S. Waters would cover her ass. Make certain any tracks, fabric, hair, prints, bullet casings she might leave behind were expunged.

Her only issue: killing Stanton here and now meant that locating the Southwoods documents could prove to be more difficult.

February 1964, two days after the Morales killings, five military police officers showed up at her door, scoured her Miami apartment, and bagged every item that might be connected to Southwoods. Simultaneously the same routine went down with each of the other members of the planning and execution teams. Even the generals on the Joint Chiefs got the treatment. Orders coming straight from LBJ. The president was pissed. Majorly pissed.

Because of that quick action, no Freedom of Information request was ever going to uncover the scheme. Every document was shredded. At least that's what they'd thought.

Stanton claimed he still had a copy. He'd only been a bit player. Unlikely he'd been given any paperwork. Though now that she thought about it, she supposed Lansky could've leaked it to him.

There was no way around it. She had to take his threat seriously. In the long term the document could be far more damaging than the photograph. But the two together could set off a nuclear fission that would blow apart dozens of careers. And send people to Leavenworth, or worse.

Pauline settled into her nest, checked the Glock, patted the spare clip in her jacket pocket. All set.

The phone in her pocket vibrated.

She drew it out, flipped it open. A text message from Runyon. Good boy, staying in touch.

Folowd Thrn and Snk to Key Biscayn then Cielo house. Ten minit inside. Lft Cielos, hding north. Hvnt had a clr shot yet. Will take them down shortly. R

Key Biscayne? What the hell were they doing at Key Biscayne? But worse, they had gone to see Miguel Cielo, that poisonous old man. Where'd they learn his name? Old and sick, he might say anything. Deathbed shit. Just waiting for someone to walk in so he could get it off his chest. She should've followed Thorn and Snake and Runyon. She'd tailed the weak sisters. Goddamn it to hell.

So what to do?

Go forward, do a hurry-up job on these three, or break off and head back to Miami, where the real action was unfolding? She took out her list of names. Read down it, weighing her alternatives. The hotter scene was clearly in the city. The greater threat. If she left Stanton on his own down here, he might just succeed in taking out Sugarman and the Collins woman himself. Stanton doing Pauline's work for her. Then later on she could make a deal with King for the Southwoods papers. Once she had them in hand, that would be the end of the mayor.

That seemed the cleaner option. Cut and run.

But then again, she'd driven all this way. It was an hour back to the city. She was here. She was invested. Why not just get it done, pop all three and get the hell back to Miami afterward?

It was a simple logical choice. She was usually so good with logic.

CHAPTER THIRTY

"Listen, Mr. King," Sugarman said. "Lower the pistol, okay?"

"Call me *Stanton*."

They were still facing off in the hallway. Sugarman had moved forward to stand at Alexandra's side. Stanton King's aim was fixed squarely on her chest.

"Maybe we could go in the living room?" Sugar said. "Sit down, talk?"

"No photograph? I didn't think so. But I came anyway. I convinced Runyon we should split up. I needed to get away from that man. Oh, he's masterful with ignitions. He fired up a Cadillac in the motel lot, then took my Jag. I'm no good with practical things like that. Though I admire it in others, the Runyons of the world. Men who can hot-wire cars, field-strip rifles, overthrow dictators."

"Mr. King?"

"Sure, let's go in the living room. Maybe you can throw together some breakfast. I'm famished. It's been a very long night. You don't have any bagels, by any chance, do you? Cream cheese? I'd love some bacon."

With King bringing up the rear, they adjourned to the kitchen, and Sugarman and Alex set to work preparing breakfast on one side of the island while Stanton sat on a stool on the other side and watched.

"I think I'm coming undone," he said. "The stress, you know."

"You do seem a little lost," said Alex.

"I'm a dead man," he said.

"How so?"

Alexandra cracked eggs into a skillet, broke their yolks with a spatula, swirled them together, then looked back at King.

"Oh, they'll kill me. I know too much. I've seen too much. I'm dead."

"Who's going to kill you? Pauline?"

"Oh, God. You know about Pauline? You must be very good."

"Is that who you're afraid of?"

"This could be my last chance," he said, "to bump my karma in the right direction. You believe in karma?"

"Sometimes," Alex said.

"I tried," Stanton said. "I tried all that Buddhist stuff, but it never really took hold. I guess I'm just too damn Western."

Sugarman popped two slices of bread into the toaster and glanced at her, with a "How you doing?" wrinkle in his brow. She nodded at him.

"Is Pauline after you?" Sugar got down three plates from the high shelves and spread them out across the island's tile countertop.

"Don't try to play me, Mr. Sugarman. If I want to confess, I'll do it in my own way."

"Your gun, your rules," said Sugar.

Alexandra was stirring the eggs. Stanton looked around the room.

"If I confess, it won't make your lives any easier. People will try to kill you if you know about Southwoods."

"Southwoods?" Alex said.

Stanton King stared out the French doors, withdrawing into a grave silence. His gaze moved beyond the landscape at hand, beyond the watery distance, the sky and the hazy horizon.

Then he swallowed once and closed his eyes, and when he opened them again he seemed changed, resolved and melancholy, like a man who has let go of his last hope of forgiveness.

"I was just twenty-seven," he said. "What does anyone know when they're so young?"

"This is when you were mayor?" Alex said.

"Yes, I'd been mayor for a year when I fell in love. Desperately, wretchedly in love. And I acted unwisely. I traded everything for that woman. A Faustian exchange. My career, my future, my dreams, my pride. Everything I had, I swapped for Lola Henderson. A woman who was simply an illusion. A terrible, icy fantasy. Isn't it strange? When you're twenty-seven, everything seems possible. Then one wrong choice and your life is forever altered. One miscalculation."

"How can love be anything but good? The great vibrant fuel of life. Like a rocket lifting off, that rush, that excitement, an explosion of joy. But like that missile rising from the earth, one little nudge, one jostle, the slightest disturbance in the trajectory, and that great ship will simply sail off into oblivion. That was me. That was us, Lola and me. A rocket to oblivion."

"How so?" Alex said.

He stared into Alexandra's eyes with a frank and bottomless despair.

"I purchased my wife. I didn't win her love. I bought and paid for her."

Alexandra turned the heat off under the eggs, set the spatula aside.

"Eight hundred thousand dollars. It virtually depleted the family fortune. I gave it as a bribe to Meyer Lansky so he would kill the man my wife truly loved."

"Morales," Sugar said.

"Yes, Jorge Morales."

"Morales was Lola's lover?"

"Oh, yes, he was one of many who shared her bed. But Morales was the love of her life. When he threw her away, she despised him for it. She loved him and she hated him. And begged me to make her pain go away."

Alexandra looked over at Sugarman. His expression was as neutral as if he heard things of this sort every day.

"And what's this Southwoods deal?" Sugar said.

"They're all connected. Lola, love, Southwoods. It's all part of the same dreadful stew. I wouldn't have known about Southwoods if it weren't for Lola. She and Lansky were pals. He liked having her around, such a beautiful woman. Just after Morales jilted her, Lola heard Lansky discussing Southwoods, then she got an idea and came to me and asked if I could help. It was all her doing. Making Morales the target. But Lansky needed persuading. He wanted to go back to Cuba very much and thought Morales was a poor choice. That's what the eight hundred thousand was for. So even if Southwoods failed, Lansky would have something in his pocket."

"Southwoods was a CIA operation?"

Stanton nodded.

"Why does the CIA give their target selection to a mobster?"

"Oh, they were all kids," Stanton said. "The ones running the show, they were in their twenties, fresh-faced, naive. It was their first mission. They were doing this with minimal oversight. It was a rogue operation, run by some general up the chain. Caufield and the others were virtually on their own. They didn't know the lay of the land or who to trust. The Cuban exiles were telling them one thing, local Anglos another, blacks another. They knew Lansky better than anyone else. The CIA had worked with him in Havana. To Caufield, Lansky seemed larger-than-life. She trusted him. She was even a little in awe. He knew Miami better than she did, and he spoke her language. Finally, I suppose she believed he was patriotic and wouldn't steer her wrong."

"Lansky and the CIA teamed up to kill Morales," Alex said. "That's what you're saying."

Stanton King nodded, then glanced out the French doors at the lagoon and the sea beyond. Going back there, that time, that place. He frowned and shook his head hard, as if to clear a sour taste.

"Did you go along that night with Runyon and Humberto and the others?" Sugarman was buttering the toast, keeping his voice low and sincere. The concerned interrogator. Helpful, interested, but not pushing it.

"God, no. I went home after the fight and waited. But morally I might as well have been there. I was there in spirit. I have blood on my hands just the same. I knew what was going to happen. I aided and abetted a mass murder. Sitting there at the boxing match, knowing the Morales family only had a few hours to live."

His voice was growing fainter as he spoke, as though with every sentence he were receding further into that time he described.

"Lola begged me. She was in such agony, I couldn't refuse. Almost a million dollars so Lansky would execute her lover. And Morales's wife as well. It was the wife who put an end to the affair and Lola detested her, too. I thought I wanted Morales dead. I thought it would end her heartache and she'd turn to me. That her gratitude would eventually become love."

The room was silent for a moment. Stanton King looking off at nothing.

Then he said, "My God, I'm crazy, aren't I? Crazy as a goddamn loon."

Stanton made a weary smile, and he looked at Sugar, then Alex, an impossible plea in his eyes. The ruby color drained from the birthmark on his cheek, and for a moment it disappeared into the flesh around it.

"We're going to have to take you in," Alex said. "You know that."

"I know. Yes, I know. I'm ready whenever you are."

Sugarman said, "What exactly was the CIA trying to achieve? Why kill Morales? What's this all about?"

"It was a terrible plan, terrible. Sick and evil."

Stanton resettled on his stool. His eyes strayed out the French doors again, and seemed to come into focus on something nearby. Alex turned to follow his line of sight but saw nothing unusual.

When she turned back around, the glass in one of the doors exploded and Stanton King's head jerked hard to the side and he coughed. From his lips a pink vapor bloomed. He fell forward onto the countertop, and his pistol twirled across the white tile. As it was going over the edge, Alex snatched it.

In the instant she ducked to make the grab, a second slug slammed into the side of the refrigerator exactly where she'd been standing. Electrical sparks spewed from the dented hole.

A third round gouged a trail across the face of the cabinet and sent Sugarman sprawling to the floor. A fourth raked the stove, and the fifth blasted apart a mirror across the room.

Then the shooter ceased. There was only the trickle of glass and the sizzle of sparks from the guts of the fridge and the pounding in Alexandra's ears.

Stanton King coughed another time and a moment later his dead weight shifted and his body tumbled from the stool onto the kitchen tile floor.

By then she and Sugar were squatting side by side between the stove and the breakfast island. Near his collar blood seeped through the fabric.

"A nick," he said.

"Let me see."

But he raised a hand to wave her off.

"A nick."

It was clear from the sound of the blasts and the shattered glass in the French door that the shooter was in the woods near the lagoon.

"Your weapon, where is it?"

"Down the hall in my laptop bag." His voice was raspy.

"You take this. I'll get it."

Alexandra held out King's .45.

"I'll get mine. I know where it is. You stay here, Alex."

"You're okay? You're sure?"

"One way to find out."

Sugarman held his left hand hard against his neck and rose.

When he was gone, Alex duckwalked to the end of the counter. From there she had a view out the doors to the lagoon and the mangroves and scrub palmettos that formed the border of Thorn's property. To make those five shots, the shooter had to be in one of two clumps of shrubbery.

But a smart man would've repositioned himself already.

If it were Alex, she'd slip around to the front of the house. That was the brazen approach. What a pro would do. Enter through the door that Stanton used. Just walk in. A slow prowl while the two civilians cowered in the kitchen. Reload, strike again before the targets could regroup.

She cut back to the long hallway. Her arm ached and a ligament or tendon in her neck was badly strained from the weight of the cast—a sharp crick burned deep in the meat of her shoulder. Alex held the pistol in her good hand and advanced down the hall.

Inside one of the bedrooms she heard Sugar moving around. She didn't wait for him but got to the door to the foyer, flattened her back against the wall. A long breath, another, listening for the latch to click.

She waited another half a minute. She checked the wall for shadows but saw nothing. Just the coatrack, an old windbreaker hanging there. A brass pot on the floor with two umbrellas in it.

She lowered the .45 from the ready position.

She must've had it wrong. The shooter wasn't coming through the front. Maybe he was gone, or maybe he was circling the house to break into one of the bedrooms on the north side. Sugarman was taking too long.

Alex turned and made a first step back down the hall toward the bedrooms when she heard the latch. She pressed her back to the wall and raised the pistol shoulder high. She heard nothing. Half a minute went by and still nothing.

The shooter was a quiet bastard. Probably waiting just inside the door to absorb the floor plan. Choosing which way to head, just as Stanton had. Forward into the house or left to the doorway where Alex stood.

Alexandra bent her knees into a half squat, inched the barrel to the edge of the door frame. She didn't count to three, didn't take a breath, just went.

The woman wasn't expecting her. She'd taken a step forward, apparently deciding to proceed into the main house.

"Lower your weapon," Alex said.

The woman was blond, slender. Wearing black chinos and a blue shirt and a dark jacket. She stared forward, her pistol still directed into the house.

"I'm not telling you again." Alex came up from her squat.

"You're Alexandra Collins, crime-scene tech with Miami PD. You're training for search and rescue, a mid-career course correction."

"And you're Pauline Caufield. Now lower the weapon. Last chance."

The woman was at least sixty, but in the right light she might've passed for ten years younger. With the bright sun flooding from the transoms, however, Alex could see the grooves around her mouth and eyes, not deep but lots of them. Frown lines, growl lines, pissed-off lines.

Pauline was still weighing her chances, the Glock's muzzle tipping down an inch. She was watching Alex in her peripheral vision the way cornered animals study their attacker just before they choose fight or flight.

Alexandra stepped to her right, exposing her cast, her full body.

"Just lower it. Stop thinking. Do it."

"Okay," Caufield said. "You win. I'm lowering."

She dipped her weapon a few inches, then fell backward, dropped hard on her butt and rocked her legs upward, sighting between her uplifted feet at Alex. Somewhere in the first half second of her evasive move, Alexandra squeezed the trigger of the .45 and got the metal click of an empty chamber. And a second click.

Stanton had held them hostage with an empty weapon.

As Caufield was settling her aim, Alex slung the pistol at her. The woman bobbed her pistol down, then brought it back. Alex was in the air by then, leaping at the federal agent who had just killed Stanton King and wounded Sugar and meant to murder her.

Alex swung her heavy cast, accelerating as she swiveled into a roundhouse blow. Then spiking the woman full in the face.

The Glock blasted. A skewer of shock waves knifed down

Alexandra's shoulder and the round tore open a seam in the plaster cast and ripped apart the sleeve of her sweater.

Alex fell back on the floor. Her ears were ringing, but she was not dead. No wound she could feel. Not yet anyway.

Pauline Caufield, on the other hand, was out. A three-inch gash etched across her hairline, and blood drooling from the cut like milk from a leaky carton. Alex pried the Glock from her hand and stood up. She patted her down and found only a tiny telescope in her jacket pocket. No ID, no keys.

Alex stood up straight, and the foyer started to spin like a sluggish carnival ride. She settled her back against the wall and ordered the whirling to cease. After a few seconds it slowed enough for her to walk.

Alex made it back into the hallway without falling. She made it five more feet, then another five, the walls breathing in and breathing out. She pushed open the door to the first bedroom, but Sugarman wasn't there. She made it to the second and shouldered that door aside.

Sugar sat on the floor, his back propped against the bed. Blood saturated the front of his shirt and was puddled around his butt.

He opened his eyes and watched her kneel down beside him.

An embarrassed smile washed across his lips.

She found a phone in a hallway, called Emergency, gave her location.

The dispatcher got the medics rolling, then said, "This is Thorn's house?"

"That's right."

"Hell, what's he into now?"

Alex had forgotten that part of Key Largo. Everybody into everybody's business. Some folks thrived on it.

"Five minutes or less," the dispatcher said. "Apply pressure."

"I know about that," Alex said, and hung up.

She opened Sugarman's collar and examined the wound.

He'd been right, it was just a nick, but it was a bad nick. Very bad. The slug had whisked across the flesh just below his jawline. The artery was perforated, and a strong current of blood was pulsing out. She pulled a pillowcase loose and pressed a corner to the gash. When the fabric could absorb no more, she kept it in place to speed the clotting and folded another piece over it to soak the rest.

As they rolled Sugar out to the ambulance, Alex noted without surprise that there was no sign of Pauline Caufield.

CHAPTER THIRTY-ONE

Pauline had double vision. Speeding up the turnpike toward Miami, seeing two eighteen-wheelers where there was one, two motorcycles, two bread trucks. Two exit signs flashing past.

It took her three tries before she punched the correct numbers.

"Need to speak to Hadley."

Two red Corvettes blew by her on the left.

"He's in a meeting," his secretary said. Someone new Pauline didn't know. They were always rotating in and out.

"Get him out of the meeting. This is urgent."

"I'm sorry, what was your name again?"

"Caufield, Pauline Caufield."

"One moment please."

Pauline watched two big white birds sail across the highway. Two suns burning in the sky, two roads running parallel before her. The blood had stopped seeping. But a bell was ringing in her throat, and something tasted rotten at the back of her mouth.

"I'm sorry, Ms. Caufield. He can't come to the phone. It's an important meeting."

"It's Pauline Caufield. Did you tell him that?"

"Yes, ma'am, I did."

"Well, go tell him again. This is the highest priority."

"I'm sorry, ma'am, Director Waters said he doesn't know a Pauline Caufield."

At thirteen she learned to pleasure herself. In her dreary, motherless house she lay beneath the sheet and comforter, hand stroking thighs. A sweet relief from the pressure knotted inside. Something new, something exciting. Something all her own.

Twice that year her daddy swung open her bedroom door and caught her in the act. Shamed her, gave her prayers to say, made her read the Testament, pointing to the terrible punishments parents were sometimes required to make. Abraham and his boy Isaac. Onan, who so displeased the Lord for spilling his seed, he was slain.

*Eye for eye, tooth for tooth, hand for hand, foot for foot,
Burning for burning, wound for wound, stripe for stripe.*

The third and final time he caught her she was fourteen. As she was rising to the crucial moment, her guilt-loving father pushed open her door as if he'd been standing in the hall waiting for her moans, the squeak of mattress springs; her father waiting outside, ready with his punishment.

He strode across the room, yanked back her sheets. He looked down at her hand tucked between her white thighs.

I warned you about this.

I warned you, yet you continue to defy me. This lewd conduct. It will spoil you for marriage. No man will have you. I will not allow this in my house. I have warned you. Over and over I have warned.

There was a glass specimen jar in his hand. He held it out, unscrewed the lid, tipped it. Inside was a papery nest crawling with wasps, frantic to defend their broken hive.

No, she said. I won't do it again. I promise. I'll stop. I will.

You promised before. I no longer trust your word.

He dropped the hive onto her loins. The stinging hive. The wasps, the wasps, the stinging hive.

Years passed and she grew wanton. More bold and daddy-hating. Eighteen, nineteen, moving quickly from boys to men and more men. Bringing his worst fears to life. Dangerous men, powerful men, some more powerful than he. Inviting them in, taking all they had. Draining them dry, casting them aside.

Until that one man, that thrilling man. A man of valor. She fell for him, fell and fell so hard. His slinky body, his insolent smile, long lashes. Sensual macho lips. A genuine man, nothing like the others. A man of action and daring.

She made her way into his bed, oh God, his bed, his body. Those hours in his arms, his breath in her ear. His ferocity, his yearning.

But no. She can't have him. Beautiful man. Can't have, can't have. The wife and children called him home. And that's final. Go away, leave me alone. Forget I exist.

With her eyes shut, she placed on her tongue the dry wafer of the past, sipped from the goblet of memory. Reliving once more that murderous night, the man who died, and that sweet girl child. The wasps, the stinging wasps seeking her out, circling her head like a venomous halo, they buzzed round her brain, swarming and swarming to return to their hive, crazy to return to their broken hive. Their broken, broken hive.

Hadley Waters couldn't do that. Could he?

Pauline Caufield was a government employee with health insurance, a pension plan, nearly forty years of service. Waters couldn't erase all that, couldn't delete her Social Security number, expunge her from the system. No way in hell. People knew her, lots of people. She had a history. She had a penthouse office in one of Miami's finest office buildings, a network of agents under her command. She had bank accounts, a Florida driver's license, a passport, a deed to her house in Belle Meade, credit cards, a leased vehicle. There was no way she could simply poof and be gone. No way in hell.

Then again, she knew that wasn't exactly true.

She'd done as much herself. Agents in the field exposed who'd had to disappear. She'd overseen the work from Langley tech support. Watching them type and delete. Erase the flickering electronic codes that held the data that gave heft to human identity. A day or two was all it took, tracking down every trace, every footprint in the sand.

Poof.

And Hadley S. Waters had access to the best tech masters in the field. Better than anyone Pauline used. He might have already done it. He might have made Pauline Caufield and all her many accomplishments evaporate.

When making an agent vanish, removing the data was step one. It was step two that chilled her. Carting off the furniture from her house, the books on her shelves, the photographs. Removing the files from her computer, the computer itself, the record albums, the letters. Emptying drawers, stripping clothes from the closets, checkbooks and old tax statements from the desk, the pots and pans, everything down to the last spoon and paper clip.

Removing all physical presence of Pauline. Making her disappear.

CHAPTER THIRTY-TWO

Ten minutes after leaving Cielo's house, battling his way through midday traffic, Thorn worked north on Le Jeune, a shady two-lane road. A dividing street: mangy Grove on the east side, tidy Gables on the west.

He peered into the rearview mirror. Still no Jaguar.

"He's back there," Snake said. "Biding his time."

"Maybe we lost him. Maybe he gave up."

"Dream on."

"What do you propose?"

Snake stared out the windshield, tapping the .38 irritably against his knee.

Finally Thorn said, "Cielo talked about being back in Havana. The *gran proyecto*. What do you make of that?"

Snake gripped his forehead one-handed and squeezed.

"When it comes to Cubans," he said, "there is only one grand project. It is the same now as it's been since the communists came down from the mountains. To return home."

"Always that," Thorn said. "Always that."

"My father was no clown," Snake said. "His men were workers, yes, that's the only thing Cielo got right. They were common men and he inspired them. He was a lousy father and husband, but he was passionate for his cause. He had a vision. He would have sacrificed anything to return to Cuba."

"Look, Snake. We're closer than we were, but we're not

there. We know their names, the five people. We know they conspired to kill your parents for a CIA operation; at least a couple of the people in the photo were at your house that night. But we don't know why."

"I don't care why."

Thorn braked for a long line of traffic waiting to cross Dixie Highway. They hadn't discussed a destination.

Snake looked out at the unmoving traffic ahead of them. He checked his rearview mirror, then threw open his door and climbed out.

"Hey!"

The .38 was clutched in his right hand. He raised it to shoulder level as he marched down the row of cars stalled behind them. Horns began to hoot. Thorn hopped out and chased after Snake.

Ten cars back, the green Jaguar was wedged between a plumbing truck and an empty school bus.

By the time Thorn caught up, Snake had gotten the drop on Runyon. Still sitting behind the wheel, the old man had his hands raised to his ears.

Drivers in nearby vehicles were abandoning ship, escaping from the madman with his weapon. There was a strange orderliness to it, like a fire drill these folks had practiced more than once.

Thorn hustled up as Snake said, "Where's my goddamn father?"

"Hey, fuck you, kid. I'm not scared of you or your asshole buddy."

Thorn leaned down for a look through the passenger window. Backseat empty. The butt of a chrome pistol visible in the map holder, wedged between his thigh and the door. An easy draw.

"He's got a gun."

Unfazed, Snake said, "Let me see your mutilated hand."

"Fuck you."

"Raise your right hand where I can see it. Do it now."

"You're in some deep shit, boy."

"I was born in deep shit," Snake said.

Behind Snake a man edged forward through the deserted cars. He wore jeans and a polo shirt, and had the square-jawed look of an off-duty cop, sworn by law to help. Thorn yelled at the guy to forget about it. He halted for a moment, making the decision of a lifetime, then took a swallow of his own spit and backed off the way he'd come.

"The hand, Runyon, show me your hand."

The old man raised it to the open window. The first two fingers had been hacked away below the middle knuckle.

"That's my work, isn't it?" Snake said.

"Pull him out of there, we'll take him with us," Thorn called. "People are on their cells; cops'll be here soon. We can sort this out later."

Snake ignored him. Fixed on the man who'd abused his sister, a member of the team who'd wasted her and his parents and sent Snake whirling off into a warped corner of the galaxy.

Snake was daring him to make a play.

Thorn had seen it too often before. The gestures men made in their final moments seemed to spring directly from the core of their character as if it were impossible for a dying man to lie. They fired off one last true picture of their soul. With Runyon, it was a final act of scorn for Snake and men like him who had never served on the front lines or worked the dark edges of espionage in distant lands. How could civilians measure up to battle-hardened men? It was a mistaken view, of course. Domestic horrors being what they were, men and women without experience of war could grow every bit as hard and dangerous as any Runyon. Just ask Thorn. Or Snake.

"You only chopped off two of the ten," Runyon said. "What're you doing, coming back for the rest, little boy?"

His hand slipped off the steering wheel and slid to the crack between the seat and door. Doing it openly, an insolent smile for Snake and his kind.

The first three rounds blew open the chest of Runyon's green Hawaiian shirt. After that, Thorn looked away.

Around them Thorn heard the screams of good citizens.

Ordinary people who minutes earlier had been running errands, keeping the fridge stocked, meeting their appointments. So many times in the past, from the safe distance of Key Largo, Thorn and his buddies had scoffed at these city folk. Their agitated lives, their callous disregard for the land and sky and natural world around them, as if they were another race of man, inferior in every way. But standing among them, Thorn felt none of that disdain. City people, island people, it made no difference. He felt an upwelling of shame that he had once been so smug and so wrong.

He turned from the Jaguar and started toward the sidewalk. Making his exit from this mess.

Then Snake was beside him. He'd taken charge of Runyon's silenced pistol and used it to poke Thorn in the ribs.

"Where you think you're going?"

"I'm done," Thorn said.

Behind them cars were jockeying for the side streets.

Snake produced a grim smile, the muzzle of the pistol riding up and down the bumps of Thorn's rib cage.

"I'm not arguing with you. Walk back to the car, or die right here."

Thorn half turned to face him. Snake skipped back a step but kept the pistol steady on Thorn's chest.

"You can cut the high-and-mighty bullshit, Thorn. You and me, we're not any different. I saw you in action yesterday. We're just a couple of killers out for a joyride."

Thorn drew a breath and let it out. He walked back to the car. Snake followed closely.

In the secret marrow of his bones, Thorn considered himself a peaceful man. Meditative, a student of sunsets and sunrises, and the trajectory of gulls and egrets and the lazy lofting flight of great blue herons. A man who hungered for nothing more than the love of a woman, the tug of a large fish on his line. Simple shit.

But the years had proved a steady contradiction. No doubt about it anymore. Thorn had been born under a doomed planetary alignment. A dozen times before, he'd been on this same steep grade. Knew the feel of the tipping point—when his trot became a gallop, the gallop grew to a crazy hurtling rush, and by God, once again he found himself sprinting over the suicidal edge, into empty air, sailing down into whatever waited below.

Snake slid in behind the wheel, and with the pistol in one hand, he whipped the Audi through a U-turn.

Sirens howled in the distance. Snake drove for ten minutes until the sirens were lost in the traffic noise. He swung into the parking lot of a 7-Eleven. He spent a moment reloading his pistol from bullets he'd been carrying in his pockets. Then he told Thorn to get out.

"What now?"

"I think you're right, we should work on the why." Snake nodded at the pay phone. "Let's find a plumber."

"Humberto? The man's been dead for forty years."

"We Hispanics tend to carry on our family business."

"We don't know if Berasategui even had a family. And if he did, what're they going to tell us we don't already know?"

"The man killed my sister. I'd like to know who he was."

Snake followed him to the phone, and Thorn leafed through the Yellow Pages. Ran his finger down the column of plumbing businesses. He saw his hand shaking. His body was flushed with adrenaline. The pistol's racket still in his ear, the big man dying behind the wheel. Thorn took a breath and stilled the shiver. The day was young.

There was one plumber with that uncommon name.

H. Berasategui. South End Plumbing. Cute.

"Call it," Snake said.

A woman answered, and Thorn asked if Humberto was in.

There was no one there by that name. He must have made a mistake.

"No Humberto Berasategui?"

She thought about it for a second, then yelled in Spanish to someone in the next room and momentarily a man's voice replaced hers.

"There's no Humberto," he said. "There's a Danny." The man was impatient, on the verge of hanging up.

"Yellow Pages say *H. Berasategui*."

"Nobody calls him that. Like I said, his name is Danny."

"Was his father Humberto Berasategui?"

The man spoke as though delivering a blow: "His father's dead."

"Murdered forty years ago?"

"Who is this?"

"Detective Mark Harris." Thorn's new career, impersonating cops.

The man was quiet for a moment. Then more Spanish yelled back and forth. He fumbled with the phone, came back on.

"Danny's on a job."

"I'm working the murder of Humberto Berasategui."

"Working the murder? Some goddamn little kid did it. All that was forty years ago, for christsakes."

"There's new evidence. I'd like to speak to Danny."

The man considered it for several seconds. Thorn stood in Snake's shadow and watched the traffic pass.

"He's on a job," the man said. "I'll beep him. He wants to talk, it's his call."

"I'll give you my cell."

CHAPTER THIRTY-THREE

Three minutes later Thorn's cell phone rang. Danny Berasategui had a quiet voice with an uncertain catch in his speech, like a boy summoned to the principal's office. In the background Thorn heard a woman's giddy laughter. She sounded so close to the phone, she might have been nuzzling the plumber's neck.

Thorn kept it short and gruff. Repeating what he'd said to the guy on the phone.

Danny considered it for a moment, then covered the receiver and asked the woman a question. She must have given her assent.

Forty-three Star Island Drive was protected by three sets of security gates. The first manned by a red-faced guard with cheap sunglasses and a cheaper grin.

"We're here to see Danny Berasategui." Thorn gave him the address.

The guard didn't have to check his book to know there was no one by that name anywhere on that posh island.

"He's a plumber," Thorn said, "working a job out here."

"A plumber? I'm going to buzz you through on the okay of a plumber?"

"Ring the house, see what the owner says."

He did, and the owner wanted to speak to Thorn.

It was a woman with such a purr in her voice, on a normal day Thorn would've felt a tingle in his gut.

"Danny's plunging my toilet," she said.

"Too much information," said Thorn.

He handed the phone back to the guard, the woman sent her furry voice into the guard's ear, and a second later the steel post rose.

The man bent to Snake's window and delivered his parting advice.

"No one likes a smart-ass."

"Wisdom for the ages," Thorn said.

Star Island was a dredged-up lozenge of marl and sand, so neatly sculpted and landscaped that Thorn found his hand flattening the front of his rumpled shirt.

Movie stars lived there, rock stars, tennis stars, a TV legend or two, and the reigning basketball superman, all planted cheek to jowl, all sharing the diamond light radiating from the bay and the white distant glow of the towers of Miami Beach. The woman Thorn talked to on the phone had probably flushed a sack of gold coins down her toilet by mistake. A reason to summon Danny.

At the second checkpoint, a black man in a Nassau cop's uniform saluted and waved them through his gate. Word had passed along. On the eastern edge of the island they located number 43, a standard-issue villa, Mediterranean style. Ten thousand square feet of view and all the other necessities. Stepping from the private guardhouse was a young woman in safari clothes and a pith helmet, a handgun strapped to her waist. She examined them through the windshield, then pointed into the walls of the estate.

"All these guards," Thorn said. "Somebody's expecting a revolution."

Snake pulled up behind a pink Rolls and got out.

Thorn was imagining Mae West in a half-open silk bathrobe, but the twenty-something woman who whisked down the steps and met them in the drive was as emaciated as a Death Valley distance runner. Thorn could never be sure about such women, whether they were super-fit or anorexic.

She wore pink shorts and a matching halter top. Her childish mouth was set in a pout as if Danny's plumbing skills had not quite satisfied her needs.

Lugging his hamper of tools, Danny Berasategui was a few steps behind. A man in his early forties, well built, in a white company shirt and stubby blue shorts. He wore a phone on his belt and several gold chains around his throat, as if jewelry were one of his accepted forms of payment.

"Would you like to come inside?" she said in her downy voice. "Have a drink. Mojito, or something."

"We can't stay," Snake said.

"Pity," the woman said. "Which of you was on the phone?"

Thorn raised a guilty hand.

"So you're the witty one," she said. "I enjoy witty men."

"We're always in great demand."

She led them to a gazebo in a grove of palms and said she'd let them talk in private. As she passed Thorn on the way back to the house, she trickled her fingers across his arm.

"You know where I am," she said. And headed away into luxury.

"Okay," Danny said when she was gone. "What the hell is this about?"

Snake said, "Your father, was he a *communista*?"

Danny stared at Snake for a moment and slowly got to his feet.

"Now, now," Thorn said. "He meant no offense."

"My father was no goddamn communist," Danny said. "I don't care what the cops said. He hated communists. Hated them with a passion."

"So noted," said Thorn.

"What else do you know about him?" Snake said.

Danny sat back down. He was shaking his head.

"Who did he work for?" Snake said. "Just tell me that."

Danny turned his eyes toward the waterway, where a white Hatteras yacht was steaming north, a redhead on the bow, waving in their direction. All the rich folks so happy to see one another.

Danny swallowed and settled himself on the white gazebo bench.

"You guys aren't cops."

"True," Thorn said.

"Who are you?"

"Interested parties."

Danny considered that a moment, his hard look relaxing by degrees.

"There's nothing to solve," he said. "A kid killed my dad. Some little boy with a machete."

Snake sat across from him, and his tongue wet the corners of his mouth.

"Got to be hard losing a dad at that age. What were you, two, three?"

"I wasn't born yet. I was in the womb. I never met my old man. But hard, yeah, sure it's hard."

Snake nodded and looked back toward the house.

"Did your father do anything besides plumbing?"

Danny kicked a toe at his bag of tools and said, "What's that supposed to mean?"

"I'm asking a simple question. Did he have another job? Another employer?"

"Who the fuck are you guys?"

"I'm the kid," Snake said. "The one with the machete. That was me."

This time Danny popped to his feet. Thorn braced himself to pull the two apart, but Berasategui closed his eyes and must have been weighing his own hurt against Snake's, because when he opened his eyes again, he filled his chest with air and blew it out, then planted his butt again on the bench.

"So what is this? You here to fuck me up?"

"No," Snake said. "Just to learn a few things. Did he work for someone on the side? Moonlighting?"

Danny looked at Snake for a long moment.

"I can't believe it. You're the kid. That fucking kid."

"I am."

For a second or two Thorn thought Danny might begin to

sob, but he fought off the emotion and turned his face to the splash of sun on the bay.

"Berasategui," Danny said. "It's a Basque name."

"So?"

Danny cleared his throat and rubbed his lips with the back of his hand, as if he meant to erase any traces of lipstick he might have missed.

"Before my father was a plumber," Danny said, "he played jai alai at the Miami Fronton. He'd played it as a boy in Bilbao, the Basque country of Spain. He was very good."

"Okay."

"When he could no longer play well enough to earn a living, he took work as a plumber, but jai alai was in his blood. He went back to the fronton every day and drank wine and hung out with the players, and he bet on the games. He became a gambler. I believe it was an addiction. Something to fill up his heart from no longer being able to play the game he loved."

"So he was in debt."

Thorn was thinking about the photograph. Humberto Berasategui. How uncomfortable he looked, how out of place. Sitting next to Pauline Caufield, down the row from Meyer Lansky.

"Yes, he was in debt."

"To bookies."

Danny nodded.

"Did you ever hear the name of Meyer Lansky?"

Danny strained under the weight of the memory.

"My mother mentioned him, yes. She was afraid. Men were coming by the house. Thugs threatened to hurt him, burn down his business."

"And then it all stopped," Thorn said.

Danny looked at him.

"How did you know that?"

"Maybe your father was forced to participate in something dangerous to wipe out his debt. It's possible it was his only way out. To join with some other people in killing Snake's family."

"To pay off a debt." Snake spoke the words as if practicing them.

"Lansky may have wanted to have his own team member aboard. In that case, your dad was there that night to save his own family. That's all."

Snake stood up, started toward the car. His face was blank, but Thorn could see the emotion clenching his shoulders.

"Wait a minute," Danny said. "You're just going to walk away? You show up, tell me you killed my old man, and then walk off? Not let me know what's going on?"

"We don't know what's going on," Thorn said. "Not yet."

Danny looked at Snake for some parting word. But there was none.

CHAPTER THIRTY-FOUR

Snake drove back across the causeway to the other Miami, the one with hourly wages and no water view. He wandered south on Dixie Highway, then turned impulsively into a neighborhood Thorn didn't know. Old bungalows from an era when only snowbirds vacationing for the winter populated these streets. He'd been inside such houses. Tiny closets, no storage. Built for Yankees living out of suitcases. Nowadays those little cottages seemed absurdly small for the families crammed into them.

"I don't see what there's left to know," Snake said.

"The grand project," said Thorn. "What that CIA gang was trying to accomplish."

"I'm going home. I'll wait for Stanton and Lola. I'll get it out of them."

"You could try, I suppose."

Snake stared out his window and chewed on it.

Thorn opened the manila envelope, drew out the Xeroxed pages. It took a couple of minutes to locate the name Sugarman had spotted.

"Shepherd Gundy," he said at last. "Military investigator who worked your parents' murder."

"Military? Why the hell was the military investigating?"

"I don't know. The FBI was into it because they believed foreign nationals were involved. And it was a homicide case with the Miami PD. Then there's this military guy."

"He's in Miami?"

"I have no idea," Thorn said. "He was stationed at Homestead Air Force Base forty years ago. He could've retired down here like some of them do, or he could be anywhere. If he's still alive, maybe we could track him down, talk to him on the phone."

Snake thought about it for a block or two.

Then he dug his cell phone from his pocket and dialed.

"It's Snake," he said. "No, I'm not coming to work. I need you to look up a guy's phone number."

According to the cab dispatcher, there was no Shepherd Gundy anywhere from Palm Beach south through the Keys. After another minute he assured Snake there was no Shepherd Gundy in Florida. No Shepherd Gundy anywhere in the contiguous forty-eight as far as Friendly Cab could tell. The name *Gundy* made only a single appearance in the South Florida listings. Gundy Creations. A phone number but no listed address.

"Worth a try," Thorn said.

Snake got the number, dialed it. It was disconnected.

"Dead end," he said. "Any other ideas?"

Thorn thought of the address in his pocket, the one Mariana Cielo had given him. It hadn't sounded promising at the time, and it still didn't.

Before he could reply, Snake called back the dispatcher and told him to look up the address of Gundy Creations in the reverse phone book. Put in a phone number, find the street.

The dispatcher came back in two minutes, and Snake repeated the address aloud for Thorn. It was somewhere in the center of the city, Overtown or Liberty City, the black ghetto. One of those areas of Miami that had been full of raucous nightlife when Thorn was a kid.

Then about the time Cassius left town with his new championship belt, Miami's city fathers decided to cut the interstate through that disposable part of town. Businesses closed forever, churches failed, homes boarded up. Forty years later it was a nearly deserted sector of the city. Breeding rats and despair.

"Tell him to do it the other way," Thorn said. "Use that address to find the phone number."

"We already got the phone number. It's disconnected."

"Try it and see."

The Overtown address did indeed have a second phone number attached to it. One line for the business, one for the home. Business line disconnected, home not. Snake hung up from the cab company and said, "Why are we doing this?"

"Okay, forget it. You don't want to know why your sister was killed. You're content with what you got."

"You're a pushy bastard. Anybody ever tell you that?"

"You're the first."

Snake punched in the number and handed the phone to Thorn.

A woman answered. She sounded southern and polite, and African American.

"I'm looking for a man named Shepherd Gundy."

"May I ask why?"

"Was he once an investigator for the military?"

She thought about it for a moment, then said, "What's this about?"

"It concerns a case he worked a long time ago."

"What case was that?"

"The Morales family. A father and mother and daughter murdered. Five others, too."

"Oh," she said, and there was another pause. "Are you a newspaper writer?"

"No, just a normal citizen."

"Well, he doesn't like reporters. I'm just warning you."

Shepherd Gundy's house was in Overtown, infamous for its race riots and street-corner drugs. In a city where Cubans and Anglos battled for all available resources, the people in that part of town had fallen to an even lower rung on the social ladder than where they once were. Odd man out, surviving on the table scraps.

Overtown had been Cassius Clay's home base for six years, between the ages of eighteen and twenty-four, while he trained for Liston. Thorn remembered that Clay stayed at a hotel named the Sir John. The motel had a swimming pool, and that's where Cassius was photographed underwater in his boxing trunks. Thorn could still picture the *Life* magazine spread, the tall, handsome Cassius, powerful as a god, submerged in that swimming pool, throwing crosses and jabs and hooks. The trails of silver bubbles his punches made through that water.

He doubted the hotel had survived. Nothing much from that era had.

Gundy's house was yellow and made of concrete block. It was on the corner of a shady street that was full of houses exactly like it, though none was quite as well maintained. A rock toss away were the low-cost housing projects and the crumbling buildings and vacant lots full of giant weeds and the carcasses of dead animals. But the street Gundy lived on seemed like an island of hope in that sea of hopelessness.

Mrs. Gundy met them at the front door. She had white frizzy hair and a quiet smile. She was tall and frail and she wore a bright green apron over her white dress. There was baking flour on her hands, which she dusted against her apron as Thorn and Snake entered.

"You're sure you're not reporters?"

"Very sure," Thorn said.

"He's tried to tell his story to a couple, and they just laughed in his face."

"Maybe he spoke to the wrong ones."

"Maybe."

She looked at the manila envelope in Thorn's hand but said nothing.

She shifted her attention to Snake. He had fallen silent and his face was busy with thought, as if he were staging his next acts of mayhem. Blood burned in his cheeks, and his chest rose and fell with seething breath.

"He's in his shop," Mrs. Gundy said. "Through the kitchen, out back. He's expecting you."

Thorn thanked her, and he and Snake were out the kitchen door when Mrs. Gundy said, "He'll claim he's writing a book about that Morales thing. But he's no writer.

Though I often wish he was, 'cause he needs to unburden himself. It eats at him, keeps him awake. So I wish you luck in getting it out."

Shepherd Gundy stood with his back to them at a scarred-up pine table. He wore a blue jumpsuit, its arms and cuffs encrusted with sawdust. Over his workbench hung an elaborately carved sign with raised letters that read, GUNDY CREATIONS. Some of those creations were displayed on the shelf in front of him.

Wood of every color and grain, carvings both abstract and tourist-shop hokey, like the tableau of a redneck with his finger hooked through a moonshine jug, stumbling over his coon dog. And there were redbirds and blue birds and jays and robins and every reef fish Thorn had ever seen, and many he had not. There were hundreds of sculptures no more than a few inches high. The abstract pieces were elegant loops and coils of wood that seemed to have been fashioned like sculptors are said to shape rock sometimes, following the seams, the veins, discovering the hidden shape inside the wood.

It was the work of someone both fanciful and reflective. A lot more than a hobby, though maybe not quite art.

"I'm writing a book on the Morales murders," Gundy said without turning around. "So I won't be giving you any hot exclusives."

Thorn stepped to his side and lay the photograph beside Gundy on his bench. He was gripping a detail knife, carving on a small ragged nugget that looked like a peach pit.

Gundy looked down at the photograph, then looked back at the object in his hand, then looked at the photograph again and set his work aside and turned around.

There was a scattering of white hair on his shiny scalp, and one or two longer hairs sprouting from his chin. His eyes were dark and glossy, the color of tobacco juice.

"She tell you about my book?"

"She mentioned it," Thorn said.

"She makes fun of it. But I intend to get it all down. People should know the truth. I think I could make a few dollars, too."

Thorn said nothing. Snake was standing in the doorway. He looked like he needed air. As though murdering one man and meeting the son of another man he'd killed long ago were starting to back up inside him, cramp his breath.

"How you boys come by this photograph?"

Gundy's chin was pulled back, his shoulders erect, and his spine was ramrod-straight. He was no taller than five-five, a bantamweight, and he was nearing eighty, but he struck Thorn as a man who could still hold his own. Some-one whom the punks that roamed his neighborhood probably knew well and no longer tangled with.

"It fell into our hands," Thorn said.

"You know what you got here?"

"Some of it," Thorn said.

"What's your name, and yours?" He looked at Snake.

"I'm Thorn. And he's Snake Morales."

Gundy nodded as if he'd known this all along. Looking at Snake for a full minute. Then he turned and picked up his knife and his carving and went over to a recliner that was crammed into the corner of his workshop. It was fake leather and was ripped along both sides, the stuffing showing. The room was hot, and the fan that revolved overhead did little to alter that.

He sat down and focused his attention on the carving.

"That a peach pit?" Thorn said.

"My brother sends them down from Georgia. He's got a dozen peach trees. All the pits a man could ever need."

"Isn't that awful hard to whittle on?"

"Softer than oak."

"You make that skew knife and that double-cut skew on the bench?"

Gundy squinted at Thorn with an investigator's prying eyes.

"You a woodworker, are you?"

"Nothing as nice as this."

"Yeah, my tools are homemade. I grind the steel, carve the handles. I can't afford the fancy stuff from the stores."

"They're obviously doing the job."

Gundy rubbed his thumb across the rough surface of the seed.

"See for yourself how hard it is."

Gundy held out the pit in one hand, the skew knife in the other.

Thorn had been carving fishing plugs for years, and his hands were practiced with smoothing the edges away, making small fish eyes and tapered fins, but nothing like the detailed work Gundy did.

He took the knife and the peach pit, looked at Gundy, then focused on the nugget of wood and dug the tip into a groove of the fruit seed. He found it more cooperative than he'd imagined. The face that Gundy had been working on had only a nose so far. Thorn scraped out the beginning of a smiling mouth, lips spread wide. It took him only a minute.

He handed the seed back, and Gundy looked at it and looked at Thorn.

"You've done this work before."

Thorn shrugged.

"I've put some hours in with knives and wood. Fishing lures."

"I see," Gundy said. "You're a practical man."

Gundy leaned out and drew open the drawer in a desk beside him and Thorn stepped over to view another display of the man's work. Dozens of peach pits were lined up in neat rows. Each was pared down into a human face. Each was different from the other, a vast range of emotions. Expressions of doubt, of joy, of contemplation. Laughter and frowns. Gundy had painted some, left others natural. Long noses and short, white men, black men, red men, Arabs and Jews. Lined up neatly like a platoon of international warriors.

"Couldn't make a go of it," Gundy said. "Wasted nearly a thousand bucks out of our nest egg, and only managed to sell about five carvings before I had to shut up my business. Isn't any great pent-up demand for whittling. Not that I could discover."

"This is a waste of time." Snake opened the screen door and stepped outside. "You can find your own way home, Thorn."

Gundy looked at him.

"Your parents were killed to start a war."

Snake halted. He turned around and looked back through the screen. Then went back inside.

CHAPTER THIRTY-FIVE

"Defensible grievances," Gundy said. "That's the term the Pentagon liked to use. He hit me, so I get to hit him back. What's good enough for the schoolyard is good enough for our nation's foreign policy."

"I'm not following you," said Thorn.

Snake came closer and eyed Gundy suspiciously.

Gundy took a breath and blew it out.

"All right, then," Gundy said. "I'll slow it down for you."

He worked his peach pit as he spoke, the air around them fragrant with sap and the lemon oils and varnishes that kept the wood shining. There was the sharp scent of epoxy underneath those natural smells.

"They brought me into it a few days after the killings. I was just a kid, never worked anything more complicated than a barroom fight or a stolen car. I took it as an honor, but that's not how it was meant. They wanted me 'cause I was just a second lieutenant, someone they could manipulate. They were just going through the motions, doing it because someone in civilian leadership was having a hissy fit and forced them to investigate. Some senator, I don't think I ever knew his name.

"Top brass didn't think I'd uncover anything useful, and when I did, they weren't much happy with it and I was relieved of duty."

"What'd you find?"

"Southwoods was its code name."

Gundy shaved at the peach pit, eyes on his delicate work.

"I came across the paperwork. Top-secret. Classified. But I read it anyway. It was my job."

"Why was the military investigating at all? It was a civilian crime."

"Not entirely," Gundy said. "Right from the get-go it was clear the killers had had military training. At least a couple did."

"You knew that from what?"

"Weapons they used, ammo. Fingerprints."

"What fingerprints?" Snake said. "Nothing I ever read mentioned prints."

"There weren't any," Gundy said. "Not the kind you could dust for."

Gundy was silent for a moment. He looked up at Thorn and took a long breath, as if he were starting to reconsider his confession.

"The two fingers left behind," Thorn said. "The ones Snake chopped off."

"Correct," Gundy said. "Took me the better part of a month, 'cause I didn't have computers doing the work like they do now. I compared the prints against military records, and a few hundred hours later a name popped up."

"The prints belonged to Edward Runyon."

Gundy stopped his whittling and stared at Thorn.

"You boys better watch yourselves. You're digging in some perilous holes."

"Southwoods," Thorn said. "Tell us about it."

"Well, now, when I got those prints back and I tracked down this Runyon fellow, he was in some special army unit, answering directly to people at the Pentagon. I tried to sit down with him and ask a few questions, and that's about the exact minute I was relieved of duty. They wanted me to do my job, but they didn't want me to do it so well I brought down the government. So that was all she wrote for my military career."

"What're you saying? My parents and sister were killed by the government of the United States?"

Gundy took a minute to answer, focused on his peach pit.

"I'm sorry to say they were, son. I'm even sorrier to say that after I learned that fact, I was unable to bring it to the attention of anyone who gave a shit."

"Southwoods," Thorn said.

"It was dreamed up by a bunch of fanatics in the State Department that called themselves the Cuba Project. Some angry old hawks who never got over the disaster at the Bay of Pigs. They ordered the Joint Chiefs to come up with war-game scenarios. That's how they sold it. Plausible actions providing justification for military intervention in Cuba."

"But it didn't work," Thorn said. "The Morales family died and no war started."

"Starting a war with only one provocation is like trying to light a log with a single match. Of course it wouldn't work. Southwoods called for a coordinated effort, several stages: attacks at Guantánamo Naval Base, sinking boatloads of rafters who were trying to make it to Miami, hijacking civil aircraft and blaming it on the communists. They were even considering shooting down John Glenn, the astronaut, blaming that on Castro, too. Half a dozen hostile acts, all of it Fidel's doing. A slow build.

"Right after the Morales murders they had another incident planned that was supposed to happen out in the Florida Straits. You two were young back then, so you might not remember our pilots flew out of Homestead Air Force Base, made regular runs down to Cuba, always staying a legal twelve miles offshore, of course, just flapping their wings in the dictator's face. Taunting.

"One day a pilot who was in on the plot would be riding at the back of the formation, tail-end Charley, they called it. He'd drift farther and farther back. Then, near the Cuban coast, he was to broadcast that he'd been jumped by MiGs and was going down. Then radio silence. The pilot would turn his plane around and fly directly west at low altitude and land at an auxiliary base. The plane would be stored in a secret hangar and a new tail number applied. With one of our fighter jets apparently shot down, the country would be at war in a week. That's not a single match anymore, that's a damn blowtorch."

"All right," Snake said. "I get the idea."

"Provocation," Gundy said. "That's what they wanted. A pretext for war. Get the American public lathered up, then go in there, throw Castro out, ship all the exiles home."

"Why didn't they do the others on their list?" Thorn said. "The fake shoot-down and all that."

"Lost their nerve, I'd say," Gundy said. "LBJ got wind of it, too. Came flying down here and tore some heads off."

"Pauline Caufield?"

Gundy sniffed and shook his head.

"I believe she ran the show, yeah. Young woman, barely out of college. She's out there supervising the murdering of American citizens so she can get a salary upgrade."

"There was a woman along that night," said Snake. "I heard her voice. She was the boss of the operation. That was Pauline Caufield? The blonde in the picture?"

Snake was standing so stiff he looked like his body had been flash frozen and might shatter with the slightest touch.

"Well, yes, that's her in the picture. But, no, I can say for certain Caufield was not along that night. Far as I know, it was five people in the raiding party. Two from this photo, that little Cuban fellow on one end and Runyon. The others who did the shooting were ones the CIA brought into it. Never got their names. That's where I ran into the stone wall."

"I heard a woman's voice," Snake said. "She said, 'Leave him, let's go.'"

"Could be true," said Gundy. "I had a couple eyewitnesses said there was a woman running with the others. But it wasn't Pauline Caufield. She had an alibi. Rock-solid."

"What was that?" Thorn said.

"She was in jail that night. Her and her buddy Meyer Lansky."

"In jail for what?"

"That's another story," Gundy said.

"We got time."

"Well, I don't have all the particulars. It wasn't central to my investigation. What I do know is, Caufield and Lansky were arrested in a vice raid on a bookie joint out on Miami Beach. Lansky was there to cover the losses on the Clay fight and ream out a few of his people. Apparently he thought he had that fight rigged. Liston was supposed to blind Clay with some stinging jelly he smeared on his gloves, then move in for the kill. Didn't work out that way."

"Clay survived."

"And Lansky lost a mountain of money."

"Caufield went to jail that night, too?"

"Wrong place, wrong time, happened to be with Lansky, although I expect I know where she was headed after that. She just stayed in the city jail overnight. Charges dismissed. Lucky break for her. Kept her clear of the Morales murders. So it wasn't Caufield that Snake heard at his house. That woman was in jail."

Thorn looked back for Snake. But he had vanished.

"You're welcome to that story if you'd like to have it," Gundy said. "I'm about ready to be shut of it myself."

Thorn thanked him for his generosity.

"We talked to a man named Miguel Cielo earlier. Did that name come up in your investigation?"

Gundy nodded.

"He told us something I didn't understand," Thorn said. "That if he'd been in charge, Morales wouldn't have been the target."

"From what I gather," Gundy said, "Cielo was campaigning for some larger, more well-connected militia group. That's what he thought. If thirty, forty people were killed, instead of just seven or eight, the outrage would be that much greater, and declaring war on Cuba would be more likely."

"These are his own people," Thorn said. "Fellow Cubans. And he's pissed off because more of them weren't killed?"

"You got it."

Thorn glanced around the orderly workshop. For years, through some dogged alchemy, Gundy had been transforming his regret and frustration into that drawer of grim, decapitated men, as well as those intricate abstract sculptures. Maybe it wasn't art. Maybe it was something better.

"I can call you a taxi if you like," Gundy said.

"Thank you, sir. I'd appreciate that."

"And by the way, I only met him five minutes ago, but that friend of yours, he looks like he means to take some justice into his own hands."

"Can't say I blame him."

"No," Gundy said. "Can't say I do, either."

CHAPTER THIRTY-SIX

As he was leaving the house, Thorn promised Gundy he would do what he could to pass along the story of the Southwoods operation to a wider audience. Both Shepherd and his wife said they'd certainly appreciate that. It was past time for the American people to know the deeds their elected officials had done, and what they might one day be capable of doing again.

"Wait a minute," Gundy said, and turned and went back into the house.

"Thank you," Mrs. Gundy said when he was gone. "Thank you, sir."

When he came back, Gundy was carrying a sheaf of papers. He held them out to Thorn.

"Something else you can slip into that envelope. Might be of use. I'm sick of having them around."

Thorn glanced at the cover sheet.

In bold print across the top it read: TOP SECRET SPECIAL HANDLING.

Below those words the subject of the memo was short and to the point: "Justification for U.S. Military Intervention in Cuba."

"Be smart with that," Gundy said. "Probably the only copy that exists."

"I'll do my best."

Thorn gave the taxi driver the address on the pink slip

Mariana Cielo had pressed on him. The last stop on the stations of the cross. He sat and looked out the window as the cab rolled through the decayed heart of Miami, heading south past Jackson Memorial Hospital toward the greener neighborhoods.

Thorn hoped that Shepherd Gundy's unburdening would do him some good. Get him an extra hour or two of sleep at least. He meant what he'd told the old couple, that he had every intention of trying to expose Southwoods and anybody still alive who might have had a connection to those events. Though, honestly, he had no idea how he would manage any of that.

The address Mariana Cielo had given him was a block off Flagler in the heart of the residential section of Little Havana. Thorn asked the Haitian driver to wait out front, and he agreed to.

Except for the windows, the house was exactly like every other one on the block. Small, brightly painted, with a tiny attached garage, a single stunted tree in the yard. The grass was freshly mowed and edged, a gardenia bush by the door showing a few early blooms.

The jalousies, however, were from a distant era. Narrow louvered slats that cranked open to snag the breeze. Panes so flimsy, they'd shatter with the accidental brush of a child's passing. Snap one in half, then stick your hand inside to unlatch the door or window, walk right in. Burglary 101.

All the other houses on the street were heavily barred, and some probably had the new bulletproof glass. Alarm-company signs were planted in every yard like miniature tombstones marking the grave of a bygone age.

But the house Thorn walked up to appeared to be unprotected, as though it held some special exemption in the neighborhood that no thief in his right mind would dare challenge.

He knocked and knocked again but heard only silence inside. He was turning to go when the door cracked open and a woman in a gray nun's habit peeked out at him. She was milky-skinned and there was a curl of blond hair showing at

the edge of her hood. She was a few years younger than
Thorn, in her early forties perhaps.

"Could I help you?"

"I was given this address."

"Were you now? And why was that, do you suppose?"

The nun spoke with an Irish lilt, and her big-lipped smile
was rich with mischief.

"I'm not sure why. The woman who directed me here said
this was some kind of shrine, that it would help me with the
problem I'm looking into."

"A shrine, is it? Well, now, I suppose it might be described that way. What sort of problem is it you're working on?"

Thorn drew the photo from the envelope and handed it to
her and she studied it for several moments, then tipped her
smile his way.

"I wouldn't know anything about a boxing match."

"No, ma'am. It's the people in the stands, row three, I'm
interested in. Those fans watching. About an hour after this
picture was taken, some of those people committed an extreme act of violence."

The smile drained from her lips.

"When are we talking about here?"

"February 1964. It took place here in Miami, a father and
mother killed, and their daughter as well. In a neighborhood
a lot like this."

"Are you meaning the Morales family? Jorge and María?"

Thorn stared into her green eyes and said yes, the Morales
family.

"Then it's not a neighborhood a lot like this," the woman
said. "It's a neighborhood exactly like this."

She stepped back and swung open the door.

"I haven't had any visitors before," she said. "But I'll do
my best to answer what you'd like to know. Step right in."

The living area was paneled with dark fake wood like the
waiting room of a cut-rate dentist. Low-slung sectional
couches in a bright orange-and-red stripe faced an even lower
round coffee table. Danish modern, Thorn believed. The shag

rug was avocado green and ended abruptly at the edges of the living room, where the speckled terrazzo took over.

He wasn't sure what odor it was that so clearly evoked the decade of the sixties. Maybe some fiber in the shag rug or the musty, suffocating scent given off by so much paneling.

He went forward into the room and felt the swirl of déjà vu. Though he knew full well he'd never been in that house before, he had been thinking about the place a good deal in the past two days. Imagining what the house must have looked like and sounded like and felt like on that February night in 1964 when the killers poured through the front door and began firing.

On the wall above the Magnavox radio console there was an oil painting of a handsome hippie Jesus, his hands folded in prayer. A Cuban flag curtained a window in the Florida room. *La Estrella Solitaria,* the Lone Star. Red triangle, blue and white stripes. It gave the air a purple glow. Bookshelves were suspended from the ceiling on metal rods. No books, but a dozen black-and-white photos faced the front door.

Thorn stepped close. The girl, Carmen, was about thirteen at the time of the last snapshots, and she had cherubic cheeks and bright eyes that stared into the camera with a fervor that was edged with something like panic. Carlos was short and had blunt features and a leering grin. Snake looked distant and thoughtful and maybe mildly depressed. Jorge Morales, the young father, was a tall, whippy man who favored white shirts, the sleeves rolled three-quarters. His cigarettes dangled like a gangster's. Various tough-guy poses. The mother, María, appeared startled and out of place, as if she'd wandered into each photograph at the last second and would wander off again when the roll had been advanced. A woman of slender build with pretty eyes, short brown hair and a wincing smile.

"This is the Morales family."

"Yes, it is."

"Pardon me, my name is Thorn."

"I'm Sister Sharon, Sharon McElvoy. I'm on loan from St. Michael the Archangel. This house is a special project of the monsignor's. I'm new to this assignment, so you'll forgive me if I can't answer all your questions."

He was standing in the center of the room, his eyes panning back and forth across the photos and furnishings. Absorbing the room's vibrations, which seemed to radiate from the walls like painfully loud music.

Thorn tilted his head back and saw the faded patches in the paint where putty had been used to fill in the craters. Fist-size cavities in the cement where bullets had punched a half foot deep before losing steam. They were everywhere. Thorn lost count at twenty.

Thorn stared into the sunporch, where toys were scattered about on the bare terrazzo. A baseball glove, rubber soldiers, a Barbie in a wedding gown, Ken gazing fondly at his adorable bride. A deck of playing cards and a checkers board.

"I don't understand," he said. "What's going on here?"

"It's a sad house, that I know. Bad things happened here, as you described." Sister Sharon moved across the living room, drifting toward the hall. "We've tried to bring a little sunshine to the place without disturbing the original decor too much. She doesn't like it when we change things around. She gets very upset."

"Who is that?"

"I thought you knew. I thought that's why you'd come. To meet Carmen."

Thorn followed her down the hallway to a young girl's bedroom. There was a white spread on the bed, a collection of stuffed animals clustered on the pillow. A rhino, a duck, a camel. It was on that floor that Runyon's two severed fingers fell. And it was that window they climbed through, Snake and Carmen.

Thorn went to the window and looked out at the freshly mown yard and the street beyond. The lawn where Snake and Carlos and Carmen had run for their lives. Where Humberto Berasategui paid off his debt to Meyer Lansky by firing his pistol and striking down the young girl. Where Snake raised up with the machete and killed the small man with the pencil mustache, hacked him to death on the lawn of his childhood home.

"Carmen is alive?"

The sister smiled quietly and led him out of the room and farther down the hallway. At the master bedroom, she pushed open the door and stepped aside. Thorn looked in and saw a woman in her mid-fifties wearing the same nun's habit that Sister Sharon wore. She was kneeling before an altar that had been erected against the far wall. A gold crucifix hung above it, and on the cross the figure of Christ writhed in agony.

Carmen heard them. She turned and saw Thorn, and her body stiffened like a startled fawn.

"It's all right, Carmen, he's a friend." Sister Sharon moved past Thorn and went to Carmen's side and took the woman's hand in hers and stroked the back of it.

Carmen's face was as childlike as it had been in the photographs on the living-room shelf. Unlined, untanned, a blush in her round cheeks. Her hair was black and glossy, as were her eyes. While her right eye tracked Thorn carefully, her left eye didn't move. It was locked in place. Either it was an orb of glass or some essential muscles had been snipped. A button-shaped depression marked her temple on the same side as the bad eye.

The panicky look passed and her features fell instantly into a dull repose. An expression that settled so naturally on her face, it was clear this was her prevailing mood.

Sister Sharon steered her back to the kneeling bench, and Carmen resumed whatever prayer she was capable of.

Outside in the hallway with the door shut, Thorn said, "She's brain damaged?"

Sister Sharon nodded.

"She's lost the power of speech. She can neither write nor read. Her memory seems to be gone, though she does have nightmares now and then. One can only imagine what she must be reliving. But she can feed herself and she moves quite well. She doesn't require a great deal of care."

"Who else knows about her?"

"Why is that an issue, Mr. Thorn?"

"I've been working alongside her brother, Snake. He believes Carmen's dead. As far as I know *everyone* believes she's dead."

"I'm not sure of the exact history, why it was decided Carmen should live here under parish protection. All that was determined long before I arrived in Miami. But from what I gather, when Carmen was first in the hospital, officials at the time were worried about her safety and made the choice to keep her condition confidential. I believe it was the mayor of Miami who took a personal interest in Carmen's situation and felt it best she receive private care. Her needs have since been supervised by a very generous benefactor. A woman who is a great friend of my church. Part of her tithes are stipulated to be spent by the parish for Carmen's care. Beyond those arrangements, I know nothing more."

In the living room Thorn took another pass by the photographs. The déjà vu had slackened but not gone away. He studied the photos one by one, seeing Carmen as she'd been as a child. Her starched white blouses, her chaste smile. A Bible in her hand in more than one. A rosary, a catechism. The trinkets of religious devotion.

Thorn doubted that Stanton or Lola had been worried about Carmen's safety. What worried them was their own. That Carmen might be able to give a full description of the man who fondled her in her bedroom before Snake intervened. If the cops had an accurate drawing of Edward Runyon, someone might have come forward and the whole operation might have been exposed.

Then Thorn noticed, high on a shelf, a photograph he had missed before. He had to reach up and take it down to view it clearly. It was a color shot of Jorge Morales with his hip cocked against the fender of a chromed-up Studebaker. His arm was slung around the shoulders of a pretty young woman with bright red hair. He wore baggy tan trousers and a loose blue shirt that rippled in the wind. The handsome woman beside him had on checked capri pants and a dark sleeveless blouse. One hand reaching up to rein in her tossing hair.

Jorge's free hand rested on the sleek hood of that fancy car, and the look of smug possessiveness in his eyes might be assigned to his feelings for either the fine automobile or the woman, or perhaps some combination of both.

The woman, in contrast, was gazing at Jorge's profile with such intensity, there was no mistaking the object of her devotion.

"Is this your benefactor?" Thorn asked the sister.

"Her wish is to remain anonymous."

"But this is her. This red-haired woman. This beauty."

"I won't deny it," the sister said.

"Has Carmen ever seen this?"

"That's why it's kept on a high shelf. The lady brought it and put it there for reasons of her own. But apparently the image upset Carmen the one time she noticed it. We can't take it down, because the lady drops by now and then and always looks for it. So it's there, up high, out of sight."

"Her name is Lola, isn't it? Lola King."

The woman said nothing, but her smile was sufficient.

That house of horrors had become a convent, a place where the girl's beliefs in a heavenly order could be lived out in everlasting isolation. A timeless, cloistered existence that was sustained by Lola and Stanton King's unflagging guilt. Or some mutation of parental love that was so twisted, Thorn couldn't quite get hold of it.

They had raised two of the survivors in their own home, and cared for the third in this never-never land. While some might consider their motives big-hearted and pure, to Thorn it all stank of murder.

He was headed for the door and a breath of fresh air when a small detail hiding within one of the photographs registered.

He walked back to the shot of Jorge and Lola leaning against the car and held up the boxing photo next to it.

"What is it?" Sister Sharon asked.

"I'm no expert on women's clothes," he said.

When Sharon came to his side, Thorn touched Lola's checked capri pants in the color photograph, then touched the woman's trouser leg that was barely visible in the boxing photo. The woman's right leg was pressed against Meyer Lansky's left. The boxing photo had been cropped to exclude the rest of the woman who sat beside the mobster. All but that leg.

"I am no expert, either," the sister said. "But yes, they appear remarkably alike. And the shoes as well."

The shoes in both photos were black and had silver buckles the size of half dollars. It wasn't DNA, but it was plenty. Lola had been Lansky's date for Clay versus Liston. Which meant that it was almost certainly Lola who went along with Runyon and Humberto that night to watch her lover die for the crime of abandoning her.

If there was more proof floating out there somewhere, Thorn felt no further need to search for it.

He thanked the sister and went out into the hot sunlight.

Sister Sharon stood in the doorway for a moment, waiting for some last word, an expression of gratitude or censure. But Thorn was fresh out of emotion. He was just relieved to be outside in the lively air.

CHAPTER THIRTY-SEVEN

Sister Sharon called the monsignor, and the monsignor called her. The monsignor called to say a man had been at the house. A man had been asking questions, looking at photographs. And he had met the young lady. Carmen. A man. A man in the house.

After the man left, the nun felt bad that she'd opened the door to a stranger. The nun thought the monsignor should know. The monsignor thought Lola should know as well. Felt that Lola should know about the man coming into the house. The man had showed a great interest in that photograph, the color one. Lola leaning against a car.

Lola listened to the monsignor and said nothing in reply.

It was the queen's sacred duty to dominate. Without a dominant queen, the hive could not function. If the ruling queen died, another female wasp immediately asserted herself and dominated. Without a queen, there could be no workers, no drones, no laying of eggs in the cells, no feeding of larvae with the dead insects she brought. There could be no defense of the hive. Without a queen, the hive was in mortal jeopardy. The hive was exposed. The hive, the hive.

The monsignor called to say a man had entered the house. A blond man, tanned and tall. An invader. The monsignor apologized. The nun was new on the job and she'd been caught off guard and wasn't sure she'd done right. The monsignor thought Lola should know, should know. The monsignor thought she should know.

Sweet Jesus. The nest was cracked. The center exposed, its sticky gold. The stinging swarm with nowhere to go. Sting sting but nowhere to go. A buzzing cloud around her head, a halo of poison. Nowhere left to go.

The drone of wasps, their stingers erect—everywhere she looked was a gray blur.

Wasps defended their hive. It was their destiny, their blood oath. They defended even broken ones. Even hives lying asunder. They would never give up. Under attack, they would sting and sting. They would even kill members of their own colony, any threat to the hive, any threat at all.

Lola hung up the phone. She stood for a long while, thinking. Then she opened the box of pellets. She loaded pellets into the eight-shot rotary magazines. She loaded every magazine she had. Twelve, thirteen, fourteen. She loaded and loaded.

She stood at the attic slats, wooden louvered slats, and looked out at the yard below, the pool, the patio, the driveway to the street.

Beside her, hanging from a single filament, the papery nest was hectic. Wasps came and went, returned and left again, killing their prey and feeding the hive. Feeding, killing, feeding, killing. Egg, larva, pupa, adult. The metamorphosis was fully under way.

Snake spoke Carmen's name in the quiet sanctuary of the Church of the Little Flower. He spoke her name, but she made no reply. She had no counsel, no encouragement, no consolation. The big room swelled with silence.

Snake paged through Carmen's Bible. He read a passage, read another, but none of it made sense. Snake shut the Bible and thought of Cassius. He thought of the noble young man who was so flamboyant, so serious at the core.

But Snake was no Cassius and never had been. All they shared was that both were once outsiders, unwelcome in a foreign land. Cassius had fought his way into the hearts of his enemy. Those who once despised him ultimately embraced him and crowned him as their own. He'd earned it all by sweat and stamina and courage. He grew strong and stronger, and his smile lit up the stages of the world. Cassius was a winner, a champion, a man triumphant. And look at Snake. Opposite in every way.

At the front of the church the old woman who'd been in the confessional drew the curtain aside and hobbled down the aisle. Snake took his turn inside the ornate box. The purple curtain drew back and Father Meacham's profile appeared.

"Forgive me, Father, for I have sinned."

Father Meacham looked at Snake through the grate.

"I killed a man today. I shot him in the chest. His name was Edward Runyon. He was the man who molested my sister just before she was shot down. I killed him and I feel no regret. When I leave here today I'm going to hunt down the rest who were involved. I know their names now. I'm going to track them down and kill each one. Stanton King and Lola King and Pauline Caufield and any others who get in my way."

Father Meacham was staring wordlessly at Snake.

"I descended to the bottom of the bottomless cave, and I shined my light in the face of the monster. I found out what happened and why. Now I will have my vengeance."

Father Meacham closed his eyes, bowed his head, and was silent.

"Does God have anything he wants to say to me, Father?"

Snake riffled the pages of Carmen's Bible and stared at the priest. Several moments passed without response.

"No?" Snake said, and rose to his feet. "I didn't think so."

Snake waited a moment more, then walked down the aisle to the exit. He left the Bible behind in the confessional. He had no further use for it. The truth had not set him free. Perhaps more killing would.

Sugarman had lost a dangerous amount of blood. It was touch and go.

"Touch and go? Are you saying he could die?" In the backseat of the taxi, Thorn pressed the cell phone hard against his ear. Alexandra sounded far away. It was difficult for Thorn to tell if it was just a poor connection or if the frailness of her voice signaled the new condition of their bond.

"That's all they've told me, just what I've told you."

"And Stanton King is dead?"

"That's right."

"Pauline Caufield is injured and on the run."

"On the run, or on the attack. I don't know. She's obviously desperate. She's probably got a concussion. Beyond that, I can't say."

"When will you know more about Sugar?"

"He should be out of surgery in a couple of hours."

"And you?"

"They have to do the arm again, new pins, cast. I'll be all right."

"They're giving you something for the pain?"

She was silent for several seconds, and Thorn thought he'd lost her.

"You still there?"

"Yes," she said. "They're doing what they can about my pain."

The taxi driver pulled onto St. Gaudens Road. Stanton King's street. Lola's street. Snake and Carlos's street.

"Alex. I'm so goddamn sorry."

"I'm sorry, too, Thorn."

The line was filled with the buzz of silence, then a click ended it.

They're doing what they can about my pain. The careful phrasing wasn't lost on Thorn. The sort of pain that tormented the tissues of the body could be remedied or dulled. But the kind of hurt Alex was referring to could not be lessened by drugs or any man-made potion. From her tone, Thorn doubted that time or any comfort he might offer would do much good, either.

Thorn counted out the fare and added a tip.

Carrying the manila envelope, he walked to the front

gates of Stanton King's estate and looked down the drive. The gray Audi that Snake and he had been using was parked some distance from the front door. Near the Audi, a white Ford sedan with dark windows had rammed into the unforgiving trunk of an oak tree. Its grille was crumpled, and wisps of steam from its radiator coiled into the lower branches. The white Ford didn't wear government plates, but it might as well have.

Thorn held his position and surveyed the grounds.

He had seen the house before in the photographs from the forty-year-old newspaper. The photos had presented it in an idyllic light—an opulent refuge for the two boys who'd lost their parents and sister in an explosion of violence. But the dwelling Thorn saw before him now was anything but idyllic.

The house was quiet and loomed with a faded nobility over its neighborhood. The Spanish mission architecture was reminiscent of some ancient Palm Beach hotel built for men in white suits and women in wide-brimmed hats and sun veils who played croquet and took their tea while European waiters tended to their every whim.

But the King estate was in the last stages of disintegration. The lawn was ragged, the paint washed out and patchy. The pink roof tiles were crumbling and blackened by mildew. Screens were ripped or missing entirely from the windows. It was the sort of house and grounds that required constant attention and an uninterrupted cash flow, and it obviously had been receiving neither for a very long time.

When grand old ladies like this one fell into such a sad state, it was time to sell the land and take the real estate winnings elsewhere. But people like Stanton King didn't abandon South Florida. They had spent too many years setting their roots in that rocky, forbidding ground. Roots that tough and tangled in the limestone and coral rarely gave way.

Thorn stepped through the gate and onto the King property. Miles away over the Atlantic, dark clouds were muscling together and sliding upward toward the sun. Pulses of lightning brightened within the cloud banks, making muffled gray explosions. The clouds churned and roiled and half the sky had turned a frosty gray, while the other half was still bright blue.

It was weather that could swing either way: hours of raging storms with jagged shoots of lightning, or a day of perfect springtime sun. But even if it stayed out there and didn't roll ashore, the black squall had an unsettling effect, flickering and rumbling like a distant battlefield. A reminder of the indifferent generals perched high above the human fields of war.

This sunny driveway where Thorn stood was not where he wanted to be, and this was not what he wanted to be doing. But he was no longer factoring in his own desires. He was acting on behalf of Lawton Collins, and in service to Mr. and Mrs. Shepherd Gundy, and for a girl who'd lost her life forty years ago but lingered in a dreary, unending twilight.

Snake Morales was on that list, too. His sister, Carmen, was still alive. Lola and Stanton, out of spite or some other brand of selfishness, had not informed him of the fact. Not that there was much hope that such news would heal Snake's injuries; still, it seemed a small measure of justice that Thorn should pass the knowledge on.

Ten yards into King's estate he saw the first sprinkle of blood on the flagstones. A few steps ahead was another spatter, and a yard beyond that was still more. A trail that headed directly toward the front door.

He touched the toe of his boat shoe to the closest dots of blood and smeared. They were only minutes old.

Squinting into the afternoon light, he tried to read the trail's meaning. He took another step and changed his angle and saw that ten feet ahead the path of dark specks divided briefly, then rejoined. Which said that it was the track of not just one injured party, but two. The second had followed the path of the first but had lurched at least once along the way.

Thorn was stepping closer to the house, past the first dash of blood, when something plucked at his shirtsleeve and he felt a stunning jolt in his right biceps.

He staggered backward. The pain was intense, but after a

second or two he found that it was localized, no more than a quick jab with an ice pick.

At the spot of the wound the sleeve of his denim shirt was pocked. He rubbed a finger against the throb and felt a lump embedded just below the skin.

He retreated another step, then another, till he was two paces behind the first spray of blood. He peered up at the house but saw no sign of life. With a finger he widened the rip in his shirt, then he set his teeth and squeezed the flesh around the lump. He had to use his fingernail to dig the object free.

He held it in his palm. The lead pellet had a flattened base, while its business end was sharpened to a nasty point. It resembled a squat steeple glistening with blood.

Ammo from an air rifle of some sort. Apparently the state-of-the-art BB gun was a hell of a lot more potent than the plinkers of Thorn's youth.

He looked up at the house again, scanning the windows for any movement. One by one he tracked across them but saw no shadow, no silhouette, no twitch.

Another pellet stung his throat but didn't lodge, and while he was scooting farther back, another skimmed the side of his temple. Thorn moved away another step, then halted. He watched the projectiles hit and skid and ricochet a few feet ahead of him. A new shot every other second. He stood there, safely out of range, and rubbed at the aching knot on his arm and wiped the smear of blood from his neck.

The pellets pinged against the flat rocks at his feet and skittered into the grass. He counted eight shots, then there was a pause of ten or fifteen seconds, apparently for reloading. Then the shooting resumed. This clearly wasn't a pump-action single-loader. It was a semiautomatic with a magazine, eight pellets per clip. Each shot was sent flying by a burst of pressurized gas.

Fifty feet was the distance to the front of the house. If the shooter was as skilled as the previous shots suggested, Thorn figured he might take one or two more hits before he made it across. Fewer if he was lucky, more if he was not. Stumbling or stalling out from pain was not an option. Worst case, a pellet would find his eye.

He could try the back side of the house, or search for another entry point south. But the shooter might have those sides covered just as well or better.

He lifted the tail of his shirt and tucked the manila envelope under his belt. He set his feet, chose his course, lifted a hand to defend his eyes, and broke into a sprint.

CHAPTER THIRTY-EIGHT

Inside the front door he halted and took stock. The rump of a pellet protruded from his left palm. He pinched it out and tossed it on the rug. His earlobe was torn and bled down his neck like a botched piercing. Somehow a third slug had caught him high in the shoulder. He twisted his arm in that direction, bent his wrist backward, but could only graze the spot with his fingertips. No way to dig the sucker out.

Thorn leaned against the foyer wall and got his breath.

After a minute he drew out Alexandra's cell phone and flipped it open. Summoning the cops was the rational choice. It would have been Sugarman's method. And clearly that made more sense than forging on, unarmed, into an unknown house and another spray of lead. The accumulated pain was starting to swirl his thoughts. His vision was going in and out of focus, and his breath was ragged and burned his throat.

He stared at the phone's keypad and punched in 911, but on the first ring he heard a groan from the adjacent room. A woman in serious pain. He clicked the phone shut, shoved it in his pocket, and pushed himself off the wall.

The blood trail he'd been following divided a few feet on. One track led into the room where the woman's voice was coming from, and the other traveled up the stairs.

In the study, slumped in a leather wingback chair, he found a trim blond woman speaking to herself in a voice so shrill and quaking, it seemed not quite human. The front of her blue shirt was soaked with blood and her lips were smeared with red, as if she'd been feasting on fresh kill.

She lifted her chin and gazed at Thorn. Her left eye was swollen shut. There were welts on her left cheek where the pellets had struck and bounced away. One slug had punctured her throat. The wound was a ragged tear whose edges fluttered as the woman breathed.

With her good eye, she watched Thorn approach, then extended her open hand as if begging for alms.

Her voice was moist and nearly unintelligible.

She spoke the word twice before Thorn understood that she was demanding he hand over the photograph.

"You're Pauline Caufield."

She sputtered Thorn's name.

"Who's shooting?" he said.

The woman's wild one-eyed gaze shifted to the doorway and the foyer beyond. Her voice was a faint gargle.

"Lola," she said. "The bitch."

The decent, caring thing to have done was call for paramedics. But Thorn was no longer feeling virtuous toward these people. Let them suffer, let them bleed, let them kill one another off one by one. It was still less than they deserved. People so depraved by political zeal, so embittered from being ditched by a lover, that they'd sacrificed an entire family for career advancement and personal revenge. Together they'd struck down eight souls one winter night and left the survivors to bleed to death slowly over the years. No end, however agonizing, would be fair repayment. Let her suffer, let her die by slow degrees. She had earned the fate.

The staircase was carpeted with an Oriental pattern, worn away to the fabric backing where generations of footsteps had passed.

The blood trail Thorn followed up the stairs was surely Snake's. Fired at by his own adoptive mother for reasons Thorn could not imagine. Some poisoned logic, some madness that drove a woman to shoot at the boy she'd raised as a son. It really didn't matter anymore. Nothing mattered but bringing this to a close. There was no wisdom to be had. No insight into the human condition. Thorn wanted only to shut this engine down and go home to Key Largo and stare at the sky.

On the landing of the second floor, the trail led to the right, down the carpeted hallway. Thorn looked for a place to set aside the envelope with the boxing photo and the Southwoods documents he'd gotten from Gundy, and the Xeroxes.

He propped it against the wall at the head of the stairs. Then he turned back to the blood and followed it down the corridor until, ten feet later, it came to an abrupt stop. A shut door was to his right, and to his left was a window that looked out on oak branches.

He swung to the door and twisted the knob, threw it open, and ducked back behind the wall. But no lead pellets came flying out. He stayed there half a minute, then peeked around the edge. It was a bedroom with a four-poster in the center. Cardboard boxes were stacked on the comforter, old newspapers piled along one wall, a set of dining chairs heaped in a corner. A storage room. Empty except for a moth that fluttered through the dust motes illuminated by a single window.

Thorn returned to the hallway. A mockingbird trilled a song on a branch just outside. He heard the low hum of traffic roll in from Main Highway, and the rumble of that black squall still out at sea. But nothing else.

He looked up at the ceiling and saw the attic cord dangling at arm's length. A knob at its end.

That explained the commanding angle the shooter had. A sweeping view from one side of the house to the other. It also made clear the pellet implanted in his shoulder. Lola had fired straight down at him as he was just feet from the front door.

The wound in his shoulder muscle and the one in his palm and the other in his biceps thumped in unison. The light in the hallway dimmed and came back full strength as if some major appliance had cycled on and off. The plaster walls swayed and the floor felt shaky beneath his feet.

Thorn touched the phone in his pocket. As wobbly as he

was, he still didn't want assistance. It was, after all, just an old woman with a high-powered BB gun. Nothing he couldn't handle on his own.

Thorn reached up and took hold of the knob to the swing-down steps. He forced himself to take two measured breaths before he yanked the cord.

The springs creaked and the trapdoor separated from the ceiling and tilted down toward him. Then it all came at once. As the door swung open, the cord broke from his grip and the stairs began to clatter down, and in the next instant a human body tumbled on top of him and drove him to the floor.

The back of Thorn's skull smacked the carpet and the light in the hallway fluttered to twilight, then slowly revived. The man who was sprawled on top of him was muscular and heavy and pinned Thorn flat to the floor as if by his weight alone he meant to crush the air from Thorn's lungs.

When his eyes finally cleared, Thorn shoved at the man's chest, heaved, and punched until he realized the body wasn't punching back. He swiveled to the right and pried himself loose, thrusting the man away.

Snake Morales rolled onto his stomach and was still. Threads of blood leaked from both his ears. Somehow Lola had managed to disable him long enough to fire her pellet gun into his brain.

The air flooding down from the attic was hot and dry and full of dust and the smell of rat shit and rotting wood. Thorn took hold of the handrails and mounted the steps.

He was prepared to take as many pellets as required to rush Lola and disarm her. But she didn't fire, didn't make a sound as he surfaced into the overheated air. She was sitting in a rocking chair that was wedged into the far corner of the space.

She wore a brown shapeless robe with gold bands around its sleeves. Sandals on her feet and a single gold chain around her neck. She had the look of banished royalty. A queen dethroned and exiled to the prison tower. Her red hair was loose and hung across her shoulders. In her lap the black molded air pistol was trained at Thorn's face.

He'd been stared at by more than his share of freak jobs and killers, but he'd never felt so invaded by a pair of eyes. Thorn tried to reconcile this woman sitting before him with the amorous beauty who'd been leaning against that fancy car, staring at the profile of her lover, Jorge Morales. But no vestige of that devoted woman in the photograph looked out of the remote and glassy eyes of Lola King. As though sometime after that photo was taken, when Jorge Morales cast her off, whatever fragile connection Lola had maintained with humankind was severed.

Thorn stood his ground and measured the distance to her rocker.

The gears that operated the stairway must have been on some kind of spring-loaded return. For as Thorn took his first step toward Lola, the trapdoor cranked and heaved, then slammed heavily shut behind him. He whirled toward the noise and realized as he was going around that this must have been the same mistake Snake had made. A diversion that gave Lola just enough time to rise from her rocker, step close to Thorn's head, and point her pistol into the dark, welcoming center of his ear.

Thorn fell away from the shot and wrecked her aim by just an inch or two. The pellet tore into the muscles of his neck. A bolt of voltage ran down both arms, and he felt a warm numbness spread across his back. He rolled away onto the plywood floor. Lola followed him, attacking with two more shots that planted bits of lead near the base of his spine.

He found his feet, ducked his head, and rammed his shoulder into her gut and drove her backward, his arms wrapped around her narrow waist. A football tackle. He shoved her toward the front of the house, toward the wall of louvered slats she'd used as her hunter's blind. He meant to ram her as hard as space and strength allowed, hammer her backbone against the timbers of the attic wall. Knock her unconscious or paralyze her; it hardly mattered.

But the floor-to-ceiling wooden louvers were as decayed as the rest of that old house and the frame gave way as

Lola's backside smashed against it. Wood gone soft and useless from years of neglect. It offered no resistance but exploded in a gust of chalky powder, and Thorn was suddenly standing on his tiptoes, tilting forward, two floors above the flagstone drive with nothing but his balance keeping him and Lola in place.

They teetered for another few seconds in that grim embrace, with Thorn still gripping her around the waist, his shoulder planted in her belly, fighting for his equilibrium while Lola held perfectly still, suspended thirty feet from the earth.

Inches from his eyes a wasp nest hung from a timber like a gray paper flower, the wasps circling their hive on full alert.

In his arms Lola released the one-handed clutch she'd taken on the back of his shirt and twisted her torso in his grasp. Thorn was just about to win the battle against gravity, tipping his weight back toward the safety of the attic, when he felt the hot muzzle of her air pistol settle against his ear and screw down tight.

He let her go. Gave a shove and stepped back. She fired twice as she fell. One pellet struck him square in the forehead and knocked him back against the trapdoor. He lay there for a moment, stunned. Then under the strain of Thorn's weight, the stairway door began to open.

He lifted his head, struggled to rise like a boxer trying to beat the count. But his head sagged back and the floor continued to give way. One final time he tried to roll to safety but was too weak, too slow.

Beneath him the steps swung open and unfolded, and Thorn thumped and rolled down them to the corridor and came to rest beside Snake Morales.

When his head cleared a little, Thorn reached out and touched a finger to Snake's throat but found no pulse, only a quickly fading warmth. Thorn drew back his hand and closed his eyes, and his last feeling before spiraling down into oblivion was something close to brotherly remorse.

It was ten or fifteen minutes before he moved again. First

opening his eyes, sorting out his location, and the events of the previous half hour. Lola plunging two stories to the driveway. The origin of the knot in the center of his forehead.

He got to his knees and decided that was plenty far enough for the moment. The mockingbird outside the window continued to sing as if the world had been proceeding just fine without Thorn being conscious of it.

He struggled to his feet and started for the stairway, but it moved away from him, then moved again and again after that. So he settled for the wall where he'd left the envelope and planted his butt against it and rode it to the floor and eased himself down onto the worn carpet.

He picked up the envelope and set it in his lap.

A lone wasp buzzed by his face and dropped on the rug at his feet. For a moment it explored the frayed carpet, then finding no useful nourishment, it lifted off and sailed at the windowpane. It bumped against the glass and vectored off in another direction and was gone.

Outside that window Thorn saw the black storm had been coaxed north by steering currents. The raging clouds, the booms of thunder, the ragged spears of lightning paraded just offshore. Marching up the state to find another point of attack.

Feeling no great sense of urgency, Thorn decided to stay right where he was until the walls of the house stopped moving. Then he would try another time to stand, to walk, to leave, and make his way back home to Key Largo.

CHAPTER THIRTY-NINE

Sugarman and Thorn and Alex briefly occupied nearby rooms at Mariners Hospital in Tavernier. Sugar required surgery to repair his lacerated artery, and hours of transfusions. Thorn was sitting beside his bed when Sugar finally woke and smiled and asked what day it was and fell back asleep before Thorn could reply.

Fifty-three stitches were needed to sew up all the holes in Thorn's hide. Some nerves had been compromised in his back, and the pain he felt seemed distinctly out of proportion to the size and number of his wounds.

Alex was transported up to Baptist Hospital in Miami, where new surgery on her arm and shoulder took place. After twenty-four hours Sugar and Thorn were discharged from Mariners and they went together to Thorn's house to recuperate.

Ballistics showed the pistol used to murder Alan Bingham was the same one that cut down Lawton Collins and wounded Alexandra. The .22 revolver had not yet been recovered, but with Alexandra's testimony, the blame for both deaths was placed squarely on the Morales brothers.

Alex claimed to have passed out immediately after being shot and therefore had not witnessed the clubbing death of Carlos. She was holding to that assertion despite serious attempts to shake her statement by the county's lead homicide detectives. It was her parting gift to Thorn, protecting him from the legal jeopardy he had rightly earned.

Furthermore, the investigators and DA decided that after fatally shooting Snake Morales with a pellet gun, Lola King, apparently in a fit of despair, had thrown herself from the second-story attic of her Coconut Grove mansion. Blood-stains in the study of the house, especially those on a leather wingback chair, remained a mystery, as did similar stains on the second-floor landing near the stairway.

A sniper in the Key Largo woods had killed Stanton King and wounded Sugarman, then vanished. In the hospital Alexandra Collins named the shooter as Pauline Caufield, and hours later a woman matching her description was stopped at Miami International, trying to buy a first-class ticket to Quito, Ecuador, with an invalid passport. Pauline Caufield's name was on the federal no-fly watch list, but somehow the slender blond woman managed to escape air-port authorities and was the subject of an ongoing manhunt.

The next day's paper carried the story of the King family's disintegration. But without any mention of the Southwoods op-eration, the story lacked a centerpiece motive. Sugarman's cell phone rang constantly and a couple of reporters showed up in Thorn's driveway, but he told them that Sugar was not yet ready to talk. The police took preliminary statements and promised to delve further when Sugar was up to the task. But they didn't seem particularly inspired. They had Lawton's killer and they had a murder-suicide explanation for Snake and Lola, and seemed in no hurry to complicate their investigation.

Alexandra persuaded Dan Romano, her old boss at Homi-cide, to use the Miami PD computer to run a background check in hopes of narrowing down Caufield's current where-abouts, but the data available on Pauline Caufield was nonex-istent. A woman who appeared to be even more anonymous than Thorn. Even the white Ford left behind at the King es-tate was a dead end. It was registered to TransAmerica Con-struction Corporation, but no one at the company had ever heard of an employee by the name of Caufield.

As to the shooting death of Edward Runyon on Le Jeune Road, dozens of eyewitnesses came forward to positively identify Snake Morales as the man who gunned him down while he sat in his green Jaguar. However, there was far less agreement on the description of Snake's sidekick in that shooting episode.

Some witnesses portrayed him as tall and blond and decidedly Anglo. Others were sure he was short and dark and Hispanic. A prominent attorney who had been passing by the scene at that precise moment, a man named Mo Chonin, was willing to stake his reputation on the fact that Snake's accomplice was a stocky woman with tattoos covering both arms. The end result was that no artist's sketch of Thorn was ever posted and no one from law enforcement had come knocking on his door. At least so far.

Alexandra called several times to check on Sugar, and even though Thorn spoke to her on each of those occasions, nothing intimate passed between them. Alex responded to each of Thorn's apologies and his attempts to discuss their future with long, unbroken silences. She was not unfriendly, but that was the most he could say. He truly couldn't blame her. Maybe a year from now, when her suffering had slackened, there might be a chance for them. But Thorn wasn't holding out much hope.

He lay in the sunshine and nursed warm beers, and spent the long hours while Sugarman was drowsing thinking the situation through. At this point he was free to simply walk away from the whole affair, lucky to have survived with as little scarring as he had. But he had made a vow to Shepherd Gundy and his wife, and every hour that passed without his taking action made the simmer of guilt in his belly grow.

On their second day out of the hospital, he and Sugar were finishing breakfast on the dock that rimmed the lagoon. Thorn with his shirt off, letting his wounds take some air before he cleaned them again and refreshed the bandages. From his tumble down the stairs, he'd bruised some muscles and done some undiagnosed harm to internal organs. It hurt to stand up or sit down or lie on the bed. Hurt to go up stairs or go down them. There wasn't a position he'd found that didn't hurt. But he was still looking.

Sugarman had just finished reading the latest piece in the *Herald*. A follow-up from the day before, mostly a recounting of what they already knew, with a few quotes from Stanton King's neighbors, who were appalled such violence could happen on their lovely street.

"The tribute to Lawton, that was nice, very moving."

"Not long enough by half," Thorn said.

Thorn watched a platoon of pelicans riding the morning breeze.

"What you should do, you should send a dozen roses to the clerk at the porn shop. She must've had a crush on you, stashing the baseball bat or whatever the hell she did with it. Not to mention giving the cops a bad ID."

Thorn considered a quip about the biker granny and her piercings, but he couldn't force it out. He wasn't feeling lighthearted, might not get back to that state for a while.

Thorn picked up the last greasy curl of bacon and slipped it into his mouth. It hurt to eat. Chew, swallow. It hurt to think about eating.

They looked out at the lagoon for a while. Thorn worked on easing down slow breaths. One, two, three. See how many he could string together before Alex came back into his head. Her smile, her touch, her long limbs, the way she never strayed an inch from what was real and true. And then, hell, there was Lawton, too, something the old guy said, one of his pronouncements, one of his wacky jibes.

Thorn waved a gnat away. He cleared his throat and tapped a finger against Sugarman's laptop lying on a table between them.

"Could you show me something?"

"On the computer?"

"Yeah, that thing with the photographs you were doing last week."

Sugar gave him a wary look, then sighed, switched on the machine, and took Thorn through the steps of locating photo files and opening them.

Thorn was leaning over his shoulder, watching Sugar work the mouse pad to bring up photographs of his twin daughters.

"What're you up to, Thorn? What's going on in that head of yours?"

"I'll tell you. Just not right now."

He finished the lesson to Thorn's satisfaction, then Sugar stood and walked out to the dock. He was still weak and moved like a man twice his age, but the doctors agreed he was in remarkable shape, considering he'd practically been drained of blood.

"Well, I'll be damned," Sugar called.

"What?"

"Your friend's back."

Thorn hobbled out to the dock.

A large snook was cruising the rocky ledges of the lagoon.

"Couldn't be," Thorn said.

"Looks like the same one to me."

"What's it been, less than a week, she's got three lures in her lip already."

"Four," Sugar said. "Like she came back for you to clean her up again."

"Or she's just showing off."

"What're you going to do?"

Thorn watched the snook wavering through the clear water. Tough old warhorse looking for trouble.

"Let her be," Thorn said. "Just let her be."

About midnight, when Sugar began to snore in the guest room, Thorn stole through the house and carried the envelope with the photo and the papers out to his VW.

An hour later he parked half a block down the street from Alexandra's. He turned into her walk and went to her front door. At the rear of the house, a single light burned in her bedroom. He didn't let himself picture her or what she might be doing this late, alone.

Thorn stood on her porch and looked up at the roofline

overhead. He'd fixed her leak at least, left her with some minor improvement. He stared at the patch of grass where he'd dropped on Carlos Morales's back and stabbed him with the electric drill. Where he'd met Snake and first seen the photograph of the Liston-Clay fight. Where he and Lawton headed off to rescue Alex.

Through the front door Thorn heard the click of Buck's nails coming down the hardwood floor of the hallway, then the dog began to snuffle at the edge of door as he caught Thorn's scent. He whined once, then scratched a paw at the handle.

Thorn drew a breath and let it out. He slipped the cell phone from his pocket and lifted the lid of Alex's mailbox and settled the phone inside. He turned and walked back to the sidewalk, then crossed that dark, empty street.

Yellow crime-scene tape still stretched across Alan Bingham's front door. It took Thorn less than a minute to pry open a back window and crawl inside the photographer's house.

Thorn found Bingham's computer in a study piled with books. He didn't turn on lights but used the streetlamp's glow to guide him.

Permeating the house was the harsh, acrid reek of a death chamber: gunfire and ashes and blood. Thorn sat down at Bingham's desk and found the switch to power up the computer.

It was minutes later that Thorn located the folders containing Alan Bingham's digitally preserved photos. Not the high-quality resolution of the originals, but when Thorn enlarged them so they filled the entire computer screen, they were vivid and impressive. Below each photograph Alan Bingham had typed notes to himself, the kind of things one might scribble on the backs of old snapshots to remind oneself later who these people were and why they'd mattered so much at one time. The year, the date, the location, people's names.

Thorn hadn't actually known what he was looking for. He'd had a notion that he wanted to find an uncropped version of the boxing shot that included Lola King to positively confirm what he already believed.

It took him half an hour, scanning through files and fold-ers until he found one labeled *Cassius-Liston, '64,* and clicked it open.

He sat back in Alan Bingham's chair and studied the image for several moments. It was better than he'd hoped. Lola was sitting in full view beside Meyer Lansky, and on the other end of their group there was a man with slick brown hair and a movie-star jawline seated next to Humberto Berasategui.

The caption beneath the photo named all but one of the people in row three. Five names Thorn already knew. Lola, Lansky, Runyon, King, Berasategui. Alan Bingham had not discovered Pauline Caufield's name, but he did know the one person Thorn didn't. The new man sitting beside Humberto was conventionally handsome and wore the relaxed smile of someone who had never suffered a doubt in his life. His name was Hadley S. Waters.

Thorn located the printer and switched it on and made a copy of Bingham's uncropped photo.

He was trying to understand the meaning of what he'd just discovered. Bingham obviously knew who most of those people were and must have had some inkling that he'd cap-tured on film an odd gathering, to say the least. Whether Alan knew more than that or suspected anything so extreme as what turned out to be the truth, Thorn could only guess. Bing-ham's decision to include the photo in his exhibit may have been based on nothing other than aesthetic grounds, with the intriguing sidebar that some of the people in row three had become familiar public figures. What Bingham knew or may have suspected was a mystery that died with him.

It took Thorn another few minutes to locate the Internet search engine Sugarman preferred. In the empty slot, he typed *Hadley S. Waters* and sat back and looked at the screen fill up with information. Current director of the CIA. Lead-ing contender for the Republican presidential nomination. Numerous photographs of Mr. Waters standing next to world leaders.

Thorn switched off the computer and climbed back out the window with his loot. He drove along the deserted streets to downtown Miami, located the main office building of the *Herald,* and parked in the visitors' lot.

From two A.M. to sunrise Thorn scribbled on the legal pad he'd brought along. He made his handwriting as legible as possible and tried to keep his grammar under control and his sentences short and to the point.

Combining what Sugar had told him about the origin of Southwoods and the bribe Stanton King made to Meyer Lansky, Thorn sketched out the entire story. A woman scorned by her lover. Jorge Morales committing the unforgivable sin of rejecting Lola Henderson. And then a man so in love with Lola, he was willing to exhaust his family fortune to have his rival murdered in an attempt to win Lola's affection. That personal story had fused with the political one. A group of young covert operatives trying their best to provoke a war.

Thorn kept it to the facts alone, leaving out speculation and guesswork about motives and avoiding any cheap psychologizing.

He was no practiced writer and had to wad up half the sheets on the pad before he was satisfied with his effort. Five double-spaced pages that spelled out the history of everything he knew, everything Gundy had told him and everything Sugar and Alex had learned. He left out only a couple of small self-incriminating parts. The baseball bat, the gentle shove he gave Lola, assisting her on her last flight. He included what little he knew of Pauline Caufield, and her boss and former co-conspirator, Mr. Hadley S. Waters.

When he finished, the sun was breaking free of the Atlantic, and the Miami sky was rosy and streaked with stripes of darker pink and a few bright golden tendrils that coiled off the edges of the first clouds of the day.

As the morning shift flooded into the office building, Thorn joined them and managed to scoot past security and make his way to the sports desk.

He found the office he was looking for and entered. The secretary behind the desk was sipping coffee and listening to a talk show on the radio. She turned it down and asked Thorn if she could help him.

"Is Mr. Pope in?"

"Mr. Pope is on assignment. A golf tournament. Something I can do?"

"Could you see he gets this?"

Thorn handed her the envelope. Battered and blood-stained, it was stuffed with his own writing and Bingham's uncropped photo and the one he'd displayed in his exhibit. Also there was the top-secret Southwoods document and the Xeroxed pages that included Mr. Pope's own articles about Cassius from the winter of 1964.

"It's not exactly a sports story," Thorn said. "But there's sports in it. A famous boxing match that happened not ten minutes from where we're standing. And there's murder and treason and some other things I don't fully understand. It might call for a little more digging. And for sure it's going to require some guts to take on the people the story will expose."

The woman stared at him, and her hand drifted toward her phone as if she meant to summon security.

"I've always admired Mr. Pope's writing. The way he gets straight to the truth. No wasted words, no bullshit. He strikes me as an honest man. This might not be a story he wants to write himself, but if he doesn't, I know he'll pass it on to the right person."

The woman's hand drew back from the phone.

"Is there a number where you can be reached?"

"Not really," Thorn said. "I'm more of a pay-phone kind of a guy."

She smiled uncertainly and he smiled back and left the office. He walked outside to his car, started the old wreck, and headed off. At this time of the morning it would take an hour and a half to work his way through the traffic back home to Key Largo.

He planned to spend the rest of the day sitting on his dock, staring at the sky. Maybe later on in the afternoon, if the spirit moved him, he'd tie a bonefish fly or two, then take the skiff out and test them on the flats. See if the old magic was still there.

Read on for an excerpt from the next book by

JAMES W. HALL

HELL'S BAY

Coming soon in hardcover from St. Martin's Minotaur

Twist for twist, curve for curve, the two-lane road tracked the ancient meander of the Peace River through the sun-battered Florida scrubland. Steering one-handed, Abigail Bates reached up and cocked her rearview mirror off-center to better ignore the white pickup riding her bumper.

She eased back in the leather seat and held the Jaguar to thirty-five and returned to spying on the river through the cypress and pines. In the full sun its dawdling current threw off a silver glow against the riverbank trees and lit the belly of a great blue heron as it slid upstream with ungainly ease. Kingfishers stood watch in the highest branches of the pines, each bird staking out a stretch of water. From the southwest a warm wind breathed through the foliage, shifting leaves and smoothing down the tall grasses.

To her mind, this landscape had a stern grandeur, but go fifty miles west and pluck an average sunbather off the white sands of Siesta Key, drop them on the seat beside her, and most would be hard-pressed to find a trace of beauty in that stark countryside. *Godforsaken* was how she had described it as a defiant teen, seventy years before, serving out her childhood in the land of cattle prairies, citrus groves, pine flatwoods, cypress swamps, and marshes. Back then this wilderness was home to a wealth of scrub jay, sandhill crane, little blue heron, indigo snakes, and any number of species that these days were near extinction. Extinct as well

were the leathery cowmen who'd settled that land—
roughneck dreamers like her father and his father before
him. Although they'd never been glamorized by moviemak-
ers, Florida wranglers like her ancestors were cracking
whips over vast herds of cattle a half century before long-
horns grazed the prairies of the West.

Despite her youthful scorn of that rugged terrain and its
rural isolation, eventually Abigail succumbed to her old
man's coaching and learned a measure of appreciation for
the hardscrabble aesthetics of the place.

Apart from the garish aberration of Orlando, the vast interior of the state was thought by most to be a desolate waste-
land. Finding champions for those millions of acres of scrub
and palmetto and cypress swamp was nearly impossible. Indeed, that lack of care and legal scrutiny was in large measure what allowed Abigail's family to amass their empire.

As she steered the car around another sweeping bend, her
foot softened on the gas pedal. On the gravel shoulder a
bloated possum lay on its back, its paws reaching skyward as
if pleading to the indifferent sun. Unperturbed by Abigail's
car, a pair of buzzards plucked at the remains.

If she'd had any sense, she would've braked hard,
U-turned, and headed back to the penthouse on Longboat
Key. She was a firm believer in omens, and if that possum
wasn't one, she didn't know what was.

But damn it, for months she'd promised her granddaughter she'd complete this journey, take a firsthand look at what
was at stake. Not that a three-hour paddle down the Peace
River was going to alter her decision a whit.

Despite the prickle of unease, she pushed on, and in another ten minutes she saw in the distance her first waypoint,
the canoe outfitter's shack.

A good half mile in advance she put on her blinker for the
benefit of the yahoo behind her. As she made her turn into
the gravel lot, the truck thundered past, and she glimpsed the
driver, a woman with chalky skin and a long braid.

She parked in front of the dilapidated cabin with a rusty
sign over the door: CANOE SAFARI. The man who stuck his

head out the doorway at the sound of her car had blond hair that trailed across his shoulders and a scraggle of hair on his chin.

He stepped into the doorway and watched her climb out of the Jaguar. Except for the creaky knees and the steady throb in her left hip, she judged herself as supple as any woman half her age.

For this outing she'd chosen one of her long-departed husband's fly-fishing shirts with all the silly pockets and air vents, a pair of frayed jeans, and pink Keds. She'd pinned her silver hair into a bun and fit a Marlins cap atop. In that getup and the right light she might pass for seventy.

With a squint of wariness the man watched her cross the gravel lot.

"Help you?"

"I'm looking to rent one of your boats."

He gazed at her for several seconds as if waiting for her to break into a grin and admit she was only teasing.

She stepped closer and said, "In case you're wondering, I'm eighty-six. I'm fully insured, but if it'll make you feel easier, I'll sign a release."

The man drew a strand of hair off his cheek and looped it behind his ear.

"What's your fancy? Red boat or one of the yellows?"

It was agreed that the young man, Charlie Kipling, would rendezvous with her downstream at the state park landing at noon and would haul out the canoe and return her to this spot. That would give Abigail a three-hour drift down the Peace, quite enough time to take in the views and remind herself what the fuss was about. All she'd have to do was paddle a few lazy strokes now and then to keep the boat straight.

After she was safely aboard a scarlet beauty, Charlie squatted ankle-deep in the water, holding the stern. He had a simple smile but seemed more weary than a man his age or profession ought to be.

She looked down the corridor of tea-stained water and trickled her fingers through the warm stream. Two canoes slipped past, father and son in one, mother and daughter in the other. The kids chattering to each other while the adults paddled, everyone snug in orange life preservers.

"It's as lovely as I remember."

"Oh, it's picturesque," he said. "For the moment, anyway."

She gripped the paddle, waiting for him to release her into the current.

"But things keep going like they been, won't be long before I'll be shopping for another river."

She held his eyes, and after a few seconds she watched them harden and grow bleak. Once again she'd been recognized.

He licked his lips and licked them again as if fetching for a curse.

"I'll be damned. You're that woman, Bates International."

"That would be me. Abigail Bates. Nice to meet you." She didn't bother holding out a hand.

"Well, goddamn it all to hell."

"Go on," she said. "Say your piece."

"I've seen you at the meetings, sitting with that shithead lawyer, Mosley."

"Nothing's settled yet."

"That's a damn lie. It's a done deal. Train's left the station. It's already chugging down the rails; there's no turning that big-ass monster around. From the governor on down, the fix is in. Permits approved. Those meetings are just for show. Letting people think they got a choice in the matter when we got no choice in hell."

She sighed and shook her head and looked into the river's wavering shine. What he said was true, of course. The meetings were a sham. The people would be patiently listened to, but ultimately the decision was not theirs. Such as it was, such it had always been. The few deciding for the many.

She wanted to reach out and give the young man a reassuring pat but felt sure he'd swat her hand away.

"This river's been taking care of itself for a long, long time."

"Never been any threat like this. Not even close. Already

this year it's down another foot. It'll be a dribble before you people are done."

Abigail stared out at the steady current. She'd heard it all before, every dire prediction.

"Anyway, it's more than the damn river," he said. "Way more than that. It's where the river goes, what it does. All the people who depend on it whether they know it or not. Goddammit, I don't believe you just walked right up and thought you could rent one of my canoes."

"Maybe I should've called in advance. You could've written a speech."

"Or brought my gun."

He held her eyes for a moment, then his face went pale and he swung away as if appalled by his own rage.

Abigail bent to her bag and dug out the Beretta.

She gripped it by the barrel and offered it. She'd been shooting all her life but only lately started carrying a pistol as the death threats mounted.

"There's no safety. Just aim and shoot."

Charlie Kipling pivoted back and stared at the pistol. His shoulders shook as if he'd felt a cold draft across his back. He looked into Abigail's eyes. Then with the mix of dread and boldness a man musters to snatch up a snake, he shot out his hand and wrenched the pistol from her grasp. He fumbled with the Beretta briefly before he found the grip.

It surprised her. The young man had struck her as another spineless tree-kisser with no muscle behind his convictions. But as she watched him raise the trembling muzzle and direct it at her body, Abigail drew a resolute breath and saw again that damn possum on the side of the road, a clear warning that any country girl should've taken seriously.

Charlie was panting, a bright sheen of sweat on his cheeks.

"If I took you down, I'd be a hero to a lot of people."

"I'm sure you would."

She watched his eyes flick right and left as if consulting the river spirits.

"If I thought it'd make any difference, I'd do it."

"I'm not trying to talk you out of it," she said.

A gold dragonfly whisked between them.

Over Charlie's shoulder, Abigail saw a minivan pull into the lot and park beside her Jaguar. After a moment, the side door slid open and three girls leapt out, followed by two young mothers in shorts and T-shirts.

Charlie glanced over at the arrivals, keeping his aim fixed on Abigail.

The red-haired woman in the lead noticed the pistol in Charlie's hand and swept up the children and herded them back to the van.

"Hey!" the other woman called out and took a couple of steps toward Abigail. But her friend shouted and she whirled and trotted back to the van.

"You lost some paying customers," Abigail said.

After the van screeched onto the highway, Charlie tipped the pistol toward the muddy bank and fired. Muck spattered the side of the canoe and dotted Abigail's shirt sleeve. He gritted his jaw and squeezed the trigger again and again. When he'd emptied the clip he dropped her pistol into the shallow water at his feet where it sank to the bottom and gleamed within the swirl of mud like the flash of fish scales.

The glow drained from Kipling's face.

"Noon at the ramp," he said, his voice vacant as a sleep-walker's.

Then he shoved her canoe out into the moving water, and Abigail straightened it and felt the current take hold. She tested her stroke, port side then starboard, felt her heart struggling to regain its cadence.

If Kipling didn't show, it was no tragedy. She'd phone her security people in Sarasota to come fetch her. An hour drive, no problem. But she believed Kipling's fury was spent, and he had every intention of keeping the appointment—if only to present his case in a more calculated manner.

A hundred yards downstream she turned and looked back, and he was still standing in the shallows watching her go. After a moment, he swatted at a bug near his ear, then turned back to his pine shack.

She traveled almost an hour downstream before her killer appeared.

By then Abigail Bates had spotted three deer in the brush along the river. An eagle, four osprey, a red-tailed hawk feasting on a plump dove, numerous ibis, a handful of limpkins, and a large creature rooting in the shrubs along a section of private farmland. Probably a feral hog, one of the descendants of the creatures Hernando de Soto's conquistadors had introduced centuries before.

Despite the tannic tint, she could see the bottom of the river in most places, twenty to thirty feet deep, and the fish were visible—a snook, one huge catfish, bass, bream, hundreds of minnows flicking by in nervous, synchronized schools.

Because it was midweek and not yet tourist season, the river traffic was light. Only a single kayaker passed her, a stalwart young woman in a skimpy swimsuit who was paddling with the sharp, focused strokes of an athlete in training. The air smelled of snakes and damp mud and an occasional gust of a sharp, insistent citrus scent that made her think of a teenage boy's first cologne.

A few feet ahead the river narrowed, and the cypress and pine and flowering shrubs crowded close to the water's edge. Abigail steered the canoe around a tight corner. And there, standing about ten yards to her right on an outcropping of rock, was a woman with flesh so white her body might have been carved from cheap soap.

She was long and bony and wore a green one-piece bathing suit.

Abigail paddled two hard strokes on the starboard side to angle away from the woman's perch on the bank, though at this narrowed spot, the shoreline where she stood was only twenty feet away.

When the canoe was almost abreast of the woman's position, she dove. Five feet down she frog-kicked toward the canoe with powerful strokes.

When she surfaced nearby, a mouthful of water drooled from her lips. She treaded water and gave Abigail a cheerless stare. The woman had heavy eyebrows, a braided rope of coal-black hair, hollow cheeks, and harsh cheekbones. She was in her late thirties and had the gaunt look of one who'd known more than her share of rough treatment. Peasant genes. Italian, maybe Greek. A woman who would be a great attraction for certain peckerwoods in the region—men with a fascination for the exotic.

Almost certainly this was the driver of the pickup truck who had tailgated her to the canoe shack. After Abigail turned off, she'd driven down the highway until she'd come to this place where the canoe would be pinched between two banks. Perfect spot for an ambush.

No crime of impulse. This was not the sort of woman who carried a swimsuit in her pickup for river frolics. Which meant she'd followed Abigail with full knowledge of her destination and had brought the required equipment. Abigail's lungs hardened. Only one person knew where she had been headed today. Only one who might have betrayed her.

For a moment they floated parallel, eyeing each other in silence.

At that juncture, with two solid strokes she could be a boat-length beyond the woman, and it would be a race downstream.

But she hesitated, for it had never been Abigail's way to dodge a battle. A fighter as a girl, a fighter still. You didn't swerve from conflict. You took it on and overcame. Those were her daddy's lessons passed on from a long line of hardass daddies. Back down once, it becomes a way of life.

She shifted her grip on the paddle, finding a hold that once, many years before, she'd used with a garden spade to hack off a rattler's head.

The swimmer blew a mist from her lips and slid toward the canoe on an angle that would bring her into range in a second or two.

The moment was gone when Abigail might have fled, and a ghost of gloom swelled within her for she saw she'd erred.

She should have raced this lanky woman to the next bend, used the river's flow to her advantage. But she'd behaved the way old people so often do. A stubborn attachment to habit. Failure to adapt. She'd made that mistake a lot lately. Treating the new world as if it were still the old.

With two precise strokes the woman closed the gap, and her hand shot out for the edge of the canoe. Abigail chopped the paddle blade against her bony wrist and knocked her away. While she recovered just out of range, there was another window for escape. But again Abigail faltered.

Sculling one-handed, the young woman rubbed at her damaged flesh and squinted at Abigail with the stony indifference of one who'd absorbed greater pain than any this old woman could deliver.

"Last chance," Abigail said. "Go back where you came from."

The woman smiled bleakly, then glided to the bow and took hold. With that effortless act, she had Abigail in her control. No way in hell could she work her way forward in that tippy vessel to attack the woman.

"How long can you hold your breath?" The woman's voice had a country flavor.

"What?"

"Thirty seconds, forty? How long?"

The woman rocked the canoe back and forth as if testing its balance. Abigail gripped both gunwales and held on. At each tip she was only a degree or two from going over.

"Tell me what you want. I can make it happen. Whatever it is."

"What I want," she said, "is to see how long you can hold your breath."

Like she was taking down a steer at branding time, the woman slung her arm across the prow and twisted the boat onto its side, and Abigail slid across the metal bench and sprawled headlong into the river.

The woman looped an arm around Abigail's waist, securing her with a grip both solid and restrained, as if determined to leave no crime-scene bruise. Abigail balled her hands and hammered at the rawboned woman, but she absorbed the blows with the forbearance of a parent enduring a child's tantrum.

Blind beneath the river, all she could make out was a fizz of bubbles as the woman dragged her toward the sandy bottom, ten feet, fifteen, swimming with one arm, the other locked around her waist. Strong as any man her size, this woman seemed at home beneath the surface, knifing down with an easy power.

As they sank, the water cooled. A swirl of dizzy light spun around her, then she released half the air in her lungs, the glittering froth lifting in a cloud to the surface.

Doing that for the woman's benefit. If she could make her body go limp, the woman might mistake her for dead and drop her guard.

Through slitted eyes, she saw where the woman was dragging her.

A cypress root that bowed out from the bank like the handle of a large door, the door to a bank or some impressive office building like so many Abigail herself had entered. A woman of authority. Doormen holding them open for her. The long car waiting while she did her business.

Abigail watched the young woman take hold of the root as if she meant to open that door for Abigail, show her into the next world.

Above her the riverbank jutted out and put them in shadows and out of view of any passing paddler. She willed herself motionless, though the pain in her chest was vicious and her consciousness was dimming fast.

After a moment more, the woman relaxed her grip and Abigail thought she'd fallen for her ruse. She jerked hard against the woman's hold, threw an elbow at her face. It missed. She tried a savage kick, but that failed too. The toe of her sneaker wedged in a crevice and came off.

In that spasm of exertion Abigail lost control of her lungs and watched with black horror as a final bubble burped from her mouth, and rose shining toward the sun.

She felt her mouth slacken as the iron in her veins dissolved. Letting go of her ferocious determination, letting go of everything. Her lungs filled and she felt the gentle tug of the current across her flesh. Abigail Bates shivered hard and surrendered.